'Can't sleep?'

The Italian's silky voice penetrated her spinning thoughts and Keira could tell from the shifting weight on the mattress that Matteo Valenti had turned his head to talk to her. She swallowed. Should she pretend to be asleep? But what would be the point of that? She suspected he would see through her ruse immediately—and wasn't it a bit of a relief not to have to keep still any more?

'No,' she admitted. 'Can't you?'

He gave a short laugh. 'I wasn't expecting to.'

'Why not?'

His voice dipped. 'I suspect you know exactly why not. It's a somewhat *unusual* situation to be sharing a bed with an attractive woman and having to behave in such a chaste manner.'

Keira was glad of the darkness which hid her sudden flush of pleasure. Had the gorgeous and arrogant Matteo Valenti actually called her *attractive*? And was he really implying that he was having difficulty keeping his hands off her? Of course he might only be saying it to be polite—but he hadn't exactly been a model of politeness up until now, had he?

'I thought you said you didn't find me attractive?'

'That's what I was trying to convince myself.'

In the darkness, she gave a smile of pleasure. 'I could go downstairs and see if I could get us some more tea.'

'Please.' He groaned. 'No more tea.'

'Then I guess we'll have to resign ourselves to a sleepless night.' She plumped up her pillow and sighed as she collapsed back against it. 'Unless you've got a better suggestion?'

One Night With Consequences

When one night…leads to pregnancy!

When succumbing to a night of unbridled desire
it's impossible to think past the morning after!

But, with the sheets barely settled,
that little blue line appears on the pregnancy test and it
doesn't take long to realise that one night of white-hot
passion has turned into a lifetime of consequences!

Only one question remains:

How do you tell a man you've just met
that you're about to share more than just his bed?

Find out in:

Claiming His Christmas Consequence by Michelle Smart

The Guardian's Virgin Ward by Caitlin Crews

A Child Claimed by Gold by Rachael Thomas

The Consequence of His Vengeance by Jennie Lucas

Secrets of a Billionaire's Mistress by Sharon Kendrick

The Boss's Nine-Month Negotiation by Maya Blake

The Pregnant Kavakos Bride by Sharon Kendrick

A Ring for the Greek's Baby by Melanie Milburne

Engaged for Her Enemy's Heir by Kate Hewitt

The Virgin's Shock Baby by Heidi Rice

Look for more **One Night With Consequences** stories
coming soon!

THE ITALIAN'S CHRISTMAS SECRET

BY
SHARON KENDRICK

MILLS & BOON

First Published in Great Britain 2017
By Mills & Boon, an imprint of HarperCollins*Publishers*
1 London Bridge Street, London, SE1 9GF

© 2017 Sharon Kendrick

ISBN: 978-0-263-92543-2

Sharon Kendrick once won a national writing competition by describing her ideal date: being flown to an exotic island by a gorgeous and powerful man. Little did she realise that she'd just wandered into her dream job! Today she writes for Mills & Boon, featuring often stubborn but always *to die for* heroes and the women who bring them to their knees. She believes that the best books are those you never want to end. Just like life…

Books by Sharon Kendrick

Mills & Boon Modern Romance

A Royal Vow of Convenience
The Ruthless Greek's Return
Christmas in Da Conti's Bed

One Night With Consequences

The Pregnant Kavakos Bride
Secrets of a Billionaire's Mistress
Crowned for the Prince's Heir
Carrying the Greek's Heir

Wedlocked!

The Sheikh's Bought Wife
The Billionaire's Defiant Acquisition

The Billionaire's Legacy

Di Sione's Virgin Mistress

The Bond of Billionaires

Claimed for Makarov's Baby
The Sheikh's Christmas Conquest

At His Service

The Housekeeper's Awakening

Visit the Author Profile page
at millsandboon.co.uk for more titles.

For the vivacious and beautiful Amelia Tuttiett—
who is a great raconteur and always fun to be with.
She is also a brilliant ceramic artist.

Thanks for all the inspiration, Mimi!

CHAPTER ONE

'MR VALENTI?'

The woman's soft voice filtered into Matteo's thoughts and he made no effort to hide his exasperation as he leaned back against the leather seat of the luxury car. He'd been thinking about his father. Wondering if he intended carrying out the blustering threat he'd made just before Matteo had left Rome—and if so, whether or not he could prevent it. He gave a heavy sigh, forcing himself to accept that the ties of blood went deeper than any others. They must do. He certainly wouldn't have tolerated so much from one person if they hadn't been related. But family were difficult to walk away from. Difficult to leave. He felt his heart clench. Unless, of course, they left you.

'Mr Valenti?' the soft voice repeated.

Matteo gave a small click of irritation and not just because he loathed people talking to him when it was clear he didn't want to be disturbed. It was more to do with the fact that this damned trip hadn't gone according to plan, and not just because he hadn't seen a single hotel he'd wanted to buy. It was as much to do with the small-boned female behind the steering wheel who was irritating the hell out of him.

'*Cos' hai detto?*' he demanded until the ensuing silence reminded him that the woman didn't speak Italian, that he was a long way from home—in fact, he was in the middle of the infernal English countryside with a woman driver.

He frowned. Having a woman chauffeur was a first for him and when he'd first seen her slender build and startled blue eyes, Matteo had been tempted to demand a replacement of the more burly male variety. Until he reminded himself that the last thing he needed was to be accused of sexual prejudice. His aristocratic nostrils flared as he glanced into the driver's mirror and met her eyes. 'What did you say?' he amended, in English.

The woman cleared her throat, her slim shoulders shifting slightly—though the ridiculous peaked cap she insisted on wearing over her shorn hair stayed firmly in place. 'I said that the weather seems to have taken a turn for the worse.'

Matteo turned his head to glance out of the window where the deepening dusk was almost obscured by the violent swirl of snowflakes. He'd been so caught up in his thoughts that he'd paid scant attention to the passing countryside but now he could see that the landscape was nothing but a bleached blur. He scowled. 'But we'll be able to get through?'

'I certainly hope so.'

'You hope so?' he echoed, his voice growing harder. 'What kind of an answer is that? You do realise that I have a flight all geared up and ready to go?'

'Yes, Mr Valenti. But it's a private jet and it will wait for you.'

'I am perfectly aware that it's a *private jet* since I happen to own it,' he bit out impatiently. 'But I'm due at a party in Rome tonight, and I don't intend being late.'

With a monumental effort Keira stifled a sigh and kept her eyes fixed on the snowy road ahead. She needed to act calm and stay calm because Matteo Valenti was the most important customer she'd ever driven, a fact her boss had drummed into her over and over again. Whatever happened, she mustn't show the nerves she'd been experiencing for the past few days—because driving a client of this calibre was a whole new experience for her. Being the only woman and the more junior driver on the payroll, she usually got different sorts of jobs. She collected urgent packages and delivered them, or picked up spoilt children from their prep school and returned them to their nanny in one of the many exclusive mansions which were dotted around London. But even mega-rich London customers paled into insignificance when you compared them with the wealth of Matteo Valenti.

Her boss had emphasised the fact that this was the first time the Italian billionaire had ever used their company and it was her duty to make sure he gave them plenty of repeat business. She thought it was great that such an influential tycoon had decided to give Luxury Limos his business, but she wasn't stupid. It was obvious he was only using them because he'd decided on the trip at the last minute—just as it was obvious she'd only been given the job because none of the other drivers were available, this close to Christmas. According to her boss, he was an important hotelier looking to buy a development site in England, to expand his growing empire of hotels. So far they had visited Kent, Sussex and Dorset—though they'd left the most far-flung destination of Devon until last, which wouldn't have been how *she* would have arranged it, especially not with the pre-holiday traffic being what it was. Still, she wasn't being employed to sort out his schedule for him—she was here to get him safely from A to B.

She stared straight ahead at the wild flurry of snowflakes. It was strange. She worked *with* men and *for* men and knew most of their foibles. She'd learnt that in order to be accepted it was better to act like one of the boys and not stand out. It was the reason she wore her hair short—though not the reason she'd cut it in the first place. It was why she didn't usually bother with make-up, or wearing the kind of clothes which invited a second look. The tomboy look suited her just fine, because if a man forgot you were there, he tended to relax—though unfortunately the same rule didn't seem to apply to Matteo Valenti. She'd never met a less relaxed individual.

But that wasn't the whole story, was it? She clutched the steering wheel tightly, unwilling to admit the real reason why she felt so self-conscious in his company. Because wasn't the truth that he had blown her away the moment they'd met, with the most potent brand of charisma she'd ever encountered? It was disturbing and exciting and scary all at the same time and it had never happened to her before—that thing of looking into someone's eyes and hearing a million violins start playing inside your head. She'd gazed into the darkest eyes she'd ever seen and felt as if she could drown in them. She'd found herself studying his thick black hair and wondering how it would feel to run her fingers through it. Failing that, having a half-friendly working relationship would have satisfied her, but that was never going to happen. Not with a man who was so abrupt, narrow-minded and *judgmental*.

She'd seen his expression when she'd been assigned to him, his black gaze raking over her with a look of incredulity he hadn't bothered to disguise. He'd actually had the nerve to ask whether she felt *confident* behind the wheel of such a powerful car and she had been tempted to coolly inform him that yes, she was, thank you very much. Just as she was confident about getting underneath the bonnet and taking the engine to pieces, should the need arise. And now he was snapping at her and making no attempt to hide his irritation—as if she had some kind of magical power over the weather conditions which had suddenly hit them from out of the blue!

She shot a nervous glance towards the heavy sky and felt another tug of anxiety as she met his hooded dark eyes in the driver's mirror.

'Where are we?' he demanded.

Keira glanced at the sat-nav. 'I think we're on Dartmoor.'

'You think?' he said sarcastically.

Keira licked her lips, glad he was now preoccupied with staring out of the window instead of glaring so intently at her. Glad he was ignorant of the sudden panicked pounding of her heart. 'The sat-nav lost its signal a couple of times.'

'But you didn't think to tell me that?'

She bit back her instinctive response that he was unlikely to be an expert on the more rural parts of the south-west since he'd told her he hardly ever visited England. Unless, of course, he was implying that his oozing masculinity was enough to compensate for a total lack of knowledge of the area.

'You were busy with a phone call at the time and I didn't like to interrupt,' she said. 'And you said…'

'I said what?'

She gave a little shrug. 'You mentioned that you'd like to travel back by the scenic route.'

Matteo frowned. Had he said that? It was true he'd been distracted by working out how he was going to deal with his father, but he didn't remember agreeing to some guided tour of an area he'd already decided wasn't for him, or his hotels. Hadn't it simply been a case of agreeing to her hesitant suggestion of an alternative route, when she'd told him that the motorways were likely to be busy with everyone travelling home for the Christmas holiday? In which case, surely she should have had the sense and the knowledge to anticipate something like this might happen.

'And this snowstorm seems to have come from out of nowhere,' she said.

With an effort Matteo controlled his temper, telling himself nothing would be achieved by snapping at her. He knew how erratic and *emotional* women could be—both in and out of the workplace—and had always loathed overblown displays of emotion. She would probably burst into tears if he reprimanded her, followed by an undignified scene while she blubbed into some crumpled piece of tissue and then looked at him with tragic, red-rimmed eyes. And scenes were something he was at pains to avoid. He liked a life free of drama and trauma. A life lived on his terms.

Briefly, he thought about Donatella waiting for him at a party he wasn't going to be able to make. At the disappointment in her green eyes when she realised that several weeks of dating weren't going to end up in a swish Roman hotel bedroom, as they'd planned. His mouth hardened. He'd made her wait to have sex with him and he could tell it had frustrated the hell out of her. Well, she would just have to wait a little longer.

'Why don't you just get us there as safely as possible?' he suggested, zipping shut his briefcase. 'If I miss the party, it won't be the end of the world—just so long as I get home for Christmas in one piece. You can manage that, can't you?'

Keira nodded, but inside her heart was still racing faster than it should have been considering her sedentary position behind the wheel. Because she was rapidly realising that they were in trouble. Real trouble. Her windscreen wipers were going like crazy but no sooner had they removed a thick mass of white flakes, there were loads more their place. She'd never known such awful visibility and found herself wondering why she hadn't just risked the crowds and the traffic jams and gone by the most direct route. Because she hadn't wanted to risk a displeasure she suspected was never very far from the surface with her billionaire client. Matteo Valenti wasn't the kind of person you could imagine sitting bumper to bumper on a road of stationary traffic while children in Santa hats pulled faces through the back windows. To be honest, she was surprised he didn't travel round by helicopter until he'd informed her that you got to see a lot more of the natural lie of the land from a car.

He seemed to have informed her about quite a lot of things. How he didn't like coffee from service stations and would rather go without food than eat something 'substandard'. How he preferred silence to the endless stream of Christmas songs on the car radio, though he didn't object when once she changed the station to some classical music, which she found strangely unsettling—particularly when a glance in the mirror showed her that he had closed his eyes and briefly parted his lips. Her heartbeat had felt *very* erratic after that particular episode.

Keira slowed down as they drove past a small house on which an illuminated Santa Claus was driving his sleigh above a garish sign proclaiming *Best Bed & Breakfast on Dartmoor!* The trouble was that she wasn't used to men like Matteo Valenti—she didn't imagine a lot of people were. She'd watched people's reactions whenever he emerged from the limousine to cast his eye over yet another dingy hotel which was up for sale. She'd witnessed women's gazes being drawn instinctively to his powerful physique. She'd watched their eyes widen—as if finding it hard to believe that one man could present such a perfect package, with those aristocratic features, hard jaw and sensual lips. But Keira had been up close to him for several days and she realised that, although he looked pretty perfect on the surface, there was a brooding quality underneath the surface which hinted at danger. And weren't a lot of women turned on by danger? As she clamped her fingers around the steering wheel, she wondered if that was the secret of his undeniable charisma.

But now wasn't the time to get preoccupied about Matteo Valenti, or even to contemplate the holidays which were fast approaching and which she was dreading. It was time to acknowledge that the snowstorm was getting heavier by the second and she was losing control of the big car. She could feel the tyres pushing against the weight of the accumulating drifts as the road took on a slight incline. She could feel sweat suddenly beading her brow as the heavy vehicle began to lose power and she realised that if she wasn't careful...

The car slid to a halt and Keira's knuckles whitened as she suddenly realised there were no distant tail lights in front of them. Or lights behind them. She glanced in the mirror as she turned off the ignition and forced herself to meet the furious black stare which was being directed at her from the back seat.

'What's going on?' he questioned, his tone sending a shiver rippling down Keira's spine.

'We've stopped,' she said, turning the key again and praying for them to start moving but the car stayed exactly where it was.

'I can see that for myself,' he snapped. 'The question is, *why* have we stopped?'

Keira gulped. He must have realised why. Did he want her to spell it out for him so he could shovel yet more blame on her? 'It's a heavy car and the snow is much thicker than I thought. We're on a slight hill, and...'

'And?'

Face facts, she told herself fiercely. You know how to do that. It's a difficult situation, but it's not the end of the world. She flicked the ignition and tried moving forward again but despite her silent prayers, the car stubbornly refused to budge. Her hands sliding reluctantly from the wheel, she turned round. 'We're stuck,' she admitted.

Matteo nodded, biting back the angry exclamation which was on the tip of his tongue, because he prided himself on being good in an emergency. God knew, there had been enough of those over the years to make him an expert in crisis management. Now was not the time to wonder why he hadn't followed his instincts and demanded a male driver who would have known what he was doing, instead of some slip of a girl who didn't look strong enough to control a pushbike, let alone a car this size. Recriminations could come later, he thought grimly—and they would. First and foremost they needed to get out of here—and to do that, they needed to keep their wits about them.

'Where exactly are we?' he said, speaking slowly as if to a very small child.

She swivelled her head to look at the sat-nav for several silent seconds before turning to meet his gaze again.

'The signal has cut out again. We're on the edge of Dartmoor.'

'How close to civilisation?'

'That's the trouble. We're not. We're miles from any-where.' He saw her teeth dig into her lower lip as if she were trying to draw blood from it. 'And there's no Wi-Fi connection,' she finished.

Matteo wanted to slam the flat of his hand against the snow-covered window but he sucked in an unsteady breath instead. He needed to take control.

'Move over,' he said roughly as he unclipped his seat belt.

She blinked those great big eyes at him. 'Move over where?'

'Onto the passenger seat,' he gritted out as he pushed open the car door to brace himself against a flurry of snowflakes. 'I'm taking over.'

He was pretty much covered in ice by the time he got into the car and slammed the door shut, and the bi-zarre thought which stuck in his mind was how deli-ciously warm the seat felt from where her bottom had been sitting.

Furious for allowing himself to be distracted by something so basic and inappropriate at a time like this, Matteo reached for the ignition key.

'You do know not to press down too hard on the accelerator, don't you?' she said nervously. 'Or you'll make the wheels spin.'

'I don't think I need any driving lessons from some-one as incompetent as you,' he retorted. He started the engine and tried moving forward. Nothing. He tried until he was forced to surrender to the inevitable, which deep down he'd known all along. They were well and truly stuck and the car wasn't going anywhere. He turned to the woman sitting beside him who was staring at him nervously from beneath her peaked cap.

'So. Bravo,' he said, his words steeped in an anger he could no longer contain. 'You've managed to get us stranded in one of the most inhospitable párts of the country on one of the most inhospitable nights of the year—just before Christmas. That's some feat!'

'I'm so sorry.'

'Saying sorry isn't going to help.'

'I'll probably get the sack,' she whispered.

'You will if I have anything to do with it—that's if you don't freeze to death first!' he snapped. 'If it were down to me, I would never have employed you in the first place. But the consequences to your career are the last thing on my mind right now. We need to start working out what we're going to do next.'

She reached into the glove compartment for her mobile phone but he wasn't surprised to see her grimace as she glanced down at the small screen. 'No signal,' she said, looking up.

'You don't say?' he said sarcastically, peering out of the window where the howling flakes showed no signs of abating. 'I'm guessing there's no nearby village?'

She shook her head. 'No. Well, we did pass a little B&B just a while back. You know, one of those places which offer bed and breakfast for the night.'

'I'm in the hotel trade,' he said silkily. 'And I'm perfectly aware of what a B&B is. How far was it?'

She shrugged. 'Less than a mile, I'd guess—though it wouldn't be easy to reach in this kind of conditions.'

'No kidding?' Matteo eyed the virtual white-out which was taking place outside the window and his heart thundered as he acknowledged the real danger of their situation. Because suddenly this was about more than just missing his flight or disappointing a woman who had been eager to make him her lover; this was about survival. Venturing outside in this kind of conditions would be challenging—and dangerous—and the alternative was to hunker down in the car for the night and wait for help to arrive tomorrow. Presumably she would have blankets in the boot and they could continue to run the heater. His lips curved into a grim smile. And wasn't the traditional method of generating heat to huddle two bodies together? But he gave the idea no more than a few seconds' thought before dismissing it—and not just because she didn't look as if she had enough flesh on her bones to provide any degree of comfort. No. To take the risk of staying put while the snow came down this fast would be nothing short of madness, for there was no guarantee anyone would find them in the morning.

He ran his gaze over her uniform of navy blue trousers and the sturdy jacket which matched her cap. The material curved over the faint swell of her breasts and brushed against her thighs and was hardly what you would call *practical*—certainly not appropriate to face the elements at their worst. He sighed. Which meant he would have to give her his overcoat and freeze to death himself. 'I don't suppose you have any warmer clothes with you?'

For a few seconds, she seemed to brighten. 'I've got an anorak in the boot.'

'An anorak?'

'It's a waterproof jacket. With a hood.' She removed her peaked chauffeur's cap and raked her fingers through her short dark hair and Matteo felt inexplicably irritated by the brief smile which had lightened her pale face.

Was she expecting praise for having had the foresight to pack a coat? he wondered acidly.

'Just get it and put it on,' he bit out. 'And then let's get the hell out of here.'

CHAPTER TWO

KEIRA HAD TO work hard to keep up with Matteo as he battled his way through the deep snow because his powerful body moved much faster than hers, despite the fact that he'd insisted on bringing his suitcase with him. Thick, icy flakes were flying into her eyes and mouth and at times she wondered if she was imagining the small lighted building in the distance—like some bizarre, winter version of an oasis.

Despite putting on the big pair of leather gloves he'd insisted she borrow, her fingers felt like sticks of ice and she gave a little cry of relief when at last they reached the little house. Thank heavens she *hadn't* imagined it because she didn't like to think about Matteo Valenti's reaction if she'd brought him here on a wild goose chase. He might have insisted on her borrowing his gloves, but even that had been done with a terse impatience. She saw his unsmiling look as he kicked a pile of snow away from the wooden gate and pushed it open, and she stumbled after him up the path to stand beneath the flashing red and gold lights of the illuminated sign overhead. She was shivering with cold by the time he'd jammed his finger on the doorbell and they heard some tinkly little tune playing in the distance.

'Wh-what if…wh-what if nobody's in?' she questioned from between teeth which wouldn't seem to stop chattering.

'The light's on,' he said impatiently. 'Of course somebody's in.'

'They m-might have gone away for Christmas and left the lights on a timer to deter burglars.'

'You really think burglars are going to be enticed by a place like *this*?' he demanded.

But their bad-tempered interchange was brought to a swift halt by the sound of a lumbering movement from within the house and the door was pulled open by a plump, middle-aged woman wearing a flowery apron which was smeared with flour.

'Well, bless my soul!' she said, opening the door wider as she peered out into the gloom. 'You're not carol singers, are you?'

'We are not,' answered Matteo grimly. 'I'm afraid our car has got snowed in a little way down the road.'

'Oh, you poor things! What a night to be outside! Come in, come in!'

Keira felt like bursting into tears of gratitude as Matteo's palm positioned itself in the small of her back and propelled her inside the bright little hallway. During the seemingly endless journey here, she'd been convinced they weren't going to make it, and that their two frozen figures would be discovered the next day, or the day after that. And hadn't she been unable to stop herself from wondering whether anyone would have actually *cared* if she died?

But now they were standing dripping in a small hallway which had boughs of holly and strands of glittery tinsel draped absolutely everywhere. A green plastic tree was decked with flashing rainbow lights and from a central light hung a huge bunch of mistletoe. Keira's eyes were drawn in fascination to the row of small, fluffy snowmen waddling in a perfectly symmetrical line along a shelf—her attention only distracted by the realisation that puddles of water were growing on the stone tiles beneath their feet. Years of being told to respect property—especially when it *wasn't your own*—made Keira concentrate on the mess they were making, rather than the glaringly obvious fact that she and her bad-tempered Italian client were gate-crashing someone else's Christmas.

'Oh, my goodness—look at the floor!' she said, aware of the faint look of incredulity which Matteo Valenti was slanting in her direction. 'We're ruining your floor.'

'Don't you worry about that, my dear,' said the woman in her warm West Country accent. 'We get walkers coming in here all the time—that'll soon clean up.'

'We'd like to use your phone if that's okay,' said Matteo, and Keira watched as the woman looked at him, her mouth opening and closing comically as if she'd only just realised that she had six feet three inches of brooding masculine gorgeousness in her house, with melting snow sliding down over his black cashmere coat.

'And why would you want to do that, dear?' questioned the woman mildly.

Matteo did his best not to flinch at the overfamiliar response, even though he despised endearments from complete strangers. Actually, he despised endearments generally. Didn't they say that you always mistrusted what you weren't used to? Suppressing a frustrated flicker of anger at having found himself in this intolerable situation, he decided he needed to own it. Better to calmly spell out their needs, since his driver seemed incapable of doing anything with any degree of competence. 'Our car has become imbedded in the snow just down the road a little,' he said, directing an accusing glare at the woman who was currently pulling off her bulky waterproof jacket and shaking her short dark hair. 'We should never have taken this route, given the weather. However, what's done is done and we can't do anything about that now. We just need to get out of here, as quickly as possible, and I'd like to arrange that immediately.'

The woman nodded, her bright smile remaining unfaltering. 'I don't think that's going to be possible, dear. You won't get a rescue truck to dig you out—not tonight. Why, nothing's going to get through—not in these conditions!'

It was the confirmation of his worst fears and although Matteo was tempted to vent his rage, he was aware it would serve no useful purpose—as well as insulting the woman who'd been kind enough to open her house to them. And she was right. Who could possibly get to them tonight—in weather like this? He needed to face facts and accept that he was stuck here, in the middle of nowhere—with his incompetent driver in tow. A driver who was staring at him with eyes which suddenly looked very dark in her pale face. He frowned.

Of all the females in the world to be stranded with— it had to be someone like her! Once again his thoughts drifted to the luxurious party he would be missing, but he dismissed them as he drew in a deep breath and forced himself to say the unimaginable. 'Then it looks as if we're going to have to stay here. I assume you have rooms for hire?'

The woman's wide smile slipped. 'In December? Not likely! All my rooms are fully booked,' she added proudly. 'I get repeat trade all through the year, but especially at this time of year. People love a romantic Christmas on Dartmoor!'

'But we need somewhere to stay,' butted in Keira suddenly. 'Just until morning. Hopefully the snow will have stopped by then and we can get on our way in the morning.'

The woman nodded, her gaze running over Keira's pale cheeks as she took the anorak from her and hung it on a hook. 'Well, I'm hardly going to turn you out on a night like this, am I? Especially not at this time of the year—I'm sure we can find you room at the inn! I can put you in my daughter's old bedroom at the back of the house. That's the only space I have available. But the dining room is completely booked out and so I'm afraid I can't offer you dinner.'

'The meal doesn't matter,' put in Matteo quickly.

'Maybe if you could send something to the room when you have a moment?'

Keira felt numb as they were shown up some rickety stairs at the back of the house, and she remained numb as the landlady—who informed them that her name was Mary—opened the door with a flourish.

'You should be comfortable enough in here,' she said. 'The bathroom is just along the corridor though there's not much water left, and if you want a bath, you'll have to share. I'll just go downstairs and put the kettle on. Make yourselves at home.'

Mary shut the door behind her and Keira's heart started racing as she realised that she was alone in a claustrophobic space with Matteo Valenti. Make themselves at home? How on earth were they going to do that in a room this size with *only one bed*?

She shivered. 'Why didn't you tell her that we didn't want to share?'

He shot her an impatient look. 'We are two people and she has one room. You do the math. What alternative did I have?'

Keira could see his point. Mary couldn't magic up another bedroom from out of nowhere, could she? She looked around. It was one of those rooms which wasn't really big enough for the furniture it contained. It was too small for a double bed, but a double bed had been crammed into it nonetheless, and it dominated the room with its homemade patchwork quilt and faded pillow cases on which you could just about make out some Disney characters, one of which just happened to be Cinderella.

There were no signs of Christmas in here but on every available surface seemed to be a photo. Photos of someone who was recognisably Mary, looking much younger and holding a series of babies, then toddlers, right through gangly teenagers until the inevitable stiff wedding photos—and then yet more babies. Keira licked her lips. It was a life played out in stills. A simple life, probably—and a happy life, judging by the smile which was never far from Mary's face. Keira was used to cramped and cluttered spaces but she wasn't used to somewhere feeling homely—and she could do absolutely nothing about the fierce pang of something which felt like envy, which clutched at her heart like a vice.

She lifted her eyes to meet Matteo's flat gaze. 'I'm sorry,' she said.

'Spare me the platitudes,' he snapped, pulling out the mobile phone from the pocket of his trousers and staring at it with a barely concealed lack of hope. 'No signal. Of course there isn't. And no Wi-Fi either.'

'She said you could use the landline any time.'

'I know she did. I'll call my assistant once I've removed some of these wet clothes.' He loosened his tie before tugging it off and throwing it over the back of a nearby chair, where it dangled like some precious spiral of gunmetal. His mouth hardened with an expression of disbelief as he looked around. '*Per amor del cielo!* Who even uses places like this? We don't even have our own bathroom.'

'Mary told us we could use the one along the corridor.'

'She also told us that we'd need to share a bath because there wasn't enough hot water!' he flared. '*Sharing a bath? Not enough hot water?* Which century are we supposed to be living in?'

Keira shrugged her shoulders awkwardly, suspecting that Matteo Valenti wasn't used to the vagaries of small-town English landladies, or the kind of places where ordinary people stayed. Of course he wasn't. According to her boss, he owned luxury hotels all over his own country—he even had some scattered over America, as well as some in Barbados and Hawaii. What would he know about having to traipse along a chilly corridor to a bathroom which, like the rest of the house, obviously hadn't been modernised in decades?

'It's an English eccentricity. Part of the place's charm,' she added lamely.

'Charm I can do without,' he responded acidly. 'Good plumbing trumps charm every time.'

She wondered if he was deliberately ignoring something even more disturbing than the bathroom facilities…or maybe she was just being super-sensitive about it, given her uneasy history. Awkwardly she raked her fingers through her spiky hair, wondering what it was which marked her out from other women. Why was it that on the only two occasions she'd shared a bed with a man, one had been passed out drunk—while the other was looking at her with nothing but irritation in his hard black eyes?

He was nodding his head, as if she had spoken out loud. 'I know,' he said grimly. 'It's my idea of a nightmare, too. Sharing a too-small bed with an employee wasn't top of my Christmas wish list.'

Don't react, Keira told herself fiercely. And don't take it personally. Act with indifference and don't make out like it's a big deal.

'I expect we'll survive,' she said coolly, then began to rub at her arms through the thin jacket as she started to shiver.

He ran a speculative gaze over her and an unexpected note of consideration crept into his voice. 'You're cold,' he said, his eyes lingering on her thighs just a fraction too long. 'And your trousers are soaking.'

'You don't say?' she said, her voice rising a little defensively, because she'd never been very good at dealing with unsolicited kindness.

'Don't you have anything else you can wear?' he persisted.

Embarrassment made her even more defensive and Keira glared at him, aware of the heat now staining her cheeks. 'Yes, of course I do. I always make sure I carry an entire change of clothes with me whenever I embark on a drive from London to Devon,' she said. 'It's what every driver does.'

'Why don't you skip the sarcasm?' he suggested. 'And go and take a hot bath? You can borrow something of mine.'

Keira looked at him suspiciously, taken aback by the offer and not quite sure if he meant it. Without his cashmere coat he stood resplendent in a dark charcoal suit which, even to her untutored eye, she could tell was made-to-measure. It must have been—because surely your average suit didn't cater for men with shoulders as broad as his, or legs that long. What on earth could Matteo Valenti have in his suitcase which would fit *her*? 'You carry women's clothes around with you, do you?'

An unexpected smile lifted the corners of his mouth and the corresponding race of Keira's heart made her hope he wasn't going to do a lot of smiling.

'Funnily enough, no,' he said drily, unzipping the leather case. 'But I have a sweater you can use. And a soap bag. Here. Go on. Take it.'

He was removing the items from his case and handing them to her and Keira was overcome by a sudden gratitude. 'Th-thanks. You're very kind—'

'*Basta!* Spare me the stumbling appreciation. I'm not doing it out of any sense of *kindness*.' His mouth hardened. 'This day has already been a disaster—I don't want to add to the misery by having you catch pneumonia and finding myself with a wrongful death suit on my hands.'

'Well, I'll do my best not to get sick then,' she bit back. 'I'd hate to inconvenience you any more than I already have done!'

Her fingers digging into his sweater, Keira marched from the room to the bathroom along the corridor, trying to dampen down her rising feelings of anger. He really was the most hateful person she'd ever met and she was going to have to endure a whole night with him.

Hanging his sweater on the back of the door, she quickly assessed the facilities on offer and for the first time that day, she smiled. Good thing *she* was used to basics. To her the avocado-coloured sink and bath were nothing out of the ordinary, though she shuddered to think how Mr Cynical was going to cope. When she'd been growing up, she and her mother had lived in places with far worse plumbing than this. In fact, this rather tatty bathroom felt almost *nostalgic*. A throwback to tougher times, yes, but at least it had been one of those rare times when she'd known emotional security, before Mum had died.

Clambering into the tiny bath, she directed the leaking shower attachment over her head and sluiced herself with tepid water before lathering on some of Matteo's amazing soap. And then the strangest thing started happening. Beneath her massaging fingers she could feel her nipples begin to harden into tight little nubs and for a moment she closed her eyes as she imagined her powerful client touching her there, before pulling her hands away in horror. What on earth was *wrong* with her?

Leaving the plug in situ and climbing out of the tub, she furiously rubbed herself dry. Wasn't the situation bad enough without her fantasising about a man who was probably going to make sure she got fired as soon as they reached civilisation?

She put on her bra, turned her knickers inside out and slithered Matteo's grey sweater over her head. It was warm and very soft—it was just unfortunate that it only came to mid-thigh, no matter how hard she tugged at the hem. She stared into the mirror. And the problem with that was, what? Was she really naïve enough to think that the Italian tycoon would even *notice* what she was wearing? Why, judging from his attitude towards her up until now, she could probably waltz back in there completely naked and he wouldn't even bat those devastatingly dark eyelashes.

But about that Keira was wrong—just as she'd been wrong in making the detour via Dartmoor—because when she walked back into the bedroom Matteo Valenti turned around from where he had been standing gazing out of the window and, just like the weather outside, his face froze. It was extraordinary to witness, that unmistakable double take when he saw her, something which never normally happened when Keira walked into a room. His eyes narrowed and grew smoky and something in the atmosphere seemed to subtly shift, and change. She wasn't used to it, but she wasn't going to deny that it made her skin grow warm with pleasure. Unless, of course, she was totally misreading the situation. It wouldn't be the first time, would it?

'Is everything okay?' she asked uncertainly.

Matteo nodded in response, aware that a pulse had begun to hammer at his temple. He'd just finished a telephone conversation with his assistant and as a consequence he'd been miles away, staring out of the window at the desolate countryside and having the peculiar sensation of realising that nobody could get hold of him—a sensation which had brought with it a surprising wave of peace. He had watched his driver scuttle off towards the bathroom in her unflattering navy trouser suit, only now she had returned and...

He stared and swallowed down the sudden lump which had risen in his throat. It was inexplicable. What the hell had she done to herself?

Her short, dark hair was still drying and the heat

of the shower must have been responsible for the rosy flush of her cheeks, against which her sapphire eyes looked huge and glittery. But it was his sweater which was responsible for inflicting a sudden sexual awakening he would have preferred to avoid. A plain cashmere sweater which looked like a completely different garment when worn by her. She was so small and petite that it pretty much swamped her, but it hinted at the narrow-hipped body beneath and the most perfect pair of legs he had ever seen. She looked…

He shook his head slightly. She looked *sexy*, he thought resentfully as lust arrowed straight to his groin, where it hardened and stayed. She looked as if she wanted him to lay her down on the bed and start kissing her. As if she were tantalising him with the question of whether or not she was wearing any panties. He felt he was in a schoolboy's fantasy, tempted to ask her to bend down to pick up some imaginary object from the carpet so he could see for himself if her bottom was bare. And then he glared because the situation was bad enough without having to endure countless hours of frustration, daydreaming about a woman he couldn't have—even if he was the kind of man to indulge in a one-night stand, which he most emphatically wasn't.

'*Sì*, everything is wonderful. *Fantastico*,' he added sarcastically. 'I've just made a phone call to my assistant and asked her to make my apologies for tonight's party. She asked if I was doing something nice instead and I told her that no, I was not. In fact, I was stuck on a snowy moor in the middle of nowhere.'

'I've left you some hot water,' she said stiffly, deciding to ignore his rant.

'How will I be able to contain my excitement?' he returned as he picked up the clothes he had selected from his case and slammed his way out of the room.

But he'd calmed down a little by the time he returned, dressed down in jeans and a sweater, to find her stirring a pot of tea which jostled for space on a tray containing sandwiches and mince pies. She turned her face towards him with a questioning look.

'Are you hungry?' she said.

It was difficult to return her gaze when all he wanted to do was focus on her legs and that still tantalising question of what she was or wasn't wearing underneath his sweater. Matteo shrugged. 'I guess.'

'Would you like a sandwich?'

'How can I refuse?'

'It's very kind of Mary to have gone to the trouble of making us some, especially when she's trying to cook a big turkey dinner for eight people,' she admonished quietly. 'The least we can do is be grateful.'

'I suppose so.'

Keira tried to maintain her polite smile as she handed him a cup of tea and a cheese sandwich, telling herself that nothing would be gained by being rude herself. In fact, it would only make matters worse if they started sparring. She was the one in the wrong and the one whose job was on the line. If she kept answering him back, who was to say he wouldn't ring up her boss and subject him to a blistering tirade about her incompetence? If she kept him sweet, mightn't he be persuaded

not to make a big deal out of the situation, maybe even
to forget it had ever happened and put it down to experience? She needed this job because she loved it and
things to love in Keira's life happened too rarely for her
to want to give them up without a fight.

She noticed that he said nothing as he ate, his expression suggesting he was merely fuelling his impressive
body rather than enjoying what was on offer—but Keira's hunger had completely deserted her and that was a
first. She normally had a healthy appetite, which often
surprised people who commented on her tiny frame.
But not today. Today food was the last thing on her
mind. She broke off the rim of one of the mince pies
and forced herself to chew on it and the sugar gave
her a sudden rush, but all she could think about was
how on earth they were going to get through the hours
ahead, when there wasn't even a radio in the room—
let alone a TV. She watched the way the lamplight fell
on her client's face—the hardness of his features con-
trasting with the sensual curve of his lips—and found
herself wondering what it might be like to be kissed by
a man like him.

Stop it, she urged herself furiously. Just *stop* it. You
couldn't even maintain the interest of that trainee mechanic you dated in the workshop—do you really fancy
your chances with the Italian billionaire?

A note of desperation tinged her voice as she struggled to think of something they could do which might
distract her from all that brooding masculinity. 'Shall
I go downstairs and see if Mary has any board games
we could play?'

He put his empty cup down and his eyes narrowed. 'Excuse me?'

'You know.' She shrugged her shoulders helplessly. 'Cards, or Scrabble or Monopoly. Something,' she added. 'Because we can't just spend the whole evening staring at each other and dreading the night ahead, can we?'

He raised his dark eyebrows. 'You're dreading the night ahead, are you, Keira?'

A shimmer of amusement had deepened his voice and Keira realised that, not only was it the first time he'd actually used her name, but that he'd said it as no one had ever said it before. She could feel colour flushing over her cheekbones and knew she had to stop coming over as some kind of unworldly idiot. 'Well, aren't you?' she challenged. 'Don't tell me your heart didn't sink when you realised we'd have to spend the night here.'

Matteo considered her question. Up until a few moments ago he might have agreed with her, but there was something about the girl with the spiky black hair which was making him reconsider his original assessment. It was, he thought, a novel situation and he was a man whose appetites had been jaded enough over the years to be entertained by the novel. And Keira whatever-her-name-was certainly wasn't your average woman. She wasn't behaving as most women would have done in the circumstances. She had suggested playing a game as if she actually meant it, without any purring emphasis on the word *playing*, leaving him in no doubt how she intended the 'game' to progress—with him thrusting into

her eager body. People called him arrogant, but he preferred to think of himself as a realist. He'd never been
guilty of under-assessing his own attributes—and one
of those was his ability to make the opposite sex melt,
without even trying.

He focussed his gaze on her, mildly amused by the
competitive look in her eyes which suggested that her
question had been genuine. 'Sure,' he said. 'Let's play
games.'

Picking up the tray, she went downstairs, reappearing
after a little while with a stack of board games, along
with a bottle of red wine and two glasses.

'There's no need to be snobby about the vintage,' she
said, noticing his expression as he frowningly assessed
the label on the bottle. 'It was very sweet of Mary to
offer us a festive drink and I'm having a glass even if
you aren't. I'm not driving anywhere tonight and I don't
want to offend her, not when she's been so kind.'

Feeling surprisingly chastened, Matteo took the bottle and opened it, pouring them each a glass and forcing himself to drink most of his in a single draught as
he lowered himself into the most uncomfortable chair
he'd ever sat in.

'Ready?' she questioned as she sat cross-legged on
the bed, with a blanket placed discreetly over her thighs
as she faced him.

'I guess,' he growled.

They played Monopoly, which naturally he won—
but then, he'd spent all his adult life trading property
and had learnt early that there was no commodity more
precious than land. But he was surprised when she sug-

gested a quick game of poker and even more surprised by her skill with the cards.

Matteo wondered afterwards if he'd been distracted by knowing her legs were bare beneath the blanket. Or if he'd just spent too long gazing at her curling black lashes, which remarkably didn't carry a trace of mascara. Because wasn't the truth that he was finding his pocket-sized driver more fascinating with every moment which passed? She was certainly managing to keep her face poker-straight as she gazed at her cards and inexplicably he found himself longing to kiss those unsmiling lips.

He swallowed. Was she aware that her coolness towards him was fanning a sexual awareness which was growing fiercer by the second? He didn't know—all he *did* know was that by the time they'd drunk most of the bottle of wine, she had beaten him hands-down and it was an unfamiliar experience.

He narrowed his eyes. 'Who taught you to play like that?'

She shrugged. 'Before I became a driver, I worked as a car mechanic—mostly with men,' she added airily. 'And they liked to play cards when the workshop was quiet.'

'You worked as a *car mechanic*?'

'You sound surprised.'

'I am surprised. You don't look strong enough to take a car to pieces.'

'Appearances can be deceptive.'

'They certainly can.' He picked up the bottle and emptied out the last of the wine, noticing her fingers tremble as he handed her the glass. She must be feeling it too, he thought grimly—that almost tangible buzz of *electricity* when his hand brushed against hers. He crossed one leg over the other to hide the hard throb of his erection as he tried—and failed—to think of something which didn't involve his lips and her body.

'Mr Valenti,' she said suddenly.

'Matteo,' he instructed silkily. 'I thought we agreed we should be on first-name terms, given the somewhat *unusual* circumstances.'

'Yes, we did, but I…'

Keira's words tailed away as he fixed her with a questioning look, not quite sure how to express her thoughts. The alcohol had made her feel more daring than usual—something which she'd fully exploited during that game of cards. She'd known it probably wasn't the most sensible thing to defeat Matteo Valenti and yet something had made her want to show him she wasn't as useless as he seemed to think she was. But she was now aware of her bravado slipping away. Just as she was aware of the tension which had been building in the cramped bedroom ever since she'd emerged from the bathroom.

Her breasts were aching and her inside-out panties were wet. Did he realise that? Perhaps he was used to women reacting that way around him but she wasn't one of those women. She'd been called frigid by men before, when really she'd been scared—scared of doing what her mother had always warned her against. But it had never been a problem before, because close contact with the opposite sex had always left her cold and the one time she'd ended up in bed with a man he had been snoring in a drunken stupor almost before his head had hit the pillow. So how was Matteo managing to make her feel like this—as if every pore were screaming for him to touch her?

She swallowed. 'We haven't discussed what we're going to do about sleeping arrangements.'

'What did you have in mind?'

'Well, it looks as if we've got to share a bed—so obviously we've got to come to some sort of compromise.' She drew a deep breath. 'And I was thinking we might sleep top and tail.'

'Top and tail?' he repeated.

'You know.'

'Obviously I don't,' he said impatiently. 'Or I wouldn't have asked.'

Awkwardly, she wriggled her shoulders. 'It's easy. I sleep with my head at one end of the bed and you sleep with yours at the other. We used to do it when I was in the Girl Guides. Sometimes people even put pillows between them, so they can keep to their side and there's no encroaching on the other person's space.' She forged on but it wasn't easy when he was staring at her with a growing look of incredulity. 'Unless you're prepared to spend the night in that armchair?'

Matteo became aware of the hardness of the over-stuffed seat which made him feel as if he were sitting on spirals of iron. 'You honestly think I'm going to spend the night sitting in this damned chair?'

She looked at him uncertainly. 'You want *me* to take the chair?'

'And keep me awake all night while you shift around trying to get comfortable? No. I do not. I'll tell you exactly what's going to happen, *cara mia*. We're going to share that bed as the nice lady suggested. But don't worry, I will break the habit of a lifetime by not sleeping naked and you can keep the sweater on. *Capisci?* And you can rest assured that you'll be safe from my intentions because I don't find you in the least bit attractive.'

Which wasn't exactly true—but why make a grim situation even worse than it already was?

He stood up and as he began to undo the belt of his trousers, he saw her lips fall open. 'Better close those big blue eyes,' he suggested silkily, a flicker of amusement curving his lips as he watched all the colour drain from her cheeks. 'At least until I'm safely underneath the covers.'

CHAPTER THREE

Keira lay in the darkness nudging her tongue over lips which felt as dry as if she'd been running a marathon. She'd tried everything. Breathing deeply. Counting backwards from a thousand. Relaxing her muscles from the toes up. But up until now nothing had worked and all she could think about was the man in bed beside her. *Matteo Valenti. In bed beside her.* She had to keep silently repeating it to herself to remind herself of the sheer impossibility of the situation—as well as the undeniable temptation which was fizzing over her.

Sheer animal warmth radiated from his powerful frame, making her want to squirm with an odd kind of frustration. She kept wanting to fidget but she forced herself to lie as still as possible, terrified of waking him up. She kept telling herself that she'd been up since six that morning and should be exhausted, but the more she reached out for sleep, the more it eluded her.

Was it because that unwilling glimpse of his body as he was about to climb into bed had reinforced all the fantasies she'd been trying not to have? And yes, he'd covered up with a T-shirt and a pair of silky boxers—

but they did nothing to detract from his hard-packed abdomen and hair-roughened legs. Each time she closed her eyes she could picture all that hard, honed muscle and a wave of hunger shivered over her body, leaving her almost breathless with desire.

The sounds coming from downstairs didn't help. The dinner which Mary had mentioned was in full flow and bothering her in ways she'd prefer not to think about. She could hear squeals of excitement above the chatter and, later, the heartbreaking strains of children's voices as they started singing carols. She could picture them all by a roaring log fire with red candles burning on the mantle above, just like on the front of a Christmas card, and Keira felt a wave of wistfulness overwhelm her because she'd never had that.

'Can't sleep?' The Italian's silky voice penetrated her spinning thoughts and she could tell from the shifting weight on the mattress that Matteo Valenti had turned his head to talk to her.

Keira swallowed. Should she pretend to be asleep? But what would be the point of that? She suspected he would see through her ruse immediately—and wasn't it a bit of a relief not to have to keep still any more? 'No,' she admitted. 'Can't you?'

He gave a short laugh. 'I wasn't expecting to.'

'Why not?'

His voice dipped. 'I suspect you know exactly why not. It's a somewhat *unusual* situation to be sharing a bed with an attractive woman and having to behave in such a chaste manner.'

Keira was glad of the darkness which hid her sudden

flush of pleasure. Had the gorgeous and arrogant Matteo Valenti actually called her *attractive*? And was he really implying that he was having difficulty keeping his hands off her? Of course, he might only be saying it to be polite—but he hadn't exactly been the model of politeness up until now, had he?

'I thought you said you didn't find me attractive.'

'That's what I was trying to convince myself.'

In the darkness, she gave a smile of pleasure. 'I could go downstairs and see if I could get us some more tea.'

'Please.' He groaned. 'No more tea.'

'Then I guess we'll have to resign ourselves to a sleepless night.' She plumped up her pillow and sighed as she collapsed back against it. 'Unless you've got a better suggestion?'

Matteo gave a frustrated smile because her question sounded genuine. She wasn't asking it in such a way which demanded he lean over and give her the answer with his lips. Just as she wasn't accidentally brushing one of those pretty little legs against his and tantalising him with her touch. He swallowed. Not that her virtuous attitude made any difference because he'd been hard from the moment he'd first slipped beneath the covers, and he was rock-hard now. Hard for a woman with terrible hair whose incompetence was responsible for him being marooned in this hellhole in the first place! A different kind of frustration washed over him as the lumpy mattress dug into his back until he reminded himself that apportioning blame would serve little purpose.

'I guess we could talk,' he said.

'What about?'

'What do women like best to talk about?' he questioned sardonically. 'You could tell me something about yourself.'

'And what good will that do?'

'Probably send me off to sleep,' he admitted.

He could hear her give a little snort of laughter. 'You do say some outrageous things, Mr Valenti.'

'Guilty. And I thought we agreed on Matteo—at least while we're in bed together.' He smiled as he heard her muffled gasp of outrage. 'Tell me how you plan to spend Christmas—isn't that what everyone asks at this time of year?'

Beneath the duvet, Keira flexed and unflexed her fingers, thinking that of all the questions he *could* have asked, that was the one she least felt like answering. Why hadn't he asked her about cars so she could have dazzled him with her mechanical knowledge? Or told him about her pipedream of one day being able to restore beautiful vintage cars, even though realistically that was never going to happen. 'With my aunt and my cousin, Shelley,' she said grudgingly.

'But you're not looking forward to it?'

'Is it that obvious?'

'I'm afraid it is. Your voice lacked a certain…enthusiasm.'

She thought that was a very diplomatic way of putting it. 'No, I'm not.'

'So why not spend Christmas somewhere else?'

Keira sighed. In the darkness it was all too easy to forget the veneer of nonchalance she always adopted when people asked questions about her personal life.

She kept facts to a minimum because it was easier that way. If you made it clear you didn't want to talk about something, then eventually people stopped asking.

But Matteo was different. She wasn't ever going to see him again after tomorrow. And wasn't it good to be able to say what she felt for once, instead of what she knew people expected to hear? She knew she was lucky her aunt had taken her in when that drunken joy-rider had mown down her mother on her way home from work, carrying the toy dog she'd bought for her daughter's birthday. Lucky she hadn't had to go into a foster home or some scary institution. But knowing something didn't always change the way you felt inside. And it didn't change the reality of being made to feel like an imposition. Of constantly having to be grateful for having been given a home, when it was clear you weren't really wanted. Trying to ignore all the snide little barbs because Keira had been better looking than her cousin Shelley. It had been the reason she'd cut off all her hair one day and kept it short. Anything for a quiet life. 'Because Christmas is a time for families and they're the only one I have,' she said.

'You don't have parents?'

'No.' And then, because he seemed to have left a gap for her to fill, she found herself doing exactly that. 'I didn't know my father and my aunt brought me up after my mother died, so I owe her a lot.'

'But you don't like her?'

'I didn't say that.'

'You didn't have to. It isn't a crime to admit it. You

don't have to like someone, just because they were kind to you, Keira, even if they're a relative.'

'She did her best and it can't have been easy. There wasn't a lot of money sloshing around,' she said. 'And now my uncle has died, there's only the two of them and I think she's lonely, in a funny kind of way. So I shall be sitting round a table with her and my cousin, pulling Christmas crackers and pretending to enjoy dry turkey. Just like most people, I guess.'

There was a pause so long that for a moment Keira wondered if he *had* fallen asleep, so that when he spoke again it startled her.

'So what *would* you do over Christmas?' he questioned softly. 'If money were no object and you didn't have to spend time with your aunt?'

Keira pulled the duvet up to her chin. 'How much money are we talking about? Enough to charter a private jet and fly to the Caribbean?'

'If that's what turns you on.'

'Not particularly.' Keira looked at the faint gleam of a photo frame glowing in the darkness on the other side of the room. It was a long time since she'd played make-believe. A long time since she'd dared. 'I'd book myself into the most luxurious hotel I could find,' she said slowly, 'and I'd watch TV. You know, one of those TVs which are big enough to fill a wall—big as a cinema screen. I've never had a TV in the bedroom before and it would be showing every cheesy Christmas film ever made. So I'd lie there and order up ice cream and popcorn and eat myself stupid and try not to blub too much.'

Beneath the thin duvet, Matteo's body tensed and not just because of the wistfulness in her voice. It had been a long time since he'd received such an uncomplicated answer from anyone. And wasn't her simple candour refreshing? As refreshing as her lean young body and eyes which were *profundo blu* if you looked at them closely—the colour of the deep, dark sea. The beat of his heart had accelerated and he felt the renewed throb of an erection, heavy against his belly. And suddenly the darkness represented danger because it was cloaking him with anonymity. Making him forget who he was and who she was. Tempting him with things he shouldn't even be thinking about. Because without light they were simply two bodies lying side by side, at the mercy of their senses—and right then his senses were going into overdrive.

Reaching out his arm, he snapped on the light, so that the small bedroom was flooded with a soft glow, and Keira lay there with the duvet right up to her chin, blinking her eyes at him.

'What did you do that for?'

'Because I'm finding the darkness…distracting.'

'I don't understand.'

He raised his eyebrows. 'Don't you?'

There was a pause. Matteo could see wariness in her eyes as she shook her head, but he could see the flicker of something else, something which made his heart pound even harder. Fraternising with the workforce was a bad idea—everyone knew that. But knowing something didn't always change the way you felt. It didn't stop your body from becoming so tight with lust that it felt like a taut bow, just before the arrow was fired.

No,' she said at last. 'I don't.'

'I think I'd better go and sleep in that damned armchair after all,' he said. 'Because if I stay here any longer I'm going to start kissing you.'

Keira met his mocking black gaze in astonishment. Had Matteo Valenti just said he wanted to *kiss* her? For a moment she just lay there, revelling in the sensation of being the object of attraction to such a gorgeous man, while common sense pitched a fierce battle with her senses.

She realised that despite talking about the armchair he hadn't moved and that an unspoken question seemed to be hovering in the air. Somewhere in a distant part of the house she heard a clock chiming and, though it wasn't midnight, it felt like the witching hour. As if magic could happen if she only let it. If she listened to what she wanted rather than the voice of caution which had been a constant presence in her life ever since she could remember. She'd learnt the hard way what happened to women who fell for the wrong kind of man— and Matteo Valenti had *wrong* written on every pore of his body. He was dangerous and sexy and he was a billionaire who was way out of her league. Shouldn't she be turning away from him and telling him yes, to please take the armchair?

Yet she wasn't doing any of those things. Instead of her eyes closing, the tip of her tongue was sliding over her bottom lip and she was finding it impossible to drag her gaze away from him. She could feel a molten heat low in her belly, which was making her ache in a way which was shockingly exciting. She thought about the holidays ahead. The stilted Christmas lunch with her aunt beaming at Shelley and talking proudly of her daughter's job as a beautician, while wondering how her only niece had ended up as a car mechanic.

Briefly Keira closed her eyes. She'd spent her whole life trying to be good and where had it got her? You didn't get medals for being good. She'd made the best of her dyslexia and capitalised on the fact that she was talented with her hands and could take engines apart, then put them back together. She'd found a job in a man's world which was just about making ends meet, but she'd never had a long-term relationship. She'd never even had sex—and if she wasn't careful she might end up old and wistful, remembering a snowy night on Dartmoor when Matteo Valenti had wanted to kiss her.

She stared at him. 'Go on, then,' she whispered. 'Kiss me.'

If she thought he might hesitate, she was wrong. There was no follow-up question about whether she was sure. He framed her face in his hands and the moment he lowered his lips to hers, that was it. The deal was done and there was no going back. He kissed her until she was dizzy with pleasure and molten with need. Until she began to move in his arms—restlessly seeking the next stage, terrified that any second now he would guess how laughingly inexperienced she was and push her away. She heard him laugh softly as he slid his fingers beneath the sweater to encounter the bra which curved over her breasts.

'Too much clothing,' he murmured, slipping his hand round her back to snap open the offending article and shake it free.

She remembered thinking he must have done this lots of times before and maybe she should confess how innocent she was. But by then he'd started circling her nipples with the light caress of his thumb and the moment passed. Desire pooled like honey in her groin and Keira gave a little cry as sensation threatened to overwhelm her.

'Sta' zitto,' he urged softly as he pulled the sweater over her head and tossed it aside, the movement quickly followed by the efficient disposal of his own T-shirt and boxers. 'Stay quiet. We don't want to disturb the rest of the house, do we?'

Keira shook her head, unable to answer because now he was sliding her panties down and a wild flame of hunger was spreading through her body. 'Matteo,' she gasped as his fingers moved down over her belly and began to explore her molten flesh. He stoked her with a delicacy which was tantalising—each intimate caress making her slide deeper into a brand-new world of intimacy. Yet strangely, it felt familiar. As if she knew exactly what to do, despite being such a novice. Did he tell her to part her legs or were they opening of their own accord? She didn't know. All she knew was that once he started stroking his fingertip against those hot, wet folds, she thought she might pass out with pleasure. 'Oh,' she whispered, on a note of wonder.

'Oh, what?' he murmured.

'It's…incredible.'

'I know it is. Now, touch me,' he urged against her mouth.

Keira swallowed. Did she dare? He was so big and proud and she didn't really know what to do. Swallowing down her nerves, she took him between her thumb and forefinger and began to stroke him up and down with a featherlight motion which nearly made him shoot off the bed.

'*Madonna mia!* Where did you learn to do *that*?' he gasped.

She guessed it might destroy the mood if she explained that car mechanics were often blessed with a naturally sensitive touch. Instead, she enquired in a husky voice which didn't really sound like her voice at all, 'Do you like it?'

'Do I like it?' He swallowed. 'Are you crazy? I love it.'

So why was he halting her progress with the firm clamp of his hand around her wrist, if he loved it so much? Why was he was blindly reaching for the wallet which he'd placed on the nightstand? He was pulling out a small foil packet and Keira shivered as she realised what he was about to do. This might be the craziest and most impulsive thing which had ever happened to her—but at least she would be protected.

He slid on the condom and she was surprised by her lack of fear as she wound her arms eagerly around his neck. Because it felt right. Not because he was rich and powerful, or even because he was insanely good-looking and sexy, but because something about him had touched her heart. Maybe it was the way his voice had softened when he'd asked her those questions about Christmas. Almost as if he *cared*—and it had been a long time since anybody had cared. Was she such a sucker for a few crumbs of affection that she would give herself completely to a man she didn't really know? She wasn't sure. All she knew was that she wanted him more than she'd ever wanted anything.

'Matteo,' she said as he pulled her into his body.

His eyes gleamed as he looked down at her. 'You want to change your mind?'

His consideration only made her want him more. 'No,' she whispered, her fingertips whispering over his neck. 'No way.'

He kissed her again—until she'd reached that same delicious melting point as before and then he moved to straddle her. His face was shadowed as he positioned himself and she tensed as he made that first thrust and began to move, but although the pain was sharp it was thankfully brief. She saw his brow darken and felt him grow very still before he changed his rhythm. His movements slowed as he bent her legs and wrapped them tightly around his waist so that with each long thrust he seemed to fill her completely.

As her body relaxed to accommodate his thickness, Keira felt the excitement build. Inch by glorious inch he entered her, before pulling back to repeat the same sweet stroke, over and over again. She could feel her skin growing heated as all her nerve-endings bunched in exquisitely tight anticipation. She could feel the inexorable build-up of excitement to such a pitch that she honestly didn't think she could take it any more. And then it happened. Like a swollen dam bursting open, waves of intense pleasure began to take her under. She felt herself shatter, as if he needed to break her apart before she could become whole again, and she pressed her mouth against his sweat-sheened shoulder. Dimly, she became aware of his own bucked release as he shuddered above her and was surprised by the unexpected prick of tears to her eyes.

He pulled out of her and rolled back against the pillows to suck in a ragged breath. With a sudden shyness, Keira glanced across at him but his eyes were closed and his olive features shuttered, so that suddenly she felt excluded from the private world in which he seemed to be lost. The room was quiet and she didn't dare speak—wondering what women usually said at moments like this.

Eventually he turned to her, his eyebrows raised in question and an expression on his face she couldn't quite work out.

'So?'

She wanted to hang on to the pleasure for as long as possible—she didn't want it all to evaporate beneath the harsh spotlight of explanation—but he seemed to be waiting for one all the same.

She peered up at him. 'You're angry?'

He shrugged. 'Why should I be angry?'

'Because I didn't tell you.'

'That you were a virgin?' He gave an odd kind of laugh. 'I'm glad you didn't. It might have shattered the mood.'

She tucked a strand of hair behind her ear. 'Aren't you going to ask me why?'

'You chose me to be your first?' His smile now held a faint trace of arrogance. 'I could commend you for your excellent judgment in selecting someone like me to be your first lover, but it's not really any of my business, is it, Keira?'

For some reason, that hurt, though she wasn't going to show it. Had she been naïve enough to suppose he might exhibit a chest-thumping pride that she had chosen him, rather than anyone else? 'I suppose not,' she said, her toes moving beneath the rumpled bedclothes in a desperate attempt to locate her only pair of panties.

'I just hope you weren't disappointed.'

'You must know I wasn't,' she said, in a small voice.

He seemed to soften a little at that, and brushed back a few little tufts of hair which had fallen untidily over her forehead. '*Sì*, I know. And for what it's worth, it was pretty damned amazing for me, too. I've never had sex with a virgin before but I understand it's uncommon for it to be as good as that the first time. So you should feel very pleased with yourself.' He began to stroke her hair. 'And you're tired.'

'No.'

'Yes,' he said firmly. 'And you need to sleep. So why don't you do that? Lie back and let yourself drift off.'

His words were soothing but Keira didn't want to sleep, she wanted to talk. She wanted to ask him about himself and his life. She wanted to know what would happen now—but there was something in his voice which indicated he didn't feel the same. And mightn't stilted conversation destroy some of this delicious afterglow which felt so impossibly fragile—like a bubble which could be popped at any moment? So she nodded obediently and shut her eyes and within seconds she could feel herself drifting off into the most dreamy sleep she'd ever known.

Matteo watched as her eyelashes fluttered down and waited until her breathing was steady before removing his arm from where it had been resting around her shoulders, but, although she stirred a little, she didn't waken. And that was when the reality of what he'd done hit him.

He'd just seduced a member of staff. More than that, he'd taken her innocence.

Silently, he cursed. He'd broken two fundamental rules in the most spectacular way. His chest was tight as he switched off the lamp and his mind buzzed as he attempted to ignore the naked woman who lay sleeping beside him. Yet that was easier said than done. He wanted nothing more than to push his growing erection inside her tight body again, but he needed to work out the most effective form of damage limitation. For both of them.

He stared up at the shadowy ceiling and sighed. He didn't want to hurt her and he could so easily hurt her. Hurting was something he seemed to do to women without even trying, mainly because he couldn't do love and he couldn't do emotion—at least that was what he'd been accused of, time after time. And Keira didn't deserve that. She'd given herself to him with an openness which had left him breathless and afterwards there had been no demands.

But none of that detracted from the reality of their situation. They came from worlds which were poles apart, which had collided in this small bedroom on the snowy outreaches of Devon. For a brief time they had come together in mindless pleasure but in truth they were nothing more than mismatched strangers driven by the stir of lust. Back in Italy he had been given an ultimatum which needed addressing and he needed to consider the truth behind his father's words.

'Give me an heir, Matteo,' he had breathed. *'Continue the Valenti name and I will give you your heart's desire. Refuse and I will sign the estate over to your stepbrother and his child.'*

Matteo's heart kicked with pain. He had to decide how much he was willing to sacrifice to maintain his links to the past. He needed to return to his world. And Keira to hers.

His jaw tightened. Would he have stopped if he'd known he was her first? He might have *wanted* to stop but something told him he would have been powerless to pull back from the indescribable lure of her petite body. His throat dried as he remembered that first sweet thrust. She had seemed much too small to accommodate him, but she had taken him inside her as if he had been intended to fit into her and only her. He remembered the way she'd touched him with that tentative yet sure touch. She'd made him want to explode. Had the newness of it been responsible for her joyful response—and for the tears which had trickled against his shoulder afterwards, but which she'd hastily blotted away?

Suddenly he could understand the potent power wielded by virgins but he could also recognise that they were a responsibility. They still had dreams—because experience hadn't yet destroyed them. Would she be expecting him to take her number? For him to fly her out to Rome for a weekend of sex and then see what happened? Hand in hand for a sunset stroll along Trastevere, Rome's supposedly most romantic neighbourhood? Because that was never going to happen. His jaw tightened. It would only raise up her hopes before smashing them.

He heard her murmur something in her sleep and felt the heavy weight of his conscience as he batted possibilities back and forth. What would be the best thing he could do for Keira—this sexy little driver with the softest lips he'd ever known? Glancing at his watch, he saw from the luminous dial that it was just before midnight and the rest of the house had grown silent. Could he risk using the landline downstairs without waking everyone? Of course he could. Slipping from the sex-scented bed, he threw on some clothes and made his way downstairs.

He placed the call without any trouble, but his mood was strangely low after he'd terminated his whispered conversation and made his way back to the bedroom. With the light from the corridor flooding in, he stared at Keira's face, which was pillowed on a bent elbow. Her lips were curved in a soft smile and he wanted to kiss them. To take her in his arms and run his hands over her and do it all over again. But he couldn't. Or rather, he shouldn't.

He was careful not to touch her as he climbed into bed, but the thought of her out-of-bounds nakedness meant that he lay there sleeplessly for a long, long time.

CHAPTER FOUR

A PALE LIGHT woke her and for a moment Keira lay completely still, her head resting against a lumpy pillow as her eyes flickered open and she tried to work out exactly where she was. And then she remembered. She was in a strange bedroom on the edge of a snowy Dartmoor—and she'd just lost her virginity to the powerful billionaire she'd been driving around the country!

She registered the sweet aching between her legs and the delicious sting of her nipples as slowly she turned her head to see that the other half of the bed was empty. Her pulse speeded up. He must be in the bathroom. Quickly, she sat up, raking her fingers through her mussed hair and giving herself a chance to compose herself before Matteo returned.

The blindingly pale crack of light shining through the gap in the curtains showed that the snow was still very much in evidence and a smile of anticipation curved her lips. Maybe they'd be stuck here today too—and they could have sex all over again. She certainly hoped so. Crossing her arms over her naked breasts, she hugged herself tightly as endorphins flooded through her warm body. Obviously, she'd need to reassure him that although she was relatively inexperienced, she certainly wasn't naïve. She knew the score—she'd heard the men in the workshop talking about women often enough to know what they did and didn't like. She would be very grown up about what had happened. She'd make it clear that she wasn't coming at this with any *expectations*—although, of course, if he wanted to see her again when the snow had been cleared she would be more than happy with that.

And that was when she noticed the nightstand—or rather, what was lying on top of it. Keira blinked her eyes in disbelief but as her vision cleared she realised this was no illusion as she stared in growing horror at the enormous wad of banknotes. She felt as if she were taking part in some secretly filmed reality show. As if the money might suddenly disintegrate if she touched it, or as if Matteo would suddenly appear from out of hiding. She looked around, realising there *was* nowhere to hide in this tiny room.

'Matteo?' she questioned uncertainly.

Nobody came. Of course they didn't. She stared at the money and then noticed the piece of paper which was lying underneath it. It took several seconds before she could bring herself to pick it up and as she began to read it she was scarcely able to believe what she was seeing.

Keira, he had written—and in the absence of any affectation like *Dear* or *Darling,* she supposed she ought to be grateful that he'd got her name right, because Irish names were notoriously difficult to spell.

*I just wanted to tell you how much I enjoyed
last night and I hope you did, too. You looked so
peaceful sleeping this morning that I didn't want
to wake you—but I need to be back in Italy as
soon as possible.*

*You told me your dream was to spend Christ-
mas in a luxury hotel and I'd like to make this
possible, which is why I hope you'll accept this
small gift in the spirit with which it was intended.*

*And if we'd been playing poker for money, you
would certainly have walked away with a lot more
than this!*

I wish you every good thing for your future.
Buon Natale.
Matteo.

Keira's fingers closed tightly around the note and
her feeling of confusion intensified as she stared at the
money—more money than she'd ever seen. She allowed
herself a moment of fury before getting up out of bed,
acutely aware that for once she wasn't wearing her usual
nightshirt, and the sight of her naked body in the small
mirror taunted her with memories of just what she and
the Italian had done last night. And once the fury had
passed she was left with hurt, and disappointment. Had
she really been lying there, naïvely thinking that Matteo was going to emerge from the bathroom and take
her in his arms when the reality was that he couldn't
even bear to face her? What a stupid fool she'd been.

She washed and dressed and went downstairs, po-
litely refusing breakfast but accepting a mug of strong

tea from Mary, who seemed delighted to relay everything which had been happening while Keira had been
asleep.

'First thing I know, there's a knock on the door and
it's a man in one of those big four-wheel drives,' she
announced.

'Which managed to get through the snow?' questioned Keira automatically.

'Oh, yes. Because Mr Valenti ordered a car with a
snow plough. Apparently he got on the phone late last
night while everyone was asleep and organised it. Must
have been very quiet because nobody heard him.'

Very quiet, thought Keira grimly. He must have been
terrified that she would wake up and demand he take
her with him.

'And he's ordered some men to dig your car out of
the snow. Said there was no way you must be stranded
here,' said Mary, with a dreamy look on her careworn
face. 'They arrived about an hour ago—they should be
finished soon.'

Keira nodded. 'Can I pay you?'

Mary beamed. 'No need. Your Mr Valenti was more
than generous.'

Keira's heart pounded; she wanted to scream that
he wasn't 'her' anything. So the cash wasn't there to
pay for the B& B or help her make her own journey
home, because he'd already sorted all that out. Which
left only one reason for leaving it. Of course. How could
she have been so dense when the bland words of the
accompanying letter had made it perfectly clear? The
comment about the poker and the disingenuous sug-

gestion she take herself off to a luxury hotel were just a polite way of disguising the very obvious. A wave of sickness washed over her.

Matteo Valenti had *paid her for sex*.

Operating on a dazed kind of autopilot, Keira made her way back to her newly liberated car, from where she slowly drove back to London. After dropping the car off at Luxury Limos, she made her way to Brixton, acutely aware of the huge wad of cash she was carrying. She'd thought of leaving it behind at Mary's, but wouldn't the kindly landlady have tried to return it and just made matters a whole lot worse? And how on earth would she have managed to explain what it was doing there? Yet it felt as if it were burning a massive hole in her pocket—haunting her with the bitter reminder of just what the Italian really thought of her.

The area of Brixton where she rented a tiny apartment had once been considered unfashionable but now, like much of London, the place was on the up. Two days before Christmas and the streets had a festive air which was bordering on the hysterical, despite the fact that the heavy snows hadn't reached the capital. Bright lights glittered and she could see Christmas trees and scarlet-suited Santas everywhere she looked. On the corner, a Salvation Army band was playing 'Silent Night' and the poignancy of the familiar tune made her heart want to break. And stupidly, she found herself missing her mother like never before as she thought about all the Christmases they'd never got to share. Tears pricked at the backs of her eyes as she hugged her an-

orak around her shivering body, and never had she felt
so completely alone.

But self-pity would get her nowhere. She was a survivor, wasn't she? She would get through this as she
had got through so much else. Dodging the crowds, she
started to walk home, her journey taking her past one
of the area's many charity shops and as an idea came
to her she impulsively pushed open the door of one. Inside, the place was full of people trying on clothes for
Christmas parties and New Year—raiding feather boas
and old-fashioned shimmery dresses from the crowded
rails. The atmosphere was chaotic and happy but Keira
was grim-faced as she made her way to the cash desk.
Fumbling around in her pocket, she withdrew the wad
of cash and slapped it down on the counter in front of
the startled cashier.

'Take this,' Keira croaked. 'And Happy Christmas.'

The woman held up a hand. 'Whoa! Wait a minute!
Where did you—?'

But Keira was already pushing her way out of the
shop, the cold air hitting the tears which had begun
streaming down her cheeks. Her vision blurred and she
stumbled a little and might have fallen if a steady arm
hadn't caught her elbow.

'Are you okay?' a female voice was saying.

Was she okay? No, she most definitely was not. Keira
nodded, looking up at a woman with platinum hair who
was wearing a leopard-skin-print coat. 'I'm fine. I just
need to get home,' she husked.

'Not like that, you're not. You're not fit to go anywhere,' said the woman firmly. 'Let me buy you a drink. You look like you could use one.'

Still shaken, Keira allowed herself to be led into the bright interior of the Dog and Duck where music was playing and the smell of mulled wine filled her nostrils. The woman went up to the bar and returned minutes later with a glass of a brown mixture resembling medicine, which was pushed across the scratched surface of the table towards her.

'What's this?' Keira mumbled, lifting the glass and recoiling from the fumes.

'Brandy.'

'I don't like brandy.'

'Drink it. You look like you're in shock.'

That much was true. Keira took a large and fiery swallow and the weird thing was that she *did* feel better afterwards. Disorientated, yes—but better.

'So where did you get the money from?' the blonde was asking. 'Did you rob a bank or something? I was in the charity shop when you came in and handed it over. Pretty dramatic gesture, but a lovely thing to do, I must say—especially at this time of the year.'

Afterwards Keira thought that if she hadn't had the brandy then she might not have told the sympathetic blonde the whole story, but the words just started tumbling out of her mouth and they wouldn't seem to stop. Just like the tears which had preceded them. It was only when the woman's eyes widened when she came out with the punchline about how Matteo had left her a stack of money and done a runner that she became aware that something in the atmosphere had changed.

'So he just disappeared? Without a word?'

'Well, he left a note.'

'May I see it?'

Keira put the brandy glass down with a thud. 'No.'

There was a pause. 'He must be very rich,' observed the blonde. 'To be able to be carrying around that kind of money.'

Keira shrugged. 'Very.'

'And good-looking, I suppose?'

Keira swallowed. 'What does that have to do with anything?'

The blonde's heavily made-up eyes narrowed. 'Hunky Italian billionaires don't usually have to pay women for sex.'

It was hearing someone else say it out loud which made it feel a million times worse—something Keira hadn't actually thought possible. She rose unsteadily to her feet, terrified she was going to start gagging. 'I… I'm going home now,' she whispered. 'Please forget I said anything. And…thanks for the drink.'

Somehow she managed to get home unscathed, where her cold, bare bedsit showed no signs of the impending holiday. She'd been so busy that she hadn't even bought herself a little tree, but that now seemed like the least of her worries. She realised she hadn't checked her phone messages since she'd got back and found a terse communication from her aunt, asking her what time she was planning on turning up on Christmas Day and hoping she hadn't forgotten to buy the pudding.

The pudding! Now she would have to brave the wretched shops again. Keira closed her eyes as she pictured the grim holiday which lay ahead of her. How was she going to get through a whole Christmas, nursing the shameful secret of what she'd done?

Her phone began to ring, the small screen flashing an unknown number; in an effort to distract herself with the inevitable sales call, Keira accepted the call with a tentative hello. There was an infinitesimal pause before a male voice spoke.

'Keira?'

It was a voice she hadn't known until very recently but she thought that rich, Italian accent would be branded on her memory until the end of time. Dark and velvety, it whispered over her skin just as his fingers had done. Matteo! And despite everything—the wad of money and the blandly worded note and the fact that he'd left without even saying goodbye—wasn't there a great lurch of hope inside her foolish heart? She pictured his ruffled hair and the dark eyes which had gleamed with passion when they'd looked at her. The way he'd crushed his lips hungrily down on hers, and that helpless moment of bliss when he'd first entered her.

'Matteo?'

Another pause—and if a silence could ever be considered ominous, this one was. 'So how much did she pay you?' he questioned.

'Pay me?' Keira blinked in confusion, thinking that bringing up money wasn't the best way to start a conversation, especially in view of what had happened. 'What are you talking about?'

'I've just had a phone call from a…a *journalist*.'

He spat out the word as if it were poison. 'Asking me whether I make a habit of paying women for sex.'

Keira's feeling of confusion intensified. 'I don't...' And then she realised and hot colour flooded into her cheeks. 'Was her name Hester?'

'So you *did* speak to her?' He sucked in an unsteady breath. 'What was it, Keira—a quickly arranged interview to see what else you could squeeze out of me?'

'I didn't plan on talking to her—it just happened.'

'Oh, really?'

'Yes, really. I was angry about the money you left me!' she retorted.

'Why? Didn't you think it was enough?' he shot back. 'Did you imagine you might be able to get even more?'

Keira sank onto the nearest chair, terrified that her wobbly legs were going to give way beneath her. 'You bastard,' she whispered.

'Your anger means nothing to me,' he said coldly. 'For *you* are nothing to me. I wasn't thinking straight. I couldn't have been thinking straight. I should never have had sex with you because I don't make a habit of having one-night stands with strangers. But what's done can't be undone and I have only myself to blame.'

There was a pause before he resumed and now his voice had taken on a flat and implacable note, which somehow managed to sound even more ominous than his anger.

'I've told your journalist friend that if she prints one word about me, I'll go after her and bring her damned publication down,' he continued. 'Because I'm not someone you can blackmail—I'm just a man who allowed himself to be swayed by lust and it's taught me a lesson I'm never going to forget.' He gave a bitter laugh. 'So, goodbye, Keira. Have a good life.'

CHAPTER FIVE

Ten months later

'I HOPE THAT baby isn't going to cry all the way through lunch, Keira. It would be nice if we were able to eat a meal in peace for once.'

Tucking little Santino into the crook of her arm, Keira nodded as she met her aunt's accusing stare. She would have taken the baby out for a walk if the late October day hadn't been so foul and blustery. Or she might have treated him to a long bus ride to lull him to sleep if he hadn't been so tiny. As it was, she was stuck in the house with a woman who seemed determined to find fault in everything she did, and she was tired. So tired. With the kind of tiredness which seemed to have seeped deep into her bones and taken up residence there. 'I'll try to put him down for his nap before we sit down to eat,' she said hopefully.

Aunt Ida's mouth turned down at the corners, emphasising the deep grooves of discontentment which hardened her thin face. 'That'll be a first. Poor Shelley says she hasn't had an unbroken night since you moved in. He's obviously an unsettled baby if he cries so much. Maybe it's time you came to your senses and thought about adoption.'

Keira's teeth dug into her bottom lip as the word lodged like a barb in her skin.

Adoption.

A wave of nausea engulfed her but she tried very hard not to react as she stared down into the face of her sleeping son. Holding onto Santino even tighter, she felt her heart give a savage lurch of love as she told herself to ignore the snide comments and concentrate on what was important. Because only one thing mattered and that was her baby son.

Everything you do is for him, she reminded herself fiercely. *Everything.* No point in wishing she hadn't given away Matteo's money, or tormenting herself by thinking how useful it might have been. She hadn't known at the time that she was pregnant—how could she have done? She'd handed over that thick wad of banknotes as if there were loads more coming her way—and now she just had to deal with the situation as it was and not what it could have been. She had to accept that she'd lost her job and her home in quick succession and had been forced to take the charity of a woman who had always disapproved of her. Because how else would she and Santino have managed to cope in an uncaring and hostile world?

You know exactly how, prompted the ever-present voice of her conscience but Keira pushed it from her mind. She could *not* have asked Matteo for help, not when he had treated her like some kind of *whore*. Who had made it clear he never wanted to see her again.

'Have you registered the child's birth yet?' Aunt Ida was asking.

'Not yet, no,' said Keira. 'I have to do it within the first six weeks.'

'Better get a move on, then.'

Keira waited, knowing that there was more.

Her aunt smiled slyly. 'Only I was wondering whether you were going to put the mystery father's name on the birth certificate—or whether you were like your poor dear mother and didn't actually know who he was?'

Keira's determination not to react drained away. Terrified of saying something she might later regret, she turned and walked out of the sitting room without another word, glad she was holding Santino because that stopped her from picking up one of her aunt's horrible china ornaments and hurling it against the wall. Criticism directed against her she could just about tolerate—but she wouldn't stand to hear her mother's name maligned like that.

Her anger had evaporated by the time she reached the box-room she shared with Santino, and Keira placed the baby carefully in his crib, tucking the edges of the blanket around his tiny frame and staring at him. His lashes looked very long and dark against his olive skin but for once she found herself unable to take pleasure in his innocent face. Because suddenly, the fear and the guilt which had been nagging away inside her now erupted into one fierce and painful certainty.

She couldn't go on like this. Santino deserved more than a mother who was permanently exhausted, having to tiptoe around a too-small house with people who didn't really like her. She closed her eyes, knowing there was somebody else who didn't like her—but someone she suspected wouldn't display a tight-lipped intolerance whenever the baby started to cry. Because it was *his* baby, too. And didn't all parents love their children, no matter what?

A powerful image swam into her mind of a man whose face she could picture without too much trying. She knew what she had to do. Something she'd thought about doing every day since Santino's birth, and in the nine months preceding it, until she'd forced herself to remember how unequivocally he'd told her he never wanted to see her again. Well, maybe he was going to have to.

Her fingers were shaking as she scrolled down her phone's contact list and retrieved the number she had saved, even though the caller had hung up on her the last time she'd spoken to him.

With a thundering heart, she punched out the number. And waited.

Rain lashed against the car windscreen and flurries of falling leaves swirled like the thoughts in Matteo's mind as his chauffeur-driven limousine drove down the narrow suburban road. As they passed houses which all looked exactly the same, he tried to get his head round what he'd learned during a phone call from a woman he'd never thought he'd see again.

He was a father.

He had a child.

A son. His heart pumped. In a single stroke he had been given exactly what he needed—though not necessarily what he wanted—and could now produce the grandson his father yearned for.

Matteo ordered the driver to stop, trying to dampen down the unfamiliar emotions which were sweeping through his body. And trying to curb his rising temper about the way Keira had kept this news secret. How *dared* she keep his baby hidden and play God with his future? Grim-faced, he stepped out onto the rain-soaked pavement and a wave of determination washed over him as he slammed the car door shut. He was here now and he would fix this—to his advantage. Whatever it took, he would get what he wanted—and he wanted his son.

He hadn't told Keira he was coming. He hadn't wanted to give her the opportunity to elude him. He wanted to surprise her—as she had surprised him. To allow her no time to mount any defences. If she was unprepared and vulnerable then surely that would aid him in his determination to get his rightful heir. Moving stealthily up the narrow path, he rapped a small bronze knocker fashioned in the shape of a lion's head and moments later the door was opened by a woman with tight, curly hair and a hard, lined face.

'Yes?' she said sharply. 'We don't buy from the doorstep.'

'Good afternoon,' he said. Forcing the pleasantry to his unwilling lips, he accompanied it with a polite smile. 'I'm not selling anything. I'd like to see Keira.'

'And you are?'

'My name is Matteo Valenti,' he said evenly. 'And I am her baby's father.'

The woman gasped, her eyes scanning him from head to toe, as if registering his cashmere coat and handmade shoes. Her eyes skated over his shoulder and she must have observed the shiny black car parked so incongruously among all the sedate family saloons. Was he imagining the look of calculation which had hardened her gimlet eyes? Probably not, he thought grimly.

'You?' she demanded.

'That's right,' he agreed, still in that same even voice which betrayed nothing of his growing irritation.

'I had no idea that…' She swallowed. 'I'll have to check if she'll see you.'

'No,' Matteo interrupted her, only just resisting the desire to step forward and jam his foot in the door, like a bailiff. 'I *will* see Keira—and my baby—and it's probably best if we do it with the minimum of fuss.' He glanced behind him where he could see the twitching of net curtains on the opposite side of the road and when he returned his gaze to the woman, his smile was bland. 'Don't you agree? For everyone's sake?'

The woman hesitated before nodding, as if she too had no desire for a scene on the doorstep. 'Very well. You'd better come in.' She cleared her throat. 'I'll let Keira know you're here.'

He was shown into a small room crammed with porcelain figurines but Matteo barely paid any attention to his surroundings. His eyes were trained on the door as it clicked open and he held his breath in anticipation—

expelling it in a long sigh of disbelief and frustration when Keira finally walked in. Frustration because she was alone. And disbelief because he scarcely recognised her as the same woman whose bed he had shared almost a year ago—though that lack of recognition certainly didn't seem to be affecting the powerful jerk of his groin.

Gone was the short, spiky hair and in its place was a dark curtain of silk which hung glossily down to her shoulders. And her body. He swallowed. What the hell had happened to *that*? All the angular leanness of before had gone. Suddenly she had hips—as well as the hint of a belly and breasts. It made her look softer, he thought, until he reminded himself that a woman with any degree of softness wouldn't have done what she had done.

'Matteo,' she said, her voice sounding strained—and it was then he noticed the pallor and the faint circles which darkened the skin beneath her eyes. In those fathomless pools of deepest blue he could read the vulnerability he had wanted to see, yet he felt a sudden twist of something like compassion, until he remembered what she had done.

'The very same,' he agreed grimly. 'Pleased to see me?'

'I wasn't—' She was trying to smile but failing spectacularly. 'I wasn't expecting you. I mean, not like this. Not without any warning.'

'Really? What did you imagine was going to happen, Keira? That I would just accept the news you finally saw fit to tell me and wait for your next instruction?' He walked across the room to stare out of the window and saw that a group of small boys had gathered around his limousine. He turned around and met her eyes. 'Perhaps you were hoping you wouldn't have to see me at all. Were you hoping I would remain a shadowy figure in the background and become your convenient benefactor?'

'Of course I wasn't!'

'No?' He flared his nostrils. 'Then why *bother* telling me about my son? Why now after all these months of secrecy?'

Keira tried not to flinch beneath the accusing gaze which washed over her like a harsh ebony spotlight. It was difficult enough seeing him again and registering the infuriating fact that her body had automatically started to melt, without having to face his undiluted fury.

Remember the things he said to you, she reminded herself. But the memory of his wounding words seemed to have faded and all she could think was the fact that here stood Santino's father and that, oh, the apple didn't fall far from the tree.

For here was the adult version of the little baby she'd just rocked off to sleep before the doorbell had rung. Santino was the image of his father, with his golden olive skin and dark hair, and hadn't the midwife already commented on the fact that her son was going to grow up to be a heartbreaker? Keira swallowed. Just like Matteo.

She felt an uncomfortable rush of awareness because it wasn't easy to acknowledge the stir of her body, or the fact that her senses suddenly felt as if they'd been kicked into life. Matteo's hair and his eyes seemed even blacker than she remembered and never had his sensual lips appeared more kissable. Yet surely that was the last thing she should be thinking of right now. Her mind-set should be fixed on practicalities, not foolish yearn-ings. She felt disappointed in herself and wondered if nature was clever enough to make a woman desire the father of her child, no matter how contemptuously he was looking at her.

She found herself wishing he'd given her some kind of warning so she could at least have washed her hair and made a bit of effort with her appearance. Since hav-ing a baby she'd developed curves and she was shame-fully aware that her pre-pregnancy jeans were straining at the hips and her baggy top was deeply unflattering. But the way she looked had been the last thing on her mind. She knew she needed new clothes but she'd been forced to wait, and not just because of a chronic short-age of funds.

Because how could she possibly go shopping for clothes with a tiny infant in tow? Asking her aunt to babysit hadn't been an option—not when she was con-stantly made aware of their generosity in providing a home for her and her illegitimate child, and how that same child had disrupted all their lives. The truth was she hadn't wanted to spend her precious pennies on new clothes when she could be buying stuff for San-tino. Which was why she was wearing an unflatter-ing outfit, which was probably making Matteo Valenti wonder what he'd ever seen in her. Measured against his made-to-measure sophistication, Keira felt like a scruffy wrongdoer who had just been dragged before an elegant high court judge.

She forced a polite smile to her lips. 'Would you like to sit down?'

'No, I don't want to *sit down*. I want an answer to my question. Why did you contact me to tell me that I was a father? Why now?'

She flushed right up to the roots of her hair. 'Because by law I have to register his birth and that brought everything to a head. I've realised I can't go on living like this. I thought I could but I was wrong. I'm very…grateful to my aunt for taking me in but it's too cramped. They don't really want me here and I can kind of see their point.' She met his eyes. 'And I don't want Santino growing up in this kind of atmosphere.'

Santino.

As she said the child's name Matteo felt a whisper of something he didn't recognise. Something completely outside his experience. He could feel it in the icing of his skin and sudden clench of his heart. 'Santino?' he repeated, wondering if he'd misheard her. He stared at her, his brow creased in a frown. 'You gave him an Italian name?'

'Yes.'

'Why?'

'Because when I looked at him—' her voice faltered as she scraped her fingers back through her hair and turned those big sapphire eyes on him '—I knew I could call him nothing else but an Italian name.'

'Even though you sought to deny him his heritage and kept his birth hidden from me?'

She swallowed. 'You made it very clear that you never wanted to see me again, Matteo.'

'I didn't know you were pregnant at the time,' he bit out.

'And neither did I!' she shot back.

'But you knew afterwards.'

'Yes.' How could she explain the sense of alienation she'd felt—not just from him, but from everyone? When everything had seemed so *unreal* and the world had suddenly looked like a very different place. The head of Luxury Limos had said he didn't think it was a good idea if she carried on driving—not when she looked as if she was about to throw up whenever the car went over a bump. And even though she hadn't been sick— not once—and even though Keira knew that by law she could demand to stay where she was, she didn't have the energy or the funds to investigate further. What was she going to do—take him to an industrial tribunal?

She'd been terrified her boss would find out who the father of her unborn child was—because having sex with your most prestigious client was definitely a sacking offence. He'd offered her a job back in the workshop, but she had no desire to slide underneath a car and get oil all over her hands, not when such a precious bundle was growing inside her. Eventually she'd accepted a mind-numbingly dull job behind the reception desk, becoming increasingly aware that on the kind of wages she was being paid, she'd never be able to afford childcare after the birth. She'd saved every penny she could and been as frugal as she knew how, but gradually all her funds were running out and now she was in real trouble.

'Yes, I knew,' she said slowly. 'Just like I knew I ought to tell you that you were going to be a father. But every time I picked up the phone to call you, something held me back. Can't you understand?'

'Frankly, no. I can't.'

She looked him straight in the eye. 'You think those cruel words you said to me last time we spoke wouldn't matter? That you could say what you liked and it wouldn't hurt, or have consequences?'

His voice grew hard. 'I haven't come here to argue the rights and wrongs of your secrecy. I've come to see my son.'

'He's sleeping.'

'I won't wake him.' His voice grew harsh. 'You've denied me all this time and you will deny me no longer. I want to see my son, Keira, and if I have to search every room in the house to find him, then that's exactly what I'm going to do.'

It was a demand Keira couldn't ignore and not just because she didn't doubt his threat to search the small house from top to bottom. She'd seen the brief tightening of his face when she'd mentioned his child and another wave of guilt had washed over her. Because she of all people knew what it was like to grow up without a father. She knew about the gaping hole it left—a hole which could never be filled. And yet she had sought to subject her own child to that.

'Come with me,' she said huskily.

He followed her up the narrow staircase and Keira

was acutely aware of his presence behind her. You couldn't ignore him, even when you couldn't see him, she thought despairingly. She could detect the heat from his body and the subtle sandalwood which was all his and, stupidly, she remembered the way that scent had clung to her skin the morning after he'd made love to her. Her heart was thundering by the time they reached the box-room she shared with Santino and she held her breath as Matteo stood frozen for a moment before moving soundlessly towards the crib. His shoulders were stiff with tension as he reached it and he was silent for so long that she started to get nervous.

'Matteo?' she said.

Matteo didn't answer. Not then. He wasn't sure he trusted himself to speak because his thoughts were in such disarray. He looked down at the baby expecting to feel the instant bolt of love people talked about when they first set eyes on their own flesh and blood, but there was nothing. He stared down at the dark fringe of eyelashes which curved on the infant's olive-hued cheeks and the shock of black hair. Tiny hands were curled into two tiny fists and he found himself leaning forward to count all the fingers, nodding his head with satisfaction as he registered each one. He felt as if he were observing himself and his reaction from a distance and realised it was possession he felt, not love. The sense that this was someone who belonged to him in a way that nobody ever had before.

His son.

He swallowed.

His *son*.

He waited for a moment before turning to Keira and he saw her dark blue eyes widen, as if she'd read something in his face she would prefer not to have seen.

'So you played God with all our futures,' he observed softly. 'By keeping him from me.'

Her gaze became laced with defiance.

'You paid me for sex.'

'I did not *pay you for sex*,' he gritted out. 'I explained my motivation in my note. You spoke of a luxury you weren't used to and I thought I would make it possible. Was that so very wrong?'

'You know very well it was!' she burst out. 'Because offering me cash was insulting. Any man would know that.'

'Was that why you tried to sell your story to the journalist, because you felt "insulted"?'

'I did not *sell my story* to anyone,' she shot back. 'Can't you imagine what it was like? I'd had sex for the first time and woke to find you gone, leaving that wretched pile of money. I walked into a charity shop to get rid of it because it felt…well, it felt tainted, if you must know.'

He grew very still. 'You gave it away?'

'Yes, I gave it away. To a worthy cause—to children living in care. Not realising I was pregnant at the time and could have used the money myself. The journalist just happened to be in the shop and overheard—and naturally she was interested. She bought me a drink and I hadn't eaten anything all day and…' She shrugged. 'I guess I told her more than I meant to.'

Matteo's eyes narrowed. If her story was true it

meant she hadn't tried to grab some seedy publicity from their brief liaison. *If it was true.* Yet even if it was—did it really change anything? He was here only because her back was up against the wall and she had nowhere else to turn. His gaze swept over the too-tight jeans and baggy jumper. And this was the mother of his child, he thought, his lips curving with distaste.

He opened his mouth to speak but Santino chose that moment to start to whimper and Keira bent over the crib to scoop him up, whispering her lips against his hair and rocking him in her arms until he had grown quiet again. She looked over his head, straight into Matteo's eyes. 'Would you…would you like to hold him?'

Matteo went very still. He knew he *should* want that, but although he thought it, he still couldn't *feel* it. There was nothing but an icy lump where his heart should have been and as he looked at his son he couldn't shift that strange air of detachment.

His lack of emotional empathy had never mattered to him before—only his frustrated lovers had complained about it and that had never been reason enough to change, or even *want* to change. But now he felt like someone on a beach who had inadvertently stepped onto quicksand. As if matters were spinning beyond his control.

And he needed to assert control, just as he always did.

Of course he would hold his son when he'd got his head round the fact that he actually *had* a son. But it would be in conditions favourable to them both—not in some tiny bedroom of a strange house while Keira stood studying him with those big blue eyes.

'Not now,' he said abruptly. 'There isn't time. You need to pack your things while I call ahead and prepare for your arrival in Italy.'

'*What?*'

'You heard me. He isn't staying here. And since a child needs a mother, then I guess you will have to come, too.'

'What are you talking about?' She rocked the child against her breast. 'I know it's not perfect here but I can't just walk out without making any plans. We can't just go to *Italy*.'

'You can't put out a call for help and then ignore help when it comes. You telephoned me and now you must accept the consequences,' he added grimly. 'You've already implied that the atmosphere here is intolerable so I'm offering you an alternative. The only sensible alternative.' He pulled a mobile phone from the pocket of his cashmere overcoat and began to scroll down the numbers. 'For a start, you need a nursery nurse to help you.'

'I don't *need* a nurse,' she contradicted fiercely. 'Women like me don't have nurses. They look after their babies themselves.'

'Have you looked in the mirror recently?'

It was an underhand blow to someone who was already feeling acutely sensitive and once again Keira flushed. 'I'm sorry I didn't have a chance to slap on a whole load of make-up and put on a party dress!'

He shook his head. 'That wasn't what I meant. You look as if you haven't had a decent night's sleep in weeks and I'm giving you the chance to get some rest.' He forced himself to be gentle with her, even though his instinct was always to push for exactly what he wanted. And yet strangely, he felt another wave of compassion as he looked into her pale face. 'Now, we can do this one of two ways. You can fight me or you can make the best of the situation and come willingly.' His mouth flattened. 'But if you choose the former, it will be fruitless because I want this, Keira. I want it very badly. And when I want something, I usually get it. Do you believe me?'

The mulish look which entered her eyes was there for only a second before she gave a reluctant nod. 'Yes,' she said grudgingly. 'I believe you.'

'Then pack what you need and I'll wait downstairs.' He turned away but was halted by the sound of her voice.

'And when we get there, what happens then, Matteo?' she whispered. 'To Santino?' There was a pause. 'To us?'

He didn't turn back. He didn't want to look at her right then, or tell her he didn't think there was an 'us'. 'I have no crystal ball,' he ground out. 'We'll just have to make it up as we go along. Now pack your things.'

He went downstairs, and, despite telling himself that this was nothing more than a problem which needed solving, he could do nothing about the sudden and inexplicable wrench of pain in his heart. But years of practice meant he had composed himself long before he reached the tiny hallway and his face was as hard as granite as he let himself out into the rainy English day.

CHAPTER SIX

GOLDEN SUNLIGHT DANCED on her closed eyelids and warmed her skin as Keira nestled back into the comfortable lounger. The only sounds she could hear were birdsong and the buzz of bees and, in the far distance, the crowing of a cock—even though it was the middle of the day. Hard to believe she'd left behind a rain-washed English autumn to arrive in a country where it was still warm enough to sit outside in October. And even harder to believe that she was at Matteo Valenti's Umbrian estate, with its acres of olive groves, award-winning vineyards and breathtaking views over mountains and lake. In his private jet, he'd announced he was bringing her here, to his holiday home, to 'acclimatise' herself before he introduced her to his real life in Rome. She hadn't been sure what he meant by that but she'd been too exhausted to raise any objections. She'd been here a week and much of that time had been spent asleep, or making sure that Santino was content. It felt like being transplanted to a luxury spa cleverly hidden within a rustic setting—with countless people working quietly in the background to maintain the estate's smooth running.

At first she'd been too preoccupied with the practical elements of settling in with her baby to worry about the emotional repercussions of being there. She'd worried about the little things, like how Matteo would react when he discovered she wasn't feeding Santino herself. Whether he would judge her negatively, as the whole world seemed to do if a woman couldn't manage to breastfeed. Was that why, in a rare moment of candour, she'd found herself explaining how ill she'd been after the birth—which meant breastfeeding hadn't been possible? She thought she'd glimpsed a brief softening of the granite-like features before his rugged features resumed their usual implacable mask.

'It will be easier that way,' he'd said, with a shrug. 'Easier for the nursery nurse.'

How *cold* he could be, she thought. Even if he was right. Because despite her earlier resistance, she was now hugely appreciative of the nursery nurse they'd employed. The very day after they'd arrived, he had produced three candidates for her to interview—topnotch women who had graduated from Italy's finest training establishment and who all spoke fluent English. After asking them about a million questions—but more importantly watching to see how well they interacted with her baby—Keira had chosen Claudia, a serene woman in her mid-thirties whom she instinctively trusted. It meant Keira got all the best bits of being a mother—cuddling and bathing her adorable son and making goo-goo noises at him as she walked him around the huge estate—while Claudia took over the dreaded three o'clock morning feed.

Which meant she could catch up with the sleep she so badly needed. She'd felt like a complete zombie when she arrived—a fact not helped by the disorientating experience of being flown to Italy on Matteo's luxury jet then being picked up by the kind of limousine which only a year ago she would have been chauffeuring. The drive to his Umbrian property had passed in a blur and Keira remembered thinking that the only time emotion had entered Matteo's voice was when they drove through the ancient gates and he began to point out centuries-old landmarks, with an unmistakable sense of pride and affection.

She almost wished Santino had been a little older so he could have appreciated the silvery ripple of olive trees, heavy with fruit and ready for harvest, and the golden pomegranates which hung from the branches like Christmas baubles. She remembered being greeted by a homely housekeeper named Paola and the delicious hot bath she took once the baby had been settled. There had been the blissful sensation of sliding between crisp, clean sheets and laying her head on a pillow of goose-down, followed by her first full night's sleep since before the birth. And that was pretty much how she'd spent the last seven days, feeling her vitality and strength returning with each hour that passed.

'You're smiling,' came a richly accented voice from above her as a shadow suddenly blotted out the sun.

Shielding her eyes with the edge of her hand, Keira peered up to see Matteo towering over her and her smile instantly felt as if it had become frozen. She could feel her heart picking up speed and the tug of silken hunger in the base of her belly and silently she cursed the instinctive reaction of her body. Because as her strength had returned, so too had her desire for Matteo—a man who she couldn't quite decide was her jailer or her saviour. Or both.

Their paths hadn't crossed much because he'd spent much of the time working in a distant part of the enormous farmhouse. It was as if he'd unconsciously marked out different territories for them, with clear demarcation lines which couldn't be crossed. But what she'd noted above all else was the fact that he'd kept away from the nursery, using the *excuse* that his son needed to settle in before getting used to too many new people. Because that was what it had sounded like. An excuse. A reason not to touch the son he had insisted should come here.

She'd seen him, of course. Glimpses in passing, which had unsettled her. Matteo looking brooding and muscular in faded denims and a shirt as he strode about the enormous estate, conversing in rapid Italian with his workers—or wearing a knockout charcoal suit just before driving to Rome for the day and returning long after she'd gone to bed.

Another image was burnt vividly into her mind, too. She'd overslept one morning and gone straight to the nursery to find Claudia cradling Santino by the window and telling him to watch 'Papa' going down the drive. *Papa*. It was a significant word. It emphasised Matteo's importance in their lives yet brought home how little she really knew about the cold-hearted billionaire. Yet that hadn't stopped her heart from missing a beat as he'd speeded out of the estate in his gleaming scarlet sports car, had it?

'It makes me realise how rarely I see you smile,' observed Matteo, still looking down at her as he stood silhouetted by the rich October sun.

'Maybe that's because we've hardly seen one another,' said Keira, flipping on the sunglasses which had been perched on top of her head, grateful for the way they kept her expression hidden. Not for the first time, she found it almost impossible to look at the man in front of her with any degree of impartiality, but she disguised it with a cool look. 'And you're a fine one to talk about smiling. You don't exactly go around the place grinning from ear to ear, do you?'

'Perhaps our forthcoming trip to Rome might bring a smile to both our faces,' he suggested silkily.

Ah yes, the trip to Rome. Keira felt the anxious slam of her heart. She licked her lips. 'I've been meaning to talk to you about that. Do we really have to go?'

In a movement which distractingly emphasised the jut of his narrow hips, he leaned against the sun-baked wall of the farmhouse. 'We've agreed to this, Keira. You need to see the other side of my life, not just this rural idyll. And I'm mainly based in Rome.'

'And the difference is what?'

'It's a high-octane city and nothing like as relaxed as here. When I'm there I go to restaurants and theatres. I have friends there and get invited to parties—and as the mother of my baby, I will be taking you with me.'

She sat up on the lounger, anxiety making her heart thud even harder against her ribcage. 'Why bother?

Why not just leave me somewhere in the background and concentrate on forming a relationship with your son?'

'I think we have to examine all the possibilities,' he said carefully. 'And number one on that list is to work out whether we could have some kind of life together.' He lifted his brows. 'It would certainly make things a whole lot easier.'

'And you're saying I'll let you down in my current state, is that it?'

He shrugged his broad shoulders with a carelessness which wasn't very convincing. 'I think we're both aware that you don't have a suitable wardrobe for that kind of lifestyle. You can't wear jeans all the time and Paola mentioned that you only seem to have one pair of boots.'

'So Paola's been spying on me, has she?' Keira questioned, her voice dipping with disappointment that the genial housekeeper seemed to have been taking her inventory.

'Don't be absurd. She was going to clean them for you and couldn't find any others you could wear in the meantime.'

Keira scrambled up off the lounger and stared into his hard and beautiful features. He really came from a totally different planet, didn't he? One which was doubtless inhabited by women who had boots in every colour of the rainbow and not just a rather scuffed brown pair she'd bought in the sales. 'So don't take me with you,' she said flippantly. 'Leave me behind while you go out to all your fancy places and I can stay home and look after Santino, wearing my solitary pair of boots.'

A flicker of a smile touched the corners of his lips, but just as quickly it was gone. 'That isn't an option, I'm afraid,' he said smoothly. 'You're going to have to meet people. Not just my friends and the people who work for me, but my father and stepmother at some point. And my stepbrother,' he finished, his mouth twisting before his gaze fixed her with its ebony blaze. 'The way you look at the moment means you won't fit in. Not anywhere,' he continued brutally. 'And there's the chance that people will talk about you if you behave like some kind of hermit, which won't make things easy for you. Apart from anything else, we need to learn more about each other.' He hesitated. 'We are parents, with a child and a future to consider. We need to discuss the options open to us and that won't be possible if we continue to be strangers to one another.'

'You haven't bothered coming near me since we got here,' she said quietly. 'You've been keeping your distance, haven't you?'

'Can you blame me? You were almost on your knees with exhaustion when you arrived.' He paused as his eyes swept over her again. 'But you look like a different person now.'

Keira was taken aback by the way her body responded to that slow scrutiny, wondering how he could make her feel so many different things, simply by looking at her. And if that was the case, shouldn't she be protecting herself from his persuasive power over her, instead of going on a falsely intimate trip to Rome?

'I told you. I don't want to leave the baby,' she said stubbornly.

'Is that what's known as playing your trump card?' he questioned softly. 'Making me out to be some cruel tyrant who's dragging you away from your child?'

'He's only little! Not that you'd know, of course.' She paused and lifted her chin. 'You've hardly gone near him.'

Matteo acknowledged the unmistakable challenge in her voice and he felt a sudden chill ice his skin, despite the warmth of the October day. How audacious of her to interrogate him about his behaviour when her own had hardly been exemplary. By her keeping Santino's existence secret he had been presented with a baby, instead of having time to get used to the idea that he was to become a father.

Yet her pointed remark about his lack of interaction struck home, because what she said was true. He *had* kept his distance from Santino, telling himself that these things could not be rushed and needed time. And she had no right to demand anything of him, he thought bitterly. He would do things according to *his* agenda, not hers.

'Rome isn't far,' he said coolly. 'It is exactly two hundred kilometres. And I have a car constantly on standby.'

'Funnily enough that's something I *do* remember—being at your beck and call!'

'Then you will know there's no problem,' he said drily. 'Particularly as my driver is solid and reliable and not given to taking off to remote areas of the countryside in adverse weather conditions.'

'Very funny,' she said.

'We can be back here in an hour and a half should the need arise. We'll leave here at ten tomorrow morning—and be back early the next day. Less than twenty-four hours in the eternal city.' He gave a faintly cynical laugh. 'Don't women usually go weak at the knees at the prospect of an unlimited budget to spend on clothes?'

'Some women, maybe,' she said. 'Not me.'

But Keira's stubbornness was more than her determination not to become a rich man's doll. She didn't *know* about fashion—and the thought of what she might be expected to wear scared her. Perhaps if she'd been less of a tomboy, she might have flicked through glossy magazines like other women her age. She might have had some idea of what did and didn't suit her and would now be feeling a degree of excitement instead of dread. Fear suddenly became defiance and she glared at him.

'You are the bossiest man I've ever met!' she declared, pushing a handful of hair over her shoulder.

'And you are the most difficult woman I've ever encountered,' he countered. 'A little *gratitude* might go down well now and again.'

What, gratitude for his high-handedness and for making her feel stuff she'd rather not feel? Keira shook her head in frustration as she tugged her T-shirt down over her straining jeans.

'I'll be ready at ten,' she said, and went off to find Santino.

She put the baby in his smart new buggy to take him for a walk around the estate, slowly becoming aware that the weather had changed. The air had grown heavy and sultry and heavy clouds were beginning to accumulate on the horizon, like gathering troops. When eventually they returned to the farmhouse, Santino took longer than usual to settle for his sleep and Keira was feeling out of sorts when Paola came to ask whether she would be joining Signor Valenti for dinner that evening.

It was the first time she'd received such an invitation and Keira hesitated for a moment before declining. Up until now, she'd eaten her supper alone or with Claudia and she saw no reason to change that routine. She was going to be stuck with Matteo in Rome when clearly they were going to have to address some of the issues confronting them. Why waste conversation during a stilted dinner she had no desire to eat, especially when the atmosphere felt so close and heavy?

Fanning her face with her hand, she showered before bed but her skin still felt clammy, even after she'd towelled herself dry. Peering up into the sky, she thought she saw a distant flash of lightning through the thick curtain of clouds. She closed the shutters and brushed her hair before climbing into bed, but sleep stubbornly eluded her. She wished the occasional growl of thunder would produce the threatened rain and break some of the tension in the atmosphere and was just drifting off into an uneasy sleep when her wish came true. A loud clap of thunder echoed through the room and made her sit bolt upright in bed. There was a loud whoosh and heavy rain began to hurl down outside her window and quickly she got up and crept into Santino's room but, to her surprise, the baby was sound asleep.

How did he manage to do that? she thought enviously—feeling even more wide awake than before. She sighed as she went back to bed and the minutes ticked by, and all she could think about was how grim she was going to look, with dark shadowed eyes and a pasty face. Another clap of thunder made her decide that a warm drink might help relax her. And wasn't there a whole stack of herb teas in the kitchen?

To the loud tattoo of drumming rain, she crept downstairs to the kitchen with its big, old-fashioned range and lines of shiny copper pots hanging in a row. She switched on some low lighting and not for the first time found herself wistfully thinking how *homely* it looked—and how it was unlike any place she had imagined the urbane Matteo Valenti would own.

She had just made herself a cup of camomile tea when she heard a sound behind her and she jumped, her heart hammering as loudly as the rain as she turned to see Matteo standing framed in the doorway. He was wearing nothing but a pair of faded denims, which were clinging almost indecently to his long and muscular thighs. His mouth was unsmiling but there was a gleam in his coal-dark eyes, which made awareness drift uncomfortably over her skin and suddenly Keira began to shiver uncontrollably, her nipples tightening beneath her nightshirt.

CHAPTER SEVEN

THE WALLS SEEMED to close in on her and Keira was suddenly achingly conscious of being alone in the kitchen with a half-naked Matteo, while outside she could hear the rain howl down against the shuttered windows.

With a shaking hand she put her mug down, her eyes still irresistibly drawn to the faded jeans which hugged his long and muscular thighs. He must have pulled them on in a hurry because the top button was undone, displaying a line of dark hair which arrowed tantalisingly downwards. Soft light bathed his bare and gleaming torso, emphasising washboard abs and broad shoulders.

She realised with a start that she'd never seen his naked torso before—or at least hadn't really noticed it. She'd been so blown away when they'd been having sex that her eyes hadn't seemed able to focus on anything at all. But now she could see him in all his beauty— a dark and forbidding beauty, but beauty all the same. And despite all the *stuff* between them, despite the fact that they'd been snapping at each other like crocodiles this afternoon, she could feel herself responding to him, and there didn't seem to be a thing she could do about it.

Beneath her nightshirt her nipples were growing even tighter and her breasts were heavy. She could feel a warm melting tug at her groin and the sensation was so intense that she found herself shifting her weight uncomfortably from one bare foot to the other. She opened her mouth to say something, but no words came.

He stared at her, a strange and mocking half-smile at his lips, as if he knew exactly what was happening to her. 'What's the matter, Keira?' he queried silkily. 'Can't sleep?'

She struggled to find the correct response. To behave as anyone else would in the circumstances.

Like a woman drinking herb tea and not wishing that he would put his hand between her legs to stop this terrible aching.

'No. I can't. This wretched storm is keeping me awake.' She forced a smile. 'And neither could you, obviously.'

'I heard someone moving around in the kitchen, so I came to investigate.' He stared down at her empty cup. 'Is the tea working?'

She thought about pretending but what was the point? 'Not really,' she admitted as another crash of thunder echoed through the room. 'I'm still wide awake and I'm probably going to stay that way until the storm dies down.'

There was a pause while Matteo's gaze drifted over her and he thought how pale she looked standing there with her nightshirt brushing against her bare thighs and hair spilling like dark silk over her shoulders. Barefooted, she looked *tiny*—a tantalising mixture of vulnerability and promise—and it felt more potent than anything he'd ever experienced. She was trying to resist him, he knew that, yet the look in her eyes told him that inside she was aching as much as he was. He knew what he was going to do because he couldn't put it off any longer, and although the voice of his conscience was sounding loud in his ears, he took no notice of it. She needed to relax a little—for all their sakes.

'Maybe you should try a little distraction technique,' he said.

Her eyes narrowed. 'Doing what?'

'Come and look at the view from my study,' he suggested evenly. 'It's spectacular at the best of times, but during a storm it's unbelievable.'

Keira hesitated because it felt as if he were inviting her into the lion's lair, but surely anything would be better than standing there feeling totally out of her depth. What else was she going to do—go back to bed and lie there feeling sorry for herself? And they were leaving for Rome tomorrow. Perhaps she should drop her guard a little. Perhaps they should start trying to be friends.

'Sure,' she said, with a shrug. 'Why not?'

His study was in a different wing of the house, which hadn't featured in the guided tour he'd given her at the beginning of the week—an upstairs room sited at the far end of a vast, beamed sitting room. She followed him into the book-lined room, her introspection vanishing the instant she saw the light show taking place outside the window. Her lips fell open as she stood watching the sky blindingly illuminated by sheet lightning, which lit up the dark outlines of the surrounding mountains. Each bright flash was reflected in the surface of the distant lake, so that the dramatic effect of what she was seeing was doubled. 'It's...amazing,' she breathed.

'Isn't it?'

He had come to stand beside her—so close that he was almost touching and Keira held her breath, wanting him to touch her, *praying* for him to touch her. Did he guess that? Was that why he slid his arm around her shoulders, his fingers beginning to massage the tense and knotted muscles?

She looked up into the hard gleam of his eyes, startled by the dark look of hunger on his face.

'Shall we put a stop to all this right now, Keira?' he murmured. 'Because we both know that the damned storm has nothing to do with our inability to sleep. It's desire, isn't it? Two people lying in their lonely beds, just longing to reach out to one another.'

His hands had slipped to her upper arms, and as his hard-boned face swam in and out of focus Keira told herself to break away and escape to the sanctuary of her room. Yet her body was stubbornly refusing to obey. All she could seem to focus on were his lips and how good it felt to have him touching her like this. She'd never stood in a storm-lit room with a half-dressed man, completely naked beneath her frumpy nightshirt, and yet she knew exactly what was going to happen next. She could feel it. Smell it. She swayed. Could almost *taste* the desire which was bombarding her senses and making her pounding heart the only thing she could hear above the loud hammer of the rain.

'Isn't that so?' he continued, brushing hair away from

her face as the pad of his thumb stroked its way over her trembling lips. 'You want me to kiss you, don't you, Keira? You want it really quite badly.'

Keira resented the arrogance of that swaggering statement—but not enough to make her deny the truth behind it. 'Yes,' she said. 'Yes, I do.'

Matteo tensed, her whispered assent sharpening his already keen hunger, and he pulled her against his body and crushed his mouth over hers. And, oh, she tasted good. Better than good. Better than he remembered— but maybe that was because her kiss had lingered in his memory far longer than it should have done. He tried to go slowly but his usual patience fled as his hands began to rediscover her small and compact body. Before she had been incredibly lean—he remembered narrow hips and the bony ladder of her ribcage. But now those bones had disappeared beneath a layer of new flesh, which was soft and tempting and just ripe for licking.

Her head tipped back as he rucked up her nightshirt, his hand burrowing beneath the bunched cotton until he had bared her breast. He bent his head to take one taut rosebud in between his lips and felt her fingers digging into his bare shoulders as he grazed the sensitive areola between his teeth. Already he felt as if he wanted to explode—as if he would die if he'd didn't quickly impale her. Was the fact that she'd borne his child the reason why he was feeling a desire which felt almost *primitive* in its intensity? Was that why his hands were trembling like this?

'Do you know how long I've been wanting to do this?' he husked, his fingers sliding down between her breasts and caressing their silken weight. 'Every second of every day.'

Her reply was a muffled gasp against his mouth. 'Is that why you've stayed away from me?'

'That's exactly why.' He let his fingertips trickle down over her belly and heard her catch her breath as they travelled further downwards. 'You needed to rest and I was trying to be a...*gentleman*,' he growled.

'And how does this qualify as being...*oh*!' Her words faded away as he slid his hand between her legs, brushing over the soft fuzz of hair to find the molten heat beneath.

'You were saying?' he breathed as he dampened his finger in the soft, wet folds before starting to stroke the little bud which was already so tight.

He heard her give a shaky swallow. 'Matteo, this is...is...'

He knew exactly what it was. It was arousing her to a state where she was going to come any second, and while it was turning him on to discover how close to the edge she was—it was also making his own frustration threaten to implode. With a necessary care which defied his hungry impatience, he eased the zip of his jeans down over his straining hardness—breathing a sigh of relief as his massive erection sprang free. The denim concertinaed around his ankles but he didn't care. He knew propriety dictated he should take them off, but he couldn't. He couldn't wait, not a second longer.

Impatiently he pushed her back against his desk, shoving aside his computer and paperwork with uncharacteristic haste. And the moment the moist tip of his penis touched her, she seemed to go wild, clawing eagerly at his back—and it took more concentration than he'd ever needed to force himself to pull back. Through the distracting fog of desire, he recalled the condom concealed in a drawer of his desk and by the time it was in place he felt as excited as a teenage boy as his hungry gaze skated over her.

Like a sacrifice she lay on the desk, her arms stretched indolently above her head as he leaned over to make that first thrust deep inside her. And this time there was no pain or hesitation. This time there was nothing but a gasped cry of pleasure as he filled her. Greedily, he sank even deeper and then he rode her— and even the crash of something falling from the desk wasn't enough to put him off his stroke. Or maybe it was just another crash of thunder from the storm outside. Who cared? He rode her until she came, her frantic convulsions starting only fractionally before his own, so that they moved in perfect time before his ragged groan heralded the end and he slumped on top of her, her hands clasped around the sweat-sheened skin of his back.

He didn't say anything at first, unwilling to shatter the unfamiliar peace he felt as he listened to the quietening of his heart. He felt spent. As if she had milked him dry. As if he could have fallen asleep right there, despite the hardness of the wooden surface. He forced himself to open his eyes and to take stock of their surroundings. Imagine if they were discovered here in the morning by one of the cleaners, or by Paola—already surprised that, not only had he brought a woman here, but he had a baby son.

A son he had barely seen.

Guilt formed itself into an icy-cold knot deep in his chest and was enough to dissolve his lethargy. Untwining himself from Keira's arms, he moved away from the desk, bending to pull up his jeans and zip them. Only then did he stare down at her, where she lay with her eyes closed amid the debris of his wrecked desk. Her cotton nightshirt was rucked right up to expose her beautiful breasts and her legs were bent with careless abandon. The enticing gleam between her open thighs was making him grow hard again but he fought the feeling—telling himself he needed to start taking control. He would learn about his son in time—he *would*—but for now his primary purpose was to ensure that Santino remained a part of his life, and for that to happen he needed Keira onside.

So couldn't their powerful sexual chemistry work in his favour—as effective a bargaining tool as his vast wealth? Couldn't he tantalise her with a taste of what could be hers, if only she was prepared to be reasonable? Because Keira Ryan was unpredictable. She was proud and stubborn, despite the fact that she'd been depending on other people's charity for most of her life, and he was by no means certain that she would accede to his wishes. So maybe it was time to remind her just who was calling the shots. He bent and lifted her into his arms, cradling her against his chest as her eyelashes fluttered open.

'What are you doing?' she questioned drowsily.

'Taking you back to bed.'

She yawned. 'Can't we just stay here?'

He gave an emphatic shake of his head. 'No.'

Keira closed her eyes again, wanting to capture this feeling for ever—a feeling which went much deeper than sexual satisfaction, incredible though that side of it had been. She had felt so close to Matteo when he'd been deep inside her. *Scarily* close—almost as if they were two parts of the same person. Had he felt that, too? Her heart gave a little leap of hope. Couldn't they somehow make this work despite everything which had happened? Couldn't they?

Resting her head against his warm chest, she let him carry her through the house to her own room, not pausing until he had pulled back the duvet and deposited her in the centre of the soft bed. Only then did her eyelids flutter open, her heart missing a beat as she took in his gleaming torso and powerful thighs. She stared up at him hopefully. Was he going to lose the jeans and climb in beside her, so she could snuggle up against him as she so desperately wanted to do and stroke her fingers through the ruffled beauty of his black hair?

She watched as his gaze swept over her, the hectic glitter of hunger in their ebony depths unmistakable. And she waited, because surely it should be *him* asking her permission to stay? She didn't know very much about bedroom etiquette, but instinct told her that. She recognised that she'd been a bit of a pushover back there, and it was time to show the Italian tycoon that he might need to work a little harder this time.

'So?' She looked at him with what she hoped was a welcoming smile.

'That's better. You don't smile nearly enough.' His finger traced the edges of her lips as he leaned over her. 'All the bad temper of this afternoon banished in the most pleasurable way possible.' He stroked an exploratory finger over the tightening nipple beneath her nightshirt. 'Was that what you needed all along, Keira?'

It took a few moments for his meaning to sink in and when it did, Keira could hardly believe her ears. A powerful wave of hurt crashed over her. Was that all it had been? Had he made love to her as a way of soothing her ruffled emotions and making her more *amenable*? As if he were some kind of *human sedative*? She wanted to bite down hard on her clenched fist. To demand how someone so cold-blooded could possibly live with himself. But she forced herself to remain silent because only that way could she cling onto what was left of her battered pride. Why give him the satisfaction of knowing he'd hurt her? If he was going to act so carelessly, then so would she. And why be so surprised by his callous behaviour when he hadn't shown one fraction of concern for his baby son. Matteo Valenti was nothing but a manipulative and cold-blooded *bastard*, she reminded herself.

Hauling the duvet up to her chin, she closed her eyes. 'I'm tired, Matteo,' she said. 'Would you mind turning off the light as you go?'

And then, deliberately manufacturing a loud yawn, she turned her back on him.

CHAPTER EIGHT

KEIRA DIDN'T SAY a word to Matteo next morning, not until they were halfway to Rome and his powerful car had covered many miles. The fierce storm had cleared the air and the day had dawned with a sky of clear, bright blue—but the atmosphere inside the car was heavy and fraught with tension. She was still feeling the painful tug of saying goodbye to Santino, though he'd been happily cradled in Claudia's arms when the dreaded moment had arrived. But as well as the prospect of missing her baby, Keira was still smarting from what had happened the night before.

She'd woken up with a start soon after dawn, wondering why her body felt so…

Slowly she had registered her lazy lethargy and the sweet aching between her legs.

So…*used*.

Yes, used, that was it. *Used*. Vivid images had flashed through her mind as she remembered what had happened while the storm raged outside. Matteo unzipping his jeans and pushing her onto his desk. Matteo rucking up her nightdress before thrusting into her and making her cry out with pleasure. It had hardly been the stuff of fairy tales, had it? So why not concentrate on the reality, rather than the dumb romantic version she'd talked herself into when she was lying quivering beneath his sweat-sheened body?

He had cold-bloodedly seduced her after days of acting as if she didn't exist. He had invited her to witness the storm from the best vantage point in the house and, although it had been the corniest request in the world, she had agreed. Trotting behind him like some kind of puppy dog, she'd had sex with him. Again. Keira closed her eyes in horror as she remembered the way she'd clawed at his bare back like some kind of wildcat. Did her inexperience explain the fierce hunger which had consumed her and made her unable to resist his advances? Or was it just that Matteo Valenti only had to touch her for her to come apart in his arms?

And now the trip to Rome, which she'd already been dreading, was going to be a whole lot worse. Bad enough being in the kind of car she'd lusted after during her days as a mechanic—and having it driven by *someone else*—without the knowledge of how smug Matteo must be feeling. Why, he hadn't even wanted to spend the night with her! He'd just deposited her in her bed like some unwanted package and behaved as if what had happened had been purely functional. Like somebody scratching an itch. Was that how it had been for him, she wondered bitterly? Had he seen her as a body rather than a person?

'So, are you going to spend the next twenty-four hours ignoring me?' Matteo's voice broke into her rebellious thoughts as they passed a signpost to a pretty-looking place called Civita Castellana.

Keira wanted to pretend she hadn't heard him but that was hardly the way forward, was it? She mightn't be happy with the current state of affairs, but that didn't mean she had to lie down and passively accept it. Unless she was planning on behaving like some sort of victim—allowing the powerful tycoon to pick her up and move her around at will, without her having any say in the matter. It was time she started asserting herself and stopped beating herself up. They'd had sex together as two consenting adults and surely that put them on some kind of equal footing.

So *ask* him.

Take some of the control back.

She turned her head to look at his profile, trying not to feel affected by that proud Roman nose and the strong curve of his shadowed jaw. His silk shirt was unbuttoned at the neck, offering a tantalising glimpse of olive skin, and he exuded a vitality which made him seem to glow with life. She could feel a trickle of awareness whispering over her body and it made her want to fidget on the plush leather car seat.

She wanted him to touch her all over again. And when he touched her she went to pieces.

Firmly pushing all erotic possibilities from her mind, she cleared her throat. 'So why this trip, Matteo?'

There was a pause. 'You know why. We've discussed this. We're going to buy you some pretty clothes to wear.'

His words were deeply patronising and she wondered

if that had been his intention—reminding her that she fell way short of his ideal of what a woman should be. 'I'm not talking about your determination to change my appearance,' she said. 'I mean, why bring me to Italy in the first place? That's something we haven't even discussed. What's going to happen once you've waved your magic wand and turned me into someone different? Are you planning to return me to England in your fancy plane and make like this was all some kind of dream?'

His mouth hardened into a flat and implacable line. 'That isn't an option.'

'Then what *are* the options?' she questioned quietly.

Matteo put his foot down on the accelerator and felt the powerful engine respond. It was a reasonable question, though not one he particularly wanted to answer. But he couldn't keep on putting off a conversation they needed to have because he was wary of all the stuff it might throw up. 'We need to see whether we can make it work as a couple.'

'A *couple*?'

He saw her slap her palms down on her denim-covered thighs in a gesture of frustration.

'You mean, living in separate parts of the same house? How is that in any way what a *couple* would do?' She sucked in a breath. 'Why, we've barely *seen* one another—and when we have, it isn't as if we've done much talking!'

'That can be worked on,' he said carefully.

'Then let's start working on it right now. Couples aren't complete strangers to one another and we are. Or at least, you are. I told you a lot about my circumstances on the night we…' Her voice wavered as she corrected herself before growing quieter. 'On that night we spent together in Devon. But I don't know you, Matteo. I still don't really know anything about you.'

Matteo stared at the road ahead. Women always asked these kinds of questions and usually he cut them short. With a deceptively airy sense of finality, he'd make it clear that he wouldn't tolerate any further interrogation because he didn't want anyone trying to 'understand' him. But he recognised that Keira was different and their situation was different. She was the mother of his child and she'd given birth to his heir—not some socially ambitious woman itching to get his ring on her finger. He owed her this.

'What do you want to know?' he questioned.

She shrugged. 'All the usual stuff. About your parents. Whether or not you have any brothers or sisters. That kind of thing.'

'I have a father and a stepmother. No siblings,' he said, his voice growing automatically harsher and there wasn't a damned thing he could do to stop it. 'But I have a stepbrother who's married, with a small child.'

He could feel her eyes on him. 'So your parents are divorced?'

'No. My mother is dead.'

'Like mine,' she said thoughtfully.

He nodded but didn't say anything, his attention fixed on the road ahead, trying to concentrate on the traffic and not on the bleak landscape of loss.

'Tell me about your father,' she said. 'Do you get on well with him?'

Some of the tension left his body as he overtook a truck and he waited until he had finished the manoeuvre before answering. He wondered if he should give her the official version of his life, thus maintaining the myth that all was well. But if she stayed then she would soon discover the undercurrents which surged beneath the surface of the powerful Valenti clan.

'We aren't close, no. We see each other from time to time, more out of duty than anything else.'

'But you mentioned a stepmother?'

'You mean the latest stepmother?' he questioned cynically. 'Number four in a long line of women who were brought in to try to replace the wife he lost.'

'But...' She hesitated. 'None of them were able to do that?'

'That depends on your definition. I'm sure each of them provided him with the creature comforts most men need, though each marriage ended acrimoniously and at great financial cost to him. That's the way it goes, I guess.' His hands tightened around the steering wheel. 'But my mother would have been a hard act for any woman to follow—at least according to the people who knew her.'

'What was she like?' she prompted, and her voice was as gentle as he'd ever imagined a voice could be.

Matteo didn't answer for a long time because this was something nobody ever really asked. A dead mother was just that. History. He couldn't remember anyone else who'd ever shown any interest in her short life.

He could feel the tight squeeze of his heart. 'She was beautiful,' he said eventually. 'Both inside and out. She was training to be a doctor when she met my father—an only child from a very traditional Umbrian family who owned a great estate in the region.'

'The farmhouse where we've been staying?' she questioned slowly. 'Is that…?'

He nodded. 'Was where she grew up, *sì*.'

Keira nodded as slowly she began to understand. She gazed out of the window at the blue bowl of the sky. Did that explain his obvious love for the estate? she wondered. The last earthly link to his mum?

'Does your father know?' she questioned suddenly. 'About Santino?'

'Nobody knows,' he said harshly. 'And I won't let it be known until we've come to some kind of united decision about the future.'

'But a baby isn't really the kind of thing you can keep secret. Won't someone from the farm have told him? One of the staff?'

He shook his head. 'Discretion is an essential quality for all the people who work for me and their first loyalty is to me. Anyway, my father isn't interested in the estate, only as…'

'Only as what?' she prompted, her curiosity sharpened by the harsh note which had suddenly entered his voice.

'Nothing. It doesn't matter. And I think we've had enough questions for today, don't you?' he drawled. He lifted one hand from the steering wheel to point straight

ahead. 'We're skirting Rome now and if you look over
there you'll soon be able to see Lake Nemi.'

Her gaze followed the direction of his finger as she
tried to concentrate. 'And that's where you live?'

'That's where I live,' he agreed.

They didn't say much for the rest of the journey, but
at least Keira felt she knew a little more about him. And
yet it was only a little. He had the air of the enigma
about him. Something at the very core of him which
was dark and unknowable and which seemed to keep
her at arm's length. Behind that formidable and sexy
exterior lay a damaged man, she realised—and something about his inner darkness made her heart go out
to him. *Could* they make it as a couple? she wondered
as they drove through a beautiful sheltered valley and
she saw the silver gleam of the lake. Would she be a
fool to want that?

But the stupid thing was that, yes, she did want that,
because if Santino was to have any kind of security—
the kind she'd always longed for—then it would work
best if they *were* a couple. Her living with Matteo Valenti as his lover and mother to his son…would that be
such a bad thing?

Her daydreaming was cut short by her first sight
of Matteo's villa and she began to wonder if she was
crazy to ever imagine she would fit in here. Overlooking Lake Nemi, the apricot-coloured house was three
storeys high, with high curved windows overlooking
acres of beautifully tended gardens. And she soon discovered that inside were countless rooms, including a
marble-floored dining room and a ballroom complete

with a lavish hand-painted ceiling. It felt more like being shown round a museum than a house. Never had her coat felt more threadbare or the cuffs more frayed as it was plucked from her nerveless fingers by a stern-faced butler named Roberto, who seemed to regard her with complete indifference. Was he wondering why his powerful employer had brought such a scruffy woman to this palace of a place? Keira swallowed. Wasn't she wondering the same thing herself?

After ringing the farmhouse and being told by Paola that Santino was lying contentedly in his pram in the garden, Keira accepted the tiny cup of espresso offered by a maid in full uniform and sat down on a stiff and elegant chair to drink it. Trying to ignore the watchful darkness of Matteo's eyes, she found herself thinking about the relaxed comfort of the farmhouse and felt a pang as she thought about her son, wondering if he would be missing his mama. As she drank her coffee she found herself glancing around at the beautiful but cavernous room and suppressed a shiver, wondering how much it must cost to heat a place this size.

'Why do you live here?' she questioned suddenly, lifting her gaze to the dark figure of the man who stood beside the vast fireplace.

He narrowed his eyes. 'Why wouldn't I? It has a fresher climate than the city, particularly in the summer months when it can get very hot. And it's a valuable piece of real estate.'

'I don't doubt it.' She licked her lips. 'But it's *enormous* for just one person! Don't you rattle around in it?'

'I'm not a total hermit, Keira,' he said drily. 'Sometimes I work from here—and, of course, I entertain.'

The question sprang from her lips before she could stop it. 'And bring back loads of women, I expect?'

The look he shot her was mocking. 'Do you want me to create the illusion that I've been living a celibate life all these years?' he asked softly. 'If sexual jealousy was the reason behind your question?'

'It wasn't!' she denied, furious with herself for having asked it. Of *course* Matteo would have had hundreds of women streaming through these doors—and it wasn't as if he were her *boyfriend*, was it? Her cheeks grew red. He never had been. He was just a man who could make her melt with a single look, no matter how much she fought against it. A man who had impregnated her without meaning to. And now he was observing her with that sexy smile, as if he knew exactly what she was thinking. As if he was perfectly aware that beneath her drab, chain-store sweater her breasts were hungering to feel his mouth on them again. She could feel her cheeks growing warm as she watched him answer his mobile phone to speak in rapid Italian and when he'd terminated the call he turned to look at her, his hard black eyes scanning over her.

'The car is outside waiting to take you into the city centre,' he said. 'And the stylist will meet you there.'

'A stylist?' she echoed, her gaze flickering uncertainly to her scuffed brown boots.

'A very famous stylist who's going to take you shopping.' He shrugged. 'I thought you might need a little guidance.'

His condescension only intensified Keira's growing feelings of inadequacy and she glared at him. 'What, in case I opt for something which is deeply unsuitable?'

His voice was smooth. 'There is a different way of looking at it, Keira. I don't expect you've been given unlimited use of a credit card before, have you?'

Something in the way he said it was making Keira's blood boil. 'Funnily enough, no!'

'So what's the problem?'

'The problem is *you*! I bet you're just loving this,' she accused. 'Does flashing your wealth give you a feeling of power, Matteo?'

He raised his eyebrows. 'Actually, I was hoping it might give you a modicum of pleasure. So why don't you go upstairs and freshen up before the car takes you into the city?'

Keira put her empty cup down on a spindly gold-edged table and rose to her feet. 'Very well,' she said, forcing her stiff shoulders into a shrug.

'By the way,' he said as he gestured for her to precede him, 'I notice you didn't make any comment about my driving on the way here.'

'I thought it might be wise, in the circumstances.'

'But as a professional, you judged me favourably, I hope?'

She pursed her lips together. 'You were okay. A little heavy on the clutch, perhaps—but it's a great car.'

She took a stupid and disproportionate pleasure from the answering humour which gleamed from his eyes before following him up a sweeping staircase into a sumptuous suite furnished in rich brocades and velvets, where he left her. Alone in the ballroom-sized bathroom, where water gushed from golden taps, Keira dragged the hairbrush through her hair, wondering what on earth the stylist was going to think about being presented with such unpromising raw material.

But the stylist was upbeat and friendly—even if the store on the Via dei Condotti was slightly terrifying. Keira had never been inside such an expensive shop before—although in her chauffeuring days she'd sat outside places like it often enough, waiting for her clients. A slim-hipped woman named Leola came forward to greet her, dressed in an immaculate cream dress accessorised with gleaming golden jewellery and high-heeled patent shoes. Although she looked as if she'd stepped straight off the catwalk, to her credit, she didn't seem at all fazed by Keira's appearance, as she led her around the shop and swished her fingertips over rail after rail of clothes.

In the chandelier-lit changing room, she whipped a tape measure around Keira's newly abundant curves. 'You have a fantastic figure,' she purred. 'Let's show it off a little more, shall we?'

'I'd rather not, if you don't mind,' said Keira quickly. 'I don't like to be stared at.'

Leola raised perfectly plucked black eyebrows by a centimetre. 'You are dating one of the city's most eligible bachelors,' she observed quietly. 'And Matteo will expect people to stare at you.'

Keira felt a shimmer of anxiety as she tugged a blue cashmere dress over her head and pulled on some navy-blue suede boots. What possible response could she make to that? What would the stunning Leola say if she explained that she and Matteo weren't 'dating', but simply parents to a darling little boy? And even that wasn't really accurate, was it? You couldn't really describe a man as a parent when he regarded his newborn infant with the caution which an army expert might display towards an unexploded bomb.

Just go with the flow, she told herself. Be amenable and do what's suggested—and after you've been dressed up like a Christmas turkey, you can sit down with the Italian tycoon and talk seriously about the future.

She tried on hip-hugging skirts with filmy blouses, flirty little day dresses and sinuous evening gowns, and Keira was reeling by the time Leola had finished with her. She wanted to protest that there was no way she would wear most of these—that she and Matteo hadn't even discussed how long she would be staying—but Leola seemed to be acting on someone else's orders and it wasn't difficult to work out whose orders they might be.

'I will have new lingerie and more shoes sent by courier to arrive later,' the stylist explained, 'since I understand you're returning to Umbria tomorrow. But you certainly have enough to be going on with. Might I suggest you wear the red dress this evening? Matteo was very specific about how good he thought you would look in vibrant colours. Oh, and a make-up artist will be visiting the house later this afternoon. She will also be able to fix your hair.'

Keira stared at the slippery gown of silk-satin which was being dangled from Leola's finger and shook her head. 'I can do my own hair,' she said defensively, wondering if dressing up in all this finery was what Matteo usually expected for dinner at home on a weekday evening. 'And I can't possibly wear that—it's much too revealing.'

'Yes, you can—and you must—because you look amazing in it,' said Leola firmly, before her voice softened a little. 'Matteo must care for you a great deal to go to so much trouble. And surely it would be unwise to displease him when he's gone to so much trouble.'

It was a candid remark which contained in it a trace of warning. It was one woman saying to another—don't look a gift horse in the mouth. But all it did was to increase Keira's sensation of someone playing dress-up. Of being moulded for a role in the billionaire's life which she wasn't sure she was capable of filling. Her heart was pounding nervously as she shook the stylist's hand and went outside to the waiting car.

And didn't she feel slightly ashamed at the ease with which she allowed the chauffeur to open the door for her as she slid onto the squishy comfort of the back seat? As if already she was turning into someone she didn't recognise.

CHAPTER NINE

THE CLOCK WAS striking seven and Matteo gave a click of impatience as he paced the drawing room, where an enormous fire crackled and burned. Where the hell *was* she? He didn't like to be kept waiting—not by anyone, and especially not by a woman who ought to have been bang on time and full of gratitude for his generosity towards her. He wondered how long it would have taken Keira to discover how much she liked trying on lavish clothes. Or how quickly she'd decided it was a turn-on when a man was prepared to buy you an entire new wardrobe, with no expense spared. He was just about to send Roberto upstairs to remind her of the time, when the door opened and there she stood, pale-faced and slightly uncertain.

Matteo's heart pounded hard in his chest because she looked… He shook his head slightly as if to clear his vision, but the image didn't alter. She looked *unrecognisable*. Light curls of glossy black tumbled over her narrow shoulders and, with mascara and eyeliner, her sapphire eyes looked enormous. Her lips were as red as her dress and he found himself wanting to kiss away her unfamiliar lipstick. But it was her body which commanded the most attention. *Santo cielo!* What a body! Scarlet silk clung to the creamy curve of her breasts, the material gliding in over the indentation of her waist, then flaring gently over her hips. Sheer stockings encased her legs and skyscraper heels meant she looked much taller than usual.

He swallowed because the transformation was exactly what he'd wanted—a woman on his arm who would turn heads for all the *right* reasons—and yet now he was left with intense frustration pulsing through his veins. He wanted to call their host and cancel and to take her straight to bed instead, but he was aware that such a move would be unwise. He had less than twenty-four hours to get Keira Ryan to agree to his plan—and that would not be achieved by putting lust before logic.

'You look…beautiful,' he said unsteadily, noticing how pink her cheeks had grown in response to his compliment, and he was reminded once again of her innocence and inexperience.

She tugged at the skirt of the dress as if trying to lengthen it. 'I feel a bit underdressed, to be honest.'

He shook his head. 'If that were the case then I certainly wouldn't let you leave the house.'

She raised her eyebrows. 'What, you mean you'd keep me here by force? Prisoner of the Italian tycoon?'

He smiled. 'I've always found persuasion to be far more effective than force. I assume Leola organised a suitable coat for you to wear?'

'A coat?' She stared at him blankly.

'It's November, Keira, and we're going to a party in

the city. It might be warmer than back in England, but you'll still need to wrap up.'

Keira's stomach did a flip. 'You didn't mention a party.'

'Didn't I? Well, I'm mentioning it now.'

She gave the dress another tug. 'Whose party is it?'

'An old friend of mine. Salvatore di Luca. It's his birthday—and it will be the perfect opportunity for you to meet people. It would be a pity for you not to have an audience when you look so very dazzling.' His gaze travelled over her and his voice thickened. 'So why not go and get your coat? The car's waiting.'

Keira felt nerves wash over her. She was tempted to tell him she'd rather stay home and eat a *panino* in front of the fire, instead of having to face a roomful of strangers—but she was afraid of coming over as some kind of social misfit. Was this some strange kind of interview to assess whether or not she would be up to the task of being Matteo's partner? To see if she was capable of making conversation with his wealthy friends, of getting through a whole evening without dropping a canapé down the front of her dress?

Her black velvet swing coat was lined with softest cashmere and Keira hugged it around herself as the driver opened the door of the waiting limousine, her heart missing a beat as Matteo slid onto the seat beside her. His potent masculinity was almost as distracting as the dark suit which fitted his muscular body to perfection and made him look like some kind of movie star on his way to an awards ceremony. 'You aren't driving, then?' she observed.

'Not tonight. I have a few calls I need to make.' His black eyes gleamed. 'After that I'm exclusively yours.'

The way he said it sent ripples of excitement whispering over her skin and she wondered if that had been deliberate. But there was apprehension too because Keira wasn't sure she would be able to cope with the full blaze of his undivided attention. Not when he was being so... *nice* to her.

She suspected he was on his best behaviour because he wanted her to agree to his masterplan—whenever he got around to unveiling it. And although he hadn't shown any desire to parent their son, something told her that he saw Santino as his possession, even if so far he had exhibited no signs of love. Because of that, she suspected he wouldn't let her go easily and the stupid part was that she didn't want him to. She was beginning to recognise that she was out of her depth—and not just because he was a billionaire hotelier and she a one-time car mechanic. She didn't have any experience of relationships and she didn't have a clue how to react to him. Part of her wished she were still in the driver's seat, negotiating the roads with a slick professionalism she'd been proud of until she'd ruined her career in the arms of the man who sat beside her, his long legs stretched indolently in front of him.

She forced herself to drag her eyes away from the taut tension of his thighs—and at least there was plenty to distract her as she gazed out of the window at the lights of the city and the stunning Roman architecture, which made her feel as if she'd fallen straight into the pages of a guide book.

Salvatore de Luca's apartment was in the centre of it all—a penthouse situated close to the Via del Corso and offering commanding views of the city centre. Keira was dimly aware of a maid taking her coat and a cocktail being pressed into her hand and lots of people milling around. To her horror she could see that every other woman was wearing elegant black and her own expensive scarlet dress made her feel like something which had fallen off the Christmas tree. And it wasn't just the colour. She wasn't used to displaying a hint of cleavage, or wearing a dress which came this high above the knee. She felt like an imposter—someone who'd been more at home with her hair hidden beneath that peaked hat, instead of cascading over her shoulders like this.

She saw a couple of the men give her glances which lingered more than they should have done—or was that just something Italian men did automatically? Certainly, Matteo seemed to be watching her closely as he introduced her to a dizzying array of friends and she couldn't deny the thrill it gave her to feel those dark eyes following her every move.

Keira did her best to chat animatedly, hugely grateful that nearly everybody spoke perfect English, but conversation wasn't easy. She was glaringly aware of not mentioning the one subject which was embedded deeply in her heart and that was Santino. She wondered when Matteo was planning to announce that he was a father and what would happen when he did. Did any of his friends have children? she wondered. This apartment certainly didn't look child-friendly and she couldn't imagine a toddler crawling around on these priceless rugs, with sticky fingers.

Escaping from the growing pitch of noise to the washroom, Keira took advantage of the relative calm and began to peep into some of the rooms on her way back to the party. Entering only those with open doors, she discovered a bewildering number of hand-painted salons which reminded her of Matteo's villa. His home wasn't exactly child-friendly either, was it?

The room she liked best was small and book-lined—not because she was the world's greatest reader but because it opened out onto a lovely balcony with tall green plants in pots and fabulous views over the glittering city. She stood there for a moment with her arms resting on the balustrade when she heard the clip-clop of heels enter the room behind her and she turned to see a tall redhead who she hadn't noticed before. Maybe she was a late arrival, because she certainly wasn't the kind of woman you would forget in a hurry. Her green gaze was searching rather than friendly and Keira had to concentrate very hard not to be fixated on the row of emeralds which gleamed at her slender throat and matched her eyes perfectly.

'So *you're* the woman who's been keeping Matteo off the scene,' the woman said, her soft Italian accent making her sound like someone who could have a very lucrative career in radio voice-overs.

Keira left the chilly balcony and stepped into the room. 'Hello, I'm Keira.' She smiled. 'And you are?'

'Donatella.' Her green eyes narrowed, as if she was

surprised that Keira didn't already know this. 'Your dress is very beautiful.'

'Thank you.'

There was a pause as Donatella's gaze flickered over her. 'Everyone is curious to know how you've managed to snare Italy's most elusive bachelor.'

'He's not a rabbit!' joked Keira.

Either Donatella didn't get the joke or she'd decided it wasn't funny because she didn't smile. 'So when did you two first meet?'

Aware of the sudden race of her heart, Keira suddenly felt *intimidated*. As if she was being backed into a corner, only she didn't know why. 'Just under a year ago.'

'When, exactly?' probed the redhead.

Keira wasn't the most experienced person when it came to social etiquette, but even she could work out when somebody was crossing the line. 'Does it really matter?'

'I'm curious, that's all. It wouldn't happen to have been two nights before Christmas, would it?'

The date was burned so vividly on Keira's memory that the affirmation burst from her lips without her even thinking about it. 'Yes, it was,' she said. 'How on earth did you know that?'

'Because he was supposed to be meeting me that night,' said Donatella, with a wry smile. 'And then I got a call from his assistant to say his plane couldn't take off because of the snow.'

'That's true. The weather was terrible,' said Keira.

'And then, when he got back—nothing. Complete

radio silence—even though the word was out that there was nobody else on the scene.' Donatella's green eyes narrowed thoughtfully. 'Interesting. You're not what I expected.'

Even though she hadn't eaten any of the canapés which had been doing the rounds, Keira suddenly felt sick. All she could think about was the fact that another woman had been waiting for Matteo while he'd been in bed with *her*. He must have had his assistant call Donatella while she'd been in the bath and then preceded to seduce *her*. Had it been a case of *any* woman would do as a recipient of all that hard hunger? A man who'd been intent on sex and was determined not to have his wishes thwarted? What if all that stuff about not finding her attractive had simply been the seasoned technique of an expert who'd recognised that he needed to get her to relax before leaping on her. She swallowed. Had he been imagining it was Donatella beneath him instead of her?

'Well, you know what they say…there's no accounting for taste.' From somewhere Keira dredged up a smile. 'Great meeting you, Donatella.'

But she was trembling by the time she located Matteo, surrounded by a group of men and women who were hanging onto his every word, and maybe he read something in her face because he instantly disengaged himself and came over to her side.

'Everything okay?' he questioned.

'Absolutely lovely,' she said brightly, for the benefit of the onlookers. 'But I'd like to go now, if you wouldn't mind. I'm awfully tired.'

His dark brows lifted. '*Certamente*. Come, let us slip away, *cara*.'

The practised ease with which the meaningless endearment fell from his lips made Donatella's words seem even more potent and in the car Keira sat as far away from him as possible, placing her finger on her lips and shaking her head when he tried to talk to her. She felt stupidly emotional and close to tears but there was no way she was going to break down in front of his driver. She knew better than most how domestic upsets could liven up a sometimes predictable job and that a chauffeur had a front-row seat to these kinds of drama. It wasn't until they were back in the villa, where a fire in the drawing room had obviously been kept banked for their return, that she turned to Matteo at last, trying to keep the edge of hysteria from her voice.

'I met Donatella,' she said.

'I wondered if you would. She arrived late.'

'I don't give a damn when she arrived!' She flung her sparkly scarlet clutch bag down onto a brocade sofa where it bounced against a tasselled cushion. 'She told me you were supposed to be meeting her the night we got stuck in the snow!'

'That much is true.'

She was so horrified by his easy agreement that Keira could barely choke out her next words. 'So you were in a sexual relationship with another woman when you seduced me?'

He shook his head. 'No, I was not. I'd been dating her for a few weeks, but it had never progressed beyond dinner and the occasional trip to the opera.'

'And you expect me to believe that?'

'Why wouldn't you believe it, Keira?'

'Because…' She sucked in a deep breath. 'Because you didn't strike me as the kind of man who would chastely court a woman like that.'

'Strangely enough, that's how I like to operate.'

'But not with me,' she said bitterly. 'Or maybe you just didn't think I was worth buying dinner for.'

Matteo tensed as he read the hurt and shame which clouded her sapphire eyes and was surprised how bad it made him feel. He knew he owed her an explanation but he sensed that this went deeper than anything he'd had to talk his way out of in the past, and part of him rebelled at having to lay his thoughts open. But he sensed there was no alternative. That despite the ease with which she had fallen into his arms, Keira Ryan was no pushover.

'Oh, you were worth it, all right,' he said softly. 'Just because we didn't do the conventional thing of having dinner doesn't change the fact that it was the most un-forgettable night of my life.'

'Don't tell me lies!'

'It isn't a lie, Keira,' he said simply. 'It was amazing. We both know that.'

He saw her face working, as if she was struggling to contain her emotions.

'And then,' she said, on a gulp, 'when you got back—she says you didn't see her again.'

'Again, true.'

'Why not?' she demanded. 'There was nothing stopping you. Especially after you'd given me the heave-ho.'

If he was surprised by her persistence he didn't show it and Matteo felt conflicted about how far to go with his answer. Mightn't it be brutal to explain that he'd been so appalled at his recklessness that night that he'd decided he needed a break from women? If he told her that he'd never had a one-night stand before, because it went against everything he believed in, mightn't it hurt her more than was necessary? He didn't believe in love—not for him—but he believed in passion and, in his experience, it was always worth the wait. Deferred gratification increased the appetite and made seduction sweeter. And delaying his own pleasure reinforced his certainty that he was always in control.

Yet his usual fastidiousness had deserted him that snowy night when he'd found himself in bed with his petite driver, and it had affected him long after he'd returned to Italy. It wasn't an admission he particularly wanted to make but something told him it would work well in his favour if he did. What was it the Americans said? Ah, *sì*. It would buy him brownie points. 'I haven't had sex with anyone since the night I spent with you. Well, until last night,' he said.

Her eyes widened and the silence of the room was broken only by the loud ticking of the clock before she blurted out a single word.

'Why?' she breathed.

He bent to throw an unnecessary log onto the already blazing fire before straightening up to face the dazed disbelief which had darkened her eyes. He had tried convincing himself it had been self-disgust which had made him retreat into his shell when he'd returned to Rome, but deep down he'd known that wasn't the whole story.

'Because, annoyingly, I couldn't seem to shift you from my mind,' he drawled. 'And before you start shaking your head like that and telling me I don't mean it, let me assure you I do.'

'But why?' she questioned. 'I mean, why me?'

He paused long enough to let her know that he'd asked himself the same question. 'Who knows the subtle alchemy behind these things?' He shrugged, his gaze roving over her as he drank in the creamy curves of her flesh. 'Maybe because you were different. Because you spoke to me in a way that people usually don't. Or maybe because you were a virgin and on some subliminal level I understood that and it appealed to me. Why are you looking at me that way, Keira? You think that kind of thing doesn't matter? That a man doesn't feel an incomparable thrill of pleasure to discover that he is the first and the only one? Then you are very wrong.'

Keira felt faint and sank down onto the brocade sofa, next to her discarded clutch bag. His words were shockingly old-fashioned but that didn't lessen their impact on her, did it? It didn't stop her from feeling incredibly *desired* as his black gaze skated over her body and hinted at the things he might like to do to her.

Did her lips open of their own accord or did he somehow orchestrate her reaction from his position by the fireplace—like some puppet master twitching invisible strings? Was that why a hard gleam suddenly entered his eyes as he walked towards her and pulled her to her feet.

'I think we're done with talking, don't you?' he questioned unsteadily. 'Haven't I answered all your questions and told you everything you need to know?'

'Matteo, I—'

'I'm going to make love to you again,' he said, cutting right through her protest. 'Only this time it's going to be in a bed and it's going to be all night long. And please don't pretend you're outraged by the idea, when the look on your face says otherwise.'

'Or maybe you're just going to do it to pacify me?' she challenged. 'Like you did last night.'

'Last night we were in the middle of a howling storm and I wasn't really thinking straight, but today I am.'

And with that he lifted her up into his arms and swept her from the room and it occurred to Keira that no way would she have objected to such masterful treatment, even if he *had* given her the option. Because wasn't he making her feel like a woman who was completely desired—a woman for whom nothing but pleasure beckoned? Up the curving marble staircase he carried her, her ear pressed closely to his chest so she could hear the thundering of his heart. It felt like something from a film as he kicked the bedroom door shut behind them. Unreal. Just as the excitement coursing through her body felt unreal. Was it wrong to feel this rush of hungry pleasure as Matteo unzipped the scarlet dress and let it fall carelessly onto the silken rug? Or for her to gasp out words of encouragement from lips soon swollen by the pressure of his kiss?

Her bra swiftly followed and she gave a squeal of protesting pleasure as he hooked his fingers into the edges of her panties and ripped them apart and didn't that thrill her, too? Showing similar disregard for his own clothes, he tore them from his body like a man with the hounds of hell snapping at his ankles. But once they were both naked on the bed, he slowed things right down.

'These curves,' he said unevenly as his fingertips trickled over her breasts and hips.

'You don't like them?' she questioned breathlessly.

'Whatever gave you that idea? I seem to like you lean and I seem to like you rounded. Any way at all is okay with me, Keira.'

Slowly, he ran his fingertip from neck to belly before sliding it down between her thighs, nudging it lightly against her wet heat in a lazy and rhythmical movement. She shivered and had to stifle a frustrated moan as he moved his hand away. But then his mouth began to follow the same path as his fingers and Keira held her breath as she felt his lips acquainting themselves with the soft tangle of hair at her groin before he burrowed his head deep between her legs and made that first unbelievable flick of his tongue against her slick and heated flesh.

'Matteo!' she gasped, almost shooting off the bed with pleasure. 'What…what are you doing?'

He lifted his head and she saw pure devilry in his black eyes. 'I'm going to eat you, *cara mia*,' he purred, before bending his head to resume his task.

Keira let her head fall helplessly back against the pillow as he worked sweet magic with his tongue, loving the way he imprisoned her wriggling hips with the firm clamp of his hands. She came so quickly that it took her by surprise—as did the sudden way he moved over her to thrust deep inside her, while her body was still racked with those delicious spasms. She clung to his shoulders as he started a sweet, sure rhythm which set senses singing.

But suddenly his face hardened as he grew still inside her. 'How long do you think I can stop myself from coming?' he husked.

'Do you…?' She could barely get the words out when he was filling her like this. 'Do you *have* to stop yourself?'

'That depends. I do if you're going to have a second orgasm, which is my intention,' he murmured. 'In fact, I'm planning to make you come so often that you'll have lost count by the morning.'

'Oh, Matteo.' She closed her eyes as he levered himself to his knees and went even deeper.

She moaned as the finger moved between their joined bodies to alight on the tight nub between her legs and began to rub against her while he was deep inside her. The pleasure it gave her was almost too much to bear and it felt as if she were going to come apart at the seams. She gasped as pleasure and pressure combined in an unstoppable force. Until everything splintered around her. She heard him groan as his own body starting to convulse before eventually collapsing on top of her, his head resting on her shoulder and his shuddered breath hot and rapid against her neck.

His arms tightened around her waist and for countless seconds Keira felt as if she were floating on a cloud.

Had he really told her he hadn't slept with anyone else because he hadn't been able to get her out of his mind? Yes, he had. With a sigh of satisfaction, she rested her cheek against his shoulder and he murmured something soft in Italian in response.

She lay there for a long time after he'd fallen asleep, thinking that sex could blind you to the truth. Or maybe lull you into such a stupefied state that you stopped seeking the truth. He'd commented on her curves and admired them with his hands, but he'd made no mention of *why* her body had undergone such a dramatic transformation. She bit her lip. Because she'd carried his son and given birth to him—a fact he seemed to find all too easy to forget.

And she thought how—despite the heart-stopping intimacy of what had just taken place—she still didn't know Matteo at all.

CHAPTER TEN

SHE HAD TO say something. She *had* to. She couldn't keep pretending nothing was wrong or that there weren't still a million questions buzzing around in her head which needed answering.

Keira turned her head to look at the face of the man who lay sleeping beside her. It was a very big bed, which was probably a good thing since Matteo Valenti's naked body was taking up most of it. Morning light flooded in from the two windows they hadn't bothered closing the shutters on before they'd tumbled into bed the night before. From here she could see the green of the landscape which spread far into the distance and, above it, the endless blue of the cloudless sky. It was the most perfect of mornings, following the most perfect of nights.

She hugged her arms around herself and gave a wriggle of satisfaction. She'd never thought she could feel the way Matteo had made her feel. But the clock was ticking away and she needed to face reality. She couldn't keep pretending everything was wonderful just because they'd spent an amazing night together. He'd said he wanted to explore the possibility of them becoming a couple but there was more to being a couple than amazing sex. How could they keep ignoring the gaping hole at the centre of their relationship which neither of them had addressed? He for reasons unknown and she...

She turned her attention from the distraction of the view to the dark head which lay sleeping beside her. Was she too scared to ask him, was that it?

Because the most important thing was all out of kilter and the longer it went on, the worse it seemed. Matteo acted as if Santino didn't exist. *As if he didn't have a son.* To her certain knowledge, he'd never even cuddled him—why, he'd barely even asked after him.

It didn't matter how many boxes the Italian ticked—she could never subject Santino to a life in which he was overlooked. And trying to compensate for his father's lack of regard with her own fierce love wouldn't work. She'd grown up in a house where she had been regarded as an imposition and no way was she going to impose that on her darling son.

Which left her with two choices. She could carry on being an ostrich and ignore what was happening—or rather, what wasn't happening. Or she could address the subject when Matteo woke and make him talk about it. She wouldn't accuse him or judge him. Whatever he told her, she would try to understand—because something told her that was very important.

Quietly, she slipped from the bed and went to the bathroom and when she returned with brushed teeth and hair, Matteo was awake—his black gaze following her as she walked back towards the bed.

'Morning,' she said shyly.

'Is this the point where I ask whether you slept well and you lower your eyelids and say, *not really*?' he murmured.

Blushing like a schoolgirl, Keira slipped rapidly beneath the covers so that her naked body was no longer in the spotlight of that disturbingly erotic stare. It was all very well being uninhibited when the room was in darkness but the bright morning light was making her feel awfully vulnerable. Especially as she sensed that Matteo wasn't going to like what she had to say, no matter how carefully she asked the question. He drew her into his arms but she gave him only the briefest of kisses before pulling her lips away. Because he needed to hear this, and the sooner, the better.

'Matteo,' she said, rubbing the tip of her finger over the shadowed angle of his jaw.

His brows knitted together. 'Why does my heart sink when you say my name that way?' he questioned softly.

She swallowed. 'You know we have to go back to Umbria soon.'

'You think I'd forgotten? Which is why I suggest we don't waste any of the time we have left.'

He had begun to stroke a light thumb over one of her nipples and although it puckered obediently beneath his touch, Keira pushed his hand away. 'And we need to talk,' she said firmly.

'And that was why my heart sank,' he drawled, shifting his body to lie against the bank of pillows and fixing her with a hooded look. 'Why do women always want to talk instead of making love?'

'Usually because something needs to be said.' She

pulled in a breath. 'I want to tell you about when I was growing up.'

The look on his face said it all. Wrong place; wrong time. 'I met your aunt,' he said impatiently. 'Over-strict guardian, small house, jealous cousin. I get it. You didn't have such a great time.'

Keira shook her head as uncomfortable thoughts flooded into her mind. She needed to be completely honest, else how could she expect complete honesty in return? Yet what she was about to tell him wasn't easy. She'd never told anyone the full story. Even her aunt. Especially her aunt. 'I told you my mother wasn't married and that I didn't know my father. What I didn't tell you was that she didn't know him either.'

His gaze was watchful now. 'What are you talking about?'

Keira flushed to the roots of her hair because she could remember her mother's shame when she'd finally blurted out the story, no longer able to evade the curious questions of her young daughter. Would her mother be appalled if she knew that Keira was now repeating the sorry tale, to a man with a trace of steel running through his veins?

'My mother was a student nurse,' she said slowly, 'who came to London and found it was nothing like the rural farm she'd grown up on in Ireland. She was quite shy and very naïve but she had those Irish looks. You know, black hair and blue eyes—'

'Like yours?' he interrupted softly.

She shook her head. 'Oh, no. She was much prettier than me. Men were always asking her out but usually she preferred to stay in the nurses' home and watch something on TV, until one night she gave in and went to a party with a group of the other nurses. It was a pretty wild party and not her kind of thing at all. People were getting wasted and Mum decided she didn't want to stay.' She swallowed. 'But by then it was too late because someone had…had…'

'Someone had what, Keira?' he questioned as her words became strangled and his voice was suddenly so gentle that it made her want to cry.

'Somebody spiked her drink,' she breathed, the words catching like sand in her throat because even now, they still had the power to repulse her. 'She…she woke up alone in a strange bed with a pain between her legs, and soon after that she discovered she was pregnant with me.'

He gave a terse exclamation and she thought he was going to turn away in disgust but to her surprise he reached out to push away the lock of hair which had fallen over her flushed cheeks, before slipping his hand round her shoulder and pulling her against the warmth of his chest. *'Bastardo,'* he swore softly and then repeated it, for added emphasis.

She shook her head and could feel the taste of tears nudging at the back of her throat and at last she gave into them, in a way she'd never done before. 'She didn't know how many men had been near her,' she sobbed. 'She had to go to the clinic to check she hadn't been given some sort of disease and of course they offered her…' She swallowed away the tears because she saw from the tightening of his jaw that she didn't actually need to spell it out for him. 'But she didn't want that. She wanted me,' she said simply. 'There wasn't a moment of doubt about that.'

He waited until she had composed herself before he spoke again, until she had brushed the remaining tears away with the tips of her fingers.

'Why are you telling me all this, Keira?' he questioned softly. 'And why now?'

'Because I grew up without a father and for me there was no other option—but I don't want the same for my baby. For... Santino.' Her voice wavered as she looked into the hardness of his eyes and forced herself to continue, even though the look on his face would have intimidated stronger people than her. 'Matteo, you don't... you don't seem to feel anything for your son.' She sucked in a deep breath. 'Why, you've barely *touched* him. It's as if you can't bear to go near him and I want to try to understand why.'

Matteo released his hold on her and his body tensed because she had no right to interrogate him, and he didn't *have* to answer her intrusive question. He could tell her to mind her own damned business and that he would interact with his son when he was good and ready and not according to *her* timetable. Just because she wanted to spill out stuff about her own past, didn't mean he had to do the same, did it? But in the depths of her eyes he could read a deep compassion and something in him told him there could be no going forward unless she understood what had made him the man he was.

He could feel a bitter taste coating his throat. Maybe everyone kept stuff hidden away inside them—the stuff which was truly painful. Perhaps it was nature's way of trying to protect you from revisiting places which were too dark to contemplate. 'My mother died in childbirth,' he said suddenly.

There was a disbelieving pause as the words sank in and when they did, her eyes widened. 'Oh, Matteo. That's terrible,' she whispered.

Matteo instantly produced the self-protective clause which enabled him to bat off unwanted sympathy if people *did* find out. 'What is it they say?' He shrugged. 'That you can't miss what you've never had. And I've had thirty-four years to get used to it.'

Her muffled 'But…' suggested she was about to disagree with him, but then she seemed to change her mind and said nothing. Leaving him free to utter the next words from his set-piece statement. 'Maternal death is thankfully rare,' he bit out. 'My mother was just one of the unlucky ones.'

'I'm so sorry.'

'Yes,' he said. 'I think we've established that.' He chose his words carefully. 'I've never come into contact with babies before. To be honest, I've never even held one, but you're right—it isn't just inexperience which makes me wary.' His jaw tightened. 'It's guilt.'

'Guilt?' she echoed, in surprise.

He swallowed and the words took a long time in coming. 'People say they feel instant love for their own child but that didn't happen to me when I looked at Santino for the first time. Oh, I checked his fingers and his toes and was relieved that he was healthy, but I didn't *feel* anything.' He punched his fist against his heart and the words fell from his lips, heavy as stones. 'And I don't know if I ever can.'

Keira nodded as she tried to evaluate what he'd told her. It all made sense now. It explained why he'd thrown a complete wobbly when she'd kept her pregnancy quiet. What if history had grimly repeated itself and she'd died in childbirth as his mother had done? Nobody had known who the father of her baby was because she'd kept it secret. Wasn't it possible that Santino could have been adopted by her aunt and her cousin and grown up without knowing anything of his roots?

She felt another wrench as she met the pain in his eyes. What must it have been like for him—this powerful man who had missed out on so much? He had never experienced a mother's love. Never even felt her arms hugging him in those vital hours of bonding which followed birth. Who had cradled the tiny Matteo as the cold corpse of his mother was prepared for her silent journey to the grave, instead of a joyous homecoming with her newborn baby? No wonder he'd been so reluctant to get close to his little boy—he didn't know *how*.

'Didn't your father make up for the fact that you didn't have a mother?'

His mouth twisted and he gave a hollow laugh. 'People cope in their own way—or they don't. He left my care to a series of young nannies, most of whom he apparently slept with—so then they'd leave—or the new stepmother would fire them. But it didn't seem to matter how much sex he had or how many women he married, he never really got over my mother's death. It left a hole in his life which nothing could ever fill.'

Keira couldn't take her eyes away from his ravaged face. Had his father unconsciously blamed his infant son for the tragic demise of his beloved wife—would that explain why they weren't close? And had Matteo been angry with his father for trying to replace her? She wondered if those different stepmothers had blamed the boy for being an ever-present reminder of a woman they could never compete with.

And blame was the last thing Matteo needed, Keira realised. Not then and certainly not now. He needed understanding—and love—though she wasn't sure he wanted either. Reaching out, she laid her hand on his bunched and tensed biceps but the muscle remained hard and stone-like beneath her fingers. Undeterred, she began to massage her fingertips against the un-yielding flesh.

'So what do we do next, now we've brought all our ghosts into the daylight?' she questioned slowly. 'Where do we go from here, Matteo?'

His gaze was steady as he rolled away from her touch, as if reminding her that this was a decision which needed to be made without the distraction of the senses. 'That depends. Where do you want to go from here?'

She recognised he was being open to negotiation and on some deeper level she suspected that this wasn't usual for him in relationships. Because this *was* a relationship, she realised. Somehow it had grown despite their wariness and private pain and the unpromising beginning. It had the potential to grow even more—but only if she had the courage to give him the affection he needed, without making any demands of her own in return. She couldn't *demand* that he learn to love his son, she could only pray that he would. Just as she couldn't demand that he learn to love *her*. 'I'll go anywhere,' she whispered. 'As long as it's with Santino. And you.'

She leaned forward to kiss him and Matteo could never remember being kissed like that before. A kiss not fuelled by sexual hunger but filled with the promise of something he didn't recognise, something which started his senses humming. He murmured something in objection when she pulled back a little, her eyes of *profondo blu* looking dark and serious, but at least when she wasn't kissing him he was able to think straight. He didn't understand the way she made him feel, but maybe that didn't matter. Because weren't the successes of life—and business—based on gut feeling as much as understanding? Hadn't he sometimes bought a hotel site even though others in the business had told him he was crazy—and turned it into a glittering success because deep down he'd known he was onto a winner? And wasn't it a bit like that now?

'I will learn to interact with my son,' he said.

'That's a start,' she said hesitantly.

The look on her face suggested that his answer had fallen short of the ideal—but he was damned if he was going to promise to love his son. Because what if he failed to deliver? What if the ice around his heart was so deep and so frozen that nothing could ever penetrate it? 'And I want to marry you,' he said suddenly.

Now the look on her face had changed. He saw surprise there and perhaps the faint glimmer of delight, which was quickly replaced by one of suspicion, as if perhaps she had misheard him.

'Marry me?' she echoed softly.

He nodded. 'So that Santino will have the security you never had, even if our relationship doesn't last,' he said, his voice cool but certain. 'And so that he will be protected by my fortune, which one day he will inherit. Doesn't that make perfect sense to you?'

He could see her blinking furiously, as if she was trying very hard to hold back the glitter of disappointed tears, but then she seemed to pull it all together and nodded.

'Yes, I think marriage is probably the most sensible option in the circumstances,' she said.

'So you will be my wife?'

'Yes, I'll be your wife. But I'm only doing this for Santino. To give him the legitimacy I never had. You do understand that, don't you, Matteo?'

She fixed him with a defiant look, as if she didn't really care—and for a split second it occurred to him that neither of them were being completely honest. 'Of course I understand, *cara mia*,' he said softly.

CHAPTER ELEVEN

KEIRA HEARD FOOTSTEPS behind her and turned from the mirror to see Claudia in a pretty flowery dress, instead of the soft blue uniform she usually wore when she was working.

'Is everything okay with Santino?' Keira asked the nursery nurse immediately, more out of habit than fear because she'd been cradling him not an hour earlier as she had dressed her baby son in preparation for his parents' forthcoming marriage.

Claudia smiled. 'He is well, *signorina*. His father is playing with him now. He says he is teaching him simple words of Italian, which he is certain he will remember when eventually he starts to speak.'

Keira smiled, turning back to her reflection and forcing herself to make a final adjustment to her hair, even though she kept telling herself that her bridal outfit was pretty irrelevant on what was going to be a purely functional wedding day. But Matteo's father and stepmother were going to be attending the brief ceremony, so she felt she had to make *some* sort of effort. And surely if she did her best it might lessen their

inevitable disbelief that he was going to marry someone like her.

'What kind of wedding would you like?' Matteo had
asked during that drive back from Rome after she'd
agreed to be his wife.

Keira remembered hedging her bets. 'You first.'

She remembered his cynical laugh, too.

'Something small. Unfussy. I'm not a big fan of weddings.'

So of course Keira had agreed that small and unfussy would be perfect, though deep down that hadn't
been what she'd wanted at all. Maybe there was a part
of every woman which wanted the whole works—the
fuss and flowers and clouds of confetti. Or maybe that
was just her—because marriage had always been held
up as the perfect ideal when she'd been growing up.
There had been that photo adorning her aunt's side-
board—the bouquet-clutching image which had stared
out at her over the years. She recalled visiting for Sunday tea when her mother was still alive, when attention
would be drawn to Aunt Ida's white dress and stiff veil.
'Wouldn't you have loved a white wedding, Bridie?' Ida
used to sigh, and Keira's mother would say she didn't
care for pomp and ceremony.

And Keira had thought she was the same—until
she'd agreed to marry Matteo and been surprised by
the stupid ache in her heart as she realised she must play
down a wedding which wasn't really a wedding. It was
a legal contract for the benefit of their son—not something inspired by love or devotion or a burning desire to

want to spend the rest of your life with just one person, so it didn't really count. At least, not on Matteo's part.

And hers?

She smoothed down her jacket and sighed. Because even more disturbing than her sudden yearning to wear a long white dress and carry a fragrant bouquet was the realisation that her feelings for Matteo had started to change. Was that because she understood him a little better now? Because he'd given her a glimpse of the vulnerability and loss which lay beneath the steely exterior he presented to the world? Maybe. She told herself not to have unrealistic expectations. Not to wish for things which were never going to happen, but concentrate on being a good partner. To give Matteo affection in quiet and unobtrusive ways, so that maybe the hard ice around his heart might melt a little and let her in.

He was doing his best to change, she knew that. In the busy days which followed their return from his Roman villa, he had meticulously paid his son all the attention which had been lacking before. Sometimes he would go to Santino if he woke in the night—silencing Keira's sleepy protests with a kiss. Occasionally, he gave the baby a bottle and, once, had even changed his nappy, even though he'd protested that this was one task surely better undertaken by women.

But as Keira had watched him perform these fatherly duties she had been unable to blind herself to the truth. That it *was* simply a performance and Matteo was just going through the motions. He was being a good father, just as he was a good lover—because he was a man who excelled in whatever he did. But it was duty which motivated him. His heart wasn't in it, that much was obvious. And as long as she accepted that, then she'd be fine.

She turned away from the mirror, wondering if there was anything she'd forgotten to do. Matteo's father, Massimo, and his wife, Luciana, had arrived only a short while ago because the traffic from Rome had been bad. Since they were due at the town hall at noon, there had been little opportunity for Keira to exchange more than a few words of greeting and introduce them to their new grandson. She'd been nervous—of course she had—she suspected it was always nerve-racking meeting prospective in-laws, and most people didn't have to do it on the morning of the wedding itself.

Massimo was a bear of a man, his build bulkier than Matteo's, though Keira could see a likeness around the jet-dark eyes. Her prospective stepmother-in-law, Luciana, was an elegant woman in her fifties, who had clearly embraced everything facial surgery had to offer, which had resulted in a disturbingly youthful appearance.

Keira picked up her clutch bag and went downstairs, her heart pounding with an anxiety which seemed to be increasing by the second. Was that because she'd seen Luciana's unmistakable look of disbelief when they'd been introduced? Was she wondering how this little Englishwoman from nowhere had wrested a proposal of marriage from the Italian tycoon?

But the expression on Matteo's face made Keira's stomach melt as she walked into the hallway, where everyone was waiting. She saw his eyes darken and the edges of his lips curve into an unmistakable smile of appreciation as he took her cold hand in his and kissed it.

'Sei bella, mia cara,' he had murmured softly. *'Molta bella.'*

Keira told herself he was only saying it because such praise was expected of the prospective groom, but she couldn't deny the feeling of satisfaction which rippled down her spine in response. Because she *wanted* him to look at her and find her beautiful, of course she did. She wasn't stupid and knew she couldn't take his desire for granted. Someone like her was always going to have to work to maintain it. Leola the stylist had been dispatched from Rome with a selection of wedding outfits and Keira had chosen the one she felt was the most flattering but also the most *appropriate*. Steadfastly pushing away the more floaty white concoctions, she had opted for functional rather than fairy tale. The silvery-grey material of the dress and jacket reminded her of a frosty winter morning but there was no doubt that it suited her dark hair and colouring. Only the turquoise shoes and matching clutch bag provided a splash of colour—because she had refused all Leola's inducements to carry flowers.

At least Massimo Valenti seemed enchanted by his grandson. Keira travelled in one of the cars with him to the nearly town and watched as he spent the entire journey cooing at the baby in delight. It made her wonder why he hadn't been close to his own son—but there was no time for questions because they were drawing up outside the town hall where Matteo was waiting to

introduce her to the interpreter, which Italian law demanded.

Twenty minutes later she emerged from the building
as a married woman and Matteo was pulling her into
his arms, his hands resting on either side of her waist—
but even that light touch was enough to make her want
to dissolve with lust and longing.

'So. How does it feel to be Signora Valenti?' he questioned silkily.

Her heart was pounding as she stared up into the
molten darkness of his eyes. 'Ask me again next week,'
she said breathlessly. 'It feels a little unreal right now.'

'Maybe this will help you accept the reality,' he said,
'mia sposa.'

And there, beneath the fluttering Italian flag of the
town hall, his lips came down to claim hers with a kiss
which left her in no doubt that he would rather they were
somewhere private, preferably naked and horizontal.
It set off an answering hunger and reminded Keira of
the slightly incredible fact that he couldn't seem to get
enough of her. Didn't he demonstrate that every night
when he covered her trembling body with his own? And
wasn't that *enough*? she wondered as they drove back to
the farmhouse together, her golden ring glinting as she
fussed around with Santino's delicate shawl. Was it just
her inherently cautious nature which made her wonder
if her relationship with Matteo was as superficial as
the icing sugar sprinkled over the top of the chocolate
wedding cake which Paola had baked?

Yet when he carried her over the threshold, it felt
real. And when she returned from putting Santino down

for a nap, having removed the silvery-grey jacket to reveal the filmy chiffon dress beneath, Matteo had been waiting in the shadowed hallway for her.

Pulling her into a quiet alcove, he placed his palm over her hammering heart and she licked her lips as her nipple automatically hardened beneath his touch.

'Ever wish you could just wave a magic wand and make everyone disappear?' he drawled.

She shivered as the light stroking of her nipple increased. 'Isn't that a little...anti-social?'

'I'm feeling anti-social,' he grumbled, his lips brushing over the curve of her jaw before moving upwards to tease her now trembling lips. 'I want to be alone with my new wife.'

Keira kissed him back as his words set off another whisper of hope inside her and she wondered if it was wrong to allow herself to hope, on this, her wedding day.

'You were the man who once told me about the benefits of waiting,' she teased him. 'Won't this allow you to test out your theory?'

Matteo laughed as she pulled away from him, the prim twitch of her lips contradicting the hunger in her eyes, and he shook his head slightly, wondering what kind of spell she had cast over him. He was used to the wiles of women yet Keira used none of them. She wasn't deliberately provocative around him and didn't possess that air of vanity of someone who revelled in her sexual power over a man. On the contrary, in public she was almost demure—while in private she was red-hot. And that pleased him, too. She pleased him and unsettled him in equal measure. She left him wanting more—but more of *what*, he didn't know. She was like a drink you took when your throat was dry yet when you'd finished it, you found that your thirst was just as intense.

He stroked his fingers down over her belly, his gaze steady as they stood hidden by the shadows of the staircase. Hard to believe that a child had grown beneath its almost-flat curve. 'I want you to know you are an amazing mother,' he said suddenly. 'And that Santino is blessed indeed.'

He saw the surprise behind the sudden brightness in her eyes, her mouth working as she struggled to contain herself.

'Don't make me get all emotional, Matteo,' she whispered. 'I've got to go in there and make conversation with your father and stepmother and I'm not going to make a very good impression if I've been blubbing.'

But he disregarded her soft plea, knowing he needed to express something which had slowly become a certainty. He owed her that, at least. 'I shouldn't have taken you to Rome when I did and made you leave the baby behind,' he admitted slowly. 'No matter how good the childcare we had in place. I can see now that it was a big ask for a relatively new mother in a strange country.'

He saw her teeth working into her bottom lip and he thought she might be about to cry, when suddenly she smiled and it was like the bright summer sun blazing all over him with warmth and light, even though outside it was cold and wintry.

'Thank you,' she said, a little shakily. 'I love you for saying that.'

He stilled. 'Really?'

A look of horror crossed her face as she realised what she'd said. 'I didn't mean—'

'Didn't you?' he murmured. 'How very disappointing.'

Keira told herself he was only teasing as he led her into the salon, but she felt as if she were floating on air as she took a grizzling Santino from Massimo's bear-like arms and rocked him dreamily against her chest. Had Matteo really just admitted he'd been in the wrong by taking her to Rome and told her she was a good mother? It wasn't so much the admission itself, more the fact he was beginning to accept that each and every one of them got it wrong sometimes—and that felt like a major breakthrough.

And had she really just let her guard down enough to tell him she loved him? It hadn't been in a dramatic way or because she'd expected an instant reciprocal response. She'd said it affectionately and Matteo needed that, she reckoned. How many times had he been told he'd been loved when he was growing up? Too few, she suspected.

Still high from the impact of their conversation, Keira refused the glass of vintage champagne which was offered and accepted a glass of some bittersweet orange drink instead.

But unusually, Santino grizzled in her arms and she wondered if it was the excitement of the day which was making him so fractious. Discreetly, she slipped away to the nursery to feed and change him before rocking him until he was sound asleep and carefully putting him in his crib.

She picked up the empty bottle and was just on her way out when she was startled by the sight of Luciana, who suddenly appeared at the nursery door in a waft of expensive scent. Keira wondered if she'd wandered into the wrong room or if she'd been hoping for a cuddle with Santino. But there was an odd smile on her new stepmother's face and, for some reason, whispers of trepidation began to slide over Keira's spine.

'Is everything okay, Luciana?' she questioned, hoping she sounded suitably deferential towards the older woman.

Luciana shrugged. 'That depends what you mean by *okay*. I was a little disappointed that my son and his family were not invited to the ceremony today.'

'Oh, well—you can see how it is.' Keira gave a nervous smile, because Matteo had hinted that there was no love lost between him and his stepbrother, Emilio. 'We just wanted a very small wedding.'

'Sì.' Luciana picked up a silver-framed photo of Santino and began to study it. 'And naturally, it would have been very *difficult* for Emilio.'

'Difficult?'

Luciana put the photograph down. 'In the circumstances.'

Keira blinked. 'What circumstances?'

Elegantly plucked eyebrows were raised. 'Because of the clause in my husband's will, of course.'

Keira's heart began to pound as some nameless dread crept over her. 'What clause?'

'Surely Matteo has told you?' Luciana looked surprised. 'Though perhaps not. He has always been a man who gives very little away.' Her expression became sly. 'You are aware that this house belonged to Massimo's first wife?'

'To Matteo's mother?' questioned Keira stiffly. 'Yes, I knew that. It's where she was born and where she grew up. It's one of the reasons he loves it so much.'

Luciana shrugged. 'Ever since Matteo reached the age of eighteen, Massimo has generously allowed his son to use the estate as his own. To all intents and purposes, this *was* Matteo's home.' She paused. 'But a strange thing happens to men as they grow older. They want to leave something of themselves behind.' Her surgically enhanced eyes gleamed. 'I'm talking, of course, about continuing the Valenti name. I am already a grandmother. I understand these desires.'

Keira's head was spinning. 'I honestly don't understand what you're getting at, Luciana.'

'Ah, I can see you know nothing of this.' Luciana gave a hard smile. 'It's very simple. He loves this house for obvious reasons, but he does not *own* it. And Massimo told him he intended bequeathing the entire estate to his stepson, unless Matteo produced an heir of his own with the Valenti name.' She shrugged her bony shoulders. 'I wondered if he would be prepared to sacrifice his freedom for an heir, not least because he has always shown a certain...*disdain* for women. And yet here you are—a pretty little English girl who arrived with a baby in her arms and got a wedding ring for her troubles. The perfect solution to all Matteo's problems!'

'You're saying that...that Matteo would have lost this house unless he produced an heir?'

'That's exactly what I'm saying. His gain, my son's loss.' Luciana shrugged. *'C'est la vie.'*

Keira felt so shocked that for a moment her limbs felt as if they were completely weightless. With a shaking hand, she put the empty bottle down on a shelf and swallowed, trying to compose herself—and knowing that she had to get away from Luciana's toxic company before she did or said something she regretted. 'Please excuse me,' she said. 'But I must get back to the wedding party.'

Did she imagine the look of disappointment which flickered across Luciana's face, or did she just imagine it? It didn't matter. She was going to get through this day with her dignity intact. Matteo had married her to get his hands on this property, so let him enjoy his brief victory. What good would come of making a scene on her wedding day?

Somehow she got through the rest of the afternoon, meeting Matteo's questioning stare with a brittle smile across the dining table, while everyone except her tucked into the lavish wedding breakfast. Did he sense that all was not well, and was that the reason why his black gaze seemed fixed on her face?

She was relieved when finally Massimo and Luciana left—though her father-in-law gave her the most enormous hug, which brought an unexpected lump to her throat. Leaving Matteo to dismiss Paola and the rest of the staff, Keira hurried to tend to Santino, spending far longer than necessary as she settled her baby son for the night.

At last she left the nursery and went into the bedroom but her hands were clammy as she pulled off her wedding outfit and flung it over a chair. Spurred on by Leola, she had been planning on surprising Matteo with the shortest dress she'd ever worn. A bottom-skimming dress for his eyes and no one else's. She'd wanted to wear it in anticipation of the appreciative look on his face when he saw it and to hint at a final farewell to her residual tomboy. But now she tugged on a functional pair of jeans and a sweater because she couldn't bear the thought of dressing up—not when Matteo's motives for marrying her were making her feel so *ugly* inside.

Although she would have liked nothing better than to creep into bed on her own and pull the duvet over her head to blot out the world, she knew that wasn't an option. There was only one acceptable course of action which lay open to her, but she couldn't deny her feeling of dread as she walked into the room which overlooked the garden at the back of the house, where Matteo stood beside the fire, looking impossibly handsome in his charcoal wedding suit. Don't touch me, she prayed silently, even though her body desperately wanted him to do just that—and maybe something had alerted him to her conflicted mood because his eyes narrowed and he made no attempt to approach her.

His face was sombre as he regarded her. 'Something is wrong.'

It was a statement, not a question, but Keira didn't answer straight away. She allowed herself a few more seconds before everything changed for ever. A final few seconds where she could pretend they were newly-weds about to embark on a shared life together. 'You could say that. I had a very interesting conversation with Luciana earlier.' She inhaled deeply and then suddenly the words came spilling out, like corrosive acid leaking from a car battery. 'Why didn't you tell me you were only marrying me to get your hands on an inheritance?' she demanded. 'And that this house would only become yours if you produced a legitimate child? I would have understood, if only you'd had the guts to tell me.'

He didn't flinch. His gaze was hard and steady. 'Because the inheritance became irrelevant. I married you because I care for you and my son and because I want us to make a future together.'

Keira wanted to believe him. The child-woman who had yearned for a long white dress and big bouquet of flowers longed for it to be the truth. But she couldn't believe him—it was a stretch too far. Once she'd thought he sounded like someone reading from a script when he'd been addressing a subject which would make most people emotional—and he was doing it again now.

I care for you and my son.

He sounded like a robot intoning the correct response, not someone speaking from the heart. And his lack of emotion wasn't the point, was it? She'd known about that from the start. She'd known the reason he was made that way and, filled with hope and with trust, had been prepared to make allowances for it. She bit her lip. When all the time he'd been plotting away and using her as a pawn in his desire to get his hands on this estate.

'I understand that you're known as an elusive man who doesn't give anything away,' she accused shakily. 'But how many more people are going to come out of the woodwork and tell me things about you that I didn't know? Can you imagine how it made me feel to hear that from Luciana, Matteo? To know you'd been buttering me up to get me to marry you? I thought... I thought you were doing it for your son's future, when all the time it was because you didn't want to lose a piece of land you thought of as rightfully yours! You don't want a family—not really—you've just used me as some kind of incubator!'

'But there's a fundamental flaw in your argument,' he grated. 'If inheriting the estate meant so much to me, then why hadn't I fathered a child with someone else long before I met you?'

'Because I don't think you really like women,' she said slowly. 'Or maybe you just don't understand them. You never knew your mother and she died so tragically that it's inevitable you idealised her. She would have had flaws, just like we all do—only you never got to see them. No woman could ever have lived up to her and maybe that's one of the reasons why you never settled down.' She sucked in a deep breath. 'And then I came along and took the decision away from you. A stolen night, which was never meant to be any more, suddenly produced an heir. You didn't have to go through the whole tedious ritual of courting a woman you didn't care for in order to get yourself a child. Fate played right into your hands, didn't it, Matteo? Suddenly you had everything you needed, without any real effort on your part.'

His face blanched. 'You think I am so utterly ruthless?'

She shrugged. 'I don't know,' she said, and there was

a crack in her voice. 'Maybe you do care—a little. Or
as much as you ever can. But you're missing the point.
I thought growing up without a father was difficult, but
at least I knew where I stood. It may have been grim at
times but it was honest and you haven't been honest with
me.' She swallowed. 'It feels like I'm in the shadows of
your life—like someone in the wings watching the action on stage. I see the way you are with the baby—and
with me—and it comes over as a performance, not real.
How could it be, when Santino and I were only ever a
means to an end?'

Matteo flinched as he met the accusation in her eyes,
because nobody had ever spoken quite so candidly to
him. 'For someone so tiny, you certainly don't pull any
punches, do you, Keira?'

'What's the point in pulling punches? All we have
left is the truth,' she said wearily. 'You've got what
you wanted, Matteo. We're married now and your son
has been legitimised. You have continued the Valenti
name and will therefore inherit the estate. You don't
need me any more.'

Matteo felt his chest tighten and his instinct was to
tell her that she was right—and that he *didn't* need anyone. He'd spent his whole life not needing anyone because there had been nobody there to lean on, nobody
to get close to—why change that pattern now? But some
unknown emotion was nudging at his conscience as
something deep inside him told him this was different.

'And what if I say I do need you?' he said hoarsely
as he attempted to articulate the confusion of thoughts
which were spinning around inside his head.

Her eyes widened, but he could see a wariness in their depths of *profondo blu*. 'You do?' she queried uncertainly.

The moment it took for her to ask the question was all Matteo needed to shift things into perspective, because he knew he mustn't offer her false promises or false hope. She deserved more than that. So stick to the facts, he urged himself grimly. You're good with facts. Allow her to consider all the advantages of remaining here, as his wife.

'Of course,' he said. 'And logistically it makes perfect sense.'

'Logistically?' she echoed, her voice a little faint.

'Sure.' He shrugged. 'If we're all living together under one roof as a family, it will be much better for Santino. Better than having a father who just jets in and sees him on high days and holidays.'

'There is that, of course,' she said woodenly.

'And I've married you now, Keira,' he said softly. 'I have given you the security of bearing my name and wearing my ring. Your future is assured. You don't need to worry about money ever again.'

'You think that's what it's all about?' she questioned, her voice trembling. 'Money?'

'Not all of it, no—but a big part of it. And we have plenty of other reasons to keep our marriage going.' He curved her a slow smile. 'What about the sexual chemistry which exists between us? That fact that you are the hottest woman I've ever had in my bed?'

She gasped as if she had been winded before staring at him—as if she were looking at someone she'd never seen before. 'You just don't get it, do you, Matteo? You list all the reasons I should stay with you and yet you haven't mentioned anything which really *matters*!'

He flinched with pain as he met the undiluted anger in her gaze, but at the same time a strange sense of relief washed over him as he realised that he no longer had to try. She was going and taking their child with him and he would just have to learn how to deal with that. And anyway, he thought grimly—why would he want to prolong a relationship when it could hurt like this? Hadn't he vowed never to let anyone hurt him, ever again?

'Okay, I get it. What do you want?'

With an effort he held up the palms of his hands, in silent submission, and the sudden wobble of her lips made him think she might be about to backtrack— maybe to soften the blows which she'd just rained on him, but all she said was, 'I'd like us to separate.'

He told himself it was better this way. Better to go back to the life he was used to and be the person he knew how to be, rather than chase after the glimmer of gold which Keira Ryan had brought shimmering into his life.

'Tell me what you want, in practical terms,' he said flatly.

He could see her throat constricting as she nodded.

'I'd like to return to London as soon as possible and to rent somewhere before I decide to buy,' she said, before sucking in a deep breath. 'But I want you to know that I'll take only what is necessary for our needs and you're not to worry. I don't intend to make a great hole in your wealth, Matteo.'

And even that got to him, because he couldn't even level the charge of greed against her. She wasn't interested in his money, he realised, and she never had been. She'd taken the cash he'd thoughtlessly left beside the bed and had given it away to charity. She'd fought like mad against him buying her a fancy wardrobe. She was a jewel of a woman, he realised—a bright and shining jewel. But it was too late for them. The cold, pinched look on her beautiful face told him that. So let her go, he told himself. Set her free. At least you can give her that.

'That can all be arranged,' he said. 'But in turn, I need your reassurance that I can continue to see my son.'

There was surprise on her face now and he wondered if secretly she had expected him to cut all ties with his own flesh and blood.

'Of course. You can see as much of Santino as you wish,' she said quietly. 'I will never deny you your son, Matteo, and I hope you will see him very often, because he…he needs you. You're his daddy.'

A lump rose in his throat as he moved away from the blaze of the fire.

'I'd like to say goodnight to him now,' he said and she nodded and made as if to follow him.

'Alone,' he gritted out.

But Matteo's heart was heavy as he walked towards the nursery—as if a dark stone had lodged itself deep inside his chest. The night light made the room appear soft and rosy and Matteo stared down at the sleeping child. He remembered the first time he had seen him. When he had counted his fingers and toes like someone learning basic mathematics, and had felt nothing.

But not this time.

This time he could barely make out any detail of his sleeping son, his vision was so blurred. Too late, his heart had cracked open and left room for emotion to come flooding in, powerfully and painfully. And Santino stirred as Matteo's tears fell like rain onto the delicate white shawl.

CHAPTER TWELVE

IT WAS RAINING by the time Keira got back from her walk and she had just let Charlie off his lead when she noticed the letter lying in the centre of the hall table, where Claudia must have left it. She pulled a face. Another one.

The envelope carried an Italian stamp and the air-mail sticker seemed to wink at her. Quickly, she slid it into a drawer to lie on top of all the others, because she couldn't quite bring herself to throw them away. Her reluctance to dispose of the growing pile of correspondence was just about equal to her reluctance to read them, because they were from Matteo—she recognised his handwriting. And why would she wish to read them and risk making the hole in her heart even bigger? Why was he even *writing* to her when she'd told him it was better if all correspondence took place between their respective solicitors? Why had he arrogantly elected to take no notice?

Because she was fighting like crazy not to go under. Not to give into the tears which pricked at her eyes at night when she lay in bed missing the warm embrace of her estranged husband. She was determined to pour all her energies into being there for Santino—into being the best mother she possibly could—and she couldn't manage that if her heart stayed raw and aching from thinking about Matteo all the time.

She'd wondered whether his determination to keep in close contact with his son would have faded once she and Santino had left Umbria but to her surprise, it hadn't. He'd already paid two visits and they'd only been back in England a little over a fortnight. On both those occasions she had absented herself from the house, leaving Claudia in charge of the baby—Claudia who had been happy to accompany her from Umbria when Keira had made the emotional return to her homeland.

She supposed people might think it a form of cowardice that she couldn't bear the thought of confronting the man with whom she hadn't even shared a wedding night. But that was too bad. It didn't matter what anyone else thought, only what was right for her and her son. Sooner or later she hoped she'd be able to greet him with a genuine air of indifference but for now she didn't trust herself not to burst into noisy howls of sorrow and to tell him how much she was missing him.

With the money he'd settled on her, she was renting a house. A house with a garden and a front door which wasn't shared—the kind of house in Notting Hill where she used to drop off her prep-school charges when she was working at Luxury Limos. And she'd bought a dog, too. A scruffy little thing with a lopsided ear and the saddest eyes she'd ever seen. The staff at the rescue centre had told her he'd been badly beaten and was fearful and shy, but he had taken one look at Keira and hurled himself at her with a series of plaintive yelps. Charlie was the best thing to have happened to them since they'd returned to England and had reinforced her intention to give Santino a proper childhood. The kind she'd never had—with a dog and a mother who was always waiting for him when he got home from school.

Pulling off her rain-soaked coat, she went upstairs to the nursery where Claudia was just putting Santino down to sleep. The nursery nurse straightened up as Keira entered the room and she found herself wondering why Claudia's cheeks were so pink. Walking over to the crib, Keira stared down into the sleepy eyes of her son, her heart turning over with love.

'He looks happy,' she murmured as she leaned over to plant a soft kiss on his silken cheek.

'He should be!' said Claudia. 'After you took him out for such a long walk this morning.'

'Good thing I did. At least we missed the rain,' said Keira, with an idle glance out of the window as she drew the curtains.

There was a pause. 'Would you mind if I went out earlier than planned?' asked Claudia.

'Of course I don't mind.' Keira smiled because she knew that Claudia had struck up a close friendship with a man she'd met at the Italian Embassy. 'Hot date?'

Claudia smiled as she put her forefinger over her lips and Keira was so preoccupied with tidying up the nursery that she barely registered the nursery nurse leaving the room, though she did hear the distant bang of the front door. She turned the light out and was just about to make her way downstairs when her mobile phone began to ring and she pulled it from the pocket of her jeans, frowning when she saw Matteo's name flashing up on the screen.

Fury began to bubble up inside her. She'd asked him not to write and he had ignored that. She'd asked him not to call her and he was ignoring that too! So why now, coming straight after yet another unwanted letter from him? She clicked the connection.

'This had better be urgent,' she said.

'It is.'

She frowned as she registered a curious echo-like quality to his voice. 'And?'

'I need to see you.'

She needed to see him too, but no good would come of it. Wouldn't it make her hunger for what she could never have and certainly didn't need—a man who had lured a woman into marriage just because he wanted to inherit a house? 'I thought we'd decided that wasn't a good idea.'

'No, Keira...*you* decided.'

Still that curious echo. Keira frowned. Shouldn't she just agree to see him once and get it over with? Steel her heart against her own foolish desires and listen to what he had to say? 'Very well,' she said. 'We'll put an appointment in the diary.'

'Now,' he bit out.

'What do you mean...*now*?'

'I want to see you now,' he growled.

'Matteo, you're in Italy and I'm in England and unless you've discovered the secret of teleportation, that's not going to happen.'

'I'm downstairs.'

She froze. '*What* did you say?'

'I'm downstairs.' The echo began to get louder. 'Coming up.'

Her heart slamming against her ribcage, Keira rushed from the nursery to see Matteo with his mobile phone held against his ear, making his way up the stairs towards her. His face was more serious than she'd ever seen it as he cut the connection and slid the phone into the pocket of his jeans.

'Hi,' he said, the casual greeting failing to hide the tension and the pain which were written across his ravaged features.

She wanted to do several things all at once. To drum her fists against his powerful chest, over and over again. And she wanted to pull his darkly handsome face to hers and kiss him until there was no breath left in her body.

'What are you doing here?' she demanded.

'I need to speak to you.'

'Did you have to go about it so dramatically? You scared me half to death!' She looked at him suspiciously. 'You don't have a key, do you?'

'I don't,' he agreed.

'So how did you get in?'

'Claudia let me in before she left.'

'*Claudia let you in?*' she repeated furiously. 'Why would she do something like that?'

'Because I asked her to.'

'And what you say goes, I suppose, because you're the one with the money,' she said contemptuously.

'No.' He sucked in a ragged breath. 'I'm the one with the broken heart.'

It was such an unbelievable thing for him to say that Keira assumed she'd misheard him, and she was too busy deciding that they needed to move out of Santino's earshot in case they woke him to pay very much attention to her husband's words. 'You'd better come with me,' she said.

Matteo followed the denim-covered sway of her bottom as they went downstairs, watching her long black ponytail swinging against her back with every determined stride she took. Her body language wasn't looking promising and neither was her attitude. But what had he expected—that she would squeal with delight when she saw him again? Welcome him into the embrace he had so missed—as if that whole great betrayal had never happened? His throat thickened. He had tried playing it slow and playing by her rules but he'd realised she would be prepared to push him away for ever if he let her.

And he couldn't afford to let her.

They reached a beautiful, high-ceilinged sitting room dominated by a tall Christmas tree, which glittered in front of one of the tall windows. Fragrant and green, it was covered with lights and tiny stars and on the top stood an angel with gossamer-fine wings. A heap of presents with ribbons and bows stood at the base of the giant conifer and Matteo thought it looked so homely. And yet he wasn't connected to any of it, was he? He was still the outsider. The motherless boy who had never really felt part of Christmas.

So what are you going to do about it, Valenti? he asked himself as she turned to face him and they stood looking at one another like two combatants.

'You wanted to talk,' she said, without preamble. 'So talk. Why did you sneak into my house like this?'

'You've been ignoring my letters.'

She nodded and the glossy black ponytail danced around her shoulders. 'I told you I wanted to keep all written communication between our respective solicitors.'

'You really think that my lawyer wants to hear that I love you?' he demanded, his breath a low hiss.

Her lips opened and he thought she might be about to gasp, before she closed them again firmly, like an oyster shell clamping tightly shut.

'And that I miss you more than I ever thought possible?' he continued heatedly. 'Or that my life feels empty without you?'

'Don't waste my time with your lies, Matteo.'

'They aren't lies,' he said unevenly. 'They're the truth.'

'I don't believe you.'

'I didn't think you would.' He sucked in a deep breath. 'Which is why I wrote you the letters.'

'The letters,' she repeated blankly.

'I know you got them, because I asked Claudia. What did you do with them, Keira—did you throw them away? Set light to them and watch them go up in flames?'

She shook her head. 'No. I didn't do that. I have them all.'

'Then, I wonder, could you possibly fetch them?'

Was it the word 'fetch' which brought Charlie bounding into the room, his tail wagging furiously and his once sad eyes bright and curious as he looked up at the strange man? Keira glared as she saw Matteo crouch down and offer his hand to the little dog, furious yet somehow unsurprised when the terrier edged cautiously towards him. The shock of seeing Matteo again had shaken her and weakened her defences, making her realise that she was still fundamentally shaky around him—and so she nodded her agreement to his bizarre request. At least leaving the room and his disturbing presence would give her the chance to compose herself and to quieten the fierce hammering of her heart.

Slowly she walked into the hallway to retrieve the pile of envelopes from the drawer and went back into the sitting room, holding them gingerly between her fingers, like an unexploded bomb. By now Charlie's tail was thrashing wildly, and as Matteo straightened up from stroking him the puppy gave a little whine of protest and she wondered how he had so quickly managed to charm the shy little dog. But the terrier had been discovered wriggling in a sack by the side of the road, she remembered, the only survivor among all his dead brothers and sisters. Charlie had also grown up without a mother, she thought—and a lump lodged in her throat.

'Here,' she croaked, holding the letters towards him.

'Don't you want to open them?' he said.

She shook her head. 'Not really.'

'Then maybe I'd better tell you what's in them,' he said, his eyes not leaving her face as he took them from her. 'They are all love letters. With the exception of one.'

He saw her eyes widen before dark lashes came shuttering down to cloak their sapphire hue with suspicion.

'What's that? A hate letter?' she quipped.

'I'm serious, Keira.'

'And so am I. Anyone can write down words on a piece of paper and not mean them.'

'Then how about I summarise them for you out loud?'

'No.'

But that one word was so whispered that he barely heard it and Matteo had no intention of heeding it anyway. 'Four words, actually,' he husked. 'I love you, Keira. So how about I say it again, just so there can be no misunderstanding? I love you, Keira, and I've been a fool. *Uno scemo!* I should have been honest with you from the start, but…' He inhaled deeply through his nostrils and then expelled the air on a shuddered breath. 'Keeping things locked away inside was the way I operated. The only way I knew. But believe me when I tell you that by the time I asked you to marry me, I wasn't thinking about the house any more. My mind was full of you. It still is. I can't stop thinking about you and I don't want to. So I'm asking you to give me another chance, Keira. To give *us* another chance. You, me and Santino. That's all.'

She didn't say anything for a moment and when she spoke she started shaking her head, as if what he was demanding of her was impossible.

'That's *all*?' she breathed. 'After everything that's happened? You don't know what you're asking, Matteo.'

'Oh, but I do,' he demurred. 'I'm asking you to be my wife for real. With nothing but total honesty between us from now on, because I want that. I want that more than anything.' His voice lowered. 'But I realise it can only work if you love me too. Once, in a shadowed hallway after we had taken our wedding vows, you whispered to me that you did, but you may not have meant it.'

Keira clamped her lips together to try to contain the stupid tremble of emotion. Of course she had meant it. Every single word. The question was whether he did, too. Was it possible that he really loved her, or was this simply a means to an end—the manipulative declaration of a man determined to get his rightful heir back into his life? Or maybe just pride refusing to let a woman walk away from him.

Yet something was stubbornly refusing to allow her to accept the bleaker version of his reasons for coming here today. Was it the anguish she could see in his black eyes—so profound that even she, in her insecurity, didn't believe she was imagining it? She flicked the tip of her tongue over her mouth, wondering if it was too late for them, until she realised what the reality of that would mean. Matteo gone from her life and free to make another with someone else, while she would never be able to forget him.

And she wasn't going to allow that to happen. Because how could she ignore the burning inside her heart and the bright spark of hope which was beginning to flood through her veins?

'I've tried not to love you,' she admitted slowly. 'But it doesn't work. I think about you nearly all the time and I miss you. I love you, Matteo, and I will be your wife, but on one condition.'

His body grew very still. 'Anything,' he said. 'Name it.'

She had been about to ask him never knowingly to hurt her, but she realised that was all part of the package. That hurt and pain were the price you paid for love and you just had to pray they didn't rear their bitter heads too often in a lifetime. She knew also that if they wanted to go forward, then they had to leave the bitterness of the past behind. So instead of demanding the impossible, she touched her fingertips to his face, tracing them slowly down over his cheek until they came to rest on his beautiful lips.

'That you make love to me,' she said, her voice softened by tears of joy. 'And convince me this really is happening.'

His voice was unsteady. 'You mean, right now?'

She swallowed and nodded, rapidly wiping underneath her eyes with a bent finger. 'This very second,' she gulped.

Framing her face within the palms of his hands, he looked at her for one long moment before he spoke. 'To the woman who has given me everything, because without you I am nothing. *Ti amo, mia sposa.* My beautiful, beautiful wife,' he husked, and crushed his lips down hard on hers.

EPILOGUE

OUTSIDE THE WINDOW big white flakes floated down from the sky, adding to the dazzling carpet which had already covered the vast sweep of lawn. Keira gazed at it and gave a dreamy sigh. It was unusual for snow to settle in this part of Umbria and she thought she'd never seen anything quite so magical, or so beautiful. She smiled. Well, except maybe one other time...

Looking up from where she was crouched beside the Christmas tree where she'd just placed a couple of presents, she saw Matteo walk into the room—with snowflakes melting against his dark hair. He'd been outside, putting the finishing touches to a snowman, which would be the first thing Santino saw when he looked out of his window tomorrow morning. Their son's first real Christmas, Keira thought, because last year he'd been too young to realise what was going on and she...

Well, if she was being honest, she could hardly remember last Christmas herself. She and Matteo had been busy discovering each other all over again—and finding out that things were different from how they'd been before. They couldn't have been anything *but* different once the constraints of the past were lifted and they'd given themselves the freedom to say exactly what was on their minds. Or in their hearts.

Matteo had given her the option of living in London, Rome or Umbria—and she'd opted for the sprawling Umbrian estate which had once belonged to his mother's family. She figured it was healthier for Santino to grow up in the glorious Italian countryside, especially now that they had acquired a beautiful black cat named Luca who, against all odds, had become a devoted companion to Charlie the terrier.

But it was more than that. This estate was Matteo's link with his roots. It represented continuity and stability—something which had been lacking in both their lives until now. One day Santino might listen to the call of his forebears and decide he didn't want to be a businessman, like his daddy. He might want to grow up and farm the fertile acres of this beautiful place. A place which might so nearly have disappeared from the family.

Because Keira had discovered that the very first letter Matteo had sent during their separation contained estate agent details marketing the property. He'd put it up for sale to demonstrate that the house meant nothing, if he didn't have her. They had quickly aborted the prospective sale, despite the frantic bidding war which had been taking place at the time. And had decided to make the estate their permanent home.

'What are you smiling at?' questioned Matteo softly as he walked over to the Christmas tree and pulled her to her feet.

Her contented expression didn't change. 'Do I need a reason?' She sighed. 'I'm just so happy, Matteo. Happier than I ever thought possible.'

'Well, isn't that a coincidence? Because I feel exactly the same way,' he said, his fingers beginning to massage her shoulders, their practised caress never failing to arouse her. 'Have I told you lately that I love you, Mrs Valenti?'

She pretended to frown. 'I think you might have mentioned it before you went out to build Santino's snowman. And just for the record, I love you, too. So very much.'

He bent his head and kissed her, deeply and passionately and it was some time before she broke off to graze her lips against the dark stubble of his angled jaw.

'Did you speak to your father?' she said.

'I did. And he's looking forward to Christmas lunch tomorrow. He says he'll be here soon after eleven and is bringing his new girlfriend.' His eyes gleamed down at her. 'And that we should prepare ourselves for what he calls a *significant* age gap.'

Keira giggled as she rested her head on Matteo's shoulder. Massimo had divorced Luciana in the spring and although Keira had tried to feel sad about it, she just couldn't. Not only had the older woman been a troublemaker—it transpired that she'd been unfaithful to her husband as well. And one night, soon after the decree nisi had come through and Matteo had been away on business, Keira and her father-in-law had dined together in Rome. He'd told her it wasn't a desire to manipulate which had made him threaten to disinherit Matteo if he didn't produce an heir—but concern that his son was becoming emotionally remote and would end up a rich and lonely old man.

'And then you stepped in and saved him and made him happy. Truly happy—and I cannot thank you enough for that, Keira,' he had whispered, his voice cracking a little. 'I know I wasn't a good father when he was growing up.' He had fallen silent for a moment and his eyes had grown reflective. 'I missed his mother so much and he...well, he looked so much like her, that sometimes it was painful to be around him.'

'Have you told him that, Massimo?' she had said quietly, pressing her hand over his across the table. 'Because I think you should.'

And he had. Keira closed her eyes, remembering the long overdue heart-to-heart between father and son, and the growing closeness of their relationship which had resulted.

Her mind flicked back to the present as Matteo began to caress her bottom, murmuring his appreciation that these days she almost always wore a dress. She liked wearing dresses, although she could still resurrect her inner tomboy when needed—and she suspected she was going to need to do that a lot if Santino played as much football as Matteo intended he should. 'Would you like part of your Christmas present tonight?' she whispered, snuggling up to him.

He pulled away to look at her and raised his eyebrows. 'Is that an offer I shouldn't refuse?'

'Put it this way—I'm wearing it underneath this dress and I need you to unwrap it for me. Matteo!' She giggled as he began to lead her towards the bedroom. 'I didn't mean *now*—I meant later.'

'Too bad,' he murmured, not lessening his pace by a fraction. 'Because I have something for you which can't wait.'

Actually, that wasn't quite true—he had two things for her. The first was sitting in the garage wrapped in a giant red bow ready to be untied on Christmas morning. A neglected Ferrari 1948 Spider sports car which he'd tracked down with great difficulty and at considerable expense, because she'd once told him it was her dream to restore beautiful vintage cars—and Matteo was rather partial to making his wife's dreams come true.

The second gift was rather different and he didn't give it to her until after he'd dealt with her outrageous panty thong with its matching boned bodice, which he damaged beyond repair in his eagerness to unhook it. And once he had her naked, he was distracted for quite some time…

His throat thickened with unexpected emotion as he pulled the small box from his discarded trousers and flipped open the lid to reveal a flawless white solitaire which sparkled like a giant star against dark velvet.

'What's this?' she questioned breathlessly, from among the sheets which were rumpled around her.

He lifted her left hand and slid the solitaire in place above her wedding band. 'I never gave you an engagement ring, did I? And I didn't give you a dream wedding either. A civil ceremony in a town hall was never something we were going to enjoy telling our grandchildren about.' He lifted her hand to his lips and kissed her fingertips. 'So I wondered if you'd like to renew our vows in my favourite church in Rome. You could wear a big white dress and do it properly this time, and we could throw a party afterwards. Or not—whichever you prefer. What I'm asking is, would you like to marry me again, Keira Valenti?'

Keira opened her mouth to say that she didn't care about pomp or ceremony, but that wasn't quite true. And weren't she and Matteo all about the truth, these days? She thought about something else, too, something which had been niggling away at her for a while now. Because weddings could bring people together and heal old wounds, couldn't they? Motherhood had changed her. Softened her. She realised now that her aunt might have been strict when she was growing up, but she'd given an orphaned little girl the home she'd badly needed and had stopped her from being taken into care. And didn't she owe her aunt Ida a great deal for that? Wasn't it time to invite her and Shelley to Italy, to share in her good fortune and happiness and to introduce Santino to some of *her* roots?

She wound her arms around Matteo's neck and looked into his beautiful black eyes, her heart turning over with emotion. 'Yes, Matteo,' she said breathlessly. 'I'll be proud to marry you. To stand before our family and friends and say the thing I'll never tire of saying, which is that I love you—and I'll love you for the rest of my life.'

* * * * *

'Don't you dare laugh at me!' Indignation hurtled out with those words, all but lashing at Raul, and he reluctantly pushed away the image of this woman in his bed.

'Maybe a little laughter is how we need to deal with this situation. Now, please sit down. The poor waitress has no idea if we are staying or going.' He tried to instil some order into their meeting—which didn't feel anything like a business lunch.

He liked the way Lydia's brunette hair moved: slipping over her shoulder, those loose curls bouncing with the movement, and the way she tucked it back behind her ears. There was an air of vulnerability about her, but he didn't buy into that at all. There was no way this fiery creature was vulnerable. Spoilt and used to getting her way, yes, but vulnerable? No.

'I'm not entirely sure being forced into marriage is a laughing matter.'

She fixed those gorgeous eyes on his face, her full lips pouting slightly, making him briefly wish this was a date and that by the end of the evening he would be able to kiss them.

Savagely he pushed those thoughts aside. This was not a time to become distracted. 'Then on that we agree.'

Introducing a sizzling and sexy new duet
from Rachael Thomas

Convenient Christmas Brides

Estranged brothers Raul Valdez and
Maximiliano Martinez are about to unlock some
dark and hidden secrets. But with Christmas
around the corner first comes seduction!

Lydia Carter-Wilson finds herself blackmailed into
an engagement by Raul Valdez in

Valdez's Bartered Bride

Available now!

Maximiliano's life is turned upside down when his
estranged wife announces she is carrying his heir in

Martinez's Pregnant Wife

Coming soon!

VALDEZ'S
BARTERED BRIDE

BY
RACHAEL THOMAS

MILLS & BOON

First Published in Great Britain 2017
By Mills & Boon, an imprint of HarperCollins*Publishers*
1 London Bridge Street, London, SE1 9GF

© 2017 Rachael Thomas

ISBN: 978-0-263-92543-2

Rachael Thomas has always loved reading romance, and is thrilled to be a Mills & Boon author. She lives and works on a farm in Wales—a far cry from the glamour of a Mills & Boon Modern Romance story—but that makes slipping into her characters' worlds all the more appealing. When she's not writing, or working on the farm, she enjoys photography and visiting historical castles and grand houses. Visit her at rachaelthomas.co.uk.

Books by Rachael Thomas

Mills & Boon Modern Romance

The Sheikh's Last Mistress
New Year at the Boss's Bidding
Craving Her Enemy's Touch
Claimed by the Sheikh
A Deal Before the Altar

The Secret Billionaires

Di Marcello's Secret Son

One Night With Consequences

A Child Claimed by Gold
From One Night to Wife

Brides for Billionaires

Married for the Italian's Heir

The Billionaire's Legacy

To Blackmail a Di Sione

Visit the Author Profile page
at millsandboon.co.uk for more titles.

For Marie Dry and the happy memories
of the fun time we spent in Madrid and Seville.

PROLOGUE

Middle of September, two months earlier.

'DO YOU REALLY expect me to go through with it?' Raul Valdez's voice thundered around the room, his Spanish words fluid and fast.

'The debt needs to be repaid and, whether you like it or not, the contract your father made before his death with Henry Carter-Wilson still stands. As a member of the board I insist upon it.' Carlos's voice ripped through Raul, increasing his anger to an explosive level.

Raul swore savagely as he glared at the older man. 'Come on, Carlos, we go back further than that.'

'As a long-standing family friend, I urge you to stop looking for someone who doesn't want to be found and marry the girl—as your father obviously intended.'

'Marry her?' Raul couldn't believe he was hearing this, from Carlos of all people.

'Repay the debt, then file for a divorce once the two years are up.'

Rage charged through Raul like a bull. How could his father have done this? But that wasn't a question he needed to ask. He'd never been able to gain his father's approval, had tried all his life to no avail. This was just one more stab at the son he'd never wanted.

'You make it sound so easy.' Raul drew in a deep breath and marched to the windows looking out over Madrid, basking in the late summer sunshine. On paper it did look easy, but marriage was the one thing he'd never wanted.

'It is,' Carlos replied, his tone neutral and matter-of-fact. 'Two years living with a woman who, you've got to admit, is very beautiful, then you can file for a divorce.'

'I have no intentions of marrying anyone. Ever.' Raul strode across the office, the constraint of the walls making him feel more like a caged animal, trapped against its will. Anger at what his father had done mixed with the fear of being controlled by him still becoming a potent cocktail.

Raul stopped pacing and looked out over Madrid again, trying to control his temper. He stayed like that for several minutes, his back resolutely turned to Carlos Cardozo, the man who had been there for him more than his father ever had. *His* father. That was a joke.

He'd always known he'd been a disappointment to his father, but never had he expected such revelations after his sudden death. He'd never suspected his father had hated him, but then he'd never suspected his father had had another family—another son.

'The only other option you have is to find your half-brother.' Carlos's calm voice brought him out of his dark thoughts and back to the present with a sharp jab of shock. 'Which would mean sharing your inheritance—everything you have built this banking enterprise up to be.'

Raul whirled round. This had been a detail his father's lawyer had revealed, one he'd kept secret since that day. How did Carlos know? 'You know about him?'

'Yes.' Carlos looked him in the eye, challenging him to ask more.

'How long?' Raul took the challenge.

'Long enough to know how this is affecting you now.' Carlos's voice softened a little as he walked over to him.

Raul had been in ignorance of his half-brother's existence until his father's will had been read out two months ago. It seemed Carlos had known the full facts of his father's double life long ago.

'And you didn't think I should know?' His anger rallied again as he glowered at Carlos, the taste of deception filling his mouth with its bitterness.

'I never knew your father would make finding him a condition to you inheriting. Or that he would attach such a huge financial incentive to that task.'

Huge financial incentive.

That was an understatement.

'That or marry a woman I barely know.' Raul glowered at Carlos, suspicion rising at just how much this man knew.

'Marriage would be the easier option.'

'Is that so?' Raul seriously doubted that. Besides, his brother was out there somewhere.

'It is. You are your father's son. Marriage will be easy for you. Far better than to share all you've worked for.'

Raul turned away again. His world had been tipped upside down and then inside out. In order to inherit the financial company he'd built into a world player, he had to clear one very large debt by either marrying the

debtor's daughter, or by acknowledging his half-brother
and bringing him into the business as an equal, which
would unlock funds that would clear the debt and keep
the board of directors happy. If the debt wasn't settled,
the company would be sold to the highest bidder.

The fact that his father had even kept those funds
hidden exposed the depths of calculation he had gone
to, but that he was prepared to risk his company if the
debt wasn't settled, to risk the jobs of all the people
who worked for Banco de Torrez, was a step too far.
What the hell had he been doing loaning that kind of
money and why was Carlos the only one privy to such
information?

'I could have told you my father would be so calculating, so manipulative—had I known about his *other
life*.' Raul found himself snarling those last two words,
hating the anger that sliced through him with the sharp-
est of blades.

'He's your father—doesn't that count for something?' Carlos reached for him; the false show of sympathy and understanding in that gesture was too much.
Raul moved away. This man was not the friend he'd always thought—not to him anyway.

'I'm done with my father, so much so that I don't give
a damn about inheriting his company. I have built my
own as well as expanded his. I don't need this.' Raul
marched towards the door. As far as he was concerned
the discussion was over; there was nothing more to say.

'What about your mother?' Carlos's next words
halted his steps, kept him from walking out for good.

Raul remained with his back to Carlos, breathing
deep and slow, clenching his fingers into tight fists at
his sides. His mother was the only reason he'd spent

the last two months trying to find his half-brother, not wanting the press—or anyone else—to get to her first with the revelation of her husband's secret life. It would finish her.

'You can't walk away, can you, Raul? You can't risk her finding out by reading salacious gossip in the press?' Carlos challenged. Again. Damn him. The man knew just how to twist the situation, how to manipulate him.

Raul whirled round to face Carlos again. 'No, I damn well can't. If not for my mother's happiness, then for all the jobs which depend on me settling this debt by either finding my half-brother or marrying a spoilt little rich girl. Either way I despise my father for it.'

'So why not take the easy option and marry this Lydia girl?'

'That will never happen,' Raul spat officiously at him. After the example he'd seen of marriage, he would rather welcome a stranger into his life, into his father's company. Hell, as far as he was concerned, his brother could have it all if it kept people in work and his mother in ignorance of his father's past actions. He didn't need any of it.

'The board are getting nervous, Raul. They think you've lost your influence, especially after the Lopez deal fell through.' Carlos touched yet another raw nerve, ratcheting up the desire to prove him and every damn member of the board wrong. One lost deal didn't spell the end.

'I haven't given up on that yet, just as I haven't given up on the search for my half-brother.' Raul glared angrily at Carlos, resenting the challenge the man was issuing, inadvertently or not.

'Either way, the debt needs to be settled before the end of the year. Sooner if possible.'

'That's just over three months away. I'll find my half-brother before then, settle the damn debt and keep the scandal from my mother.'

'If you don't, you will have to meet Lydia Carter-Wilson.' Carlos spoke carefully. Quietly.

'If she is anything like she was ten years ago, I would rather lose my father's business.' Raul baulked at the memory of the simpering sixteen-year-old girl on the verge of womanhood who'd looked at him like an adoring puppy. Was that when his father had started loaning funds to hers?

'What about all those people who will lose jobs? Shutting down companies isn't who you are, Raul. Saving them and building them up, giving the people who work within them, a secure life. That's who you are and I've never known you to refuse a challenge yet.' Carlos spoke the truth, but Raul was too angry to acknowledge it right now.

'I need more time.'

'If you haven't found your half-brother by the end of November, I will expect you to announce your engagement to Lydia Carter-Wilson.'

'What if the lady is unwilling?'

Carlos laughed, defusing the tension somewhat. 'You will find a way, Raul. Your charm with the ladies has never failed you yet.'

CHAPTER ONE

Late November

LYDIA MENTALLY BRACED HERSELF for battle, because this was one fight she was not prepared to lose. Over the twenty-six years of her life, she'd perfected the art of hiding her emotions and now she intended to use it fully. Raul Pérez Valdez wouldn't know what had hit him. Ten years ago he'd made her feel totally insignificant, like nothing more than a spoilt little rich girl, and she hated him for that. Ever since she'd gone to live with her grandmother as a child, she'd worked hard to shake off that label.

Any moment he would arrive and walk through the diners of one of London's top restaurants to the intimate candlelit table he'd arranged, referring to it as neutral territory in his blunt email. The mood she was now in, he was going to need every bit of help he could get from the chosen venue, which was anything but neutral if his reputation of romancing women was true. It was very much a setting he would be at home in, whereas she was distinctly uncomfortable in such surroundings, having avoided anything remotely romantic after witnessing so many relationships turn sour, including her own supposed happy ever after.

Irritation filled her as the minutes ticked by. He was late. The time he'd appointed had already passed. Was the man intending to make her suffer even more? Make her so nervous she could easily jump at her own shadow? Or had he decided against the ludicrous deal his father had concocted with hers? Did this mean she was free to go back to her life and not honour the conditions of that deal she'd unwittingly been dragged into? Her father had reached an all-time low with that deal, leaving her to pay the price.

Except she'd had enough. She didn't owe her father anything, not after all the years of ignoring her, unless it suited his latest negotiations, of course. Like the time she'd been paraded as a sixteen-year-old in front of the man she was about to meet, as if she was some sort of bait. That plan had failed—or so she'd thought.

With a huff of irritation, Lydia picked up her purse from the small round table and stood up to leave. She wasn't wasting any more time waiting for Raul Valdez. If he wanted her father's debt settled, he could chase around London after her.

'Going somewhere?' The sultry accent snared her senses and she turned and looked up into the face of a man so handsome he couldn't possibly be the perpetrator of such dire circumstances. He'd changed, but from the intent look in his inky black eyes she knew without a doubt this was Raul Pérez Valdez, CEO of the Spanish investment bank her father had defaulted to in the most spectacular way.

Every sculpted angle of his face, from the high cheekbones to the Romanesque nose and the deep-set eyes, sent her body's senses spinning into overdrive. Memories of being an impressionable girl on the brink of womanhood collided with that reaction and she was unable to quell the erratic racing of her pulse, or the shiver of something she quickly dismissed as nothing more than attraction.

'We had a meeting ten minutes ago.' Her sharp words did nothing to this specimen of cool reserve. The heavy brows lifted slightly in disbelief—or was it amusement? She couldn't tell. The intensity in his eyes increased, but she was determined he wouldn't use his well-known charm on her. She glared at him, hoping the icy cold-ness she was renowned for showed in all its glory. She wasn't an impressionable sixteen-year-old any more.

'For my lateness, I apologise.' He held the back of the chair she'd just vacated, the expression on his face showing he expected her to sit back down.

Lydia tried to remain focused as she looked up at him, hating the way excitement sparked inside her as his dark eyes travelled down her body, making her display of cold demeanour extremely difficult. She stood boldly as his gaze seemed to rip the black fitted skirt and busi-nesslike white blouse from her. Each second that ticked by increased her vulnerability, raising it higher than it had ever been, and the urge to fight back kicked in. If he was going to blatantly inspect her, she'd return the compliment.

With huge effort she dragged her gaze from the black depths of his eyes, taking in the clean-shaven face, then to the strong neck encased in a pristine white shirt col-lar, intensifying the olive tones of his skin. His hair was thick and as dark as coal and his broad shoulders gave her the impression they were strong enough to carry any problems. His arms flexed tantalisingly beneath the fine cloth of his suit as he stood and leant slightly on the back of the chair, his cold stare barely masking his irritation.

How would it feel to be held within the strength of those arms? Her pulse leapt at the thought and she fought hard again to quell the instant attraction that had stirred the woman in her she'd long since hidden away. This was not the time to indulge in silly romantic notions and most definitely not with this man, one who'd made his thoughts of her plain many years ago.

'If this meeting was as important as you led me to believe, you would not have been late, Mr Valdez.' Her anger at the way her body had reacted as she'd taken in every detail of this man, and the thoughts that had raced through her mind at the idea of being held in those strong arms, made her voice crisp and sharp.

That impressive control didn't waver.

'You and I are in a position which I am certain neither of us want, Miss Carter-Wilson, and, as I have the solution, I suggest you sit down.' She saw his jaw flex as he clenched his teeth, the only sign she was challenging his outward display of patience.

'The position we are in? You mean the bizarre conditions your father attached to the contract he forced my father to sign?' That sensation of helplessness she'd been fighting for several weeks surfaced again and her voice rose rapidly with each word.

'Exactly that.' The calmness of his voice, together with the silky rich accent, jarred her senses, increasing her wildly overactive anxieties.

'There is no way it can be enforced.' She knew she was beginning to babble, the panic of everything almost too much, and she bit back further words. He had to think she was calm and in control, had to think he'd met his match. His equal.

'If you sit down we can discuss this rationally.' He gestured to the chair, his brow rising in question—or was it amusement?

Unable to keep a sigh of discontent from escaping, she sat down. The need to be in charge, to control the situation she was virtually drowning in, forced her to speak again before he'd sat opposite her at the small and inappropriately intimate table, complete with a red rose and candle.

'I think you need to explain just what kind of business contract your father tricked mine into signing. It is inconceivable that in the twenty-first century two people can be forced to marry because of such devious tactics.' She took a deep shuddering breath, hardly able to comprehend that this nightmare was actually happening.

'That is why I'm here—'

Lydia cut across him, angry at the stupidity of her father for signing a contract with such dire conditions and, even more so, at this cool specimen of male splendour for being so calm and pragmatic about it. 'Mr Valdez, I don't care what is in the contract. I'm not going to marry you. Not ever.'

His dark brows rose and she thought she saw a hint of a smile on his lips. Even worse, his reaction sent a skitter of something she'd never experienced hurtling through her and her pulse leapt just from having that sexy hint of a smile, which had sparked briefly in his eyes, directed at her.

'At least we agree on that.' He sat back in his chair, his dark eyes locking with hers, full of challenge. 'You may be assured I have absolutely no desire to make a spoilt little rich girl my wife.'

So his opinion of her hadn't changed. 'I am no such thing.'

She fought hard to resist the urge to jump up and walk away; only the fact that her solicitor had told her the terms of the contract her father had signed with Banco de Torrez, however bizarre, would stand up in court, kept her from doing just that—for now.

'What about all the properties? Many of them are worth millions. Your father hid them by putting them in your name as he defaulted month after month on the agreement he'd signed with my father.' He folded his arms across his chest, serving only to emphasise the strength in them as the dark grey suit pulled over his biceps. Since when did she ever notice such things about a man?

'That is something I had no knowledge of, but, if they are in my name and worth that much, I will sell them to clear the debt.' The discovery several weeks ago of what her father had done had been just another bit of her life falling to pieces. Angry at the man who was supposed to protect her, she'd maintained a stony silence with him, to show him her disappointment and anger that once again he'd risked everything, including this time her future, her happiness.

Raul looked at her and she knew he didn't believe her. The cold lack of interest was too obvious. Was he really as ruthless in business as those reports she'd read on the Internet implied? She had hoped to strike some sort of deal with him. After all, a man who rarely dated the same woman twice was as unlikely to want marriage as she was.

'I would be more than happy to accept such an offer—'

'Good.' She stood up, content that this absurd conversation was over. 'Then you can liaise with my solicitor over the matter.'

'Do you always talk over people?' His question stopped her as she was about to leave for the second time and she looked down at him, stunned into silence, and the elusive sensation of being in control slipped further away with each erratic heartbeat. From the moment he'd arrived and their eyes had met, she'd lost that control.

Raul had never known such self-assured insolence from a woman as beautiful and alluring as the prim and proper Lydia Carter-Wilson. She certainly didn't want to hear what he had to say and wasn't prepared to listen to his suggestion for dealing with the situation they were both now in. A solution he was certain would be acceptable. Yet it was blatantly clear all this fiery beauty cared about was herself. She hadn't changed a bit since he'd met her ten years ago. Granted, she'd become a beautiful and sexy woman, but she wasn't any different. She was still a spoilt little rich girl. Daddy's princess—and a liar.

He pushed down the irrational anger that engulfed him every time he thought of what his father had done. That last meddling dig at the son he'd never wanted threatened to unleash all the bitterness and contempt he'd kept hidden since his father had died five months ago. The devious old man had even known he was terminally ill and changed his will to get at him one last time.

'No, I don't, but then I've never had the dubious pleasure of lunch with a man like you.' The hot retort fired at him and he couldn't help but smile. It was definitely an inconvenience having to extricate himself from such an agreement with this woman, but he'd certainly not expected to find it so entertaining. She was a bundle of hot sparks and defiance. Just the mutinous tilt of her chin and the rapid rise and fall of her breasts as she glared at him fired something deeper than merely lust. Something he had no wish to get tangled in—ever.

She tempted him, daring him with that sexy body that begged to be made love to, and almost all rational thought slipped from his mind. But he was not his father. He would not be drawn by the lure of sex. His playboy reputation was deserved, but only as part of his armour, his defence in order to remain emotionally intact and very single.

'And what would a man like me be?' He taunted her, enjoying the fire of annoyance that flared in those green eyes, reminding him of the fresh leaves of spring on the trees in Retiro Park, in his city of birth, Madrid.

'A man who thinks he only needs to smile at a woman to have her falling at his feet—or into his bed.' The slight nod of her head, the little *so there* gesture, as she finished speaking made laughing at her impossible to resist.

'My bed?'

'Don't you dare laugh at me.' Indignation hurtled out with those words, all but lashing at him, and he reluctantly pushed away the image of this woman in his bed.

'Maybe a little laughter is how we need to deal with this situation. Now, please sit down. The poor waitress has no idea if we are staying or going.' He tried to instil some order into their meeting, which didn't feel anything like a business lunch.

He watched as she turned to look at the waitress who was approaching their table for the second time. He liked the way Lydia's brunette hair moved, slipping over her shoulder, the loose curls bouncing with the movement, and the way she tucked it back behind her ears. There was an air of vulnerability about her he didn't buy into at all. There was no way this fiery creature was vulnerable. Spoilt and used to getting her way, yes, but vulnerable, no.

'I'm not entirely sure being forced into a marriage is a laughing matter.' She fixed those gorgeous eyes on his face, her full lips pouting slightly, making him briefly wish this were a date and that by the end of the evening he would be able to kiss them. Savagely he pushed those thoughts aside. This was not a time to become distracted.

'Then on that we agree.' He beckoned the waitress forward with a subtle move of his hand and watched as Lydia took the menu, appearing to use it as a shield. Against him or the situation? He watched her long lashes lowering as she read and took the opportunity to study her further. Her skin was pale, making it obvious she hadn't spent the summer in one of her Mediterranean properties. The menu shook very slightly in her hands and he wondered if it was possible for such an audacious woman to be nervous. Much more likely to be anger, he decided, anger that was directed firmly at him. Anger was good, because then at least they could sort out this mess their fathers had selfishly created for them.

As she gave her order her voice became soft and

gentle, not at all like the hard and sharp tones he'd been treated to so far. How would she sound if they were here as lovers? Would that softness be beguiling him to take her home and to his bed?

Alarmed by the train of his thoughts yet again, he dragged his mind back to the truth of the situation and placed his order. Employing all the charm he'd perfected as his armour, he smiled at the waitress.

'So, how exactly do you propose to deal with this situation?' The softness had gone and the question fired at him with force. Had she meant to use that word? Propose was the last thing he intended to do. He focused his attention back to the woman opposite him, the woman his father had decided would make him a suitable wife simply because of the substantial properties that she owned and her misfortune to have such a reckless and weak father.

He kept his gaze fixed on the pale beauty of her face, watching for any signs of compliance. 'You have considerable property assets and these were the security used by your father. The terms are more than clear, as I have already informed your lawyer.'

'I have said that I am more than happy to sell them in order to raise the funds required.' She cut across him again, stemming the flow of his well-prepared proposition.

'If that were possible, it would be the most sensible option. Unfortunately, my father has used this security as part of his conditions of his will.' The outrageous terms his father had insisted on still infused him with rage as fiercely as the day he'd discovered what his father had done. A final jab at his son, even after his death, to get just what he wanted.

'His will?' The sharp intake of breath left him in no doubt this was not a piece of information she was aware of. 'I'm sorry about your loss. I had no idea.'

'Please don't waste your sympathy on me.' He pushed away memories of his childhood, of never being able to be what his father wanted, never knowing how to please him and having no idea why. At least that mystery had been solved. 'My father and I were not close.'

That was an understatement. He'd lost all respect for his father over ten years ago when he'd taken his womanising to a new level, having affairs with young models and actresses who craved the limelight and high life his name and wealth could give them. The fact that everyone expected him to be just as much of a playboy had irritated him at first, until he'd learnt to use that as defence to keep women at an emotional distance.

The beautiful brunette who'd been dragged into the latest battle his father had set regarded him sceptically, the spell only broken by the arrival of their wine. He smiled at the waitress as he sampled the wine, aware of Lydia's scrutiny with every breath he took. 'Very good, thank you.'

'Yes, I can see any sympathy would be a waste of time.' Her barbed words flew at him and inwardly he baulked at her directness, but refused to let it show. He was more than used to keeping his emotions away from the scrutiny of others, used to putting on a show of uncaring detachment, and right now that suited him perfectly.

'So, shall we discuss our options?' Before she could once again talk over him or correct him, he launched directly into all that needed to be said. 'I have no wish to marry anyone, least of all you, but the terms of my father's will are very clear. Upon my father's death, our marriage is the only way your father's debt can be repaid—unless you have such a large sum of money saved?'

'Why can't I just sell the properties?' Her eyes widened with disbelief and her hand came to her face, the tip of one finger dragging across her bottom lip in a very distracting way. He watched as the pink-painted nail dug into the plumpness of her lip, wishing he could sample that plumpness against his lips.

Again he urged his mind back to the situation. Perhaps he was more like his father than he'd ever imagined. The thought sickened him. 'Although the properties are in your name, the terms of the transfer your father carried out means you cannot sell them, that they only remain yours until your marriage, at which point they will become your husband's property.'

'What?' She pressed her fingertips against her mouth, as if to stem the shocked flow of words, and her neat brows furrowed into a frown. He wasn't falling for that.

'Hard to believe, but I'm afraid it's true. It's also a fact my father sought to exploit when he made his will, just months before he died. I am not happy to have inherited your father's debt and with it you as my bride.' He recalled his lawyer's face, full of apology, and the words that had proved beyond doubt how much his father must have disliked him.

'I tried to persuade him against it, but he was adamant.'

'What century are we in?' Her shock had turned to anger and she flung her hands out over the table, palms upwards in exasperation. 'Just what did they think they were doing?'

'It appears we have both been little more than pawns in their game and it's time now to take control, to thwart whatever it was they each intended.'

'At least now we are on the same page. I have no intention of marrying someone who wants me for what I have. I almost travelled that road and I'm not going there again.' Her burst of irritation held a hint of passion, intriguing him in a way he was far from comfortable about.

'Are you holding out for love, Lydia?' It was the first time he'd used her name and it shocked him how he liked to say it as he looked into her beautiful face. If circumstances were different, he'd be tempted to reach out and push her hair back from her face, revealing her beauty. But he couldn't go there. He didn't seek the confines of marriage, so for now it was better to hide behind the mask of a hardened businessman.

Lydia's pulse leapt as he said that word and looked into her eyes. The unyielding blackness of his sent skitters of awareness all over her. Every part of her body was tuned into his, every move he made only intensified it, but the mention of love halted all that, as if she'd just careered into a brick wall.

'I have no intention of wasting my time holding out for love.' She bristled at the memory of the man she'd thought she'd loved, the man she'd believed had loved her until she'd discovered he'd also been in the habit of loving as many other women as he could. By that point she and Daniel were engaged. This had rankled her father and, just to show him she'd make her own decisions in life, she'd accepted Daniel's apology. Something she deeply regretted. It would have been almost preferable to have her father look at her with that *I told you so* expression than the humiliation after Daniel had left her because she no longer had anything to offer him, something her father had made very clear to him, although at that point she'd not understood exactly what he'd meant.

Now she did. It was the contract her father had signed with Raul Valdez's father, using her as his leverage, his security.

'So cynical, Lydia. Are you not in search of your Mr Right, the man to live happily ever after with?' His accented voice sent a shiver of awareness over her and she knew a flush of colour had spread over her face.

Who was he to mock such dreams? He was a complete playboy.

'Once bitten, twice shy, as they say.' She couldn't help the light and flirty tone of her voice and to hide her embarrassment she took a sip of her wine. 'But that is not why we are here, to discuss such nonsense as love, Mr Valdez, is it?'

'No, we are not.' He snapped the words out, his accent sharp, and she sensed the impatience in him. Or was it irritation? 'We are here because your father defaulted on his loan.'

Before he could say any more Lydia cut across him once more, not missing the frown of annoyance, which gave her a strange sense of satisfaction. 'And because your father saw fit to use that default in the most devious and unethical way.'

'I agree,' he said and leant forward in the seat, his dark eyes penetrating hers, preventing her from doing anything other than looking into them, but they were cold and she shivered slightly. 'That is why we are here. To extricate ourselves from a marriage I certainly don't want and it would seem you share that view.'

'I still don't see why I can't just sign some of the properties over to you, or sell them and clear the debt.' She wished now she'd had a proper meeting with her solicitor instead of the rushed phone call. She hadn't understood all he'd told her and in all honesty she couldn't believe what her father had done.

'You do not own them, Lydia. They are only yours until you marry, at which time they will pass into the legal possession of your husband.'

She recalled an argument with her father almost a year ago, one of those rare meetings of father and daughter. He'd been smugly pleased with his latest plot to manipulate her into marriage for the good of his company. He'd told her he had found her a husband and that this time she would have no choice but to do as she was told. She'd refused, telling him she and Daniel were engaged, but that had been no deterrent to the lows her father had stooped to in order to save himself from financial ruin. She'd had no idea his vast property portfolio had been put into her name until her marriage.

'By that you mean you.' She put down her wine glass and glared at him, everything clear at last. 'Your father added the marriage clause in his will to trick my father.'

'I consider it more of a shrewd tactic to safeguard the considerable amount of money he had loaned to your father's business. He must have been sure your father wouldn't obtain such levels of funding through the usual channels and added the extra condition in his will, should the debt remain unsettled in the event of his death.'

'I hardly think forcing either of us into marriage is shrewd or businesslike. It's medieval.' She stumbled over the words as she realised how futile they were and when a smile tugged at the corners of his lips she wished she were bold enough to get up and walk away.

'After our marriage, all the properties will become mine and therefore the debt will be repaid and the board of directors satisfied. The only issue is that we must remain married for two years—living together.'

'Are you actually suggesting we get married, just to clear the debt? I thought you were against any such idea as much as I am.' Lydia couldn't take it in. Married. To this man. For two years.

'That depends on how much you want to help your father.'

Lydia didn't have to think very hard on that one. She didn't want to help her father, but she did want to protect his mother, her grandmother. The woman who'd cared for her, loved her as a daughter. She was the only reason she was still here having this discussion.

'Of course I want to help my father, but I will not marry anyone to do that.' She wasn't about to enlighten Raul Valdez to the fact that her father had tried several times to push her into a marriage that would financially benefit him. The fact that this man's father could possibly succeed where hers had failed was not a pleasant prospect.

'In that case you will be interested to hear of my solution.' Her attention was caught not only by his words, but by the tone of his voice.

'Which is?'

'I suggest we make the marriage and clear the debts. We can lead separate lives whilst living in the same place. After two years, I will not contest a divorce.' He sat back in his chair, the expression on his handsome face close to being smug.

'Is that the best you can do?' Irritation surged through her. Had he met her here to put forward a suggestion that was at the moment the only obvious conclusion? She was so angry with her father. He could have warned her of this, months ago. He must have known he couldn't make the repayments. Now she understood why he'd made it so easy for her to keep up her annoyed silence. He'd gone to ground, hiding like a coward. 'Why have you left it five months to contact me? You must have been made aware of the will conditions months ago.'

'I had other, more pressing issues to deal with.'

'Such as?'

He looked at her as if assessing her ability to be trusted and, just as when he'd first swept his gaze over her, the scrutiny did strange things to her. 'I have been trying to contact a family member whose existence I only discovered upon the reading of the will. If found, that person would offer a very different option for both of us and there is a large financial reward which can be used to clear your debts, but I have as yet been unable to find that person.'

'So, in the meantime, you thought you'd come and force me into a two-year marriage.' Irritation rushed through her. They weren't getting anywhere.

'I am still intending to search for that person, but your father has not made any further payments and has managed to evade all attempts at a meeting. I now have no choice. The board is calling for settlement of

the debt. They will not wait any longer. Our engagement must be announced.'

He sat back and sipped the last of his wine, the calm
and unruffled exterior unsettling her more than she
cared to admit. 'There are agencies for such things.'
The confusion on his face as she derailed the topic was
priceless and for a brief moment she wanted to laugh.
'Finding missing family members, that is.'

'If you wish to make it public, then yes, there are.'
He clenched his jaw as he finished speaking.

'You want to find someone yet keep it secret?' That
made no sense whatsoever and at the same time intrigued her. Who did this power-hungry man wish to
contact and why?

'It is not something I want the press to get hold of.'
The annoyed growl of his voice gave her immense satisfaction but as she took a sip of wine an idea filtered
through her mind. Genealogy was something she was
very interested in and she'd spent long happy hours
helping friends trace their family roots back many generations. Was it possible she could provide what this
man wanted? Maybe there was a deal to be made here?

'That sensitive, is it?' She toyed with him, like a cat
who had stumbled upon a mouse, enjoying the sensation, even if only briefly, of power.

'Yes, as a matter of fact it is, but it bears no relevance
to our discussion.' The curt tone of his voice blended
with his accent and she wondered what he would sound
like if he were whispering words of love. Except a man
like him didn't indulge in love—only lust.

'Supposing I was able to find this family member—
discreetly, of course.'

'You?' The surprise in his deeply accented voice sent

a smile of satisfaction spreading across her lips. He obviously thought she was nothing more than an empty-headed socialite, who did nothing but party and shop.

'Yes, me. It could clear the debt and relieve us of the need to get married.' It was also far more than that for her. She wanted to hold on to all she'd worked for in life and if this man could sweep in and demand the properties her father had put in her name, would he then want all she had? Her business?

'Go on.'

'I happen to have a passion for genealogy.'

'A passion?' His brows rose and a shiver of awareness spread all over her as he said the word, giving it a totally different connotation from the context she'd meant. 'Now you have aroused my interest. But how can it help with this matter?'

Much to her disgust heat rushed to her cheeks and yet again she lifted her chin and fixed him with a piercing glare. She couldn't let it show just how much he was affecting her, how he was making her stomach flip and her heart pound like a lovesick teenager. Not when she'd sworn she'd never indulge in such nonsense. Hadn't her time with Daniel been enough to warn her off?

'I'll make a deal with you, Mr Valdez. If I find this person, all the debts will be cleared without the need for marriage.'

'That's a massive charge for such a service when I could hire an agency, as you say.'

'But would you have the confidentiality you require?' She waited, hardly able to breathe, the anticipation immense. Had she actually managed to dig her way out of the mess her father had landed her in?

'It's still a high price, Miss Carter-Wilson. Are you

sure you can deliver?' He leant forward, his forearms on the table, his long tanned fingers holding the stem of the wine glass.

'Yes.' She crossed her fingers beneath the table and smiled boldly at him.

'How long?'

'That depends on many things. Months at least.'

'You don't have months.' The brittleness of his tone made her blink rapidly.

'Weeks, then.'

'Four at the most.' He assessed her again and she wondered if he sensed her panic.

'In that case you have yourself a deal—but be warned, if this is leaked before I am ready, or you are not successful, then I will want full and immediate payment of the debt, which would mean you as my wife.'

'That threat won't be necessary, Mr Valdez.' She kept her voice firm as she put out her hand to shake on the deal. 'I suggest we meet again as soon as possible, then you can give me any information you already have before you return to Spain.'

'If you are investigating my family, I will be keeping a close watch on what you are doing. Which means, Miss Carter-Wilson, *you* will return to Madrid with me.'

CHAPTER TWO

Raul could hardly believe the surprising deal he was about to agree on with this woman. He'd been immediately captivated by her beauty, but had pushed that aside, unable to think past the terms of his father's will or the fact that it appeared ever more likely that he was going to have to do the unthinkable and marry.

He had no desire to get married to any woman. Least of all one his father had tricked him into marrying. The last thing he needed right now was the constant temptation that this woman would represent if she came back to Madrid with him. From the moment he'd first seen her, annoyed and angry at his late appearance, he'd been fighting the pull of attraction that insistently demanded satisfaction.

He couldn't act on it, not when it was the one thing his father had wanted, obviously considering him as much of a womaniser as he had been. Did his father recall the time he and Lydia had met? Had she been part of his plans even then? But what was there to gain from two years of marriage? That was the part that didn't yet make sense.

As he'd arrived at the busy London restaurant, decked out for Christmas, the one thing he hadn't anticipated was that Lydia would hold cards of her own—and be more than willing to put them into play.

Had she sensed how much he needed to track down Max? Did she really have the connections to trace people or was family history just the passing fancy of a rich girl with too much time on her hands? He had little option but to trust her now and cursed himself for having confided in her. Her offer of a deal, even one as outrageous as that, was one he wasn't able to refuse. Not now she could walk away and spill the long-kept family secret he'd only recently discovered. There would of course have to be a back-up plan, one that would mean he wasn't about to risk his business reputation now that he'd finally proved he was not the same man as his father to those that mattered in the business world.

Until recently, he'd been unable to work alongside his father and had started buying up small and struggling businesses, turning them around and either selling them on or trading their shares. It was far more than just the banking business his father had operated. It was a way of helping people and now the Lopez deal was back on the table. His biggest yet.

'You want me to come to Madrid? To drop everything at this time of year just so that you can trace a long-lost relative?' Lydia's shock-infused words dragged him back to the hustle and bustle of the busy London restaurant.

'And what keeps you so busy, Lydia? Parties? Shopping? All of that happens in Madrid too.' Annoyance filled each word. He hadn't expected instant compliance from her, but he had anticipated she'd be ready to do anything to avoid her father's debts.

'Don't assume you know me.' Her eyes sparked angrily at him.

'I don't assume anything other than you will come to Madrid, trace the person I am looking for and settle your debt. Unless you wish to be married before Christmas?'

'I will not go to Madrid on your whim.' She pulled back her hand before he could shake on the deal and he had to suppress the urge to smile. He liked the anger that sparked in her eyes brighter than the Christmas lights of London. He liked the way her lips parted in almost total contrast to that anger. What he didn't find so appealing was his questionable urge to kiss those lips until desire replaced the anger in her eyes.

'Then there is only one alternative open to us.' He let his words hang heavily between them and for the briefest of seconds it was only the two of them. The noise of the other diners slipped away and all he could hear was the rhythmic thump of his heart. He couldn't let her walk away now. He had to find Max as discreetly as possible—and quickly.

'Which is?' The brittle words snapped from her and he became aware of everyone around them once more.

She scowled at him, suspicion in those sexy green eyes, and he decided perhaps it wouldn't be so very bad to be bound in marriage to such a fiery beauty. Two years living as her husband would at least be entertaining.

'You or your father must settle the debts—in full. By the end of the year.'

'By the end of the year? That's little over a month away.'

'The debt must be settled, Lydia, by either full payment or marriage.'

'Believe me, Mr Valdez, if I could make the payment I would, but I can't.'

A spark of fury rose in her voice and a smile pulled at his lips. Instantly her mouth pressed into a firm line of annoyance, which only made the urge to smile at her greater.

'Then you have no alternative but to come back to Madrid and either find the person I am looking for, quickly and discreetly, or announce our engagement. The terms of my father's will state there is a financial reward for finding that person. Enough to cover the debt.'

She shook her head in denial, her soft dark hair bouncing invitingly on her shoulders, snagging his attention all too easily. 'No, I won't leave London now. I can't.'

'A lover?'

'Not that it's any of your business, but no.'

'Then you will become my wife and settle your father's debts—unless your claim is true.'

He wouldn't enlighten her yet to the fact that they would have to be seen as a couple, seen to be preparing for their nuptials. Carlos had insisted that would be the only way to satisfy the board of directors that he was calling in the debt, that his bride was willing.

'If I am not about to waltz off to Madrid with you, I am hardly likely to agree to a marriage, whatever the conditions attached to the deal my father signed.'

He watched as her eyes narrowed with anger and her lips pressed together and as much as he wanted to kiss those lips until they softened he knew he never could.

That would be indulging a side of him he had no wish to explore, be it playboy or something more emotionally involved.

However, her father's debt was to be settled, she was well and truly off-limits and he certainly didn't need the complication of having to resist an ill-timed attraction. He needed the board off his back, to know the debt would be settled. Then he could resume his search for Max, which now seemed much more hopeful if Lydia Carter-Wilson did really have a passion for family history. But what would she make of his family, of the tangled web of deceit that had corrupted recent generations?

More to the point, could he trust her? If this got out it could undo all the good work he'd done to prove to the business world he was a man of morals and high values. A man to be trusted.

'I can of course call in the debt right now.' He could almost feel the angry vibe coming across the table at him and wondered what her reaction would be if they hadn't been having this conversation in such a public place. Would she have given vent to her anger or would she have been as controlled as he was?

'You wouldn't dare.' The whispered words had a hiss of anger in them and his body responded wickedly, the earlier urges to kiss her returned in full force. Only the desire to be different from his father had made him accept the somewhat desperate bargain Lydia had made. It would be a high price, but one worth paying if it avoided the messy tangle of marriage.

'Don't underestimate me, Lydia.' He knew he sounded hard, more of a snarl, but he had to instil such aggression. He needed to make this deal, because he had never expected to be filled with lustful need for the woman he might well have to make his temporary wife.

'It is you who underestimates me, Mr Valdez.' Despite the anger that still simmered in her eyes he detected a hint of compliance in her voice.

'I never underestimate anyone I do business with and you are certainly no different.' He wouldn't tell her that he'd done his homework on her, found out all he needed to know about the woman who could become his wife. 'Whatever deal we strike, it is for business and nothing more.'

'Nothing at all?'

'No, nothing. It will be a marriage in name only and will end in exactly two years.'

'Before I commit myself, I think you had better tell me exactly who it is I am locating for you.' The frivolous tone of her voice belied the inner turmoil he could see playing out in those expressive eyes. He doubted she could hide anything from him and he certainly hadn't missed that spark of attraction that had briefly showed through all the irritation he'd witnessed in their depths. Her pretty face was so expressive he could read every emotion that crossed it, including the attraction that had sprung as instantly to life as when they'd first met.

Whatever it was sizzling between them, she was as aware of it as he was.

'I am not sure I can trust you yet.' He veered towards caution. She could take the secret he'd uncovered, which would blow his family wide open, and sell it to the press for a huge amount. Maybe not enough to clear her father's debts, but it would still damage his business and his father's, which was precariously positioned with share prices falling since his sudden death. He would not allow it to happen—whatever the cost. He was more than prepared to sacrifice his bachelor status—temporarily—to calm the nerves of the board.

'Then you have wasted my time and yours.' The crispness of each word jarred his senses and he quickly tried to rationalise the situation.

With one call to the press she could destroy his family and his business, but it would ultimately drag her father into the limelight. She appeared to have as little desire for an arranged marriage as he did and even professed to have the skills and knowledge he needed to trace his half-brother. But would she be discreet?

His father had been manipulative to the end. If Lydia successfully found Max, the half-brother he'd never known anything about, then he could claim the money, clear her debts and release them both from the need to marry. His father had excelled himself this time, but had his plan been to force him to marry or bring his unknown half-brother into the business?

'Your father has a debt to pay, Lydia, and I am collecting it—from you. If you can indeed trace the person I am looking for, make contact without arousing the suspicion or interest of the media, then your father's debt will be cleared immediately. Marriage in any form will not be necessary.'

'If you are so against the idea of marriage too, why don't you just pay it off now?' That was exactly the question he'd put to Carlos and his legal team and even now he could feel the cold fear sink through him as he recalled Carlos's reply.

'Such an action will invalidate the will and your father's business will no longer be yours. Failure of

any kind to clear the debt will result in the business being sold.'

He had to convince Lydia. There was no way he was letting anyone get his hands on a company he'd painstakingly expanded. 'When I find the person I am looking for it unlocks funds, more than enough to clear your father's debts.'

'So this is all about money? Silly me, I thought you had sentimental reasons for wanting to find this person.' The accusation in her eyes was clear, but she could think what she liked. He'd never have to see her again after this.

'Yes, it's about money—as all business is.'

'So, who is this person? Is it a love child you abandoned and now want to bring out into the open?'

Such an accusation made it clear she'd researched him too and believed him to be as much of a playboy as his father had been. Maybe that was for the best. She didn't seem the type to enter into brief affairs merely to satisfy a sexual attraction. This was a woman who would demand so much more from a lover, whatever her earlier protestations had been.

'It is a love child, yes.' He flaunted the truth before her, aware of the conclusions she was making.

'I hate men like you.' She snapped the words at him and he smiled lazily. He hadn't fathered any children. That was something he'd been extremely careful of, but he enjoyed seeing the anger mix with contempt, filling her eyes, again letting him know exactly what she was thinking.

'Not as much as I dislike women who jump to conclusions.' He sat and watched the questions race across her face. 'It is not my child.'

'So if it's not your love child, whose is it?' Her fine brows rose elegantly in question and the satisfaction that danced in her eyes told him she thought he was lying.

'As I have said, it is not mine.' He wasn't ready to give her the secret that had stayed hidden for so many years. All the times he'd tried to be the son his father had wanted had been in vain and now, with the discovery of Max, his half-brother, it had all become perfectly clear why.

'You are going to have to tell me, if I am to trace this person.' A haughty note had entered her voice. She thought she'd got him on the run, thought she now held the power. Never. But he'd allow her to think that. For a while at least.

'It is my father's son I wish to find.'

Lydia's stomach plummeted. She'd been challenging him, pushing him to reveal his true self to her, and it had just backfired spectacularly. The fierce expression on his face warned her she'd gone too far, pushed too hard. Would he now revoke the offer, force her to find an extortionate amount of money to settle her father's debt? Or worse, marry him?

Suddenly she was that awkward sixteen-year-old again being introduced to Raul by her father. She'd smiled at him, pleased to know that someone closer to her own age would be at the dinner party her father had insisted she attend with him, but Raul had looked down at her with barely concealed lack of interest.

Not that that had stopped the heady attraction she'd instantly had for him and she'd been glad she'd chosen the fitted black dress that had made her feel taller, more attractive and much more grown up. Stupidly, she'd hung on every word Raul had said as they'd been placed next to one another at the dinner table. She'd liked him—more than liked him—and had wanted him to notice her, to like her too. She'd wanted to be more than friends and had already wanted him to be the one she experienced her first kiss with.

All evening she'd tried everything to get his attention, even trying to use her classroom Spanish.

'If you can't say it correctly, don't bother.' The high and mighty put-down had done just that, crashing all the dreams of a friendship, or more, with him.

'I don't have much call to use the language,' she'd retorted, her cheeks flaming with embarrassment. How had she thought him nice? How had she even begun to imagine that he might like her, might want to be friends, go on a date?

'Then I suggest you stick to your usual shopping and partying and give languages a miss.'

'But I'm going to study languages at university,' she'd replied with a gauche smile.

He'd looked at her then, his dark eyes locking with hers, and she'd held her breath, wondering if he was teasing her—teasing her because he liked her.

'Don't. You clearly don't have any talent for Spanish, exactly what I'd expect from Daddy's little princess who does nothing other than look pretty.' The scathing tone of his voice as his gaze had travelled down her had left her in no doubt that he didn't like her, that he despised her and all he thought she was.

She'd bit back a temper-fuelled retort and vowed that one day, she'd tell him exactly what she thought of him and she'd do it fluently in his language. If he thought she was a spoilt little thing, that was fine by her, but her sense of injustice didn't leave her, not even when she and her father left the dinner party. It had stayed with her, adding to all the insecurities her father had instilled in her.

Now she looked at Raul, ten years older, anger at what her father had done mixed with sympathy for this proud man. Her father's deception, the way he'd forced her mother to leave with his detached and cold ways, his constant need to make the next million before losing it again, seemed minor compared to the family secret Raul had just revealed.

'I'm sorry, I had no idea.' Her voice softened, but it did nothing to the feral expression on Raul's face. He was a man who didn't show softer emotions, that much was clear.

'I have only just discovered the existence of my half-brother. He and I are due to inherit from my father's estate.'

'I don't understand.' She was perplexed by the unveiling of the last few minutes. 'Your father must have known about him, to have included such conditions in the will.'

'He knew. He also knew that I wouldn't want to marry anyone, least of all the daughter of one of his debtors.'

'We have both been set up.' Shock set in and the full implications of the situation she was in finally hit home. How could her father have been so cruel? How could he have used her like this? She could almost imagine him concocting this strange deal with Raul's father. Two heartless men together.

'It would appear so. My father knows that money will motivate me over marriage.'

She tried not to feel insulted, tried not to feel glad that there was a way out of this mess and once she was out of it she'd insist her father sold the properties to repay the debt that, as far as she was concerned, he would still have to Raul. Debts had to be honoured.

'I need to find my brother, preferably without any media attention. I have no wish for the circus they can create or to expose my father's weakness, which will push the company further into the wrong kind of spotlight, not to mention destroy my mother.' His eyes were harder than ever, like a heavy thundercloud about to unleash its fury. Did he hate the brother he'd never met?

Questions raced through her mind, but one had to be asked. 'So why trust me, someone you barely know, with such sensitive information?'

'Because you're as against the idea of marriage as I am and claim to have what I need. Added to that, you are your father's only hope of clearing his debt without dragging his long-standing family name through the bankruptcy courts. That in itself should ensure your compliance with my request.'

He was right about that. If there had been another way to settle this she wouldn't have even met with him today. Her relationship with her father was strained to say the least, but she didn't want the family's name brought into disrepute. Her grandmother might be elderly, but it would break her heart and after what her mother and father had done to her with their selfish actions she would never do anything to upset the only person in the world who had shown her genuine love and affection.

'And there is no other way?'

He paused for a moment and, although those dark

eyes were focused on her, she was sure his thoughts were far away. A pang of sympathy zipped through her for him. How would she feel if she suddenly discovered that she had a half-brother or sister?

'I either find my half-brother or we must marry.' His accented voice was sharp as he set out the alternative and totally obliterated that misguided sympathy.

At least any marriage that did have to be made would be purely for the purpose of transferring her property assets to settle the debt. The fact that he wouldn't contest a divorce went some way to settling the unease that still ran through her. He obviously didn't have any intention of making her truly his wife.

So why did disappointment filter through her? Surely she had got over that teenage crush? He might be handsome and possess a lethal charm, if the waitress's reaction to him was anything to go by, but succumbing to his looks and charm was unthinkable. She would never give him the satisfaction.

As if to prove the point, their meals arrived and that skilful charm once again melted the waitress into a puddle. Lydia shook her head in disbelief and looked down at the food she suddenly had no appetite for.

'I don't need to go to Madrid with you. I can work from here.' She had her own business to run and in the final weeks before Christmas it would be busy. Added to that the idea of going to Madrid with this man was not one she welcomed, but the prospect of marriage, even if it was only on paper, was infinitely more unappealing.

'Your enthusiasm for my company warms me.' He mocked, but there was a hint of a mischievous smile on his lips, which she couldn't help but respond to. 'But you will come to Madrid. That is non-negotiable.'

Raul watched the battle play out in those expressive eyes. He could see every twist and turn of her doubt and reluctance, mirroring all he'd felt when he'd realised just what his father had done.

'Neither of us have much choice in this arrangement.' He tried to avoid becoming sidetracked by her long lashes as they lowered over her eyes, shielding his view into her soul. He hadn't expected to find a solution to the problem of tracing his half-brother when he'd made arrangements to meet her, just as he hadn't expected to find the spark of desire from the very first moment he'd seen her, anger sparking from her as she prepared to leave.

'Before I go anywhere with you, or make any kind of formal agreement, I will need a written contract, Mr Valdez. I need it in writing that if I find your brother, my father's debts will be settled.' She hesitated. 'And if the worst happens and we have to marry, it will be nothing more than a deal on paper.'

So she didn't trust him either. He admired her courage to sit there and demand a contract for the repayment of her father's debt. 'I will have it drawn up and you can sign it as soon as we arrive in Madrid.'

He'd already decided they would leave tomorrow as he had no intention of giving her too much time to begin enquiries into the whereabouts of his half-brother, Max. He might not yet have given her any details, but he couldn't risk her discovering the full extent of his father's treachery, not until he could be sure she wouldn't leak the story to the press. He had no intention of putting his mother, the only person to have shown him genuine love, through such a public humiliation.

His father had treated him and his mother badly. For eight years he'd led a double life, deceiving not only his wife and son, but another woman and child. Raul remembered the day his mother had found out about his affair. He could still hear the hurt echoing from the past as she'd told his father the marriage was over, that he could do what he liked but she and her son were staying where they belonged. That was the start of the coldest example of marriage he'd ever seen. What if he too was destined for the same?

Now that he'd discovered his father had turned his back on a child and its mother, Raul wanted to deal with it. He'd grown up with a father in his life and another child hadn't. It didn't sit well and he was determined to do all he could to make some kind of amends for the past. He only wished his father were here to listen to the tirade of angry words he had for him. Given his father's reputation, it was worryingly possible that more children had suffered the same fate.

He sat back and pressed his fingers together in a steeple, forcing all the hurt and rejection from his childhood down, trying hard to keep those negative emotions out of play. Now was not the time to relive that constant feeling that he'd never be good enough for his father, no matter what he did.

He had two choices. To ignore his half-brother and marry Lydia to settle a debt or take Lydia's offer, find Max and hopefully free them of need to marry. He didn't have to think too long about that answer. His father might have wished Max away by ignoring him, but he didn't want to do that—just as much as he didn't want to enter into the negative binds of marriage. If his father thought the threat of sharing his inheritance would be enough to force him into marriage, he had miscalculated—badly.

'What if I don't find your brother?' The question slipped innocuously from her lips and he looked at them, briefly wondering how they'd taste and feel beneath his.

He bit down on such traitorous thoughts, focusing instead on the shock of all he'd discovered yet had been unable to uncover himself. 'Half-brother.'

'Half-brother, brother…what difference does it make? What if I don't find him?'

'It makes a great deal of difference, Lydia. You too are an only child. How would you feel if you'd just discovered you had a sibling?'

'That's not what we are discussing,' she fired hotly back at him.

'If you don't find my half-brother within four weeks, then you will become my wife and your father's debts will be cleared.'

'For two years.' The dejection in that statement almost got to him. Almost.

He nodded. '*Sí*. After which you can file for divorce.'

'Four weeks is not very long to undertake such a task,' she said as she took a sip of her wine, the action once again drawing his attention to her lips, causing his mind to wander in directions it shouldn't be going in. 'And it will be Christmas too.'

'All the more reason to succeed. Four weeks is all you have. If you fail, Lydia, you will become my wife on Christmas Eve.'

CHAPTER THREE

MADRID WAS THE last place Lydia had expected to find herself and Raul's overpowering presence made it seem even more unreal, as if she were in the middle of a dream—or a nightmare.

The flight to Spain on his private jet had been difficult and with just the two of them she'd wondered what they were going to talk about. Thankfully he'd used the time to read over some paperwork and she'd given the outward appearance of relaxing even though inside she'd been a jumbled mess of questions. Now however, as they travelled in the back of his chauffeur-driven car through the bustle of the city's streets, lit up with festive cheer even in the late afternoon, she couldn't escape the fact that his full attention was focused on her.

'How long do you anticipate it will take to find my brother?' It was the first time he'd referred to him not as his half-brother and she wondered why, when he was notorious for being a playboy himself, he had been so affronted by the discovery of another sibling. But then she knew better than most that families could portray a façade of happiness when underneath secrets and lies were hidden away. It was an art she too had now perfected.

'I have no idea, not until you can give me some more information, but don't forget this is not my profession. Researching family history is just an interest of mine. I'm not claiming to be an expert.' She didn't like the way his eyes narrowed, a sign she'd quickly realised was one of irritation. Neither did she like the rush of panic that swept over her. What if she failed?

You can't fail, so you're not going to.

'What *is* your profession?' The glacial tone of his voice held scorn and she had to fight hard against the urge to smile smugly at him because one thing was certain and that was the fact that he still labelled her a spoilt little rich girl—Daddy's heiress who didn't know how to do anything other than party and shop.

'My profession?'

'Yes, what is it that you do each day?'

Would he be surprised if she told him that she'd graduated from university with an honours in Spanish? What about if she told him she'd taken her love of fashion and now had two very successful luxury boutiques? One in London and one in Paris. She'd never linked them to her family name, wanting only to succeed on her own merit. And she had. Briefly she wanted to shock him with that piece of information, but what right did he have to know everything about her? All she needed to do was trace his brother and it could be done in a matter of a week or two—if she was lucky.

'I think it's fair to say my strengths lie in the retail market.' She teased around the truth, played on what he still thought of her and couldn't help but smile as he scowled at her. Let him think what he wanted to. Far better that he thought she spent money rather than earned it. After all she was here in Madrid to settle her father's debts, so that she could move on and put the shambles that was her childhood behind her. She had only ever been an inconvenience to her mother, who now barely contacted her, and her father had always been a shadowy figure in the background of her life. It had been her grandmother who'd brought her up.

'You will of course find plenty of opportunity for such retail strengths here in Madrid.' The icy tone of his voice was almost enough to make the sun race behind the gathering rain clouds. If he tried hard enough he might even make it snow. She smiled at the thought as she watched him, his handsome face full of undisguised annoyance. 'Especially at this time of the year.'

'Yes, but there are of course more important matters than shopping right now—like which hotel do you suggest I stay at?' She hadn't been away from home for some time and was looking forward to the luxury of time out, satisfied that her recently appointed London manager would handle almost any problem that should arise. Not that she intended to stay for an extended length of time. Once she'd handed over the information Raul Valdez had requested, she'd leave, free of debt and free of obligation—to anyone. Even if it took two weeks she'd still be back in London before Christmas.

'You will be staying with me.' His words dropped into the ocean of her thoughts, shattering them as the waves of implications spread outwards.

'With you?' She looked across the car at him, suddenly feeling trapped. There was no way she could stay with him, not when he unleashed the kind of reaction that made her doubt her ability to ignore his presence or the sizzle of attraction that rampaged through her just from one look of those sexy dark eyes. She didn't need or want the complications of a man in her life. Daniel had killed those silly dreams even if her parents' hostile marriage hadn't.

She looked away from those brooding eyes and the sensation that he could read every thought that ran through her mind. Instead she focused on the passing city streets. What was the matter with her? Since when did she go all gooey over a man? She'd never been like this before.

'I have a perfectly adequate guest suite in my apartment.' A smile teased around his lips as she looked back at him, instantly wishing she hadn't as a zip of something she really didn't want to acknowledge charged through her.

'I thought you wanted to keep your search quiet and away from the press. What if they see you and I together and come up with the wrong answer?' She scrabbled for a reason not to stay with him.

'If that does happen, our *romance* will be much more of interest than the research you will be doing.' The heavy line of his brows lifted and this time he did smile. One of satisfaction and she swallowed down against the flutter that rose swiftly from her stomach, making her head light. She wasn't a teenager being chatted up by the hottest guy she'd ever met. She was a grown woman who knew her own mind, one who would make him regret ever looking at her with such disdain.

'Our romance?' A nervous laugh escaped with those words, intensifying her anger at the situation she was in.

'The perfect cover for your investigation, no?' The car stopped and he looked at her, the flirtatious mood of seconds ago disappearing. 'Do not forget who has the debt to settle, Lydia. You are not in a position to make demands or question my decisions and we will act as if we are in a relationship, as if we both accept the terms of the contract your father signed with mine.'

Before she could hurl any retort at him, he got out of the car and seconds later her door was opened by his driver, making exactly what she wanted to say difficult, if not impossible. She had made the original bargain, striking a deal that would help her, and he had turned it around to suit his needs.

He spoke in a flourish of Spanish to the driver; the sexy undertones of his voice in a language she loved knocked her thoughts off balance. But that little nugget of information was one she'd keep to herself—for now. As the satisfaction of that thought settled over her, he turned to her and spoke softly in English, putting his hand gently in the small of her back. 'This way, *querida*.'

The sensation of his hand, barely touching her, stifled any kind of reaction and like a meek lamb she did his bidding, glancing up quickly at the old but ornate building they were entering. The sound of the almost constant flow of traffic was snuffed out as the doors closed behind them.

'I'm still not sure it is right that I stay with you. I could easily find a hotel near here and still be able to do the research.' She tried one last time to avert the course of action he seemed set on.

'You could, but you won't.' His hand moved away from her as he pressed the call button for the elevator, the firmness in his voice echoing around the large marble lobby. The elevator doors opened and he stepped inside, his handsome face set in stern lines as he looked at her. 'We do have a deal, Miss Carter-Wilson, do we not?'

Damn him, he knew she was going to say yes—had to say yes. The amusement lurking behind the darkness of his eyes showed her that. She had no other way out of the mess her father had made.

'Very well.' She joined him in the elevator, alarmed at how small it became as the doors closed and they ascended. 'But it is a deal for business, nothing else.'

'Do you think I might seduce you?' The amusement in his eyes increased and that sexy devil-may-care hint of a smile lingered at the edges of his mouth.

'Isn't that what you are renowned for, Mr Valdez?' The flirty edge to her voice was unintended and inwardly she cringed. What was it about this man that made her say and do things she never normally would? 'The waitress yesterday is testimony to that.'

He looked at her, a slight frown furrowing his brow, and she lifted her chin and glared at him. The elevator doors opened but he didn't move and she couldn't, pinned to the spot by his piercing, dark eyes.

'Is that a hint of jealousy?'

She gasped in outrage. How dared he think she was jealous, that she craved his attention? 'Absolutely not.'

Without a backward glance she flounced out of the elevator as his deep, sexy laughter chased after her. Moments later she was in a vast apartment. His apartment. His life.

Raul watched Lydia waltz into his apartment, enjoying the sway of her hips, outlined perfectly in a black skirt that hugged her body more than he suspected she'd want it to. The long black boots only emphasised her sexiness and the openness of his apartment seemed suddenly to close in on him. He'd watched many women wander around his apartment but never had he experienced the pull at emotions he kept locked away. He never let a woman close, never let her see just who he really was.

Yet somehow, Lydia had unlocked that door. He'd already told her far more about himself than he had anyone else. Was it because she was the first woman to be here for a reason other than merely sleeping in his bed? The idea of her in his bed sparked a shot of lust through him, making him want to forget the real reason she was here.

'I trust it meets with your approval,' he teased her and was rewarded with that glare of fiery passion as she turned to look at him. Would she be as inviting if his lips claimed hers in a kiss? Would she respond and match the fire of desire beginning to burn within him? He was being drawn to her by an attraction so strong even he doubted he had the power to resist its allure. But he had to—for now at least.

'Tell me, Mr Valdez, why exactly do you require my father's debt settled in such an extraordinary way when it is obvious that you have more wealth here alone than in a couple of holiday villas my father used as security?'

Was she trying to annoy him?

He moved quickly across the marble floor, his shoes tapping out an insistent rhythm as the implications of her words hit home, turning the unwanted desire into much-needed anger. 'A couple of holiday villas? Is that what you think this is about? Do you really think I am mercenary enough to call in a debt for that?'

Raul began to seriously doubt she had really grasped

just how much debt her father had got himself into. It might have been to purchase holiday villas, but it was far more than a couple. He would take her straight to his office to see for herself just what her father had done and sign the contract agreed between them. The sooner he'd tied her into a contract, the better.

'That is exactly what I think. You've turned everything around and now are practically blackmailing me. I either find your brother or marry you.'

'And which would you prefer to do, *querida*?'

'Don't call me that.' The spark of fury was palpable as she stood her ground and he recalled her atrocious attempt at Spanish the night they'd first met. Then, just as now, her green eyes blazed like priceless emeralds, calling to the lustful desire within him, and he was just as adamant as ever that he would ignore it.

'We will go to my office right now and you can see for yourself exactly what your father owes, Miss Carter-Wilson.' Irritation surged through him. How dared she accuse him of underhanded dealings? He would hang on to that irritation. Use it to wipe out the idea of things he really didn't need to feel right now. Hell, why did he have to find *this* woman so sexy?

'That sounds the most sensible option,' she tossed haughtily at him, her eyes sparking defiance and her lips pressed together in a firm angry line, just begging to be kissed into submission. 'And on the way back I will check into a hotel.'

He narrowed his eyes as he looked at her. 'You don't give up, do you?'

'No, so I suggest you show me exactly what my father owes your company and I'm sure it will prove that a few days of tracing your brother will more than cover it—and release us both from the bizarre marriage deal your father must have tricked mine into agreeing to.'

'In that case, *querida*...' he took pleasure in using the endearment again, relishing the fury that shone in her eyes as much as the opportunity to remain in control of this ridiculous situation '...we shall leave immediately and sort this out.'

Her boot heels tapped on the marble floor as she walked towards him, that superior *you don't worry me* look on her face again. 'That is the most sensible thing you have said since we met in London.'

'It is a short walk to my office.' He glanced down at the sexy high-heeled boots, trying to ignore the idea of her shapely ankles encased in them and keep his thoughts firmly on the task at hand.

'A short walk will be perfect,' she said as a hint of challenge rose in those expressive green eyes.

Determined not to be affected by her, he led the way back to the elevator and out onto the busy street. Despite her heels she kept pace with him and he slowed his slightly as he entered one of the city's plazas, lined with cafés where couples enjoyed the cool winter sun of the afternoon. What would it be like to sit and relax with her, to forget the stress of their situation and get to know one another properly?

It shocked him to realise that was exactly what he wanted to do, not in the way he'd always done with other women, but in a deep and meaningful way. That would never be an option, not now. It was better if she continued to think of him as a womaniser, especially when he sensed she was not the kind of woman to indulge in one-night stands, making her exactly the kind of woman he always avoided. Was that the reason for this inconvenient attraction? Forbidden fruit? He was stronger than that, wasn't he?

He paused outside the doors of the old town building that was home to the head office of Banco de Torrez. She looked at him and the uncertainty he saw briefly in her eyes pulled at his conscience. He silenced that conscience. There was no other way of dealing with the mess created by both their fathers.

Without a word, he pushed open the large and heavy door and entered the calm interior, which, like his apartment, was modern and spacious, belying the exterior that belonged in the city's past. As he looked down at her, he saw her delicate brows rise in question and recalled her earlier remarks, suggesting that he could just write off the debt she had to pay. He could, if he was prepared to risk a company he'd built being sold off to the highest bidder. He couldn't allow that to happen to all the people who depended on Banco de Torrez for employment. The only other option was for Lydia to find Maximiliano without luring the press closer. It was time to put her *hobby* of family history to the test.

'I will show you to the office you can work from whilst here,' he said as he stepped into the elevator, trying to ignore the close proximity they were forced into once again.

Lydia followed Raul past offices where staff members worked, some greeting him and others regarding her with mild curiosity. Did they think she was his latest mistress? That thought almost made her feet stop moving, but she forced herself to continue, trying not to care what others thought.

Finally, the glass-partitioned offices finished and they reached a more private area. Raul walked in and the luxury of what was obviously his space forced her to stifle a small gasp.

'This is where you will work.' He gestured to an office area off his. She walked in, trying to ignore the way he made her feel as he stood so close, looking out of the window, which took up almost all of one wall. Rooftops of grand old buildings nestled beneath the winter sun and she wished briefly she could explore the city, get to know it better. But she was here to work, to pay off her father's debts and finally free herself of, not only Raul Valdez, but her ill-fated honour to her father. She was here ultimately for her grandmother. There wasn't time for such frivolities and most definitely not for exploring the simmering passion between them.

'Nice, but I only intend to be here for a matter of days.' She had no idea how much her father owed, but even to her ears the fact that it would only take a few days sounded extortionate. He must be desperate to trace his brother, not for any emotional reasons, she was sure, but for the money his inclusion in the business would unlock. Raul had been brutally honest about that. It must be far greater than her father owed. Much more of a lure for a cold businessman like Raul Valdez.

He shrugged casually, a move so unexpected it aroused her suspicions. What hadn't he told her?

'I think we should discuss the extent of your father's debt before you make plans to leave Madrid, because make no mistake, *querida*, you will *not* be leaving until I consider the debt repaid, either with the information I require or your signature on a marriage document.'

Inwardly, Lydia's anger surfaced. She was not his

querida, but outwardly she remained calm and poised and she resisted the urge to reply in Spanish. She would save that pleasure for another time. 'In that case, I need to know the exact sum my father owes.'

She followed him back into his office and stood calmly waiting as he got a file out, opened it slowly and with purpose, then he looked at her as he slid it across the expanse of polished wood. The warning on his handsome face was clear and she braced herself for what was to come.

'The figure exceeds five hundred million euros.' He spoke without any emotion, any sense of surprise at the figure he mentioned. Her eyes widened in shock. How could he say that so calmly?

'And the properties used as security?' Her voice wavered and she dreaded the answer.

'Far in excess of that amount.'

How many properties had her father hidden in her name? This was much bigger than she'd imagined and with each passing hour she was getting in deeper. Too deep. It would finish her grandmother, who was recovering from a bout of ill health, if she knew how much.

'So if we married you would gain substantially more?' He nodded and she carried on whilst she still had the strength to stand. 'Why then are you prepared to accept the deal I offered? Before I knew the extent of the sums involved, I might add.'

'I want my brother found. I'd prefer the money to come from the accounts my father set up for the purpose of his devious acts than from you and our marriage. I trust you agree.'

'I agree only on that I have no wish to get married— to you or anyone.' She injected as much confidence into her voice as she could even though inside she was still reeling from shock at the amount her father owed.

'If you agree, then you must sign this confidentiality contract.'

Suspicion nudged into her mind. What was he keeping from her? 'There must be more to it than that. What are you keeping from me, Mr Valdez?'

She stood in the middle of his office and used the long-ago-perfected art of indifference as she lifted her chin and challenged him. There was a hint of anger, a hint of bristling annoyance as his gaze met hers. Then it was gone. Replaced by icy disdain.

'You are very astute, Lydia. You should be a businesswoman.' His cutting tone bounced off her toughened barrier, but inside something changed. He'd seen her as something more than an empty-headed heiress. Briefly maybe, but he'd seen the real Lydia.

'Maybe I am,' she taunted him as she walked towards him, watching as his eyes narrowed in suspicion, noticing how his dark lashes made his eyes look so very sinfully sexy. 'Which means, before I sign any contract with you, I want to know the finer details. All of them.'

'Very well.' He moved towards her and she suddenly wished she hadn't been so bold, provoking him as she'd done moments ago, because now he was far too close. She could smell the unadulterated scent of a powerful male. It scared and excited her. 'There is one more detail which needs to be agreed upon.'

'Which is?' She looked up at him, her heart thudding at his closeness. So close that if he lowered his head he could kiss her. Where had that thought come from?

'That we become engaged—immediately.'

'No,' she snapped the word back at him, defiance echoing around the room.

'I have no wish for anyone to know that I am looking for my brother—not until I am ready. The board of directors are demanding settlement of this historic, and seriously overdue, debt, and it is imperative that they believe that we are willing to marry to clear it.'

He moved a bit closer and she bit down on her bottom lip, trying to pretend the butterflies that had begun to flutter inside her weren't because of him. She had to get a grip on herself. He couldn't know that she found him attractive. Instinctively, she knew that would be dangerous.

'Why should I care about what your board of directors think?' He'd tricked her, kept this part of the terms from her until she arrived in Madrid.

'I have until the end of December to sort this matter and in order to save thousands of jobs from being put under scrutiny or worse. There is one final clause and that is if I don't find my brother or marry you, the company will be sold. It is essential that I am seen to be dealing with the debt. It is not, after all, a small debt. I'm sure even you would agree on that.'

'And if I agree to this fake engagement?' Again she challenged him.

'You will be helping not only yourself and your father, but many hundreds of ordinary families who depend on their continued employment.'

Lydia sighed. She knew when to give in gracefully. How hard could it be to pretend to be engaged to this man? All she had to do was find his brother and then this nightmare, which was getting worse by the minute, would be over.

Raul spoke again, adding to her worries. 'And if you fail to find my brother we will have already begun the process of organising our marriage, which will have to take place on Christmas Eve.'

'You've got it all planned, haven't you?' A Christmas wedding? The thought sent panic racing through her like a torrent of flood water. She had no wish to be a married woman. She'd seen how hopeless her dreams of love and happiness were. Now Raul was reinforcing how futile those dreams were.

'I am always prepared for all eventualities.'

Why did that sound so threatening? She looked up at him, his dark eyes piercing into hers, and not a trace of anything other than seriousness was on his handsome face, nothing to soften the severity of his hard expression.

For the briefest of moments, she considered walking out. This was her father's mess and he could sort it. But she knew he never would and when it all went wrong Raul would be back, only then she would have nothing to bargain with. Not if he'd already found his brother. On top of that she could almost hear her grandmother, urging her to be strong, to get through this, as she'd always done when the fear of boarding school had been her only worry in life.

It was now or not at all and she'd do it for her grandmother's sake. Not Raul's, not hers and most definitely not her father's.

'I don't doubt that at all.' She lifted her chin defiantly, pulling herself up as a new inner strength surged through her. She'd sort this and get this man out of her life. 'But why did your father set this up?'

'To force me to accept his other son or do the one thing I have always said I wouldn't do—get married.'

'Would he really do that?'

'He would. So what is it to be, Lydia? Do we have a deal?'

She wanted to ask him how he could talk of marriage in such a detached way, but instead she took his lead and walked over to the desk, picked up the pen, and with one last angry and defiant look at him she signed the paper. 'We have a deal, Mr Valdez. I will be your fake fiancée—but only for one month.'

CHAPTER FOUR

LYDIA SAT AT her desk, her gaze fixed on the view of Madrid as the December sun set across the city, her mind wandering through the ever-increasing questions about the deal she'd struck with Raul. She twisted the large diamond engagement ring on her finger, still shocked to find it there despite having worn it for over a week.

The first ten days of the fake engagement was over and she was closer to a marriage she didn't want but would have to go through with, unless she came up with something to do with Maximiliano Valdez. She'd gone down so many dead ends this week and wasn't any closer to discovering the whereabouts of Raul's brother, or even the name he used, because she was certain it wasn't Valdez. She sighed, momentarily feeling beaten. She had to come up with something soon. It was only a matter of time before Raul demanded to know what she'd found out.

'Is your work boring you, Lydia?' Raul's deep and accented voice penetrated her thoughts and she swivelled round in her chair, turning her back on the view and her questions.

He leant casually against the door frame, his arms

folded and an expression of expectancy on his face. How could he look so commanding and yet so attractive at the same time?

'I was thinking.' She tried to block that mutinous train of thought. She didn't want to think about this man like that. She mustn't.

'And are you any closer to the answer, to finding my brother?' He seemed to loom over her, his height darkening the light and airy office and, even worse than that, her heart was thudding. Was it panic that she hadn't yet got any real leads as to where his brother might be or because he was so close and she was excruciatingly aware of him?

His brows flicked up in question when she didn't respond, his eyes, so very dark, fixing her to the spot. 'Anything?'

'No.' She didn't want to elaborate on it, all too aware that now she had just over two weeks before he could demand that she became his wife and settle the debts her father had recklessly created. If she didn't find his brother, she had no other way of paying even a part of what was owed. She might have her own business, but it was still in its infancy and would never be in the league of Raul's high-earning business—or her father's debt.

He inhaled deeply, as if he was holding back on saying something, and strode to stand at the window, his arms folded defensively across his broad chest. She watched him as the silent seconds ticked by, drawn to the width of his shoulders and the shirt that strained over his muscled arms. Strong and safe arms.

She blinked in shock. Where had that come from? She looked down at her desk, making a show of stacking papers tidily, anything other than look at this virile specimen of masculinity that threatened everything she thought she was.

'Then I am afraid we have to put in motion our alternative option.' The coolness of his voice sent a shock of fear through her as if she'd just dipped her toes into the cold seas around England.

'What alternative option?' Had she missed something?

He turned to look at her, that dark and yet strangely sexy look in his eyes, and she felt the simmer of attraction build. Damn the man. Did he know what he was doing? Was he deliberately trying to disarm her?

'To go ahead with the marriage.' His voice held a note of determination despite the calm, soft tone.

'But there are three more weeks yet.' She knew she sounded panicked, but she couldn't help it. Quickly she tried to regain her inner strength, her ability to come somewhere close to matching this man's power.

'*Si*, that is true, but, as far as your father's debt is concerned, we have to be seen to be preparing for marriage in order to make the repayment of that debt.'

'By who?' she fired back at him angrily.

He moved to her desk, placed his palms on it and leant towards her. 'By the board of directors, the people who have the power to insist that the contract your father signed is adhered to, that his debt is repaid by our marriage and subsequent transfer to me of those properties around the globe you claim to know nothing of.'

He was angry; she could feel it reverberating from him and bouncing off the clean white walls of the office. She'd spoken to her solicitor, knew that her father had been advised against signing such a contract, which made it all the worse. Her father had engineered the terms just to keep himself out of trouble, placing her in the firing line. Still she couldn't help but goad this proud and powerful man.

'And you always do as you are told?' Mischief entered her voice and, briefly, she had the upper hand.

He leant lower to her, his face so close to hers that if anyone was looking in through the large window such a move could be mistaken for a lover's kiss. She held her breath, refusing to back down, refusing to lose the upper hand she had inadvertently gained.

'Do you really think I would marry you—or anyone—simply because I have been told to do so?' The words were deep and accented, his breath warm on her face, his dark eyes granite hard and fixed on hers.

No, she didn't think that at all. In fact, it had crossed her mind more than once why such a commanding and in-control man would follow the wishes of his father's will so succinctly.

She leant daringly forward, closer to him and looked into the fierceness in his eyes. 'No, I don't, so maybe now would be a good time to tell me exactly what this is all about instead of waiting three more weeks and forcing us into a marriage neither of us want. I have no wish to spend the next two years with you.'

He didn't answer. His eyes searched hers, what for she didn't know, but she couldn't help the tingle that covered her lips as if his had touched hers, brushed over them and teased them—teased her—into passionate life.

She jolted back on her chair. 'What is it all about, Raul?'

A smug smile of satisfaction teased at the lips she'd just imagined kissing hers and heat spread over her cheeks. She stood up from the desk, as calmly as she could even though her insides were somersaulting wildly as she fought, once again, the pull of attraction for this proud Spaniard.

'You know it all, Lydia.'

'I'm going home,' she announced sternly, but the questioning rise of his brows left her in no doubt of her mistake.

'By home, you mean, my home?' The deep sensuous accent did untold things to her already disturbed equilibrium.

'I have never had the luxury of calling any one place home for long. Any place I stay becomes my home—temporarily at least.' Why had she said that? Why had she given away a part of her like that? Angrily, she turned and picked up her jacket and purse.

'Join me for a drink—on the way home.' His accent had deepened, become more noticeable and far too sexy.

She turned and looked at him, the challenge in his eyes unmistakable. He expected her to refuse, to run from whatever it was that had just zinged subtly between them, changing everything. Well, she'd show him he didn't scare her, that she had the power to resist the attraction—resist him.

She smiled at him brightly. 'That would be the perfect end to the day.'

The fire in Lydia's eyes did something to him as he looked at her and Raul suddenly had the urge to spend an evening with her. A long evening. Whatever it was that had reared up like a stallion between them as he'd looked into her eyes now called to him, daring him to accept the challenge this woman presented, daring

him to take what he wanted. She was a challenge he
shouldn't accept.

He sat opposite Lydia at a café in one of the city's
most vibrant plazas, content that here they would be noticed, their status as an engaged couple brought to the
attention of Madrid's society—and subsequently Carlos,
who would inform the board, who were pushing more
strongly for settlement of her father's debt. This would
buy them both time.

He ordered wine and tapas and sat back, enjoying
the buzz of early evening in Madrid, but knowing he
would have to bring the conversation round to the finer
details for their marriage. He'd been forced to put the
marriage plan into motion because after one week it
was becoming clear that maybe she wasn't able to trace
his brother. Her *hobby* obviously wasn't as developed
as she'd led him to believe.

'I have made the official notifications for our marriage. On Christmas Eve, you and I will marry in a civil
ceremony.' She paled but before she could offer up one
of her little interruptions he continued, 'Your father's
debts will be cleared as soon as we are married, but we
must remain living as a married couple for two years.'

'I thought we didn't have to go to the extreme of
marriage.' Her eyes flashed with a spark of anger as
she looked at him, calmly taking a sip of her cool white
wine. Her long elegant fingers and vibrant red-painted
nails drew his attention. She hadn't changed since they'd
first met, just evolved into the socialite, a spoiled little
heiress who had nothing better to do than pamper and
indulge herself. Not at all the kind of woman he usually noticed. He liked more independent women, those

who didn't read too much into a smile. So why was she getting under his skin so easily?

'Only you can decide what happens, Lydia. You need to find my brother soon. Only then can your father's debts be cleared and the marriage cancelled. Fail or take too long and the marriage will have to go ahead.'

'If I decide to do something I never fail so you shouldn't trouble yourself with all those official and legal documents just to arrange a marriage that won't be necessary.'

The defiant and determined look in her eyes stirred something deep within him, something he'd kept concealed even from himself. Annoyed at the direction of his thoughts, he pushed it aside. Far better to dislike her than desire her.

'The official arrangement to marry you on Christmas Eve is my insurance policy to ensure that you don't fail.'

'You are nothing but a blackmailer,' she threw at him and looked out of the window across the plaza. Around them an increasing amount of people were filling up the tables, their laughter and talking infusing the evening with fun and vibrancy.

'I think that particular title goes to your father.' There were moments when he believed her innocence in this, believed that she knew nothing of the properties her father had bartered with. Then, when she looked at him so defiantly, so very proudly, like an heiress who had it all and knew it, he believed nothing of the sort. She certainly gave out mixed messages.

Right now she looked vulnerable and that struck a chord within him, sent questions racing through his mind. She was gambling with far more than a few properties. Like him, she was prepared to risk her freedom, risk ending up in a marriage she didn't want. But why? She didn't appear to have a conscience for the father, a man who had used her in his scheming ways. What was keeping her here, keeping her from walking away?

'And yours,' she flung at him, the spark of fire obliterating that vulnerability. 'And I don't intend to become their victim. I will do everything I can to find your brother, Raul, everything.'

'That is very honourable of you.'

'Honour doesn't come into it. Self-preservation maybe, dislike for a man such as you, very definitely.'

'Ouch.' He laughed at her, admiring the hissing wildcat barely concealed beneath those words, thinking it would be exciting to tame her. 'Where has the little kitten gone?'

'Kitten?' She looked at him, a frown on her beautiful face.

'The one who wanted nothing more than me to kiss her as we talked at your desk.'

'I did not.' The indignation was clear in her voice as she jumped to her feet; so too was the hint of colour on her cheeks. He'd known as he'd looked at her across the desk that if he'd kissed her, if he'd followed the silent requests of her lovely full lips, he would have wanted more. He'd resisted the temptation. If he'd given in so easily he would have been living up to the reputation he'd created as part of his armour, but he'd wanted to—badly.

'Sit down, Lydia. It will look as if we are as far from lovers as can be if you stand there glaring at me so intently.'

'Which is exactly what we are.' The words hissed at him, but she did at least sit down again.

'I intend for us to be seen as, if not lovers, at least friends. We are about to enter into the happy state of marriage.'

'Hah.' The false laugh that slipped so easily from her lips left him in no doubt that she too had little sentiment for marriage. 'Is there such a thing?'

'From that I deduce your parents' marriage was as unhappy as that of my parents.' Why was he talking of such things with her? He never discussed his childhood, never talked to anyone about the cold and heartless home he'd grown up in, or the constant warring of his parents as his father's indiscretions became ever more frequent and ever more public. His mother had never forgiven the double life her husband had led for over eight years of their marriage and he intended to keep his search for the child of that double life from her for as long as possible.

'It is not me who has a half-sibling to trace.'

So the kitten's claws were still unsheathed. Maybe he should have kissed her when he'd had the chance.

'True. But would you really know? Can you really say that your father has not sired another child when you spent most of your childhood with your grandparents until you went to boarding school?'

'How do you know so much about me?' Now he had her full attention.

'Did you really expect me to even consider marrying you without some background, something more than our dinner-party talk ten years ago? Your father has told me much.'

She looked at him shrewdly, her green eyes almost dark with suspicion. 'And what did you discover?'

'That maybe you are not the spoilt little rich girl you

want people to believe you are.' Now he had her attention. Her eyes blazed a furious challenge at him and who was he to refuse?

'Which means?'

'Which means, Lydia, I know you have no other choice. That at least was very clear from what he told my legal representative. Even so, we have a deal, one you will honour with either marriage or success in finding my half-brother.' He paused, letting the information sink in whilst he pushed his suspicion that there was something else, some other reason for her compliance, to the back of his mind.

'For now, that means acting as if we are preparing to unite in marriage, that we at least like each other. I have no wish for the board to pick up on any reluctance from either of us. They must not question that the debt will be settled in full, however that might be.'

'All this to save your business.' She shook her head in disbelief and it grated on him that she thought his motives for demanding the marriage appear to take place were purely selfish.

'And to save your father from ruin as well as safeguard our much-wanted state of being single.'

'Do you really expect me to believe that?'

'*Sí, querida*, I do.' The words he'd just spoken weren't lost on him. They were words he'd no intention of saying to any woman.

Lydia looked at Raul as he sat quietly, their little spat over. Around them the noise of the evening increased and a party atmosphere prevailed. The night was still young but she didn't have time to think of parties and fun. She had to find his brother and the turn of conversation, however fiery, had showed just how she could do that.

'I need to talk to your mother. She must know something.' That got his attention.

His dark eyes held hers and he looked up at her, then back out to the now busy plaza, ablaze with Christmas lights. Around them the place was full of laughter and voices, the sounds echoing up around them, making everything seem surreal. She looked at the firm set of his jaw, the fierce profile, and knew she'd touched a nerve. A very raw nerve.

'I have no wish to involve my mother in this.' Finally, he turned back to face her and she could see the coldness in his eyes. 'She knows nothing of the terms of the will and that is exactly how it will stay.'

'It may be that she has the initial lead which will help with this. After all, she was married to your father. She must know something of what happened.'

'Why do you say that?' His icy voice was full of disdain but she pushed on regardless. She had no intention of ending up married to this man in three weeks' time. By Christmas she'd be back in London and if it meant upsetting him and his mother was the only way out of it then that was exactly what she would do.

'Women usually know. I have also worked out, from the small amount of information you have given me, that you and your brother must have been born within months of each other.' She ploughed on, regardless of the deepening anger on his face. This wasn't a time for sentimental feelings of guilt. This was a time to save herself from a marriage she had no wish to make.

'Which is exactly why I have no wish to drag her into it. Imagine how it must have felt to be a new mother and know your husband was sleeping with another woman, that you'd provided the much-needed heir and were now surplus to requirements.'

Her temper boiled at the thought of the man who'd done that to his wife, Raul's mother, and then a flash of sympathy for Raul himself. Had he too grown up knowing he was merely the heir required and not the son much wanted? Was that why he was so hard, so cold and unreachable?

She pushed it aside. 'We have no other option, Raul, so when you have decided which way to proceed, perhaps you will be good enough to let me know.' She stood up and began to walk away, aware of him behind her, tossing notes onto their table and following her.

She didn't wait. She walked into the plaza, wanting only to get away from him.

'I am not accustomed to women walking away from me,' he stated harshly as he caught up with her. Did he expect her to bend to his wishes, do his bidding exactly as he wanted? No, she would never do that. She'd seen her own mother do it and then seen her leave, unable to tolerate the bullying regime any longer; she hadn't even cared that she was leaving behind her daughter. It had been her grandmother who'd looked after her from then on.

She stopped to look up at Raul, an uncomfortable thought settling over her. For the first time in her life she wondered if she too should have been the required heir or even the much-sought-after son. Had she been a disappointment and let-down to both her parents when she'd arrived? A daughter neither of them had wanted?

Suddenly her childhood made so much more sense. Bitterness swept over her and she responded, lashing out at the man who'd brought such a realisation about.

'Well you are about to find out what it's like. I'm not staying here whilst you dither about just who you want to help with finding your brother. It seems to me you would rather marry than find him. What are you afraid of, Raul? Sharing your inheritance?'

He grabbed her wrist and pulled her close against him, looking directly into her eyes. For a brief moment she thought she saw desire combined with the anger her words had induced. Her heart thumped wildly in her chest, his closeness invading every sense in her body as drops of rain began to unceremoniously fall.

He didn't care about the rain, or that they were quickly getting wet, instead he looked into her eyes, his breath as hard and fast as hers. Did he feel that powerful attraction too? The same attraction she was fighting? She couldn't allow him to know what he did to her.

'Let me go,' she demanded fiercely, wanting only to hide the spark of something very close to desire that had leapt to life inside her, despite the dousing by the rain.

She couldn't break eye contact as the rain began to fall harder; locals and tourists alike sought refuge inside the buildings of the plaza, but she couldn't move. It was as if he'd cast a spell, fixed her to the spot. She couldn't walk away, didn't want to move.

He let her hand go, but remained so very close, looming over her like a matador, and to her horror she still couldn't move, couldn't back away from him. Around them the plaza had emptied, the noise of the pre-Christmas parties replaced by the constant thud of rain onto the now soaked bricks and cobbles of the plaza. She could feel him so very close, feel the heat of his body, smell his masculine scent. For goodness' sake, she could even taste his kiss, taste what it would be like to have his lips pressed against hers.

Her hair was beginning to stick to her head, her jacket to her skin. She began to shiver, but she wasn't cold. Far more powerful sensations were racing round her body. Raul pulled off his jacket, his eyes locked on hers all the time as he placed it round her shoulders. It made it worse. She could smell him around her, feel his heat caressing her, and as the rain quickly soaked him his shirt became tantalisingly transparent, serving only to heighten his strength and masculinity—not to mention her barely veiled desire to be kissed by him.

Before she knew what she was doing or had time to think of the implications of such actions, she'd moved closer still. It was all the invitation he'd needed and within seconds she was in his arms, her own wrapped around his neck as his lips, hard and demanding, claimed hers. Her wet body clung to his, the sensation of being against him so wildly sensual as the rain continued to fall on them that she couldn't help the sigh of pleasure escaping.

His husky whisper in Spanish only added to the electrifying moment and she couldn't stop herself pressing closer still, feeling every hard contour of his body against hers.

Then sense prevailed. What was she doing? Kissing the one man she shouldn't kiss. Her enemy. What was the matter with her?

'That,' she breathed heavily as she pulled back from him and out of his arms, the rain still pounding down around them. 'That was not part of our deal.'

'Yet you can't maintain you didn't want me to kiss you, can you, *querida*?'

She shook her head as he continued. 'In fact, it was you who started it, you who moved towards me. What is a man meant to do when a woman like you kisses him? Stand there and not move?'

'I am not your *querida*.' She hurled the words at him, glaring accusingly as her heart thumped and her body pulsed with need.

'So you have said.'

'I don't want anything from you, Raul, and especially not a kiss. All you need to do is find out if your mother has any idea who it was your father had an affair with.' Desperate to rid her body of the heat that surged powerfully through it after that explosive kiss, she pulled off his jacket, allowing the rain to cool her, to dampen the desire she hadn't been able to fight.

'That may not be easy.' He glared at her, obviously fighting the same desire as she was. A man like Raul Valdez, who had a reputation for being as ruthless a lover as a businessman, surely wouldn't have to fight the attraction.

'Marrying you won't be easy either.' She spoke the truth, but now those words came from a different place than they had done when she'd first met him. She hadn't known then just how lethal a kiss from him could be.

'Very well,' he said as he looked down at her, raindrops falling from his hair, making her want to reach up and push it back from his forehead. 'I will arrange for you to meet my mother. And now I suggest we go and get dry—separately.'

'Absolutely separately. There won't be a repeat of this. Of that much I can assure you.'

CHAPTER FIVE

THE LAST THING Lydia had expected was Raul to announce they were going away for the weekend and to be driven out of Madrid, into the countryside. Even more of a shock was the fact that he had relented and agreed to take her to see his mother. In the short time she'd spent with Raul, Lydia knew he didn't do anything on a whim. Everything had a purpose. So what was this visit all about?

The question lingered in her mind until finally, after what had felt like hours of driving, due to the tension filling the car, he turned off the road. The car tyres scrunched over the gravel drive of a country villa, typically Spanish in every way. Not at all like the grandeur of his Madrid penthouse apartment.

'This is nice,' she said lightly as he turned off the engine, silence filling the car, blending with that ever-present tension as he looked at her. She'd been acutely aware of his presence next to her, of every move he'd made as he'd driven first on the busy roads away from the city and then to the quieter and smaller roads through farmland, interspersed with villages.

'My weekend retreat,' he offered as he got out of the car. She watched him walk around the front of it and towards her door, rebelliously enjoying the view of his long legs and lean body encased, as always, in a suit, which did little to hide his strength. Memories of how it had felt to be pressed against his body as rain had soaked them rushed back at her, adding to the air of expectancy zinging between them.

Aware he would think she was waiting for him to open her door, she quickly did so herself and slipped out of the low sports car. Standing outside in the fresh air of winter, she expected to feel less intimidated by him, but after the previous night and the kiss that had set fire to her whole body she was anything but. There wasn't any escape from the attraction, no relief from the sizzle of tension now.

She couldn't allow herself to be drawn in by it—by him. She had to keep in mind his motives for bringing her to Spain, to this romantic villa. It was purely money and wealth that drove him; not the need to find a brother he'd never known of, purely money. He might have all the trappings of wealth, but other than that he was no different from Daniel, wanting her for what she had, not who she really was.

'And your mother lives here?' She hoped the question was light and casual, belying the turmoil in her mind, but the look he fired her way was far from that. It was cold and calculating. Distanced yet intense.

'No, she lives about half an hour's drive into the hills.'

So she was alone with him again and this time there wouldn't be an office to escape to. 'I see.'

'You made yourself perfectly clear last night, Lydia. You have nothing to fear from being here with me.' The brusqueness of his voice backed up his words and she tried not to be disappointed as a small reckless part of her wanted him to kiss her again—and much more. She pushed that woman aside. She had to remain strong and as detached as he evidently was. It was the only way.

'So we are here purely to see your mother?'

'*Sí*. Did you think I had ulterior motives for bringing you here?' Raul's dark eyes fixed her to the spot, but the haughty façade she lived behind served her well.

'Only to increase your wealth.'

He stepped towards her, but she stood firm, retained her cool composure. 'All I want, Lydia, is for you to find my brother. Then I can secure the future of the company by settling the extortionate debts *your* father has run up and move forward in my life.'

Before she could register his words, he turned and walked towards the door of the villa. Deep within her, hidden expertly away, she trembled with shock. It might be her father's debts he wanted repaid, but he'd just confirmed he was no better than either his father or hers. This was all about greed.

He opened the door and stepped back for her to enter the villa, which was not at all what she'd expected of this hard and dominating businessman. This was more like a home. It was comfortable and welcoming, not a sleek modern angle in sight. It was the kind of place she would choose, the kind of place to finally put down roots.

Her early years had been spent moving from one house to the next. She'd never had time to settle, time to make friends before the family was on the move again. Then, if that wasn't unsettling enough, her mother had left her with her father. Luckily her grandmother had stepped in and her father had been all too ready to allow

her to live with her grandmother, the only time she'd
felt she belonged.

She pushed away that yearning need to make a place
a home, to actually belong somewhere, and focused her
attention on the reason for being here in the first place.
To ensure her grandmother didn't find out just how low
her own son had sunk.

'Then I suggest the sooner I can speak with your
mother, the better. Time is ticking away and as I have
no intention at all of marrying you in three weeks' time
I want my father's debt settled.' She tried to hide her
see-sawing emotions and appear as calm as he was,
watching as he moved around the villa, looking out of
place in his smart suit. The ruthless businessman she'd
come to know didn't fit here at all.

'You will not ask her anything directly.' Raul's firm
voice snapped in the air around them like the first clap
of thunder as a storm broke.

'Then how am I supposed to fulfil my part of the
deal?' What was he trying to hide or, more to the point,
what didn't he want her to know?

'My parents' marriage was an arranged one and even
as a young child I sensed the undercurrent of dislike
between her and my father. They barely tolerated one
another.' Each word was emotionless and matter-of-fact.
Exactly how she would describe her childhood and attempt to hide the hurt emotions of the child that still remained. Was Raul hurting too? Could it be that he was
more capable of emotions than he wanted her to believe?

'That is a scenario I am familiar with.' She dropped
the words in casually as she looked around the villa,
liking it more with each passing second.

He looked at her as he walked across the room and

opened doors to the terrace, the cool air of winter rushing in, fresh and stimulating. When his eyes met hers
seconds later, that mask of indifference was well and
truly in place. 'My father led a double life, Lydia. For
eight years he had two families.'

When she didn't speak he continued, 'I was sent to
boarding school from a very young age and never knew
family life. When I came home it was to hostilities and
stand-offs. Then one day he was gone. So although I assume my mother knows all about the affairs my father
had after that, as well as the mistress he'd lived with
and had a family with alongside ours, I would rather
she didn't have to face it head-on.'

'Fine,' she said as she watched him, tall and powerful against the backdrop of the rural room of the villa.
'I will find a way to enquire about Max without being
too obvious.'

'You will also leave her in no doubt that we are lovers. I don't want her to find out what my father has
done—ever.'

'Why did he do it? Set the terms of his will like that?'

'He obviously thought I was like him and that I
would not tolerate sharing the success of the business
with anyone. I suspect he thought I would find an enforced marriage more preferable.' The bitterness in his
voice was clear, but deep down she didn't believe he
was like that.

He looked at her, his eyes locking with hers for a moment, then walked out through the open doors onto a
terrace that boasted a pool, covered now for the colder
winter months, and, beyond that, stunning views of
the countryside.

She watched as he walked across the terrace, saw the

tension in his shoulders when he stood with his back to her, rigid and upright; sympathy filled her. She knew what it was like to grow up in a home where parents didn't even know the meaning of the word marriage, let alone love. Such an upbringing had made her yearn for love and happiness, a desire that had led to one disastrous relationship and now this, a fake engagement. Would she ever find love? Did it really exist?

'Won't it hurt your mother more when she finds out our relationship is fake?' She walked out onto the terrace, the chill of the afternoon making her shiver. Or was it the coldness coming from the man who'd kissed her so passionately she'd nearly gone up in flames?

'That is a risk I am prepared to take.' He turned to face her, the set of his jaw hard and angular. 'I'd rather she thinks my engagement failed when we go back to our lives than learn the full extent of my father's deceit and treachery.'

'As you wish.'

'It goes without saying that whatever you discover must never become common knowledge, something which you agreed to adhere to in the contract.' He turned to face her, hard lines of worry on his brow. He still didn't trust her, even though she was doing this to clear her name and her father's debts.

'You don't trust me at all, do you?'

'I never trust anyone, Lydia. Trust is like love—an empty word that people pretend to believe in.'

'Do you really believe that?' She couldn't believe the venom of his words.

'I do, but I have no wish to discuss it.' He walked from the room and she knew he meant it; the discussion was over. She only hoped his mother was easier to talk to. The sooner she found out the name his brother might be using, the sooner she could walk away from Raul and his unyielding presence.

By the time they had finished the meal with his mother later that evening, Raul was beginning to think that maybe he could trust Lydia. For the entire evening she'd put on a brilliant show of being his fiancée. She'd acted to perfection the part of a woman who loved him and wanted to be with him for the rest of her life. She'd even convinced his mother that their chance meeting just a short while ago was lovers' fate as she'd excitedly shown her the engagement ring.

'I never thought I would see the day my son fell in love.' His mother's words, said in heavily accented English. Her enthusiasm for their happiness grated on his conscience and guilt nudged at him for the lies he had told her and the lies still yet to come. He'd told Lydia he'd rather his mother think their romance had ended than know the truth, but now, seeing the happiness on her face, he wasn't so sure.

'When is the wedding?' his mother asked as she sipped at her wine.

'Christmas Eve.' Despite Lydia's subtle scrutiny, he managed to say it calmly, but didn't miss the question on his mother's face.

'Why the rush?' For a moment she grappled with her limited English.

He took Lydia's hand and looked into her eyes. 'I met the woman I love. Why wait?'

Lydia held his gaze, blushing prettily and very convincingly, then smiled up at him. A warm smile that lit up her eyes, sending those sparks of lust hurtling through him once more as memories of their kiss in the rain surfaced.

'We want to be married and, as neither of us wants a big fancy affair with lots of guests, Christmas Eve seemed perfect.'

'Then you are not...?' His mother's question died away as he turned his attention to her, pulling Lydia close against him.

'No. Goodness.' Lydia laughed and the relief on his mother's face shocked him. Did she suspect there was more to this engagement than love? Worse still, did she somehow know what his father had done with his will? She might have been a distant figure in his childhood, thanks to his father's influence, but she was still his mother and that counted for something at least. He had no wish to hurt her.

'We want to marry, as soon as possible and with the minimum of fuss.' He spoke first in fast Spanish, to ensure his mother understood, then repeated it in English as he looked at Lydia.

'And we'd like you to be there,' Lydia enthused and Raul inwardly groaned as she got carried away with the role she was acting out. One more bit of deceit to extricate himself from.

'I will be.' His mother smiled then hugged them both in turn. He watched as Lydia hugged her back, recalling the little she'd told him of her childhood. She had painted a very cold picture. Had she missed out on a mother's love?

'There is one other person we'd like at the wedding,' Lydia said softly, almost absently. Her skills for acting were very convincing. He'd have to be wary of that.

'I think I know who that might be.' His mother responded to Lydia but looked at him and he had the strange sensation of being out of control, completely at another person's mercy, something he'd long ago decided never to be again. 'His name is Maximiliano, after his father.'

To hear it confirmed—from his mother—hurt like hell. He had never been the son his father had wanted, even from the moment he'd been born. The honour of being given his father's name had been bestowed on the son he'd truly wanted.

'Do you know where we can find him?' Lydia asked, not taking her attention from his mother once. Could she sense his anger, his growing dislike for a brother he'd never known, the only son his father had wanted?

She shook her head and changed the conversation immediately to something completely different, preferring to indulge in a conversation about village life, and Raul knew the opportunity had passed. He shook his head at Lydia as she looked up at him. He didn't want his mother hounded about this. It obviously made her as angry as it made him.

He'd lost his father and she'd lost her husband. Of course she didn't want to bring her husband's love child into their lives now and she most certainly wouldn't want him at her son's wedding. No, this wasn't the way to find out about his brother.

'We need to go back to the villa,' he said, smiling at his mother, trying to ignore the shocked look on Lydia's face. He would have to find another way of tracing his brother. He was not going to have his mother's life turned upside down just because his father had made one last dig at both of his sons, pitching them against each other.

He guided Lydia towards the door, wanting to leave before something more was said to upset his mother, and was standing beneath the archway, which in summer became covered in bougainvillea, when his mother called to Lydia, who exchanged a glance with him then went back to see her. He waited, not wanting to see the moment when his mother would be duped once more into thinking he and Lydia were in love. A few minutes later, Lydia reappeared, looking as uncomfortable as he felt. At least she had a conscience.

He wanted to ask her what had been said, but decided against it. In a few weeks the fake engagement would be over and whatever it was wouldn't matter any more.

Lydia had clutched her small bag in her lap as Raul had navigated the twisty turns of the road back to his villa, aware that she was now holding the key to her freedom. His mother had pushed an old envelope into her hands and the words she'd spoken in heavily accented English still collided with Lydia's conscience. She should have put the woman at ease and spoken Spanish, but she was still uneasy about doing so after Raul's put-down and she wasn't yet ready to prove to him she was anything other than an empty-headed party girl.

She stood now, looking out over the dark countryside, wondering what exactly was in the envelope and why his mother had kept it from him all along. She'd have to wait until she was alone. The last thing she wanted to do was unleash the secret until she knew what it was and if it would help her find Raul's brother. She had to know if it really did reveal enough to enable her to walk away from Raul, her father's debts cleared. She could still hear his mother's words as she'd thrust the envelope into her hands, struggling to put what she wanted to say into English. Her eyes, as dark as her son's but much softer, had implored Lydia to listen, to hear what she had to say. It was the kind of look that crossed any language barrier.

'I have guarded this secret from my son since the day he was born and now, as the woman he loves, it is your secret to guard—or share.'

'What wise words did my mother give you?' Raul's voice made her jump as he came up behind her. His nearness set off the thudding in her heart and she tried to tell herself it was because of the secret she now held and definitely not because of the man.

'You startled me,' she said as she whirled round to face him, finding herself just that little bit too close. He looked down at her, questions and suspicion brimming in his eyes.

Today she'd seen a very different man from the hard businessman she'd first met in London and her thoughts towards him were changing. Just like her, he had every reason to portray a tough exterior to the world. But knowing this made her vulnerable to him and, worse, made it dangerous being close to a man she was undeniably attracted to. Apart from that kiss last night, she'd kept her distance and her sanity, but now, holding the key to his past and to her freedom, her resistance had slipped a little lower.

'Did she tell you anything more about my brother?' His words were soft and coaxing but fierceness in his eyes betrayed his emotions more clearly than she was certain he would have wanted.

'No, she didn't tell me anything about your brother.' Lydia embellished the truth, not liking having to lie, but until she knew what was in that envelope she couldn't tell him. Partly to protect him but more out of respect for whatever it was that his mother had concealed. She must have had a good reason for doing it, but as soon as Lydia knew she would tell him and then hopefully free herself of this ridiculous contract.

'She must have said something.' His dark eyes narrowed in suspicion and she glanced at her bag as it lay on the table behind him, holding the information about his brother that they both needed to know. For her it was freedom and for him it was nothing but gaining yet more wealth.

'She believes we are in love, Raul,' she said and walked away from him, needing to create some space around her. She needed to think and find a way to hide the ever-increasing attraction that had far more to do with a genuine interest in him than the spark of lust-filled desire he had referred to. 'She just wanted to wish us well and make sure I knew how happy she was that you'd found someone to love.'

His eyes narrowed and he said something under his breath in Spanish. Something she understood.

She thinks I love you?

Lydia ignored the stab of hurt that rushed through her. 'Of course, I didn't enlighten her to the fact that neither of us believes in love at all.'

'This is going to hurt her, when we don't go through with the marriage.' He dragged his fingers through his hair, distracting her for a moment from her misgivings, and she tried to focus her mind as he continued in that sexy accent. 'I didn't want that.'

'Then perhaps you should tell her the truth and ask

outright if she knows just who her husband was seeing, who the mother of his other son is?'

He turned to glare at her. 'My father kept another woman's presence and that of his child from my mother. I do not think she will tell us anything.'

'But she might know something.' Lydia tried to keep the desperation from her voice. She had to find his brother. The alternative was just too much to contemplate.

'No. My father deceived her in the worst possible way—and me.'

'Maybe this clause in his will is his way of making amends.' Lydia clutched at futile straws of hope, trying to smooth the roughened waters they were now on. 'Maybe he's trying to force you together, to accept one another.'

'It is a last chance of having a stab at the son he never really wanted.' Raul's voice became a growl as he tried to keep his anger in check and deep down she knew his pain. She'd been the daughter her mother and father had not wanted and the only child her mother had carried to term. She knew all about not being wanted.

Despite this she knew he was thinking out loud and for a moment she wanted to tell him about the envelope in her bag. Wouldn't he want to know its contents? She almost relented, but if she gave it to him wouldn't that give him all the power once more, when all she wanted to do was get out of the farce of an engagement and back to her life—as a single woman?

'Well, whatever it is, it's a mess I intend to get myself out of.' She spoke forcibly, trying to instil confidence into herself. She had to find a way out of this engagement. She couldn't risk ending up married to such a cold, unemotional man and, if this was it, she wasn't prepared to tell him yet.

'As do I. If you haven't come up with something within the next few days, then we will have to build on our show of an engagement. Start making more definite plans.'

'Won't that give your mother false hope? After all, neither of us plans to go through with this marriage.'

'Right now I would rather she discover that we are not in love and not getting married than discover the true extent of my father's treachery.'

'What is it you have in mind?' she asked suspiciously, not liking the calculated way his mind worked.

'We will be seen out in Madrid next week, but the best opportunity to bring a flourishing affair to the attention of the board will be at a thirtieth wedding anniversary party being given by one of them and, knowing the couple concerned, it will be a lavish affair, attended by the elite of Madrid's society. A chance for you to indulge in your favoured pastime of shopping.'

'I see, so I am to be paraded around like one of your conquests.'

'No. You will be on my arm as my intended bride. A very different thing from a conquest.' There was smugness in his voice. Damn the man. He knew exactly how to get the upper hand.

'As you wish. I will, as always, do my job to the best of my ability.' The haughty words flew from her lips and she glared challengingly at him, daring him to disagree.

'That is all I ask for, Lydia.'

'Is it?' She looked hard at him, trying to forget that all-consuming kiss they'd shared in Madrid, the kiss that, if she hadn't put a stop to it, would have become something they both wanted but couldn't have. There was no place in their so-called engagement for desire or passion. None whatsoever.

He moved towards her, making her heart leap. '*Sí*, Lydia, it is.'

She sidestepped him. 'Then I will say goodnight.'

For a moment she thought he was going to say something else, but instead he just smiled, that soft, seductive smile he'd used in his office just hours before she'd all but begged him to kiss her. 'Goodnight, Lydia.'

Before she could change her mind, she grabbed her purse from the table and went to her room. She closed the door and sat on her bed, taking out the old, yellowed envelope and looking at it for a few moments.

Finally, she opened it, the paper crinkling as she did so. It was in Spanish and she was thankful of her studies. His mother had hired a private investigator and his typewritten reports of Raul's father's whereabouts contained all she needed to track Max down.

She was free. They were free. She should tell Raul.

She walked to the door and was about to open it, but paused. What would he think when she went to look for him after the underlying tension in all he'd said before she'd come to her room? Would he think that she wanted to carry on from their kiss? No, she couldn't risk that, not after the way she had all but begged him to kiss her, to hold her close. A fierce blush rushed over her cheeks as she recalled the way she'd clung to him, pressing her body against his so wantonly.

She couldn't risk a repeat of that kiss. She had to hold on to the fact that she had all she needed to free herself of Raul Valdez and, if she wanted to, blow his controlled world apart.

CHAPTER SIX

THE INFORMATION RAUL'S mother had handed to her had been a shock, but exactly what she needed. For the last five days Lydia had kept it to herself as she'd completed her search. Now she was finally ready to tell Raul, but with the anniversary party only a few hours away she didn't know if it was the right time. She should be elated, overjoyed that the fake engagement they had entered into was not going to end with an alarmingly real two-year marriage, but the thought of coldly delivering all she now knew and walking away didn't feel right.

What was the matter with her? Two weeks ago she would have willingly hurled abuse at the hard and tough exterior that was Raul Valdez. At first, her intention had been to find out where his brother was, then deliver the information coldly. She'd wanted to make him feel as insignificant as he'd made her feel all those years ago when they'd first met. That evening had haunted her ever since, making her squirm with embarrassment each time she recalled it. Despite her desire to make him feel as insignificant, it wasn't what she wanted to do now.

Something had changed. She'd glimpsed briefly beneath that hardness and seen a very different man. The kind of man who warmed her heart and made it skip a beat. The kind of man she found attractive and she was sure that this time he was not as indifferent to her as he had once been. Not if that kiss in the rain was anything to go by.

'It is time to leave.' Raul's firm tone dragged her from her thoughts, making her instantly question if she truly had seen a different man from the powerful and controlled man who stood before her, resplendent in his tuxedo.

He looked devastatingly handsome, pulling her already stretched nerves tighter as she fought to conceal the effect he had on her. The black tuxedo hugged his body, fitting him to perfection and highlighting his strength, and the white of his shirt emphasised the olive tones of his skin. But it was his face that really made her heart flutter. The sultry and very sexy expression in his eyes, the slight curve of a smile on his lips and the raised brows as he slowly took in every detail of her silver dress filled her with excitement.

'We should talk.' She tried to concentrate, to focus on the here and now, but nerves skittered round her. Why did she feel so nervous? It wasn't as if tonight were a real date. She stepped towards him, trying to still the thud of her heart and be herself, but something had changed and that something had happened as she'd kissed him in the rain. Since then everything had been different. She'd been trying to ignore it but as she looked up at him she knew she couldn't any longer—didn't want to.

'Not now.' His incredibly sexy voice filled with control and command, but she had to tell him. She didn't want any more hidden secrets.

'But there are things—'

'Later.' He cut across her appeal. The determination in that word and the hard, feral look he gave her almost silenced her, but he needed to know what she'd found out. She couldn't keep it from him. It wasn't just because it meant they no longer had to continue with the charade of their engagement. It was something else, something much deeper, something she'd never expected to find. She pushed the thought aside. She would be totally out of her depth with this man if she indulged in such notions. Whatever it was between them it was merely lust. A strong sexual attraction. Nothing more.

'No, we must talk, now, before we go to the party.' She hated that she sounded so pleading but, now that she knew for sure the truth about his brother, he had to know. Not that it changed anything for her, but it would definitely change things for Raul.

'Lydia, we are already late. We leave now. After all, we have to convince everyone our engagement is real, do we not?'

'B-but…' she stammered over the word, unable to believe how she'd ever imagined a hidden vulnerable side to him.

'Now, Lydia. I have timed our arrival to maximum effect. Whatever you have to say can wait.'

'Very well, let's go.' She picked up her small silver clutch bag, which matched the glitz of the stunning dress she'd bought that afternoon. She should have been ecstatic to find such a dress and the contact she'd made with the designer for her own boutiques, but the contents of the envelope had been weighing heavily on her mind. They still were.

Raul's silence as they drove through the busy streets

of Madrid to one of the most prestigious hotels was difficult to say the least. He'd made it clear he didn't want to talk of anything, that arriving with maximum impact and creating a couple newly engaged was all he cared about.

Now, as she entered the large room, tables adorned with silver decorations in celebration of the couple's anniversary, Raul changed. He smiled and became very attentive. He placed his hand in the small of her back, partly touching her skin due to the backless design of the dress, and she caught her breath as a frisson of awareness raced up her spine.

She turned to look up at him and the smile of satisfaction that lingered on his lips only heightened that awareness. For the briefest of moments, his dark gaze locked with hers, desire surging through the normal granite hardness.

'A very convincing act, *querida*.' His voice was deep and so very sexy that she couldn't break that eye contact even though she wanted to. 'Now it must be continued as we greet our hosts.'

Raul guided her through the glamorous guests and she was aware of the curious glances cast their way. Either Raul was such a playboy that nobody expected him to settle to marriage or she was very different from the kind of woman he usually had at his side. Whatever it was, she was far from comfortable.

She put on a smile as he introduced her in Spanish to a couple whose love for one another was more than obvious. The tall and elegant woman, named Estela, smiled at her and spoke in Spanish.

'She said you are very beautiful, an English rose.' Raul's voice broke through her thoughts, sounding so very different from the harshness he usually adopted. All part of the show, she reminded herself.

Lydia looked at the woman and replied in Spanish, 'Thank you and congratulations.'

'Your Spanish is excellent,' Estela replied with a smile and a quick glance at Raul, as if she knew what Lydia was doing.

Beside her she could feel the shockwaves coming off Raul. That dinner party, when he'd made her feel so low, so useless, was now being paid back. He said nothing and when she turned to smile at him she knew he was furious.

'You make a very handsome couple,' Estela's husband added, defusing the charged atmosphere slightly as he put his arm around his wife's shoulders and pulled her close. 'Your father knew what he was doing, Raul.'

Lydia's gaze held Raul's, but he was stoically calm, not a trace of emotion of any kind. Just how much did the board know of their arrangement? And if they knew it all, why was there any need to act the part of lovers?

As if sensing her annoyance and her questions, Raul called over a passing waiter and handed a flute of champagne to her, then his hosts and finally took one himself.

'A toast,' he said in Spanish. 'To love. Long may it last.'

Lydia raised her glass towards the couple and joined in the toast, then took a sip of the sparkling liquid, but nearly choked on the bubbles as Raul added one more toast.

'And to the English rose who will very soon be my wife.' He looked at her and the sexy rise of his brows threw a challenge at her, daring her to disagree.

Estela spoke again, her excitement clear. 'I'm looking forward to your wedding, to seeing two people so right for each other joined in marriage.'

Two people so right for each other? Was that really how they looked? How could that be when there were so many secrets between them? So much anger?

Raul was furious. Lydia spoke Spanish—fluently? She'd been living with him for over two weeks and had not uttered a word in his language. What else was she hiding? Her ability to act a part was as good as her ability to conceal the truth.

For the last hour Raul had enjoyed having Lydia close at his side as she portrayed a woman happily engaged to him, leaving nobody in any doubt that, whilst their marriage was one that began in the boardroom of Banco de Torrez, it would definitely be continued in the bedroom.

It went against everything he believed in to admit it, but it had also stirred something within him, something deeper than merely lust or desire for a beautiful woman. It was as if they were drawn together by a connection as yet undiscovered—or was he being irrational, wanting things his childhood had shown to be impossible?

He watched her laugh with other guests, standing back to admire the sexy dress that clung like a sparkling waterfall to her body, making him want to stand beneath the cool water until he drowned. She looked amazing and there wasn't a man in the room who hadn't drunk in her beauty tonight. Her back was slightly turned to him and the daring backless dress gave him a view of soft creamy skin that he wanted to kiss and taste. Hell, he wanted a lot more than just to kiss her.

'When were you going to tell me you spoke Spanish?' he demanded as she turned to him, his annoyance at what she did to him increasing.

'You didn't ask,' she replied, reverting to English with a smile.

'Come.' The word snapped from him as he avoided being drawn in by her and dragged his thoughts back on track and away from what he would do to her if they were alone. From the way her eyes widened in surprise he had startled her with the ferocity of that one word. 'We will dance, show the cream of Madrid's society that we are uniting in marriage for more than financial gain.'

'Lie to them, you mean.' Her words were soft, her delicate accent sweet and her smile seductive, but the spark of anger in her eyes belied all she was trying to portray.

'I want to show them that we are attracted to one another. I do not think that is a lie, *querida*.' He couldn't resist taunting her with that word.

As Raul put his arms around Lydia, pulling her close against his body, a jolt of sizzling awareness sparked through him. Just what was it about this woman that made him react so acutely to her?

Her perfume invaded his senses, the sweet floral fragrance a stark contrast to the untouchable image she created in her clinging silk gown.

'What was it you wanted to tell me earlier? What other secrets have you kept from me?' He recalled her insistence at telling him something and now he was so pleased he'd waited. Whatever it was it would give him something to think of instead of focusing on the way the curves of her body moved against his as they danced. It was exquisite and torturous at the same time. Every move she made increased his awareness of her.

Soon he wouldn't be able to ignore it, wouldn't be able to use conversation to hide what he truly wanted—Lydia.

'I don't think now is the time—or place.' Her eyes, so very green, met his, but he could clearly see her anxiety within them. What was she keeping from him? A trickle of icy unease slipped down his spine.

'I disagree, *querida*.'

She moved against him, chasing away that unease, and if his voice held a note of wavering control, it was much more to do with the woman in his arms than the words she spoke.

She tensed, her gaze firmly fixed on his, the spark of defiance stirring within those green depths. 'Not here, not like this.'

'Like what? Like lovers?' He knew without a doubt that she was fighting the same attraction that was hurtling through him, roughly snuffing out the unease that had dared to surface. Right at this moment, as they stood there among the party guests, the outcome of the evening was almost inevitable, but he couldn't let desire cloud his mind, distract him from what he must do.

'I need to talk to you.'

'Only talk?' he teased, enjoying the blush that swept over her face and the way she continued to dance, as if to mask the growing and very insistent attraction. 'Are you sure about that?'

She frowned, with confusion or annoyance, he wasn't sure. 'I need to talk to you about your brother.'

His brother? Now she had his attention. 'Then talk.'

'As you wish.' She'd adopted that sexy, haughty voice that seemed to beg him to take her in his arms and kiss her, but her chosen topic halted such thoughts—for now.

'Tell me.'

'When we saw your mother, she gave me an envelope as we left.'

Finally, she was going to tell him what that exchange with his mother had been all about. He'd known something had been said, known she was keeping something from him, but he'd blanked it all out, unwilling to deal with the truth, not because he wanted to go ahead with the marriage, but because he wasn't ready to look the past in the eye. Now he couldn't put it off any longer.

'And?'

'And it contained the information I needed to find your brother. Reports from a private investigator she'd hired.'

'She knew all along?' Raul couldn't hold back the shock from his voice.

'Yes, which means your worry of hurting her is unfounded. She was trying to protect you.'

'And have you found him?'

This was what he'd hoped for ever since he'd embarked on the bizarre deal with the delectable Miss Carter-Wilson. It also meant that contract would very soon be ended—as would the need to keep her close. But the past was bearing down on him.

Lydia looked at him and he sensed she was holding something back. Eventually she spoke. 'I have, yes.'

'And he is here in Madrid?'

'I believe he is living in London at the moment.'

'Then we shall go to London.'

'No. You will go to London. There is no need for me to be part of this any more.' She looked at him, her green eyes wide and round with shock.

'*Sí, querida.* Our deal will not be complete until I have met my brother.'

The spark of fury burned in her eyes and those so very kissable lips became a firm angry line.

'That's not very fair. To change the terms of our agreement like that, Raul.'

'Our agreement is to find my brother or get married. Only seeing through one of those options will unlock the funds to clear your father's debt. This is, after all, what it's all about. Your father's debt.'

'You really are quite mercenary, aren't you?'

'Are you only just realising this?' He couldn't keep the amusement from his voice. Her directness was refreshing. Nobody had ever dared to tell him that.

'Unfortunately, yes, and that's a mistake I will now pay for.'

'We will fly to London together and once I have met my brother your part of the deal will be honoured and your father's debts will be cleared.'

'And if your brother has no wish to meet you, to be part of the family business?'

Right now this all seemed too real and Raul couldn't think past the fact that Max had been found.

'Then your father's debts will be called in immediately and at the moment I only know of one other way for you to clear them.'

Lydia glared angrily at him. How could she have felt sorry for him? She'd let her guard down, allowed his charm to defuse her anger and hostility.

'Do you know anything about your brother?' She needed to gain the upper hand, to control the way this was going.

'Only that he shares my father's name.' Raul glowered at her. Had she touched a raw nerve? What would he say when she told him all she'd discovered? And more to the point, how did she tell him?

'But he had not used his surname.'

'So, he has shunned the Valdez name.' Raul's voice sounded firm and full of irritation. 'When exactly was my baby brother born?'

'He isn't your baby brother, Raul.' All the sympathy she'd felt for him as she'd read the contents of the envelope rushed back at her and she looked into his handsome face, watching the colour drain away beneath the olive tones of his skin.

Raul merely looked at her, the shock on his face clear.

'He is older than you, Raul.' She could still feel the pain his mother must have felt, the hard underlining in black pen of Max's birth date giving away so much. 'That is probably why your father set this whole thing up. To ensure you find his heir.'

'How much older?' Shock echoed in Raul's voice.

'Four months.'

She had been so stunned by it all, by the revelations that Raul maybe wasn't the heir to his father's fortune, she hadn't been able to tell him. She'd spent the last few days checking it all out and now she knew for sure that footballer legend turned entrepreneur after a bad car accident, Maximiliano Martinez, was his brother. Two powerful and wealthy men. It was going to be some showdown when they met.

Raul pulled her closer and she gasped, the sudden movement in complete contrast to the anger shining brightly in his eyes, but she moulded herself against him, the attraction she felt too strong to ignore, as was the need to salve his obvious pain.

'What are you doing?' The words flew spontaneously from her when his hand pressed against her lower back, forcing her so close it was almost intimate—too intimate.

'Dancing with you.'

She wanted that more than anything else right now, but deep down she didn't trust herself. The intimate way he held her, the deep, desire-filled look in his eyes lured her and she couldn't allow it to happen even though she wanted it—wanted him.

He lowered his head and whispered in her ear. 'Carlos is watching us closely. I want him to see desire, show them that the deal our fathers struck has not defeated me—or you.'

She looked up at him as her heart thudded. 'Desire?' The word was barely audible as his face came so close to hers that it would be easy to tilt her chin up and kiss him. Just as she had done once before.

'Yes, Lydia, desire. Can you do that? Then we can leave, get away from all this deceit.'

'What about your plans to show we are happily engaged?' Her words were a husky whisper and, despite all her reservations, she knew the same desire that had taken over that night in the rain was pushing her on now, turning her into a different woman.

'Right now I want them to think we are so consumed by one another that we have to leave.'

Her heart went out to him. He needed to leave in order to deal with all she'd just told him. How did it feel to discover you were not your father's firstborn as you'd always believed? No wonder his father had attached such a bizarre condition to the will. He wanted his firstborn to inherit equally and had done everything in his power to ensure it happened.

Consumed by desire and sympathy, she reached up, placed her palm against his face, feeling the new growth of stubble. Her gaze became riveted to his, seeing the passion building with them. Compassion fused with passion and her attention moved to his lips, remembering the electric kiss in the rain. Had it been the sudden downpour that had made that kiss so intense, so memorable? Or the man himself?

As the questions raced through her mind and the desire to lean closer grew ever stronger, she tried to fight it. Raul didn't. With a fierce intensity his lips claimed hers, sending her mind reeling and her heart thumping and the power of that contact shot through her entire body, unlocking an unbearable need deep within her.

Silently she gave thanks that they were in the middle of a dance floor, that all around them people could surely see the fire that had sparked to life. But she wanted more and to her horror she wished they weren't at the party, wished that they were alone and able to follow the heady trail of passion to its ultimate conclusion.

Raul pulled back from her, his eyes darker than she'd ever seen them. 'I'm taking you home. Right now—and then I'm going to make love to you.'

No. That was the word she wanted to say, the word she should say, but for a moment it wouldn't come and when it did it was a breathy whisper. 'No, we can't. That's not part of the deal.'

'To hell with the deal.'

'Raul,' she pleaded even though inside her body clamoured with excitement and need for this man.

He brushed his lips so lightly over hers she almost
sighed with pleasure. 'Tonight you will be mine, Lydia.'

She had to remember what this was all about, but did
the deal really matter any more? Hadn't she done her
part? She'd found his brother, her dues were paid, her
father's debt now clear. So where did that leave her now?

Could she walk away from this moment, this man?
He'd got to her, entered her mind, her thoughts, her
very soul and, even though she knew she shouldn't, she
wanted him, wanted to be his, to feel the passion and
desire so completely.

Her heart was leading her head, her desire for him
all-consuming. 'Take me home, Raul.'

CHAPTER SEVEN

LYDIA'S HEART THUMPED and her body hummed with anticipation as Raul's car stopped outside his apartment. There was no mistaking the intent in Raul's eyes, just as she couldn't deny the need within her. A need that had boiled up rapidly, blending together with the shock that she'd been so bold, creating an intoxicating cocktail that couldn't be denied—by either of them. It was strong and powerful. The kind of attraction that, if she was honest, had sealed her fate the day they had first met.

His eyes said all that needed to be said as he got out of the car, took her hand and she stepped out into the crisp evening air. In one hungry sweep his gaze devoured her, ratcheting up the tension, the anticipation, smothering the nerves and apprehension over what she was about to do, making her want him, want this night more than ever.

He still held her hand, the heat of his touch scorching her, and without a word he led her into the building, calling the elevator. Was he still angry at what she'd told him about Max? Or was it her use of Spanish? Had he put everything but what they were about to do from his mind? Was he so focused on desire that he thought of nothing else? Could she really affect him like that?

'Raul?' His name slipped out as a question, her eyes searching his firmly set profile as the elevator took them up to his apartment. The tension in the confines of the mirrored walls all but exploded as his gaze met hers, the unconcealed desire in his eyes echoing around her from the reflective surfaces.

Hungry need met innocent desire, becoming something else, something she couldn't deny even if she wanted to. There would be no turning back now. This strong, powerful man was what she needed, even if it was for one night only.

'You have found Max so are no longer bound by our agreement.' The sharpness of his words was in total contrast to the desire burning in his eyes, making the dark depths unreadable.

'I'm not?'

'You have done what you promised, Lydia. You are free to go back to London.' There was a hint of warning in his voice, warning she had no intention of heeding.

'And if I don't want to?' Her heart went into free fall at her boldness, the likes of which she'd never known before. How could one man change her so much? 'Not yet anyway.'

She couldn't believe how shameless she sounded and knew it came from something much deeper than just passion. All she wanted now was to stay, to discover more with this man even though she'd constantly fought him and the attraction that had leapt to life between them. But why, when such an action went against everything she believed in? When he'd been the man who'd humiliated her as a sixteen-year-old?

Because you've seen beneath the tough exterior, seen who he really is.

He stopped abruptly and looked at her, the intensity in his eyes so wild, so very daring she could scarcely breathe as the elevator doors opened onto the opulent space of his apartment. 'You should only walk through these doors with me if you want me to kiss you.'

'I want that.' She searched his face, looking for the man she had glimpsed, the man who hid behind the toughened exterior of billionaire businessman Raul Valdez. 'I want you to kiss me, Raul, like you did the other night—in the rain.'

He reached out to her, his thumb and finger lifting her chin a fraction, the heat of his touch almost too much as she swallowed back the nerves that threatened once more. Just as she thought she couldn't look into his eyes any longer he moved closer, his lips so very close she could feel his breath, warm on her face.

'If I kiss you again, Lydia, it will become far more than that. I don't want a shy innocent in my bed. I want the passionate woman I know you are, the one you have kept hidden from me.'

Did he really think that of her? She drew in a breath as a rush of panic skittered over her. She might not be a virgin, but she was still innocent to the ways of a man like Raul. She had only known one other man, her ex-fiancé.

'I want to be that woman again, but this time I want more than a kiss. Much more.' She blushed at the thought, trying to put aside his obvious dislike for a woman who had very little experience of sex. She would have to continue the act of confidence and sophistication if she wanted to experience a night with this man—and she did. 'Tonight is for us, Raul.'

In answer he brushed his lips provocatively over

hers, sending a rush of heady desire round her until it unlocked the passion she'd been fighting since that first meeting in London.

Desperate to hide her inexperience, she pressed herself against his body, the answering groan as he deepened the kiss setting light to her desire again. With her hands behind his neck, her fingers in the dark hair at his collar, she pulled him to her, her tongue slipping boldly into his mouth, teasing in a way she'd had no idea she knew how to do. Raul Valdez had turned her into a very different woman.

With a swiftness that had her gasping in shock, he pulled away from her and, taking her hand in his, strode purposefully to his apartment, unaware she struggled to keep up in the heels she'd teamed with her dress.

He pushed open the door and, with a wild look in his eyes, pulled her towards him, slamming the door shut as he did so. Before she could blink, his lean hard body pressed her against the door and any doubt she had that he wanted her no longer existed. The fire of need leapt to life as he pressed himself intimately against her.

What are you doing?

The sane and sensible Lydia surfaced once more and she looked into his brooding eyes, the feral darkness almost intimidating. She pressed her palm against his chest, exerting pressure, but he didn't yield. Instead his lips came down on hers with such force her knees buckled and only the solid door and his firm body kept her upright. It was a plundering and ruthless kiss, one that swiped the sensible Lydia out of the room, and as his hands slid up her waist to her breast she knew that version of herself wouldn't come back tonight—and she didn't want her to.

* * *

Raul's hand cupped her breast and the fire of need within him raged ever higher. He must be going mad. To want a woman so much, but now it was too late. Part of him had wanted her to stop him, to act the high and mighty woman he'd first met in London and coldly rebuff him. The innocent girl she'd been all those years ago when they'd first met had been replaced by a sassy and very sexy woman. One who made it clear she wanted him as much as he wanted her.

She'd encouraged him, drawn him deeper into this madness when they had arrived at his apartment, the change in her, the lack of resistance all too clear. Was it because she now knew she was free of him, that the threat of marriage, which had at first seemed the only way to clear her father's debts, was now over?

Whatever it was, he was incapable of rational thought at this moment and he intended to take all she offered— and more. He intended to lose himself in passion, to drown in desire, because right now it was the only way to block out the hurt that had been lurking in the shadows of his life for as long as he could remember. Hurt he had no control over, but passion he did.

'This has to go.' His words were as feral as his desire and he pulled at the strap of her dress, but it didn't yield.

'So impatient.' Lydia's husky voice, full of flirtation, threatened to push him over the edge. She wriggled against him as she tried to reach behind her and unfasten the dress.

'Allow me.' He fought to calm his wayward body as he stepped back from her, placed his hands on her arms and gently began to turn her.

Her gaze met his for a split second before she willingly turned her back to him. He looked at the creamy soft skin, the sexy shape of her spine, and cursed the thin strap across her shoulder blades that had held the dress in place. Perhaps it was just as well the dress hadn't been discarded in an instant because now he had a tighter rein on the desire she ignited within him. He watched as she breathed in, deeply and evenly, then slowly he unclipped the thin silver strap.

'There's another at my waist.' Her voice was a husky whisper. She didn't move but the sexual chemistry between them was building, getting stronger with each breath she took. The air around them so charged with fire and passion that if he struck a match they'd go up in flames.

He didn't say a word as he traced his fingers down her spine, smiling with satisfaction when she arched slightly beneath his light touch. She lowered her head forwards, her hair slipping away from her neck, and all he could think about was trailing his lips against the soft skin there and down her back.

Instead he focused his attention on unfastening the dress, which had clung to her slender hips, sparkling invitingly all evening, daring him to want her. Slowly he slid his hands up her bare back, pushing his fingers beneath the straps at her shoulders, then as if in slow motion he watched the straps slide down her arms where they stopped in the bends of her elbows, preventing him from seeing her gloriously naked.

With a stab of shock, he realised she stood with her palms flat against the door of his apartment, her head lowered, her breathing deep and rapid with desire. When had he ever wanted a woman so much he hadn't been able to get further than the front door? Never. He hadn't ever wanted to claim a woman as his with the urgency that flooded him now. What was so different about this woman?

He should lead her to the bedroom before they went any further, but even as the thought flitted through his mind he dismissed it. Before he could stop himself he had moved closer to her, his hands going inside the heavy sequined material that hung loosely from her. He slipped his arms around her waist, pulling her against him and smoothing his palms over her stomach, then her ribs and then up to her breasts. The scent of her perfume, seductive rose and jasmine, only served to notch up the tension even further, heightening his need for her.

He kissed her neck and she sighed softly, but as his fingers teased her nipples the sound became distinctly more untamed. 'We should take this to the bedroom, should we not, *querida*?'

He could feel every deep and erratic breath she took as his hands caressed her breasts. Still her hands were pressed flat against his door, but the whole sensation was so different, so erotic, he could stay like this, enjoying the mounting desire, for far longer than if she were now completely naked on his bed.

'Yes.' That one word was so loaded with sexual tension he nearly groaned aloud, then she looked back at him, her green eyes so dark they resembled the depths of the forest, hidden from the sun. 'We should.'

She turned to him; the dress that had been so seductively tight over her breasts now lingered alluringly on her arms, tempting him, and he bit down on the wild desire to all but rip the silver fabric from her.

'This way, *querida*.' He held out his hand to her, giv-

ing her one last chance to back away, one last chance
to stop the madness of the desire that was flowing like
a raging river between them.

She didn't falter as she took his hand, and as they
walked towards his bedroom her heels tapped on the
hard floor. Each step she took was firm and decisive.
She wanted this as much as he did.

The urge to rush, to take her swiftly and make her
his had subsided, in its place a need to be calm, gentle.
That way he could lose himself in desire, forget the
world beyond whilst he savoured every moment of the
night with Lydia, determined to wipe out all she meant,
all she was connected to. He wanted to forget who she
really was for one night. Somewhere in the recesses
of his mind he knew she was different, knew this was
a glimpse of the kind of life, the sort of love he could
have had if his past hadn't shaped him into a hard and
emotionless man.

This was the kind of woman a man could love, the
kind of woman *he* could love if he allowed himself to.
But that would never happen. Love was a weakness and
he would never be weak.

Lydia stood in his room, the large opulent bed dominating the space, competing with the man whose hand she
had taken willingly as she'd walked with him towards
this moment. She should have turned and run, as far as
she could, when he'd given her the chance—and he'd
given enough of them. She hadn't because she wanted
this too much, wanted him, wanted this one night.

'Turn around.' The firmness of his voice was tem-
pered by the husky desire lingering in it. She did as
she was told for no other reason than she wanted to.

She wanted to go back to the moment of minutes ago when she could feel his touch, his breath warm on her neck as he'd kissed her, his body, firm and hard against hers; she wanted to believe this was something special, something more than the one night it so obviously was.

She shuddered as he placed his hands on her shoulders, sliding down her arms and taking the dress with them. The air was cool on her naked breasts as the dress slithered down over her hips and to the floor. Then, just as he had done before, his fingers trailed fire down her spine, pausing to make circles of pleasure on her skin as they reached the thin straps of her thong.

'Very sexy.' A feral depth had entered his voice and she couldn't help but smile. He certainly knew how to make a woman feel attractive and desired. Something she definitely wasn't used to.

Emboldened by the heady desire that coursed through her, she turned, scarcely giving a thought to the dress at her feet. All she wanted was to meet his passion, to lose herself in the moment.

She reached out to tug at his bow tie, pulling it slowly whilst looking directly into his eyes. 'I'm feeling a little underdressed at the moment.'

His brows rose in amusement, but his voice had become a hoarse whisper. 'I disagree, *querida*. Stilettos and those sexy panties are perfect.'

She let his tie drop against his white shirt as she moved closer, his arms pulling her against him, the soft fabric of his jacket brushing against her bare breasts. Just when she thought she couldn't stand it any longer he lowered his head; slowly and very seductively he brushed his lips over hers. Her arms wound around his neck as a soft sigh of pleasure slipped from her, only to be stolen by his lips as he deepened the kiss, giving into the fierce need that enveloped them.

With purpose he moved against her, pushing her back towards the big bed, but as her legs met it her knees buckled and she tumbled back, bringing him with her. His weight pressed her into the soft covers, the hardness of his arousal pressing insistently against her thighs, sending her desire to new heights.

'I want you, Raul.'

He looked down at her, his eyes so dark it was like looking at the velvety midnight sky and so easy to brush aside what this really was, so easy to fool herself into believing it was so much more.

He levered himself off her, looking so sexy, so handsome she wondered if she was dreaming, but the huskiness of his voice left her in no doubt that this was real.

'Nothing would give me more pleasure.' He smiled, a lazy and intoxicating smile, as he shrugged off his jacket, opened his shirt, button by button in such a teasing way she bit down hard on her lower lip as the anticipation of being his, being made love to by this virile specimen of masculinity, rushed over her.

Each breath she took as she watched him until he was completely naked was harder than the next. Her heart pounded wildly as he crossed the room with little regard for the fact that he was proudly erect. She watched as, with a hint of a smile, he opened a drawer next to the bed and took out the all-important contraception, placing the packet next to the lamp.

'For our protection, *querida*.'

How had she not even questioned that? Had he blinded her so much with desire that she'd given no thought to such necessities? She blushed as his smile widened then he moved back onto the bed, covering her completely, and the heat of his erection, with only the barrier of her skimpy panties, as it pressed against her made her gasp with pleasure.

It had never felt like this before.

'Tonight you are mine.' Raul's whispered words as he kissed her neck, his hands expertly making her body burn with fiery need, made anything else but the ultimate conclusion impossible.

His fingers hooked into the strings of her panties and she gasped as he pulled. The sound of ripping stitches as erotic as the expression on his handsome face.

'Don't forget the condom.' Her words held a hint of panic that she hoped he wouldn't notice. Now was not the time to enlighten him to the fact that she was far from experienced in the art of lovemaking, so much so she hadn't given a thought to contraception as desire had whisked her away.

He kissed her lips then looked down at her. 'Patience, *querida*. Patience.'

Then before she could say anything else his hand slid from her hip to the heated centre of her desire and she raised herself up as his touch brought a sensation she'd never known washing over her. As the torment continued she was aware of him speaking, aware of the Spanish words, but had no idea what he was saying, only that it increased the desire to dizzying heights.

In one swift move he rolled away from her, leaving her trembling in the wake of the pleasure that had just happened. She opened her eyes and looked at him. Would he have known that was the first time she'd ever known such pleasure?

He looked at her as he opened the packet, the intensity in his eyes making them so very dark. With a suggestive raise of his brows he rolled on the condom, then before she even had time to blush his body was overs her, his long lean legs pushing hers apart. Without any encouragement other than the constant hum of desire within her, she lifted her legs, wrapping them around him, lifting herself up to his possession.

With wild words in Spanish, so guttural she couldn't make them out, he thrust into her, making her gasp and press her fingernails into his back. The erratic thumping of desire exploded wildly inside her as she moved with him, taking him deeper as he claimed her, harder and faster. It was explosive, wild, but completely wonderful.

'I never thought…' she gasped as she clung to him, the waves of passion crashing harder and faster over her, making her thoughts as disjointed as her words '… it could be like this…'

He silenced her with kisses as they moved together until the world splintered and she floated above the earth, barely conscious of his wild desire-induced growl.

'Don't think,' Raul said between deep and hard breaths. 'Tonight I will not allow you to think, not when such passion, such fiery desire still hums between us.'

'It does?' Her voice trembled as he slid away from her, her body cooling, and she was able to focus once more.

His lips hovered over hers, his breath hot as he teased her. She closed her eyes, wanting his kiss and so much more. When it came the kiss was hard and demanding but he pulled back enough to look at her and she opened her eyes, trying to hide the need, the disappointment that it was over.

'It does, *querida*, and we have the whole night ahead of us.'

'All night,' she replied in Spanish, kissing him and allowing all her hungry desire to show.

CHAPTER EIGHT

THE WHISPERS OF a new day had begun to slip into the room as Lydia opened her eyes, acutely aware of the warmth of Raul's body against hers. It also confirmed to her questioning mind that last night had really happened. The exquisite passion hadn't been the dreams of a woman falling harder and harder for a man who'd coldly told her love was for fools.

Last night had been very real, deepening her feelings to newer levels, but now what should she do? Should she slip from the bed and return to her room? Slowly she moved, pushing aside the covers very carefully. She looked at Raul's watch, lying on the bedside table after it had been discarded last night. It was still early and as she watched the seconds ticking away the thump of her heart became louder.

'You are not going anywhere, *querida.*' Raul's voice, heavy with sleep, instantly stilled her then his arm wrapped around her waist, pulling her naked body back into bed and against his. He might still be in the clutches of sleep, but he wanted her, she was in no doubt of that.

'Now that is such a tempting idea.' She turned in his arms, trying to fight the rising desire in her, wanting to sound carefree and flirtatious, as if this were a situation she was used to. Last night she'd wanted him to think she was an experienced lover and now she wanted him to think she knew exactly how it went—the etiquette of waking up beside a man who had been your lover for one night only.

'The night isn't over yet.' His husky voice sent a tingle all over her as his hands slid down her body to her hips, where his fingers lightly circled on her skin, teasing her until she knew she wasn't going to be able to resist him.

She laughed brightly, fighting the urge to give into the heady desire now burning brightly within her once more. 'It's almost morning.'

'Don't tease me with your sexy body.' The Spanish words were soft and seductive as he brushed his lips against hers and she closed her eyes, imagining the kiss was because he loved her, because they were something more than one-night lovers.

She pushed against his chest with her palms, ignoring the firm muscle beneath her fingers, the soft hair she just wanted to run her hands through. Inwardly she groaned with a mixture of despair and longing, outwardly she laughed again.

'I am not a tease, Raul Valdez.' Her voice was so light, so playful it didn't even sound like her.

'You are,' he began as his hand moved up her waist to cover the firmness of her breast, making her drag in a deep breath as passion exploded inside her. 'And very sexy.'

'Sexy?' she questioned coyly, not able to believe she was being so flirtatious. Was it because she didn't want the night to end, didn't want the daylight to bring the harsh reality of having become just another one of his conquests?

He pulled her closer, his intentions emblazoned in the black depths of his eyes. Her heart raced as she surrendered to his kiss, to his caress. She wanted this so much—wanted him. She put her heart and soul into the kiss, allowing it to convey all the emotions she could never tell him.

'*Sí, querida.* Very sexy.' He whispered the words against her lips, the sensation wildly erotic. 'And now I can't let you go.'

'Is that so?' She moved daringly against him, enjoying the momentary rush of power, but not for one minute did she believe she was truly in control. That kind of mistake could be fatal with a man like Raul Valdez.

In a movement so swift she gasped, Raul pushed her back against the softness of the pillow, the weight of his naked body preventing her escape. Laughter glittered in his eyes as he looked into hers and she wanted to hang on to this moment for ever, to remember how it felt to be loved by him and to love him in return.

'You are not going anywhere, not until I have made love to you again and again.' His voice had become deep and husky, adding to the fire of desire that was rapidly burning out of control within her.

'But it's nearly morning.'

'Then we shall have all day, no, all weekend together.'

'All weekend?' Now she was shocked. Was he saying it as some kind of test for her? After all, hadn't she insisted on being his for just one night?

'Yes. One weekend of passion and I don't intend to waste a moment more of it.'

Before she could respond, offer up any kind of defence, his lips were claiming hers in a hot kiss, the heat of his body coaxing hers into submission and she knew she couldn't fight it any longer.

It had been hard to leave Lydia in bed, but as the mid-morning winter sunshine streamed into his apartment Raul had done just that. Their lovemaking had been powerful and passionate, but as Lydia had slept his thoughts had wandered. Now she was sitting opposite him as they had breakfast, the air of aloofness she often hid behind threatening to return. But he wasn't ready to end it yet.

'I thought you wanted to go to London today.' Lydia's voice held a note of uncertainty and he downed a black coffee in one go, needing the hit of caffeine to calm him. After last night's revelations—all of them—there was no way he was going to step out of this erotic interlude and into his future. For now, that could all wait. He still wanted Lydia with a burning need that made him want to drag her straight back to bed and it was the perfect defence against acknowledging the truth.

Was it her obvious innocence last night, before she'd become a bold and flirtatious lover, or a way of punishing her for being the one who'd changed his life? He didn't know. Either way, he wanted her. He wasn't about to turn his back on such an alluring companion. Not yet. She would be his for the weekend. On Monday he would return to reality and fly to London to meet his brother. Once he'd done that, Lydia would be free—he would be free. Their lives could return to normal.

Except that his never would. His would change beyond recognition. He had a brother. One he wanted to know, and it had nothing to do with money as Lydia had accused him of.

He and his brother shared the misfortune of having the same father. Didn't that count for something? He frowned as he thought of Carlos's insistence that he marry instead of looking for Max. Was that really to ensure Lydia's father didn't get away without repaying his debt or was Carlos reluctant to have two Valdez sons at the helm of the company? Was it possible there was something else going on?

'Would you rather I walked out so soon after last night?' He dragged his mind back to the present and glared at Lydia, unable to keep the annoyance from his voice that she could so easily move on from all they'd shared last night.

'But last night, you said you would be going today.'

'That was before our lovers' tryst.' He watched the glow of a blush rush over her cheeks and, even though anger was the best emotion to deal with what was to come, he smiled. 'I am not in the habit of making love to a woman and then running off into the night. We will spend the weekend together. Like lovers. Then we will go to London on Monday.'

'You want me to come with you?' She sat opposite him, her silk dressing gown doing little to hide the fact that beneath it she was naked, and he gritted his teeth against the sudden stab of lust that shot through him.

Slowly he put down his cup, then stood up and put out his hand to her. With a guarded expression in her eyes she took his hand and he pulled her to her feet, then with his free hand tugged at the belt tied loosely at her waist. The cream silk slipped apart, exposing her to his hungry gaze.

'I want nothing more than to make love to you again and again. This weekend is for us. The future can damn well wait.'

He shoved aside the agony of having that cruel confirmation that his father had never really wanted him, never really cared for him in any way. Now he knew why he'd had to put up with such a harsh upbringing, why anything he'd done had never pleased his father.

His father had never wanted him. He hadn't been the much-sought-after son and heir. That honour had fallen to Max, the son who'd taken his name, the name he should have had, just months before he'd been born. How could he ever have competed with that? Did he want to? The question lingered in his mind.

And this woman had known that cruel fact since they'd visited his mother and had kept it from him. He bit down on the anger and allowed desire to flow through him. He needed it to forget the pain. Passion and desire made very good salves for such wounds.

'We should go out, take a walk in the park or something.' There was hesitancy in her voice, which only increased his suspicion that she was far from the experienced lover she wanted him to believe her to be. Even her teasing this morning hadn't completely disguised the fact. He'd seen something in her eyes, something deep and meaningful.

Very well. He would play the part of lover and forget the real world that awaited him.

'We can.' He pulled her closer, feeling the heat of her body scorch his. 'After I've explored your sexy body, kissed every part of it and made you cry out my name as you did early this morning.'

She blushed prettily and he kissed her, tempting her,

feeling her resistance subsiding. Whatever else happened, she was his for now. But it couldn't last. He'd never wanted sentiments and emotions in his life and, despite the new and powerful draw to her, Lydia wasn't going to change that.

Lydia lay languidly in bed as darkness fell over Madrid, the apartment becoming the romantic place it had been last night, lit with only a few lamps. They had left the apartment to stroll around the cafés and bars in Madrid's plaza. But the undercurrent of sexual attraction meant that neither of them had had much appetite for food. As the winter sun had given way to the night, they'd returned to the warmth of the apartment and Lydia was hardly able to believe they were still in a lovers' limbo. She should be happy, should just enjoy it for what it was, but foolishly she wanted more—and knew it was impossible.

She'd never known such pleasure existed. Raul had shown her that lovemaking was something wonderful but she knew it wasn't lovemaking to him. It was merely lust—overwhelming desire and passion.

The sound of Raul in the shower dragged her from dwelling too much on what could never be. For Raul she knew this whole weekend was based on desire and lust. It was more than lust for her. Could it be possible that she'd fallen for him—really fallen for him? Or was it that she still felt sorry for him, still felt the pain and vulnerability she'd seen in his eyes when she'd told him about Max? As he'd looked at her, the party going on around them, all she'd wanted was to ease that pain, to be the one to make things right for him.

This morning his lovemaking had been wild and

hard, the gentle dominance of last night had turned to something more determined and Lydia had found it as exciting as their first passionate encounter. Finally, that anger had dissipated and the man who'd driven her mad with desire, making her throw caution aside and be his for the night, had returned.

She'd been bold, flirtatiously asking for more than sex, asking for something that resembled a real relationship, even though it would be only for two days. To her astonishment he had agreed and she had enjoyed his company over lunch. Had he enjoyed the day as much as her? Had he liked being a couple? And what happened now?

'Should we go out this evening?' She slipped from the bed and pulled on the silk dressing gown as he returned from the shower, a white towel around his hips, his hair dark with wetness. She couldn't take her eyes from him, he looked so sexy, so handsome.

'I think our absence from this evening's party will say so much more than our attendance.' The deep sultry tone of her voice made smiling coyly at him the only option, but deep down the worry still lingered that he was using her to prove something, to further his dealings with his board.

'What did you have planned, then?' She couldn't believe she, of all people, was being so teasing and behaving like a seductress.

'Other than to make love to the most beautiful English rose?' He moved towards her and she shivered in anticipation.

'Yes, other than that.' With a flaunting smile she stepped past him. 'I'd like to talk a little, get to know you better.'

He tensed, the muscles of his chest flexing, proving if nothing else that this weekend was only about sex. She turned her attention to knotting the belt in her dressing gown, desperate to hide her disappointment from him and, even more importantly, not question it herself.

'Very well. We shall eat here and talk over a glass of wine.'

She frowned at him, wondering what it was he had planned now, because if there was one thing she'd learnt about him it was that he always had plans. Whatever those plans were she was determined to drive the conversation the way she wanted, to find out just what the future held for her and her family. Was she really clear of debt? The one question she wouldn't ask was what the future held for them—as a couple.

'What are you going to do—about Max?' The question slipped from her as she lay in bed, casually trailing a finger across the fine cotton sheets.

He looked at her as he tossed aside the towel and put his clothes on, the blue shirt only highlighting the jet black of his hair. He was avoiding answering her. Was he hoping he could rid himself of Max in the same way he intended to rid himself of her?

He stood tall and proud, defiance coming off him in waves, and she knew without any doubt that it was most certainly not what he wanted. 'I will welcome Max into my life and the family business.'

'Because of loyalty to your father?' She pulled the sheet against her. Such a discussion needed modesty.

'No.' He finished dressing and looked at her, his gaze sweeping over her, and her skin burned as if she were completely naked to his gaze. There was desire in his eyes, but also something else, something unfathomable, something very cold. 'Out of necessity.'

The barb of his statement hit her hard and although it was powerful it at least confirmed that she and the man she'd become temporarily engaged to would soon go their separate ways. It was exactly the deal she'd made with herself as she'd given in to the temptation of desire and had truly become his lover.

'The lesser of two evils?' She taunted him, needing to counteract the pain she felt. Pain that came from feeling deeply for this man—far too deeply. 'Either welcome a brother or a wife.'

'*Sí, querida.* To prove I am not the heartless man my father assumed I was. He thought I'd find marriage preferable to bringing my brother into my life.'

Was he running from the truth now as she was? And what was his truth? With a heavy heart she knew it would not be that he had fallen in love with her, that he wanted more than this passionate weekend. She realised she was decidedly underdressed and vulnerability shivered over her as once again his gaze lingered on her.

'So I am free to go?' She dared to ask, dared to bring their lovers' weekend crashing down around her.

His brows rose and he crossed the room towards her, his height dominating the entire room, and even though she was covered only in a sheet she looked defiantly back at him. He sat on the bed next to her, reached out and stroked the backs of his fingers across her cheek in a moment so tender, so out of place, she had to blink back the urge to cry.

'But you don't want to go now, do you, *querida*? Not when the passion still burns so hotly between us.

You want to stay, to sleep in my bed and be the woman I desire.'

His seductive words stoked the slumbering fire of desire to life once more and she knew she was lost, that whatever she'd promised herself about not falling for him, she would never be able to keep it.

'What I want is for you to come back to bed,' she teased as she smiled up at him.

He moved towards her, his kiss so light, so very loving she could almost believe it was real. 'How can I resist such a seductress?'

CHAPTER NINE

THE PASSION THAT had ignited between them as they'd danced at the party two nights ago still flowed through Raul. A concept he was far from familiar with and, even though he wanted Lydia, he'd suggested they take a walk, as most people in Madrid did on a Sunday afternoon. She looked as if she belonged here, strolling with the locals, her long legs encased in white jeans and boots, the collar of her black faux suede jacket fanning out her hair around her. He had to do something to cool things down.

Tomorrow he would be stepping out of this strangeness he'd fallen into and back into his real life. He'd be in London to meet his brother. A thought that brought happiness and annoyance in equal measures.

'Have you spoken to your father?' he asked and her step faltered beside him as they entered Retiro Park; the trees bare of leaves but bathed in the winter sun, it still looked inviting. He'd spent many hours here, first as a young boy and then a man. Sometimes he'd had the company of a woman, but it had never been to avoid the lure of taking one to his bed yet again.

'No. That is a conversation for another day. What about you? Have you said anything to your mother yet?'

He glanced at her as she successfully turned the tables on him and a spark of admiration shot through him. Lydia was more than a match for him. He liked that. Not that it changed a thing. Tomorrow it would end. It was what they'd planned—what they wanted.

'I think it will be better to tell her when I have met my brother, seen what kind of man he is. I insist on protecting her from this as much as possible.' As he spoke she took his arm and moved closer to him and to the outside world they looked no different from any other couple in love strolling through the park.

It wasn't what he wanted. Love and other such ill-fated emotions weakened even the strongest man and, combined with the desire he had for Lydia, Raul sensed that it would be all-consuming—and lethal. No, it was not something he wanted or needed in his life.

'I admire that in you.' She spoke softly and he looked down at her, to see she was watching him. The distance he was hoping to create between them slipped away as she smiled, openly and honestly. Hell, he wanted to kiss her.

A fierce fire leapt to life within him, filling his whole body with something he didn't want, something he couldn't deal with. He'd known desire before, many times, but never like this. Could it be he'd crossed the boundary and was straying into a place he had no intention of being?

He focused his mind on the conversation, ignoring the undertones of something much more devastating. 'That I care for my mother? The woman who raised me, protecting me from the true knowledge of my father's secret life?'

Saying it aloud to Lydia brought it all home to him.

How much his mother must have suffered because of the man she'd married, not out of love, but out of duty and honour to her family.

He saw it all differently. He could hear again Lydia proudly telling him she had no intention of marrying him. All it did was back up the relief that she'd fulfilled her part of the deal and had found Max, unlocking the funds to clear the debt, funds that he strongly suspected his father had thought would never be unlocked.

'But that is not wrong, Raul.' She looked at him, a strange and powerful expression in her lovely green eyes. If he didn't know how fiercely she opposed the idea of marriage and how she agreed on his philosophy of love, he could be fooled into thinking she was in love. With him.

'Wrong or not, it is not up for discussion.' He held her gaze for a second longer, then turned to walk on. They were drawing attention, he realised. 'Let us walk.'

She fell quickly into step beside him, her black boots making a gentle sound on the path, and feeling her body against his as they walked felt so right, so natural. For the briefest of moments, he wondered why he didn't want this closeness, this total commitment.

Because it will never last and pain will follow it.

He could still clearly remember just what such pain had done to his mother when she'd discovered his father had led a secret life. It was the kind of pain that went hand in hand with that elusive emotion love and it had convinced him that, despite all his mother had claimed about their marriage being arranged, she'd loved his father.

He would never be that weak. He would never open himself up to such pain.

'The park is beautiful at this time of the year, is it not?' He diverted his thoughts and the topic of conversation onto more neutral territory.

'It is, even when it is so cold.' She snuggled against him. Was she cold or getting too comfortable? 'It's lovely, thanks.'

'A nice way to end our weekend, no?' He felt her glance up at him, but he kept his attention firmly ahead. Was it possible she was reading more into this moment?

'Yes,' she said and walked on, looking anywhere but at him, convincing him he must have been mistaken. At least she agreed and there wouldn't be any drama when they returned to their lives. This would be just a weekend affair.

Lydia breathed in the cold air, relishing the gentle breeze on her face as she walked, her arm linked in Raul's, through Retiro Park. The soft luxury of his camel cashmere coat was warm and inviting, but not nearly as much as Raul. The wind was cold, but it focused her thoughts, stopped her from believing this affair would ever be anything more than just a weekend. One that was almost over. It had been a magical interlude, which had shown her what loving a man could be like, even though she knew this man would never allow anyone close enough to love him or to love himself.

'We will go to London tomorrow.' As if he'd sensed her thoughts, taken lead from them, Raul said the words that spelt the end of whatever it was that had happened between them since the night of the party.

'So this is goodbye?' She kept walking, looking ahead of her down the long tree-lined path, noticing the red squirrels that cheekily followed them from tree to tree in the hope of treats. Normally she would have remarked upon it, taken pleasure in such a moment, but not today—not now. She wanted to be as detached as he was, her words as emotionless and empty and, whilst she was happy that she'd achieved that, inside she was breaking apart.

'*Si, querida.*' His Spanish accent was deeper than ever and the use of the now all too familiar term of endearment no longer irritated. She glanced up at him, his profile strong and unyielding. 'It is time to return to our lives.'

She should be elated. Her father's debts were to be cleared without the need to enter into a marriage more in keeping with the kind of historical novels she'd loved as a teenager. Tomorrow she would return to London and she and Raul would never have to see one another again. So why did that feel so difficult? As foolish as it was, she had fallen in love with a man who was as cold and incapable of love as his father had evidently been.

'I will of course require written proof that my father's debts are settled. I don't want to be hounded again.' The pain of her realisation made her lash out, made her want to hurt him too. But could you ever hurt a man so incapable of emotions?

'Hounded?' He pulled her to a halt and looked down at her, the spark of anger once again in his eyes. Inwardly she sighed. It seemed she brought out the worst in this man.

She lifted her chin defiantly; the barrier she usually hid behind, the one she had lowered over the last few days, slid perfectly back into place. He would never know her true feelings for him. Never. 'Yes, hounded.'

He narrowed his eyes, their dark depths searching

her face. 'In that case, after tomorrow's meeting with my brother, you will be pleased to know I will have no further cause to *hound* you, as you so nicely put it. Our engagement will be over.'

'Then you should have this back.' She pulled her arm free of his, the comfortable companionship of moments ago gone for good. It was for the best and, trying to push down the pain, she slid the engagement ring from her finger. 'I have no need of it any longer.'

The expression on his face held a hint of that amusement she found so annoying but, even so, a twinge of regret raced through her. The last few days had been so different, the pressure to be anything but herself had disappeared and she'd felt more comfortable with him than she had with anyone. The thought of giving it up saddened her. Was what they'd shared over the last few days what being in a real relationship felt like? Was that the closest she would ever come to knowing love?

'And I do?' The imperious question held such command that the birds in the trees above them seemed to stop singing, as if waiting to see what would happen next.

'Next time you need a convenient fiancée you will have the ring ready and at your disposal.' All the hurt she'd felt echoed in her words, despite her trying to keep it in.

His eyes darkened with anger and with a satisfied smile she turned and began to walk once more. It took seconds for him to join her.

'I had thought you were different.'

'From what?' She kept her voice light and flirtatious, determined he shouldn't guess at the hurt that was lancing through her, the broken and unattainable dreams this weekend had brought to light.

'From the spoilt little rich girl I first met at the dinner party. From the demanding woman who'd waited for me in the restaurant three weeks ago.' The silky softness of his voice almost disguised the underlying disgust at just who he thought she really was.

'Maybe that was part of the act.' She didn't look at him. She didn't dare. She focused on the long path ahead of them, trying instead to wonder what the other people walking in the park were doing. Wondering if they were happy and in love as she'd almost begun to believe she might be. What a fool she'd been.

The night of the dinner party, when she'd first met Raul, she'd acted to a role she'd thought her father had wanted her to play. It had been one last futile attempt at bridging the ever growing gap between her and her father. It had also been what had made Raul look at her with distaste. From that moment onwards, she'd done as her grandmother had always advised and been herself.

'You have acted your part of loving fiancée very well, *querida*. I for one was convinced.' This time, a steely undertone reverberated in every word, but still she walked, not daring to look up at him and certainly not daring to stop, to have those dark eyes fix on hers and see the truth of her feelings for him.

'It was what was expected, was it not, in order to convince the board that we were prepared to marry?' She quickened her step. Maybe if they left the park they could leave this topic behind.

'Then I applaud you. You even fooled me, especially when you were in my bed.'

She stopped and whirled round to face him. Didn't

he have any idea that these last few days had not been about the deal? They had been about letting go, being herself—being with him, the man she'd fallen ever harder for. How dared he bring that up, make it sound as if she'd bartered with herself, sold her body, just to clear her father's debts?

'At least you cannot deny I have kept my part of the deal.' The angry words flew at him but to her utter annoyance her response amused him, serving only to make her even angrier.

Raul smiled as the glitter of anger sparkled in her eyes, far more dazzling than the ring she'd just given back to him. With the afternoon sun shining through the bare branches of the trees above them and then dancing in her hair, she looked so very beautiful. Once again, that need to have more, to find more with this woman, surged forwards. He savagely pushed it down, hid it behind a sharp retort.

'No, I cannot,' he said curtly. 'Even when we were alone you maintained the act of attraction, carried it through to a most satisfying conclusion.'

She paled and a spike of guilt lanced at him. This was the one and only woman he'd wanted to get close to, get to know better, and yet he was emotionally pushing her away, wounding her with his words. It just proved he wasn't a man who should settle down, who should be given the responsibility of someone's heart, someone's deepest emotions. Whether he liked it or not, he was far too much like his father.

'I despise you, Raul—for everything you have done.' She pulled herself free of his hold and began to march away.

'Where are you going, Lydia?'

He watched the sway of her hips in the white jeans that hugged her legs allowing him to see and appreciate her. It also reminded him how it felt to have them wrapped around his body as he'd made her his—even if it was only for the weekend.

She turned and faced him once more, her pretty face set in the firm grip of anger. 'Nothing would induce me to stay a moment longer in your company, Raul. I'm going back to London—today.'

For the briefest of seconds, he floundered, then control and coldness returned. 'You agreed we would return together.'

'I have things to attend to, Raul.' The ice in her voice chilled him far more than the winter wind that had begun to sweep through the park.

'What things?'

'I have dress selections to make.'

'Ah, but of course, the busy life of a socialite—shopping is your prime concern.' He couldn't keep the sarcasm from his voice as he walked towards her, closing the distance once again. Her green eyes glittered watchfully as he moved closer still. If he reached out now he could stroke the soft skin of her face, slide his finger beneath her chin, lifting it up, and then he would be able to kiss her.

'That just proves you don't know me at all.' Her angry words halted the desire-driven thoughts of kissing her once more.

'So, what is it you have hidden from me?' Suspicion slipped over him and he narrowed his eyes as she continued to glare challengingly up at him. 'Are you still the spoilt girl I first met, concerned only with parties and shopping?'

'I was almost seventeen, Raul. It's what teenagers do. Yes, I party sometimes, I'm also often out in London, but it is business, Raul. You of all people should know that necessity.' A hint of satisfaction spread over her face, forcing her lips to stretch into a smile.

'And what business would this be?' Now he was intrigued. He'd always thought there was more to Lydia Carter-Wilson than she allowed people to see, but why had she hidden it from him?

'I have several successful ladies' fashion boutiques, one in London and one in Paris. I had thought to open one here in Madrid. I even made a useful contact whilst shopping for the silver dress I wore to the party.'

He couldn't say anything; his mind had instantly gone back to Friday evening, to dancing so very close with her and then taking her home, where he'd removed the dress.

Lydia continued her self-satisfied attack as he struggled momentarily against the memory of that night. 'But that would mean running the risk of seeing you again, so I will forget that idea.'

'And why did you keep this from me as well as your ability to speak my language?' Finally, he pushed the erotic memory to one side.

'The truth?'

'Yes.'

'You hated me when we first met and it made me think my grandmother's advice was right—to just be myself.'

His mind raced back to that moment at the dinner party when they'd first met. The way she'd made him feel, the effect her smile had had on him had shocked him and he'd covered it all up with a brusque uninterested manner.

'So you learnt Spanish and formed a business because of that night?' Guilt rushed at him.

'I have worked hard to prove myself, to be my own person, and I was not about to allow my father, or you, to take that from me. As far as I was concerned his debts would be paid by the properties he'd hidden in my name and not my business. Of course now I know it would never have been enough.'

'And what if marriage had become necessary? What if you hadn't located my brother?'

'Then I would have married you, if it meant saving the one thing I'd worked hard for. My life. My independence.'

'So was this weekend a practice for the honeymoon?'

Fury leapt to her eyes; the smile that had lingered seductively on her lips disappeared. 'This weekend was a mistake. A very big mistake. Now, if you will excuse me, I need to pack and book a flight to London.'

'I have planned that we will go on my jet tomorrow.'

'You are, but I'm going now—alone.'

CHAPTER TEN

THE GREY RAIN-FILLED sky of London matched Raul's mood as he glared out of his hotel window at the sky-line, impressive even in this weather. All last night he'd tossed and turned, haunted by the memory of one week-end with a woman who had changed his life far more than he cared to admit. Just as he refused to acknowledge that he missed her, that he hadn't wanted to let her go.

Yesterday, he'd watched Lydia march off through the park not realising how serious she was about leaving Madrid until they'd returned in silence to his apartment where she'd promptly booked a flight. The temptation to stop her, to try and make her stay, had been almost too much for him—until he'd reminded himself that such ideas were a sign of total weakness. Not only did he not indulge in such emotions, but she was the woman who had kept secrets from him, secrets that had not been hers to keep.

She'd packed, left and within an hour he had been alone. Silence had hung heavy around him as he'd brooded over their weekend, his rational thoughts accepting it had been exactly as she'd claimed. A mistake. For both of them. He'd allowed her to get close, expose depths of his emotions he'd never intended to be shown, only to find she was as manipulative and cold as him. Hell, what else had she lied about? Had all that talk of her family, her childhood been to lull him into a false sense of security whilst she dug deeper into his past?

With an angry growl he turned away from the view of London, feeling more like a caged animal. Coffee and distraction were what he needed right now. He had to focus his mind, put Lydia totally out of it. He had to forget her. Especially today. He was to meet his brother, the son his father had truly wanted. With a feral oath slipping from him, he left the luxurious hotel suite, intent on seeking the company of unknown businessmen at breakfast and the normality that had left his life the moment Lydia had entered it.

The aroma of strong coffee focused his mind as he sat at breakfast, although food was the last thing he wanted. The bitterness of the black liquid spiked his senses, bringing the controlled man he'd become back into play. Exactly what he needed to be, today of all days. He couldn't allow himself to dwell on the events of the weekend, not now at least.

In a bid for distraction he picked up one of the newspapers, but it wasn't the headline that caught his attention, it was the photo of Lydia looking every bit the socialite on a night out. Suspicion and a spark of lust slammed into him hard as he gritted his teeth firmly and looked at the image. A growl of Spanish slipped from him as he read the headline.

Blackmailed into an engagement by Spanish billionaire looking for unknown half-brother!

The paper shook as he held it, his fingers tightening on the offending pages until they hurt. She'd sold him out. Lydia had gone from his bed straight to the press. Was that why she'd been so keen to leave Madrid, to leave him? Before the headlines broke?

He shouldn't read it, shouldn't give it even the smallest bit of his attention, but his eyes began quickly to scan the words even though his emotions, and maybe even his heart, warned against it.

London heiress Lydia Carter-Wilson has been unable to keep the dark family secrets of Spanish business mogul Raul Peréz Valdez.

'Raul was shocked to discover he had an older brother,' a reliable source informed.

The only heir to his father's estate has just discovered the existence of a brother, who will now share the inheritance of his father's company, Banco de Torrez. The blackmailed bride-to-be is honouring a contract her father had signed with the late Maximiliano Valdez in order to pay off family debts.

Legitimate son, Raul, seems more than happy to marry instead of sharing his inheritance with his half-brother.

A curse left his lips without any thought for those around him. She'd even shamed her father. What kind of a woman did that? A mercenary one who only thought of herself.

Right at this moment he was trapped in a bubble of anger. He'd trusted Lydia, allowed her into his family and, if he was brutally honest, his emotions. She'd got to him on a level he'd never known—and then she'd done this.

He pulled out his phone and with savage satisfaction pressed Lydia's number. Infuriatingly, she didn't answer and as the message system kicked in he almost cut the connection, but sense prevailed. The sooner she realised he knew what she'd been up to, the better, but first there was time for a little of her own medicine. Deceit.

'Lydia. There are papers to sign for your father's debt. I will see you at twelve forty-five, before I meet Max at one.'

With a satisfied smile he ended the call. He had no doubt she would be there. Just as he had no doubt she would try and deny all knowledge of the article. After all, hadn't she kept Max's whereabouts from him for several days before enlightening him—only then she'd made seduction the main game plan? What would her plan be today?

It seemed Miss Carter-Wilson was as cold and calculating as he was and would do anything to extract herself from the debt her father had tied her to—but this time she'd gone too far. This time she'd played with the wrong man and for that she would pay.

Lydia's heart sank as she entered the smart hotel, the large Christmas tree mocking her as it sparkled. With Christmas a week away, carols filled the hotel with joy and happiness. She was far from feeling anything like that, knowing this meeting with Raul would be so much more difficult than that first one almost three weeks ago. She hung up her coat in the cloakroom and walked over to the mirror, where, feeling the need for more armour, she reapplied her lipstick then looked at her reflection.

She'd changed in the last three weeks. She might not look any different from the woman who had first met Raul, but she was. She'd had her heart broken—exactly what she'd spent all her adult life trying to avoid. Now, thanks to her father's bad business dealings and one impulsive weekend with Raul Valdez, she felt totally out of control even though she looked far from it. She took in a deep breath and smoothed her hands down the bold red skirt of the suit she'd spent time selecting this morning. Just as she had done on their first meeting, she'd dressed with care, wanting to exude a confidence she was far from feeling, and now she'd seen the headlines in today's papers she needed every bit of help she could get.

Had Raul seen them too?

He couldn't have seen it. He'd never have calmly left a message to meet her just to sign papers if he had. Would he?

He is capable of anything.

That thought echoed round in her mind as her heels tapped out a solitary beat across the elegant lobby towards the restaurant where Raul would soon meet his brother. The fact that he'd arranged to meet her so close to that meeting must surely mean all he wanted was a few papers signed. She clung to that hope as she entered the restaurant, strangely empty of any other dinners. When she saw him sitting calmly waiting for her at a table in the middle of the room, she knew that was a mistaken idea. He was dressed immaculately in a charcoal-grey suit, but nothing could detract from the air of superiority and total control he exuded.

He rose from his seat and stood waiting for her; the angry set of his handsome face left her in no doubt he had seen the headlines. Her futile hope slithered away, taking with it the remainder of her confidence as his dark eyes glared accusingly at her, his anger palpable even at this distance.

She walked towards him, her head held high, trying to match his strength, to show he didn't intimidate her at all. As she got closer her confidence faltered and she stopped halfway across the room, glad now that they were the only people there. She glanced around, just to check.

'I booked the entire restaurant to ensure I had the privacy I needed.' Raul sounded calm, approachable, but she wasn't fooled. She could detect the steely edge lurking beneath the surface. Calm he might be, but he was definitely far from approachable.

She turned to face him, looking into those dark eyes she'd lost her heart to, trying to bring confidence from deep within her. 'I got your message.'

'And I have seen your salacious kiss and tell in the papers this morning.' He went straight in for the kill, his voice now harder than the gleam of anger in his eyes, but she remained resolutely still, meeting his gaze and the accusation within it head-on. Inside she trembled but outside she was strong and defiant. The armour that had served her well for many years deflected most of the pain.

'I'm very sorry to disappoint, but I am not the source of your embarrassment.' She raised her brows at him in a show of high-handedness as she said that final word, then continued before he had a chance to say anything,

'Surely a man like you is used to sidestepping such stories in the papers.'

'About my lovers, yes.' He let the barbed words hang in the air and she refused to react, refused to think that one day she too could be linked to him as one of his lovers—exactly what she'd never wanted to be. 'About my fiancée, no.'

Fury boiled up inside her. 'I am not your fiancée. Not any longer. I kept my side of the deal.'

'On that I beg to differ.' The superiority in his voice rankled but she maintained a stony silence, forcing him to continue. 'You have shared the story of my half-brother with someone and now it is everywhere. You broke the terms of our contract, Lydia.'

'I have not shared it with anyone,' she blurted out, hurt that he could accuse her of such a thing after all they'd shared.

Raul laughed. A cold, cynical laugh, which sent a shiver of worry all over her, chilling her to the core. 'Do you really expect me to believe that, *querida*? You were so strong-willed, so against any kind of affair, yet suddenly you changed. You became a passionate woman intent only on desire. You used the mutual attraction between us to drag out more of the story.'

'I did not.' Indignation fired the retort at him but as he moved away from the table and came towards her, his dark eyes watching her closely, she regretted the outburst. Was that what he thought their weekend affair had been? When she'd been enjoying the gentle truce between them, the deeper understanding she'd gained of him as they'd talked about their pasts, he'd been satisfying a more basic need. How stupid had she been to fall for his act of vulnerability, to feel sorry for him?

He came very close to her, walking around her, his shoulder almost touching hers, as if they were about to start dancing. Not a slow sedate dance like the night of the party, but a wild passionate dance. A tango filled with anger.

Quickly she looked away and wished that other diners were here. At least it would stop the intimacy of this meeting, but that was not possible because Raul had, yet again, manipulated the situation to suit him. What kind of man booked out an entire restaurant?

One in total control—of everything.

'You begged me to take you to my bed.' The hardness in his eyes didn't match the silky seductive sound of his voice and a tremor of awareness sizzled over her. Why did she still feel like this? How could he still have such a hold on her—on her heart?

'I felt sorry for you.' She was shocked at that last thought, her gaze met the fury of his and, once again, she wished the impetuous words unsaid. Still she held his gaze, her chin lifted mutinously in a desperate attempt to hide the real reason she'd wanted to be with him, hide the love that had been impossible to ignore as it had blossomed during those two blissful days.

'So, it was pity sex.' He turned and walked away from her and she could see the tension in his shoulders as clearly as she could feel it bouncing around the empty restaurant. Then he whirled round to face her. 'That is even worse.'

'I don't care what kind of sex it was, Raul; I did not sell your story. Just tell me what was so important so I can go before your brother arrives. I will leave and we will never have to see one another again. You can move on with your life, safe in the knowledge you have safeguarded the company, destroyed my father and kept all you wanted.'

Around the room the air prickled with challenge as she glared at him. She wanted to tell him it was far from pity sex, that it had been much more about falling for him—falling in love. But that would be futile. This man didn't want love in his life. Inwardly, she groaned. How had she been so stupid? To think this man could ever feel anything for her?

'I'm afraid that will not be possible, Lydia.' The tone of his voice had changed again. He sounded dangerous and icily calm as he moved back towards her.

'What do you mean?' She held her ground, stood firm in the high black patent heels she'd chosen for added height, added confidence.

'What I mean, Lydia, is that you have broken the agreement you signed. The one that stated you would not share any information with anyone else.' Menace laced every word as he stopped a short distance from her, as if he didn't dare come any closer. He hated her now. She could see it in his eyes, hear it in his words and feel it surrounding her.

'Why would I do that?' From the moment she'd arrived in Madrid she'd become caught up in Raul's story and even more caught up in the man himself. She'd wanted to help, wanted to be the one who made a difference to his life.

'You tell me. I have lost a lucrative contract over this and who knows? I may well have lost my brother before I gained him.' Pain lashed through her. He didn't care at all that they'd lost the closeness they'd found in Madrid or that they were losing each other with each angry word he spoke.

'I'm sorry, but it wasn't me.' Outwardly, she remained strong. Detached. Inside, she was falling to pieces and she wanted this moment to end.

'I don't need your damn pity—in any form.' He rounded on her and she closed her eyes against the agony that was ripping her heart into shreds. How had she ever thought it might be possible that one day they could become more than just an affair? She couldn't stay a moment longer and listen to him, feel how much he hated her.

'And I don't need this.' With a toss of her head, her hair flinging out around her, she turned and started to walk away.

'If my brother doesn't arrive at one as arranged, then all you have done will have been in vain. Your moment of glory—or is it revenge?—will be for nothing.' Raul's steady voice halted her steps and she turned to face him. Was he holding her responsible for Max not turning up?

She looked at her watch. Less than ten minutes until Max should arrive. But what if he didn't?

'If my brother doesn't arrive, your father's debts will remain unpaid and our engagement deal will stand.' His words were hard and grating, his handsome face full of anger.

'You can't force me to marry you.' She matched his anger as she flung the words at him.

'I can and I will.'

Lydia looked to the door of the restaurant, hoping to see a man striding through, but nothing. 'No, I've done all I can do. I've found him for you. It's not my fault if he doesn't show up.'

'Isn't it?' The accusation was clear. He blamed her. She looked again at her watch. In five minutes she would know her fate. In five minutes she would have lost the man she'd fallen in love with, because whatever happened next she knew, without doubt, that he hated her.

Raul watched Lydia as she looked at the time. He saw the colour drain from her face and a brief wave of compassion surged over him. Savagely, he pushed it back. He didn't have room for compassion or any other kind of emotion that would make him want to go and take Lydia in his arms.

Any moment now his brother would walk into the restaurant and he would have to face the man who had taken his place in his father's affections even before he himself had been born.

'I should go.' Lydia's words rushed him back to the present.

'You will stay, Lydia. If he doesn't turn up then—' Raul's words were cut off by the noise of the door opening and his heart thumped as he looked beyond Lydia to see a member of hotel staff entering the room.

'Your guest is here, sir.'

All he could hear was the beat of his pulse in his ears and then his amazingly calm voice. 'Show him in.'

'It is just as well you booked the entire restaurant.' Lydia's remark gave him an anchorage as he waited for his brother to arrive.

'*Sí*, I prefer to conduct my affairs in private—unlike you.' The barb of his reply made those beautiful green eyes widen, just as they'd done that night they'd become lovers when he'd finally slipped the silver dress from her gorgeous body.

Why was he thinking about that now? He'd known

she would be a distraction, which was why he'd let her walk away from him, let her think she had the upper hand. But that damned story she'd sold had changed that. Now she would pay for her loose tongue.

'I didn't sell that story, Raul.' Her gaze locked with his and despite the defiance in her stance, in the proud tilt of her chin, he could hear the pleading in her voice, a plea that distracted him from all other thought.

'Then who the hell did?' A deep male voice crashed into the tension that had built between him and Lydia, as if striking all ten pins on a bowling alley in one fatal blow.

He heard Lydia gasp and drag in a deep breath as he turned and looked his brother in the eye for the first time. It was like looking at himself and he clenched his teeth hard; the hope that his father had got it all wrong vanished with one glittering look from his firstborn son.

'It certainly wasn't me.' Lydia began to speak again, fast bubbling words, which as far as he was concerned underlined her guilt in red, not because she had genuinely wanted to help him because of her deepening feelings for him. 'I want the debt settled. I want out of your life.'

'Then get out, Lydia,' Raul snapped without even looking at her. Now was not the time for Lydia's nervous chatter.

His brother's gaze didn't leave his face, didn't break the contact and there was no way he was going to back down, give this man the upper hand. It seemed an eternity as he stood there assessing and being assessed by the half-brother who had taken his place in his father's affections, who'd become the only son he'd ever wanted.

He should hate him for it.

Lydia moved closer to him. Every nerve in his body felt it—heightened to even the smallest movement from this woman. It wasn't right that she had such power over him. He heard the crinkle of paper but remained resolutely locked in eye combat with his half-brother. He couldn't bring himself to think his name, much less say it. Not whilst the anger and pain of his childhood years surged through him.

'You should have this.' Lydia's whispered words finally caught his attention and he looked at her, then at the old, discoloured envelope she held out to him. 'It's from your mother.'

In that moment it was just the two of them—him and the woman who had slipped under his defensive barrier and into his heart, rendering him as weak as a newborn colt. The very same woman who'd betrayed him in the most spectacular way. And it hurt—like hell. He'd watched his mother's heartache at his father's betrayal as he'd grown from a boy into a man, seen it all around him and vowed never, ever, to be the victim of such emotions.

Now he too knew the bitter taste of betrayal from a loved one.

He took the envelope in a firm, decisive move then looked into those green eyes he'd thought so sexy, so full of something special for him. His lip curled into a snarl. 'I never want to see you again. Ever.'

Lydia burst through the door of the restaurant, desperate to leave the charged atmosphere of the room. She couldn't bear to stand there and see the anger in Raul's eyes, anger that made him despise her.

She swiped at a tear as it sprang from her eye and

pulled all her anger to the fore, smothering the need to cry. 'Damn Christmas tree.' She brushed her hair back with both hands and raised her chin as she glared at the offending fir tree, decked out in gold with twinkling lights. 'What are you looking so happy about?'

'Are you okay?' A female voice came from behind her and Lydia whirled round to see a woman sitting in one of the large comfortable armchairs of the foyer, looking anything but comfortable if her perched position on the edge of the seat was anything to go by.

'Y-yes. Sorry,' Lydia stammered, realising how silly she must have looked to the glamorous redhead as she'd rushed out and begun her tirade at the Christmas tree. 'It's that time of year for stress overload, I guess.'

'Tell me about it,' the other woman said and Lydia relaxed a little, feeling as if she'd met a kindred spirit. 'A man?'

'The very same.' Lydia smiled, noticing how pale the redhead looked beneath her heavily applied make-up, as if she too was trying to hide something.

The woman smiled, but as raised male voices echoed from the restaurant both women looked at the door. For a moment Lydia wondered if she should say something. Was the beautiful woman waiting for Raul's brother? She decided against it. Raul was nothing to do with her any more. She'd found his brother and had unlocked the funds that would pay off her father's debt. She was free to go.

With that thought racing in her mind she rushed from the hotel, conscious of her hurried footsteps echoing after her and even feeling the redhead's curious gaze. Or was she just being fanciful? Was she in such a heightened state of emotions she wasn't thinking clearly?

The cold December wind took her breath away as she stood on the streets, the London traffic whizzing by, oblivious to the turmoil she was in. People passed her, some bumping her as she walked slowly in a daze of disbelief, not even aware of where she was going. Everyone around her seemed to be caught up in the buzz of Christmas and all she could do was think about what she'd lost.

The man she loved hated her. She'd seen it in his eyes. There was no doubt.

Christmas Eve was a week away. Now was no time to be nursing a broken heart. She pulled her coat tighter around her in an attempt to keep the cold at bay, but inside she was already frozen, her heart turned to ice by one look of contempt from Raul, and his last words played in her head like a Christmas carol turned sour.

'I never want to see you again. Ever.'

CHAPTER ELEVEN

RAUL COULDN'T COMPREHEND how alike he and Max were. There was no disputing they were brothers. It wasn't just the dark hair, which Max wore shorter, or the piercingly dark eyes, but the way he stood. Every line in his body was poised and commanding. Raul had not only met his brother, but his match, of that he was in no doubt, but right now he was far too angry with Lydia for her deception.

Because of her he'd lost a big deal and she'd caused him and Max unnecessary embarrassment. He wanted to believe she hadn't sold his story, that she hadn't used their passionate affair in order to gain all the information she could about the story of his brother and his father's double life, but it was just too coincidental. She'd gone from not wanting anything to do with him to seeking a passionate affair. He'd thought it had been desire driven, but he'd been wrong. Very wrong.

'Was that necessary?' his brother's voice fired accusingly at him. 'There was no need to be so hard on her.'

'Don't you dare presume that as my older brother you can tell me what I can and can't do.' Raul hurled the angry words back at Max. Thanks to Lydia and her indiscretion, this whole meeting had catapulted out of control. He couldn't even think clearly at the moment, saying the first thing that came to him in such an un-controlled way, he didn't even recognise himself.

'Now we get to the crux of it.' Max strode towards him, the same purposeful strides he would use if he weren't rooted to the spot with shock and anger at the sudden realisation that Lydia had gone. Not just left the hotel, but gone. Out of his life for good.

Focus, he demanded himself. Now was not the time to reminisce over a love affair that had ended. Now was the time to focus on his future, to move forward from the lies his father had inflicted on him—and Max. To do the one thing his father had thought him incapable of—welcoming his brother into his life.

'That minor detail has nothing to do with it,' he shot back at Max, instantly regretting the anger in his words.

'Then you had better tell me what the hell it is you want from me so that you can go and sort out your love life.' Max's dark eyes, so like his own, pinned him to the spot and he resented his brother's inference that he and Lydia were lovers.

'We are not lovers.' He glared angrily at his brother, refusing to accept that maybe he was right. Damn him, he'd been in his life all of five minutes and already he was telling him what to do.

'That's not how it looked to me.' Max flicked an eyebrow up and a trickle of calm began to defuse the angry tension that arced between them like an ugly steel bridge, connecting them, connecting their past and their future, yet neither daring to cross it.

Raul sighed. 'I didn't ask you to come here to talk about me and Lydia—'

'I should hate you right now,' Max said, cutting off

his words, blatantly attempting to take back control. He also echoed his own feelings exactly. He too should hate Max. Hate him for being the son his father always wanted, hate him for being given his father's name and most of all hate him for denying him his father's love.

But Max hadn't had a father's love either. He hadn't seen his father since he was eight years old, if all Carlos had told him was true.

Raul frowned. How did Carlos know so much? 'And do you? Hate me?'

'No.' Max turned and walked away. 'Neither of us are to blame. There is only one man who can take the blame for this, and, as always, he's too much of a coward to deal with it himself. He's left us to deal with the aftermath. Just as he walked away from my mother and I.'

Raul knew he was scowling as he digested this nugget about his brother's childhood. The tone of his voice, the way he referred to their father gave away so much. Was it possible he too had suffered the effects of being the son of a man incapable of love for his son?

'Did he ever contact you again?' Raul had to know, had to hear it for himself.

'No—and for that I am grateful. My life was better without him.' Max's voice was hard. Controlled. But he spoke the truth, Raul didn't need any convincing of that.

'So, brother, where do we go from here?' Raul asked, knowing that whatever he did now he had to get Max on side, had to get him to accept his share of the inheritance his father had left equally between them—especially as he'd turned Lydia out of his life so harshly and she was the only other hope of paying the debt the board wanted settled.

'I'm not big on emotional commitment.' Max moved closer to him, echoing his own sentiments exactly. 'The love of a father, or even a woman, is overrated as far as I am concerned.'

Raul smiled, accepting they were already so alike. 'My sentiments precisely.'

'The young lady seemed pretty certain she didn't sell the story, but someone did.' Was Max accusing him?

'I lost a big deal because of it. I'd hardly do that.'

Max's brows rose, in a way that was like looking at himself in the mirror. 'Then I suggest we work together to find out just who has it in for us.

'The media will be watching closely to see what happens next. There are probably bets on somewhere as to what we will do, but I'll wager that nobody, least of all our so-called father, would expect us to leave the past exactly where it is and move forwards—together.'

Raul held out his hand to shake on the deal Max was offering. It was far more than he'd hoped for, but if Max could put aside the past, so could he. 'Brothers.'

'Brothers,' Max replied and took his hand, their gazes locking. Then to Raul's relief and shock, Max let go of his hand and slapped him on the back. 'Brothers.'

Lydia had known exactly what she needed to do as she left Raul and his brother glaring like angry bulls at one another. She'd hailed a black cab to the station for the next train to Oxford. This time her father would face up to what he'd done. This time she was well and truly in charge. This time he'd pay. Not just for her, but for Raul—and Max.

Meeting Raul for the first time had made her grow up. Spending the weekend as his lover had given her clarity. Thinking of him spiked her heart with pain. How had she fallen in love with a man who could use her as savagely as her father had done?

She pushed the thought aside as the train pulled out of the station and a bitter December wind whistled down the platform as she wondered if she'd done the right thing.

Of course you have. He can't get away with not paying his debt.

The short taxi ride from the station to her father's home, one she'd hardly spent any time at recently, gave her just enough time to pull the last bit of confidence she had left and ready herself for seeing her father. Once that was done, she could go home and sleep away the pain of her broken heart, knowing she'd done all she could to make things right. Although they'd never be right for her again.

'I wasn't expecting you so close to Christmas.' Her father's voice boomed at her as he raised his head from whatever it was he was engrossed in at his desk. She heard the door being clicked shut as his maid retreated. Had she sensed the power of his daughter's determination?

'And I wasn't expecting to be made a scapegoat for your so-called deals.' She bit back a tirade she'd love to shower on him, wanting the implications of what she'd just said to sink in first. Would he defend himself or her?

'Ah.'

'Yes, ah.' She walked towards the desk, looking him in the eye and not missing the startled widening of his. He might not have been expecting to see her today, but he'd certainly never thought she'd be so mutinous.

'I thought you'd come to tell me you are about to marry the Valdez heir or, judging by the headlines today, I'd hazard a guess it's to congratulate me on a cunning plan which has made you a very wealthy woman and saved my neck.'

'How could you?' Her anger erupted, mixed together with the pent-up grief of losing the man she loved, even though deep down she knew she'd never had him at all. To him their time together had been merely a diversion. All that hurt tipped out onto her father. 'You used me. How could you? I will never forgive you.'

'Now hang on a minute.' He jumped up from his chair, papers sliding to the floor, his face red with anger. 'You now have properties worth millions.'

He'd walked right into her trap. 'Do I?'

'I did it for you, Lyd.' She hated it when he shortened her name and bit back the retort she'd like to hurl at him. He had to think she was softening, that she was complying with what he'd obviously planned from the outset.

'So I can do what I want with them?' she asked thoughtfully as he sat back down, looking relaxed again, believing he'd smoothed the rough water. 'Are you sure?'

'Quite sure, Lyd.' She smarted again beneath the fake endearment. 'Spend Christmas and New Year in the sun, then once the dust has settled you can transfer them back to me and we will have made millions. It can be our little investment.'

How devious could he get? How had she never noticed before just what he was like?

Because you have grown up.

'I might just do that,' she said with a smile on her

face that was so hard to achieve. 'In actual fact I think I will fly out to one of them tomorrow.'

'That's my girl. I knew you'd see sense.' The condescending tone sickened her but she played her part to the end.

'Now, if you will excuse me, I've got packing to do.'

As her father's laughter trailed after her Lydia felt numb. She had lost her father long ago, and today she'd lost the man she'd fallen in love with. But the truth was she'd never been loved by Raul.

'Have a good time and Merry Christmas.' The belated words trailed down the wood-panelled hallway of his latest home and briefly she longed to slip back in time, to the home she'd grown up in, before her parents had parted company and she'd gone to live with her grandmother. But just as going back to the time she'd spent with Raul was impossible, so was going back to the small window of happiness in her childhood. The only way was forwards, even if it was fraught with pain.

'I will.' If he only knew what she really had planned for his little *investment*, he wouldn't be so happy. First she would call her solicitor and get enough of the properties transferred into Raul's name to cover the debt that, as far as she was concerned, her father still owed. After that she would sell the rest and give it all to charity. She wanted nothing to do with them. Only then did she feel she could move on from her disastrous first taste of love.

Raul had gone straight to the bar after his brother had left and ordered a whisky. He'd needed the hot fire of the amber liquid, not because of the way things had

gone with Max, but because of the way things had gone
with Lydia.

As the image of her lovely face swam into his mind
he remembered the envelope she'd all but thrust at him
and pulled it from his pocket. He placed it on the bar
and ordered a second drink. The young woman behind
the bar smiled at him as she placed the drink next to the
envelope, but it was a smile wasted on him now. There
was only one woman's smile he wanted to see but he
had to remember what she'd done, the story she'd sold.

Unable to believe the duplicity of Carlos, the only
other person who knew the secrets of the past, or his
blatant admission when challenged, he and Max had
come up with their own exclusive to sell to the press.
The proceeds were to be split equally between their
favoured charity projects of Sports for Youngsters and
Community Rebuild. The fact that they both headed
charities proved yet another similarity between them
and highlighted just how different they both were from
their father. Except that Raul shared the fatal flaw of
being unable to love, to give his heart to anyone.

He reached for his second drink, then paused, his
hand over the envelope. Was he ready to read its contents? What was in it that was so bad his mother had
never told him? He cursed beneath his breath. Why
hadn't he ever broached the subject with her? He ignored the drink and the oblivion it lured him with and
picked up the envelope.

Around him the bar became busy with Christmas
shoppers and businessmen and women. The noise level
rose as everyone chatted against the backdrop of traditional carols, but he didn't hear any of it. The forthcoming festive season was the last thing on his mind

as he read, first the torn pages of what must have been his mother's journal and then a letter, written to him by his mother, dated on his tenth birthday.

Both told the story of his father's deception, of the brother he would never know and of her family's insistence that they remain married or she would be disinherited and his double life exposed. Now her acceptance of his father's behaviour made sense and the realisation that her story was out there in the world of the media made talking to her essential.

He'd rather do it face to face, be able to see her expression and be there to offer comfort, but London was nearly a three-hour flight from Madrid. There was only one option, so he moved away from the bar, to a quieter corner and took out his phone, waiting whilst the call he least wanted to make connected.

Just as he wondered if he'd done the right thing his mother's voice sounded across the miles, her Spanish words grounding him. 'I was expecting your call.'

'Then you will know why I am calling.' He didn't ask, but made it clear he was stating a fact. He had no wish to hurt his mother, to drag up what must be a painful past, but he had to know the truth and it seemed, if nothing else, Lydia had been right about one thing. His mother was the best person to ask.

'As soon as I saw you and Lydia together I knew it was time.' Raul frowned. Where was this leading? Whatever it was she had to tell him had nothing to do with Lydia now and he was about to say just that when his mother spoke over his thoughts. 'I could see how much she loves you—and how much you love her.'

He should correct her, should tell her she'd got it all wrong. How could anyone have imagined there was love between them? 'I need to know why you kept the truth of Max from me.'

'When you were young it was to try and mend things between you and your father, to try and keep the family together—for you, not anyone or anything else.'

A noisy group of couples sat at the table next to him, full of the joys of the festive season, but he couldn't end the call now, he had to continue. 'There was never any love lost between me and my father and now I know why. He already had a son—and had given him his name.'

'I knew about the baby, but not the name,' she carried on, her voice beginning to waver, and he wished there weren't so many miles between them for this conversation. 'I only found that out when his double life was exposed and you were so young and not getting on with your father, I couldn't give you more reasons to fall out with him.'

'You must have known it would come out?' Raul snapped, ignoring the curious glance from the party next to him, turning his back on them and their happiness. He picked up his glass of whisky, about to take a long swig, when his mother answered.

'That's why I waited until you had the support of a woman who loves you.'

He cursed loudly in Spanish. 'Lydia and I are not in love. We were forced into marriage because of a clause in the damn will. Her father's debts and my father's need to drag up the past forced us into an engagement.'

He heard his mother gasp. 'He did that to you?'

'Unless I found Max and shared the inheritance. Yes, he did that.' Raul's voice was granite hard and he tightened his grip around the glass so much he thought he might actually break it. 'With help from Carlos.'

'Carlos? I can't believe he would stoop so low, but your father, yes.'

'There will be no wedding, Mother. Lydia found Max, thanks to the information you gave her, and unlocked the funds Father had set aside as a reward for acknowledging Max as my older brother. He gambled on the fact that her father wouldn't repay the debt and that I'd rather track down his firstborn son than get married.'

It angered Raul to think that his father had known him so well, played him to the very end, but in taking up that challenge he'd hurt others. His mother for one, but the fact that he'd hurt Lydia enough to make her hate him was too much.

'He'd engineered it all, knowing he wouldn't have long left?' The shock in his mother's voice was so clear he could imagine her sitting in her favourite chair and the expression on her face.

'Every last detail.'

'None of that changes the fact that Lydia loves you. Don't lose her, Raul, don't throw away your happiness.' His mother pleaded with him and now he was glad he wasn't standing before her. How long would she keep up this particular argument?

'I am not in love with Lydia.' He snapped the words in rapid Spanish, again causing others to look his way.

'Then maybe you are more like your father than you imagine.'

Raul gritted his teeth. He wasn't having this conversation. Not now. Not here like this. Not when he'd just sent Lydia out of his life for good. 'I can't talk any more.'

'Talk to her, Raul—for me.'

He cut the call without giving his mother any further

opportunity to increase the pain that raged inside him like a wild animal, pain from the deceit of the past as well as the deceit of the present.

He downed the whisky in one go and then slammed the glass down on the table. Lydia loved him? Not possible. She was as cold and calculating as he was—and also now financially very well off with her new property portfolio. Did that mean they were well matched? Or was she hiding the real Lydia as much as he kept his true emotions hidden?

He thought back to their time together in Madrid and ultimately to that passionate weekend. He had been happy then, even forgetting the need to find Max as he'd lived the lie of being Lydia's lover. But had it been a lie? Was the elusive emotion of love the reason he'd been so happy in Madrid, so like a completely different version of himself?

As Christmas carols began to fill the bar again, jingling with merriment, he finally had the nerve to question himself, question just what it was that had sparked into life between him and Lydia from their very first meeting here in London. He thought back to the hard and cruel words he'd hurled at her just moments before she'd run out of his life. He could still hear the feral growl in his voice, as if it were being played alongside the bright and cheery carols.

An angry curse slipped from him and he strode to the bar, ordering another whisky and swigging it back in one. He glared at his reflection in the mirrored wall of the bar, distorted by the array of optics. He'd been a fool to think Lydia would betray him. He knew she would never willingly drag herself through the mire of the press and was as much a victim as he and Max. He also knew now that the passion they had shared, one so strong and powerful, like nothing he'd ever known, was not born out of lust—but love.

The unthinkable had happened. He'd fallen in love.

Lydia Carter-Wilson, his fake fiancée, was the woman he wanted to marry, the woman he wanted to have children with—and he'd sent her away.

Raul left the bar, the cold wind whipping at his coat as he crossed the busy street, dashing in front of black cabs. It wasn't the whisky that had dulled his senses, making him careless, but the loss of the woman he loved.

CHAPTER TWELVE

FIVE DAYS HAD passed since Lydia had last seen Raul and still his words echoed in her mind, haunting her day and night. The expression on his face, the pure anger directed at her, was there each time she closed her eyes. Whatever she did she couldn't get away from him, from thinking about him or from the misguided love she still had for him. But she had to and in an attempt to move on, to rebuild her life, she'd chosen to be at work, needing the distraction of ladies wanting glamorous party dresses, and, with only one weekend until Christmas, it was sure to be busy.

She'd read the headlines this morning, seen the picture of happiness Raul and Max had portrayed to the world through the lens of the press. They were pleased to have found each other and would move forwards together in a business they had both inherited as well as continue with their own businesses. It all looked too good to be true and she wondered how much of it was indeed true. How much of it was yet more business deals struck, more acting the part for the media or board of directors?

Was Max as hard and mercenary as Raul? Judging by what she'd seen just a few days ago, the stand-off she'd left in full swing, she suspected they were very alike. They were both hard and emotionless men who would stop at nothing to get what they wanted.

The door of the salon opened, bringing with it the noise of traffic from Knightsbridge and a rush of crisp, cold air. She didn't turn immediately, but continued with her task of ensuring the party dresses were displayed to their full potential, giving the customer a moment or two to browse. A few moments later, she pinned on a smile she was far from feeling and turned to greet her customer.

That smile froze on her lips as she took in Raul, standing in all his male magnificence in the centre of her boutique, watching her with narrowed eyes. What did he want now? Hadn't he hurt her enough already?

'I have nothing to say to you, Raul.' She glared at him, daring him to stay, daring him to try and say anything to her. She'd cried so much already and had been totally weakened by his cold words as she'd tried to explain what had happened. She'd been on the brink of telling him that she'd never do such a thing to the man she loved, but, thankfully, his curt remark had cut that off midsentence, reminding her how foolhardy she'd been.

At least she hadn't been given the chance to tell him how she really felt, that she loved him and all she'd done had been out of love for him.

'But I have much to say to you, Lydia.' He didn't move; like a matador preparing for the fight, he stood firm, his strong maleness so out of place amidst the sparkle of the dresses.

'Nothing I want to hear.' She turned her back on him and picked up a gold sequined top, hoping he would turn and leave. She closed her eyes against the pain as she heard his steady footsteps. He was leaving. So much for wanting to speak to her.

She listened, shock coursing through her as the bolt slid on the door of the shop and then the blind rolled slowly and purposefully down. What was he doing? She whirled round, still clutching the gold top, her fingers crushing the sequins as she pressed them hard around the padded hanger.

The self-satisfied expression on his face intensified her anger and as his brows rose in that familiar and very alluring way, her heart thumped wildly. Why did he have to look so sexy, so completely gorgeous?

'The boutique is *not* closed.' She fired the words at him, infusing them with anger, desperate to sound firm and as in control as he appeared to be.

'It is very much closed. At least until I have said what I came to say.' He moved towards her and she watched, unable to take in what was happening or why he was here.

'My assistant will be back very soon.'

'She can wait.' The curt reply was as sharp as it was hard, but she glared at him, meeting the challenge that was very definitely in his eyes head-on.

'Very well. Say your piece and then leave. I have no wish to prolong this any longer than is needed.' She tried to make her voice portray how uninterested she was to hear what he had to say, but her last words wavered, giving away the turmoil of emotions she now had rushing through her. But then Raul was the steeliest and most unemotional man she had ever met and she doubted he'd pick up on her minefield of emotions.

His brows rose and the flicker of a smile pulled at his lips so briefly she thought she'd imagined it. He moved closer. 'I know that you didn't sell the story.'

Relief flooded her, but it was short-lived and she couldn't smile at him, didn't want to take his harshly delivered statement as an apology. 'So after everything you said to me in front of your brother, you think you can just turn up and say you'd made a mistake without a word of apology?'

'I have just said I was wrong.' His eyes hardened with the glitter of anger as he spoke. Well, he wasn't the only one who was angry.

'But you can't say you are sorry, can you, Raul?' She challenged him, pushed him to feel something. 'You can't say it because you don't feel it. You are so cold, so emotionless.'

'Being so emotionless, as you say, is what has made me so successful.' The retort sparked back at her and she glared at him. 'But if it makes you happy, then I am sorry. I now know you did not sell the story.'

She wanted more than that. Wanted to hear him say he couldn't live without her, that he should never have sent her away—that he loved her. She wanted him to feel something for her.

'And how did you come to this conclusion?' The terse words slipped easily from her lips. She was finally getting her emotions under control, managing to hide them away, and discussing the story was safer than anything else right now.

'The source was revealed to me.' He paused, as if waiting for her to say something, to respond, and she wasn't going to disappoint him. 'My father had enlisted the help of a close friend, a member of the board, but he proved to be as corrupt as my father and his silence has now been assured with a hefty payment.'

'Of course. Power and wealth can buy you just about anything, can't it?' Lydia's words, spoken in perfect Spanish, cracked harder than any whip as they lashed at him. But she was right—and she despised him for it. Pain slashed through him, cutting deeper than a sword. He'd never known anything like it. To hear such an accusation from the woman he loved—and in his own language.

'Not always.' He tried to gentle his emotions, to remember why he was here in the first place. Another war of words with Lydia wouldn't achieve anything other than to push her further out of his reach. The exact opposite of what he wanted.

'Ah, so there is something the mighty Raul Valdez wants that money can't buy.' The sarcasm of her words stung the wound his pain had opened and he gritted his teeth against it and the truth of her words.

'Yes.' The word sounded feral, even to him, and the lift of her delicate brows made it clear she thought so too. Hell. Why couldn't he just tell her? Why couldn't he say the words? Tell her that he wanted her—loved her? Had he been so void of emotion for so long that he could no longer say what he felt? This was harder than any deal he'd ever won or lost, but, whatever happened, he couldn't lose, not now. 'There is something I very much want.'

Her eyes narrowed and she put the gold top back on the rail, averting her gaze and deliberately taking her time. When she looked back at him her expression was as neutral as the day he'd first seen her in the restaurant in London. She gave nothing away as once again she spoke in Spanish, reminding him of that dinner party, punishing him for his hurtful remark. 'And what has this to do with me?'

He moved towards her and her eyes widened, blinking rapidly a few times, but she didn't step away, didn't break eye contact. 'It is you I want, Lydia.'

He'd said it. He'd actually admitted that he wanted someone, needed someone. For the first time in his life, after years of hiding his heart, hiding his emotions, he'd told the woman he loved, the woman he wanted, just how he felt.

'No.' Lydia glared at him, angry sparks in her eyes, deepening the green of them, making them so intense that he couldn't help but look into them. He saw pain behind the anger. Pain he'd caused. But there was something else.

'No?' Incredulity at the show of emotions in her eyes almost made saying anything impossible. 'What do you mean, "No"?'

'I mean I have no intention of having any more to do with you. I was a fool to think we ever had any kind of future and even more of a fool to think that…' The passion of her outburst, again in Spanish, surprised him, as did the sudden faltering of her words. It was the only hint that his mother had been right, that this woman did feel something for him and was as good at hiding that as he was.

'To think what, Lydia?' he jumped in quickly, not wanting that small opening to pass by. It might be the only chance to find out how this woman truly felt, to find out if she had the same feelings for him as he had for her.

'That you cared about me.' She marched past him, her shoulder brushing against his upper arm she moved so quickly. He heard the blind being pulled roughly up, heard the bolt being slid back into place and as he turned to her he saw her wrench open the door. 'But I was wrong.'

'Is that why you lodged the deeds of most of the properties with your solicitor, putting them all into my name?' He watched her as she lifted her chin, mutinous defiance filling her body as she stood there by the open boutique door, angry green eyes blazing at him.

'I honour my debts.' Defiance sparked like flint on stone in every word she said, starting a fire of emotions. 'Fully.'

'And your promises?' He raised his voice as he fought against the noise of the London traffic. 'Do you honour those too?'

'Of course I do. Now please go. Leave.'

He took a few steps to her, getting so close he could smell her perfume, the same as she'd worn at the party. Memories of the dance leapt to life in his mind, hotly followed by those of that passionate night when she'd been his.

'Leave. Go,' she said in Spanish, the words hard and cruel, twisting the knife in his heart. The finality of the words too much, but he couldn't go.

He took her hand from the door, his eyes locked with hers. 'You made a promise to me, Lydia. You were my fiancée.'

'That wasn't a promise.' Her voice was barely a whisper as she looked up at him, her eyes searching his. Was she looking for the same emotion in his that he was searching for in hers? Love. 'That was nothing more than a deal—or blackmail.'

'And if it became something more?' Tentatively he asked, ignoring the laughter from a couple passing by the shop, his attention firmly fixed on the woman he loved.

'It could never be more, Raul. You can't give yourself or your heart. You made that very clear. We had an affair, nothing more, but it's over.'

She shut the boutique door, the traffic noise dimming as she glared accusingly at him. She was right. He couldn't give his heart, couldn't allow himself to feel any soft emotions and definitely not love. But that had been before she'd turned his world upside down, shaking his heart into life.

Lydia turned from him, taking his silence as agreement, but as she walked away he knew he couldn't leave it there, couldn't give up.

'I was wrong.' He strode after her, wanting to reach for her, wanting to force her to look at him, to listen to him.

She stood very still, her back to him, and the seconds ticked by as he waited. Finally, she turned and looked up at him, weariness in her eyes. 'So was I.'

He was losing. The one battle in his life he had to win and he knew he was losing it—losing her. He had to say the words he'd never said to anyone. It was the only hope he had of making her understand. 'I was wrong, Lydia.'

He paused and looked into those lovely green eyes, saw her blink quickly, as if tears threatened. 'I was wrong because I love you, Lydia.'

* * *

Lydia looked at the man she loved, a man she'd thought incapable of saying those words to her. But saying them wasn't meaning them. 'It's too late.'

She wanted to walk away, wanted to avoid the power of those devilishly sexy eyes, but she couldn't. All she could do was stand there and look up at him.

He shook his head. 'No, Lydia. It's not too late. I've been a fool, yes, but it's not too late.'

'I'm sorry I messed everything up just before your brother arrived, but most of all I'm sorry that my father ever got us into this mess.'

'I'm not. I've found my brother *and* the woman I love. The woman I want to be my wife.'

He was offering her everything she wanted, everything she'd dreamed of, but this was Raul Valdez, billionaire businessman who got anything he wanted by fair means or foul. She stepped back from him, away from the temptation of his potent masculinity, away from the need to feel his lips on hers just one more time. Not that once more would ever be enough, not when she loved him so completely.

A shaky laugh slipped from her. 'That's not possible. We can't.'

'We can,' he said and moved towards her, so close now that she could smell the freshness of his morning shower. Gently he reached out and cupped her cheek in his hand and she fought the urge to lean into the caress, to believe what he was saying was real.

'I've paid my debts, Raul. The contract no longer stands.' She lifted her chin and glared at him, desperately trying to ignore the heat of his touch on her face.

'To hell with the contract.'

'How can you say that when the debt instigated such a deal with me? If I hadn't been able to find your brother, I dread to think how things would be now.'

'The passion and desire between us was inevitable, Lydia. As was the conclusion.'

How could he say that so soon after saying she was the woman he loved? It was all just words for him, words to get what he wanted, when money couldn't achieve that.

Before she could say anything his lips claimed hers in a hot, searing kiss that set light to every part of her body. Her limbs weakened and her lips softened as she kissed him back as if her life depended on it as he pulled her close. She loved this man, so why couldn't she believe him? So much had happened between them in the short time they'd known each other, but could a man who'd openly condemned love really love her?

She pushed against him, breaking the kiss with such force that he was forced to let her go and she stepped quickly back. 'My father's debts are settled, not by the funds for finding Max, but by those properties my father hid in my name. They are now yours, to do with as you please. You have everything you wanted, Raul, and I have lost just about everything. Just go.'

She turned from him, the sting of tears in her eyes, and she swallowed down the need to give into them. Raul's gentle touch on her arm was the last thing she'd expected after the dominating way he'd entered the shop and then claimed that kiss. She pinched the bridge of her nose, willing the tears to stay where they were.

'That's where you are wrong, Lydia. If I have lost you, I have lost everything.' Slowly he turned her to face him and she looked up at him, into eyes that no longer held the defensive glare. This was the real Raul, the man who, for whatever reason, feared love.

'I'm sorry, Raul, I can't love a man who doesn't know how to love, how to open his heart to the most natural emotion in the world.'

'Can you give such a man a chance?' The slight waver to the deep accented timbre of his voice told her so much. It also lit the small flame of hope within her.

'You told me love was not for you. How can things have changed?' His touch on her arm seared her skin through her clothes and she longed to walk into his embrace, to accept love on his terms, but it wasn't enough.

'My mother knows we are in love.' He spoke softly, sending the conversation in a different direction and her mind into a spin of questions.

'That's because we acted the part—'

He cut her words off. 'She saw love beneath that, Lydia. My love for you and yours for me.'

She shook her head. 'No, that's not possible.'

'And Max. He saw it too.'

'You spoke of our deal to your brother?' She hadn't asked anything about that meeting, the humiliation of being sent from the room like a scolded child still very raw.

'He made it very clear I'd been too hard on you— and I was. He also told me I had much to settle with you and I'm guessing he knows that first hand, from the exchange I witnessed between him and his wife.'

'His wife? The lovely redhead waiting in the foyer?'

Raul nodded. 'And soon to be the mother of his child, but that is not important now. I have been a fool, Lydia, hiding from your love, trying to deny that I felt the same for you, seeing it as a weakness. But all that has changed.'

'It has?' The whisper her voice had become held so much hope that her heart ached.

'I've changed and it is because of you. I'd give up all my wealth, my father's inheritance, everything if it meant I could have you in my life, as my wife. I love you, Lydia.'

'I don't need anything else but your love, Raul.' He stroked his fingers down her cheek as she spoke and she closed her eyes against the sensation. When she opened them his eyes were so full of love that she wondered how they could ever have been so cold and hard. 'I love you, Raul.'

This time the kiss was gentle and loving, leaving her in no doubt that his words were far more than that. They were real, as real as their love for one another. She trembled as he took her in his arms, holding her to him so that she could hear the beat of his heart. Right here was all she'd ever wanted.

'Just one more thing.' Raul's voice was filled with emotion as he spoke and moved her from him so he could look at her.

'What is it?' Lydia looked up at him to see a smile of love on his lips and she had to resist the urge to kiss him again.

'With all the upheaval of finding Max and then losing you, I haven't cancelled our wedding.'

'But that's just days away.' Was he suggesting they get married as planned on Christmas Eve in Madrid? If he was, she knew exactly what her answer would be. She didn't need a big fancy day.

'What do you think? Should we get married?' he teased her with soft words of Spanish.

'I can't think of anything better.' She smiled and then as his lips claimed hers allowed herself to slip into the bliss of his kiss, briefly at least. There was one more small matter to settle. 'There is one condition.'

'Which is?' His eyes narrowed in suspicion, but this time the smile on his lips proved he was teasing her.

'That Max and his wife are there too.'

'That would be the best way to begin married life, with my brother beside me to witness my love and commitment to you.'

EPILOGUE

SHE WAS MARRIED. Lydia looked at her husband as he talked with his brother and her heart filled with love for Raul. It was hard to believe that three days ago in London she had been in her boutique trying to piece together her life after Raul had sent her from his so sternly. Now they were man and wife. She was married to the man she loved, the man who loved her.

Raul turned and looked at her; the hotel room they'd hired for their small wedding party faded out of focus as he smiled at her. Not only did he love her, but that love was unguarded, bared for the few close friends and family members who'd witnessed their exchange of vows. The most important being his mother and brother.

Raul crossed the room to her. He looked stunningly sexy in his black tuxedo, the red band at his waist only adding to the overall effect and matching perfectly with her seasonal bouquet. She still couldn't believe she was married to him, the man of her dreams.

He swept her into an embrace and kissed her. A long lingering kiss full of the promise of so much more and, even though his mother was in the room, she responded. How could she not? He was everything she wanted and so much more.

'You look beautiful,' he said, barely moving away from her, his forehead almost against hers, his breath warm on her face.

'You approve, then?' she teased, recalling the panic she'd gone into trying to find the perfect wedding dress the weekend before Christmas. It had been a Spanish designer she'd met earlier in Madrid who had come to the rescue. The dress fitted as if it had been made for her and the fur-trimmed hooded cape finished the 'winter bride' look perfectly.

'Of your use of a Spanish designer who created a dress almost as beautiful as you? Yes, I approve, but of you, as my wife, I more than approve.' His teasing voice left her in no doubt of how much he approved and her heart sang with joy as he kissed her again.

'It's been a perfect day,' she said wistfully.

'Even though your family are not here?'

'My grandmother is too frail to travel now, but she will meet you as soon as we return from our honeymoon, and as for my parents…' she paused, the hurt of her mother's excuses for not attending still cut deep, but her father's blunt refusal was no more than she'd expected '…let's just say time will heal. My father will get over the loss of his properties and my mother has invited us to her home in the new year.'

'So you are happy?'

'Perfectly.'

'Then it is time we went,' he said softly, a wicked gleam in his eyes. 'We will stay at my apartment for a few days, then head to London for Max's sister's birthday party. After that we will fly to the Seychelles for our honeymoon.'

She smiled at him. 'Sounds wonderful.'

'It will be. We can spend time alone and celebrate the start of a new year with our own fireworks.' The spark of mischief danced in his eyes.

'You are incorrigible, Raul Valdez, but I love you so very much.'

'And I love you too, with all my heart.'

'Do you have any idea how much it means to hear those words from you?' she teased him, interspersing her words with light kisses.

'And do you have any idea that I will be saying them to you every day from now on?'

'I'll hold you to that.'

'And I intend to show you just how much too—as soon as we are alone.'

She took his hand and looked up into his eyes. 'Let's go now, then.'

His handsome face had the sexy devil-may-care look on it and her heart melted. She loved him so very much—and he loved her. The future was theirs and full of love and happiness.

* * * * *

If you enjoyed VALDEZ'S BARTERED BRIDE,
why not explore these other stories
by Rachael Thomas?

MARRIED FOR THE ITALIAN'S HEIR
A CHILD CLAIMED BY GOLD
DI MARCELLO'S SECRET SON

Available now!

MILLS & BOON®

EXCLUSIVE EXTRACT

Reluctant Sheikh Salim Al-Noury would rather abdicate
than taint the realm with his dark secrets.

But could one exquisitely beautiful diplomat convince
him otherwise?...

Christmas means heartbreak to Charlotte, and this over-
seas assignment offers the perfect getaway. But Salim
proves to be her most challenging client yet, and his
rugged masculinity awakens untouched Charlotte to
unimaginable pleasures!

Read on for a sneak preview of Abby Green's book
A CHRISTMAS BRIDE FOR THE KING
Rulers of the Desert

She looked Salim straight in the eye. 'Life is so easy for
you, isn't it? No wonder you don't want to rule—it would
put a serious cramp in your lifestyle and a dent in your
empire. Have you *ever* had to think of anyone but yourself,
Salim? Have you *ever* had to consider the consequences of
your actions? People like you make me—'

'*Enough.*' Salim punctuated the harshly spoken word by
taking her arms in his hands. He said it again. 'Enough,
Charlotte. You've made your point.'

She couldn't breathe after the way he'd just said her
name. *Roughly.* His hands were huge on her arms, and firm
but not painful. She knew she should say *Let me go* but
somehow the words wouldn't form in her mouth.

Salim's eyes were blazing down into hers and for a
second she had the impression that she'd somehow...*hurt*
him. But in the next instant any coherent thought fled,

because he slammed his mouth down onto hers and all she was aware of was shocking heat, strength, and a surge of need such as she'd never experienced before.

Salim couldn't recall when he'd felt angrier—people had thrown all sorts of insults at him for years. Women who'd expected more than he'd been prepared to give. Business adversaries he'd bested. His brother. His parents. But for some reason this buttoned-up slender woman with her cool judgmental attitude was getting to him like no one else ever had.

The urge to kiss her had been born out of that anger and a need to stop her words, but also because he'd felt a hot throb of desire that had eluded him for so long he'd almost forgotten what it felt like.

Her mouth was soft and pliant under his, but on some dim level not clouded red with lust and anger he knew it was shock—and, sure enough, after a couple of seconds he felt her tense and her mouth tighten against his.

He knew he should draw back.

If he was another man he might try to convince himself he'd only intended the kiss to be a display of power, but Salim had never drawn back from admitting his full failings. And he couldn't pull back—not if a thousand horses were tied to his body. Because he wanted her.

Don't miss
A CHRISTMAS BRIDE FOR THE KING
By Abby Green

Available December 2017

www.millsandboon.co.uk

MILLS & BOON®

Why shop at millsandboon.co.uk?

Each year, thousands of romance readers
find their perfect read at millsandboon.co.uk.
That's because we're passionate about
bringing you the very best romantic fiction.
Here are some of the advantages of
shopping at www.millsandboon.co.uk:

* **Get new books first**—you'll be able to buy
  your favourite books one month before they
  hit the shops

* **Get exclusive discounts**—you'll also be
  able to buy our specially created monthly
  collections, with up to 50% off the RRP

* **Find your favourite authors**—latest news,
  interviews and new releases for all your
  favourite authors and series on our website,
  plus ideas for what to try next

* **Join in**—once you've bought your favourite
  books, don't forget to register with us to rate,
  review and join in the discussions

Visit **www.millsandboon.co.uk**
for all this and more today!